MEG CABOT

Princess
diaries collection

HARPER TEEN

An Imprint of HarperCollins*Publishers*

HarperTeen is an imprint of HarperCollins Publishers.

THE PRINCESS DIARIES

PRINCESS IN THE SPOTLIGHT

PRINCESS IN LOVE

ISBN 978-0-06-171568-6

MEG CABOT

The Princess diaries

HARPER TEEN
AN IMPRINT OF HARPERCOLLINSPUBLISHERS

ACKNOWLEDGMENTS

The author wishes to express her gratitude to the people who contributed in so many ways to the creation and publication of this book: Beth Ader, Jennifer Brown, Barbara Cabot, Charles and Bonnie Egnatz, Emily Faith, Laura Langlie, Ron Markman, Abigail McAden, A. Elizabeth Mikesell, Melinda Mounsey, David Walton, Allegra Yeley, and, most especially, Benjamin Egnatz.

"*Whatever comes,*" she said, "*cannot alter one thing. If I am a princess in rags and tatters, I can be a princess inside. It would be easy to be a princess if I were dressed in cloth of gold, but it is a great deal more of a triumph to be one all the time when no one knows it.*"

A LITTLE PRINCESS
Frances Hodgson Burnett

Sometimes it seems like all I ever do is lie.

My mom thinks I'm repressing my feelings about this. I say to her, "No, Mom, I'm not. I think it's really neat. As long as you're happy, I'm happy."

Mom says, "I don't think you're being honest with me."

Then she hands me this book. She tells me she wants me to write down my feelings in this book, since, she says, I obviously don't feel I can talk about them with her.

She wants me to write down my feelings? Okay, I'll write down my feelings:

I CAN'T BELIEVE SHE'S DOING THIS TO ME!

Like everybody doesn't *already* think I'm a freak. I'm practically the biggest freak in the entire school. I mean, let's face it: I'm five foot nine, flat-chested, and a freshman. How much *more* of a freak could I be?

If people at school find out about this, I'm dead. That's it. Dead.

Oh, God, if you really do exist, please don't let them find out about this.

There are four million people in Manhattan, right? That makes about two million of them guys. So out of TWO MILLION guys, she has to go out with Mr. Gianini. She can't go out with some guy I don't know. She can't go out with some guy she met at D'Agostinos or wherever. Oh, no.

She has to go out with my Algebra teacher.

Thanks, Mom. Thanks a whole lot.

Lilly's like, "Mr. Gianini's cool."

Yeah, right. He's cool if you're Lilly Moscovitz. He's cool if you're good at Algebra, like Lilly Moscovitz. He's not so cool if you're flunking Algebra, like me.

He's not so cool if he makes you stay after school EVERY SINGLE SOLITARY DAY from 2:30 to 3:30 to practice the FOIL method when you could be hanging out with all your friends. He's not so cool if he calls your mother in for a parent/teacher conference to talk about how you're flunking Algebra, then ASKS HER OUT.

And he's not so cool if he's sticking his tongue in your mom's mouth.

Not that I've actually seen them do this. They haven't even been on their first date yet. And I don't think my mom would let a guy put his tongue in her mouth on the first date.

At least, I hope not.

I saw Josh Richter stick his tongue in Lana Weinberger's mouth last week. I had this totally close-up view of it, since they were leaning up against Josh's locker, which is right next to mine. It kind of grossed me out.

Though I can't say I'd mind if Josh Richter kissed *me* like that. The other day Lilly and I were at Bigelows picking up some alpha hydroxy for Lilly's mom, and I noticed Josh waiting at the checkout counter. He saw me and he actually sort of smiled and said, "Hey."

He was buying Drakkar Noir, a men's cologne. I got a free sample of it from the salesgirl. Now I can smell Josh whenever I want to, in the privacy of my own home.

Lilly says Josh's synapses were probably misfiring that day, due to heatstroke or something. She said he probably thought I looked familiar but couldn't place my face without the cement block walls of Albert Einstein High behind me. Why else, she asked, would the most popular senior in high school say hey to me, Mia Thermopolis, a lowly freshman?

But I know it wasn't heatstroke. The truth is, when he's away from Lana and all his jock friends, Josh is a totally different person. The kind of person who doesn't care if a girl is flat-chested or wears size-ten shoes. The kind of person who can see beyond all that into the depths of a girl's soul. I know because when I looked into his eyes that day at Bigelows, I saw the deeply sensitive person inside him, struggling to get out.

Lilly says I have an overactive imagination and a pathological need to invent drama in my life. She says the fact that I'm so upset about my mom and Mr. G is a classic example.

"If you're that upset about it, just *tell* your mom," Lilly says. "*Tell* her you don't want her going out with him. I don't understand you, Mia. You're always going around, lying about how you feel. Why don't you just assert yourself for a change? Your feelings have worth, you know."

Oh, right. Like I'm going to bum my mom out like that. She's so totally happy about this date, it's enough to make me want to throw up. She goes around *cooking* all the time. I'm not even kidding. She made pasta for the first time last night in like months. I had already opened the Suzie's Chinese take-out menu, and she says, "Oh, no cold sesame noodles tonight, honey. I made pasta."

Pasta! My mom made *pasta*!

She even observed my rights as a vegetarian and didn't put any meatballs in the sauce.

I don't understand any of this.

THINGS TO DO

1. Buy cat litter
2. Finish FOIL worksheet for Mr. G
3. Stop telling Lilly everything
4. Go to Pearl Paint: get soft lead pencils, spray mount, canvas stretchers (for Mom)
5. World Civ report on Iceland (5 pages, double spaced)
6. Stop thinking so much about Josh Richter
7. Drop off laundry
8. October rent (make sure Mom has deposited Dad's check!!!)
9. Be more assertive
10. Measure chest

In Algebra today all I could think about was how Mr. Gianini might put his tongue in my mom's mouth tomorrow night during their date. I just sat there, staring at him. He asked me a really easy question—I swear, he saves all the easy ones for me, like he doesn't want me to feel left out or something—and I totally didn't even hear it. I was like, "What?"

Then Lana Weinberger made that sound she always makes and leaned over to me so that all her blond hair swished onto my desk. I got hit by this giant wave of perfume, and then Lana hissed in this really mean voice:

"FREAK."

Only she said it like it had more than one syllable. Like it was spelled FUR-REEK.

How come nice people like Princess Diana get killed in car wrecks but mean people like Lana never do? I don't understand what Josh Richter sees in her. I mean, yeah, she's pretty. But she's so *mean*. Doesn't he *notice*?

Maybe Lana is nice to Josh, though. *I'd* sure be nice to Josh. He is the best-looking boy in Albert Einstein High School. A lot of the boys look totally geeky in our school's uniform, which for boys is gray pants, white shirt, and black sweater, long-sleeved or vest. Not Josh, though. He looks like a model in his uniform. I am not kidding.

Anyway. Today I noticed that Mr. Gianini's nostrils stick out A LOT. Why would you want to go out with a guy whose nostrils stick out so much? I asked Lilly this at lunch and she said, "I've never noticed his nostrils before. Are you gonna eat that dumpling?"

Lilly says I need to stop obsessing. She says I'm taking my anxiety over the fact that this is only our first month in high school and I already have an F in something, and transferring it to anxiety about Mr. Gianini and my mom. She says this is called displacement.

It sort of sucks when your best friend's parents are psychoanalysts.

Today after school the Drs. Moscovitz were totally trying to analyze me. I mean, Lilly and I were just sitting there playing Boggle. And every five minutes it was like, "Girls, do you want some Snapple? Girls, there's a very interesting squid documentary on the Discovery channel. And by the way, Mia, how do you feel about your mother starting to date your Algebra teacher?"

I said, "I feel fine about it."

Why can't I be more assertive?

But what if Lilly's parents run into my mom at Jefferson Market or something? If I told them the truth, they'd *definitely* tell her. I don't want my mom to know how weird I feel about this, not when she's so happy about it.

The worst part was that Lilly's older brother Michael overheard the whole thing. He immediately started laughing his head off, even though I don't see anything funny about it.

He went, "*Your* mom is dating Frank Gianini? Ha! Ha! Ha!"

So great. Now Lilly's brother Michael knows.

So then I had to start begging him not to tell anybody. He's in fifth period Gifted and Talented class with me and Lilly, which is the biggest joke of a class, because Mrs. Hill, who's in charge of the G & T program at Albert Einstein, doesn't care what we do as long as we don't make too much noise. She hates it when she has to come out of the teachers' lounge, which is right across the hall from the G & T room, to yell at us.

Anyway, Michael is supposed to use fifth period to work on his on-line webzine, *Crackhead*. I'm supposed to use it for catching up on my Algebra homework.

But anyway, Mrs. Hill never checks to see what we're doing in G & T, which is probably good, since mostly what we're all doing is figuring out ways to lock the new Russian kid, who's supposedly this musical genius, in the supply closet so we don't have to listen to any more Stravinsky on his stupid violin.

But don't think that just because Michael and I are united against Boris Pelkowski and his violin he'd keep quiet about my mom and Mr. G.

What Michael kept saying was, "What'll you do for me, huh, Thermopolis? What'll you do for me?"

But there's nothing I can do for Michael Moscovitz. I can't offer to do his homework, or anything. Michael is a senior (just like Josh Richter). Michael has gotten all straight A's his entire life (just like Josh Richter). Michael will probably go to Yale or Harvard next year (just like Josh Richter).

What could *I* do for someone like that?

Not that Michael's perfect, or anything. Unlike Josh Richter, Michael is not on the crew team. Michael isn't even on the debate team. Michael does not believe in organized sports, or organized religion, or organized anything, for that matter. Instead, Michael spends almost all of his time in his room. I once asked Lilly what he does in there, and she said she and her parents employ a don't ask, don't tell policy with Michael.

I bet he's in there making a bomb. Maybe he'll blow up Albert Einstein High School as a senior prank.

Occasionally, Michael comes out of his room and makes sarcastic comments. Sometimes when he does this he is not wearing a shirt. Even though he does not believe in organized sports, I have noticed that Michael has a really nice chest. His stomach muscles are extremely well defined.

7

I have never mentioned this to Lilly.

Anyway, I guess Michael got tired of my offering to do stuff like walk his sheltie, Pavlov, and take his mom's empty Tab cans back to Gristedes for the deposit money, which is his weekly chore. Because in the end Michael just said, in this disgusted voice, "Forget it, okay, Thermopolis?" and went back into his room.

I asked Lilly why he was so mad, and she said because he'd been sexually harassing me but I didn't notice.

How embarrassing! Supposing Josh Richter starts sexually harassing me someday (I wish) and I don't notice? God, I'm so stupid sometimes.

Anyway, Lilly said not to worry about Michael telling his friends at school about my mom and Mr. G, since Michael has no friends. Then Lilly wanted to know why I cared about Mr. Gianini's nostrils sticking out so much, since I'm not the one who has to look at them, my mom is.

And I said, "Excuse me, I have to look at them from 9:55 to 10:55 and from 2:30 to 3:30 EVERY SINGLE DAY, except Saturdays and Sundays and national holidays and the summer. If I don't flunk, that is, and have to go to summer school."

And if they get married, then I'll have to look at them EVERY SINGLE DAY, SEVEN DAYS A WEEK, MAJOR HOLIDAYS INCLUDED.

Define set: collection of objects; element or member belongs to a set

A = {Gilligan, Skipper, Mary Ann}
rule specifies each element
A = {x|x is one of the castaways on *Gilligan's Island*}

Friday, September 26

LILLY MOSCOVITZ'S LIST OF
HOTTEST GUYS
(compiled during World Civ, with commentary
by Mia Thermopolis)

1. *Josh Richter* (agree—six feet of unadulterated hotness. Blond hair, often falling into his clear blue eyes, and that sweet, sleepy smile. Only drawback: he has the bad taste to date Lana Weinberger)
2. *Boris Pelkowski* (strongly disagree. Just because he played his stupid violin at Carnegie Hall when he was twelve does not make him hot. Plus he tucks his school sweater into his pants, instead of wearing it out, like a normal person)
3. *Pierce Brosnan, best James Bond ever* (disagree—I liked Timothy Dalton better)
4. *Daniel Day Lewis in* Last of the Mohicans (agree—stay alive, no matter what occurs)
5. *Prince William of England* (duh)
6. *Leonardo in* Titanic (As if! That is so 1998)
7. *Mr. Wheeton, the crew coach* (hot, but taken. Seen opening the door to the teachers' lounge for Mademoiselle Klein)
8. *That guy in that jeans ad on that giant billboard in Times Square* (totally agree. Who IS that guy? They should give him his own TV series)
9. *Dr. Quinn Medicine Woman's boyfriend* (whatever happened to him? He was hot!)
10. *Joshua Bell, the violinist* (totally agree. It would be so cool to date a musician—just not Boris Pelkowski)

I was measuring my chest and totally not thinking about the fact that my mom was out with my Algebra teacher when my dad called. I don't know why, but I lied and told him Mom was at her studio. Which is so weird, because obviously Dad knows Mom dates. But for some reason, I just couldn't tell him about Mr. Gianini.

This afternoon during my mandatory review session with Mr. Gianini, I was sitting there practicing the FOIL method (first, outside, inside, last; first, outside, inside, last—Oh, my God, when am I ever going to have to actually use the FOIL method in real life? WHEN???) and all of a sudden Mr. Gianini said, "Mia, I hope you don't feel, well, uncomfortable about my seeing your mother socially."

Only for some reason for a second I thought he said SEXUALLY, not socially. And then I could feel my face getting totally hot. I mean like BURNING. And I said, "Oh, no, Mr. Gianini, it doesn't bother me at all."

And Mr. Gianini said, "Because if it bothers you, we can talk about it."

I guess he must have figured out I was lying, since my face was so red.

But all I said was, "Really, it doesn't bother me. I mean, it bothers me a LITTLE, but really, I'm fine with it. I mean, it's just a date, right? Why get upset about one measly date?"

That was when Mr. Gianini said, "Well, Mia, I don't know if it's going to be one measly date. I really like your mother."

And then, I don't even know how, but all of a sudden I heard myself saying, "Well, you better. Because if you do anything to make her cry, I'll kick your butt."

Oh, my God! I can't even believe I said the word *butt*

to a teacher! My face got even REDDER after that, which I wouldn't have thought possible. Why is it that the only time I can tell the truth is when it's guaranteed to get me into trouble?

But I guess I *am* feeling sort of weird about the whole thing. Maybe Lilly's parents were right.

Mr. Gianini, though, was totally cool. He smiled in this funny way and said, "I have no intention of making your mother cry, but if I ever do, you have my permission to kick my butt."

So that was okay, sort of.

Anyway, Dad sounded really weird on the phone. But then again, he always does. Transatlantic phone calls suck because I can hear the ocean swishing around in the background and it makes me all nervous, like the fish are listening, or something. Plus Dad didn't even want to talk to me. He wanted to talk to Mom. I suppose somebody died, and he wants Mom to break it to me gently.

Maybe it was Grandmère. Hmmm. . . .

My breasts have grown exactly *none* since last summer. Mom was totally wrong. I did *not* have a growth spurt when I turned fourteen, like she did. I will probably *never* have a growth spurt, at least not on my chest. I only have growth spurts UP, not OUT. I am now the tallest girl in my class.

Now if anybody asks me to the Cultural Diversity Dance next month (yeah, right) I won't be able to wear a strapless dress because there isn't anything on my chest to hold it up.

I was asleep when my mom got home from her date last night (I stayed up as late as I could, because I wanted to know what happened, but I guess all that measuring wore me out), so I didn't get to ask her how it went until this morning when I went out into the kitchen to feed Fat Louie. Mom was up already, which was weird, because usually she sleeps later than me, and *I'm* a teenager, *I'm* supposed to be the one sleeping all the time.

But Mom's been depressed ever since her last boyfriend turned out to be a Republican.

Anyway, she was in there, humming in a happy way and making pancakes. I nearly died of shock to see her actually cooking something so early in the morning, let alone something vegetarian.

Of course she had a fabulous time. They went to dinner at Monte's (not too shabby, Mr. G!) and then walked around the West Village and went to some bar and sat outside in the back garden until nearly two in the morning, just talking. I kind of tried to find out if there'd been any kissing, particularly of the tongue-in-mouth variety, but my mom just smiled and looked all embarrassed.

Okay. Gross.

They're going out again this week.

I guess I don't mind, if it makes her this happy.

Today Lilly is shooting a spoof of the movie *The Blair Witch Project* for her TV show, *Lilly Tells It Like It Is*. *The Blair Witch Project* is about some kids who go out into the woods to find a witch and end up disappearing. All that's found of them is film footage and some piles of sticks. Only instead of *The Blair Witch Project*, Lilly's version is called *The Green Witch Project*. Lilly intends to take a hand-held camera down to Washington Square Park and film the tourists who come up to us and ask if we know how to get to Green Witch Village. (It's actually Greenwich Village—you're not supposed to pronounce the *w* in *Greenwich*. But people from out of town always say it wrong.)

Anyway, as tourists come up and ask us which way to Green Witch Village, we are supposed to start screaming and run away in terror. All that will be left of us by the end, Lilly says, is a little pile of MetroCards. Lilly says after the show is aired no one will ever think of MetroCards the same way.

I said it was too bad we don't have a real witch. I thought we could get Lana Weinberger to play her, but Lilly said that would be typecasting. Plus then we'd have to put up with Lana all day, and nobody would want that. Like she'd even show up, considering how she thinks we're the most unpopular girls in the whole school. She probably wouldn't want to tarnish her reputation by being seen with us.

Then again, she's so vain she'd probably jump at the chance to be on TV, even if it *is* only a public access channel.

After filming was over for the day, we all saw the Blind Guy crossing Bleecker. He had a new victim, this totally innocent German tourist who had no idea that the nice blind man she was helping to cross the street was going to feel her up as soon as they got to the other side, then pretend he hadn't done it on purpose.

Just my luck, the only guy who's ever felt me up (not that there's anything to feel) was BLIND.

Lilly says she's going to report the Blind Guy to the Sixth Precinct. Like they would care. They've got more important things to worry about. Like catching murderers.

THINGS TO DO

1. Get cat litter
2. Make sure Mom sent out rent check
3. Stop lying
4. Proposal for English paper
5. Pick up laundry
6. Stop thinking about Josh Richter

My dad called again today, and this time Mom really *was* at her studio, so I didn't feel so bad about lying last night and not telling him about Mr. Gianini. He sounded all weird on the phone again, so finally I was like, "Dad, is Grandmère dead?" and he got all startled and said, "No, Mia, why would you think that?"

And I told him it was because he sounded so weird, and he was all, "I don't sound weird," which was a lie, because he DID sound weird. But I decided to let it drop, and I talked to him about Iceland, because we're studying Iceland in World Civ. Iceland has the world's highest literacy rate, because there's nothing to do there but read. They also have these natural hot springs, and everybody goes swimming in them. Once, the opera came to Iceland, and every show was sold out and something like 98 percent of the population attended. Everybody knew all the words to the opera and went around singing it all day.

I would like to live in Iceland someday. It sounds like a fun place. Much more fun than Manhattan, where people sometimes spit at you for no reason.

But Dad didn't seem all that impressed by Iceland. I suppose by comparison, Iceland does make every other country look sucky. The country Dad lives in is pretty small, though. I would think if the opera went there, about 80 percent of the population would attend, which would certainly be something to be proud of.

I only shared this information with him because he is a politician, and I thought it might give him some ideas about how to make things better in Genovia, where he lives. But I guess Genovia doesn't need to be better. Genovia's number one import is tourists. I know this because I had to do a fact sheet on every country in Europe in the seventh grade, and Genovia was right up there with Disneyland as far as income from the tourist trade is concerned. That's probably why people in Genovia don't have to pay taxes: The government already has enough money. This is called a principality. The only other one is Monaco. My dad says we have a lot of cousins in Monaco, but so far I haven't met any of them, not even at Grandmère's.

I suggested to Dad that next summer, instead of spending it with him and Grandmère at her French chateau, Miragnac, we go to Iceland. We'd have to leave my grandmother at the chateau, of course. She'd hate Iceland. She hates any place where you can't order up a decent Sidecar, which is her favorite drink, twenty-four hours a day.

All Dad said was, "We'll talk about that some other time," and hung up.

Mom is so right about him.

Absolute value: the distance that a given number is from zero on a number line . . . always a positive

Today I watched Mr. Gianini very closely for signs that he might not have had as good a time on his date with my mom as my mom did. He seemed to be in a really good mood, though. During class, while we were working on the quadratic formula (what happened to FOIL? I was just starting to get the hang of it, and all of a sudden there's some NEW thing; no *wonder* I'm flunking), he asked if anybody had gone out for a part in the fall musical, *My Fair Lady*.

Then later he said, in the way he does when he gets excited about something, "You know who would be a good Eliza Doolittle? Mia, I think you would."

I thought I would totally die. I know Mr. Gianini was only trying to be nice—I mean, he is dating my mom, after all—but he was SO far off: First of all because of course they already held auditions, and even if I could've gone out for a part (which I couldn't, because I'm flunking Algebra, hello, Mr. Gianini, remember?) I NEVER would've gotten one, let alone the LEAD. I can't sing. I can barely even *talk*.

Even Lana Weinberger, who always got the lead in junior high, didn't get the lead. It went to some senior girl. Lana plays a maid, a spectator at the Ascot Races, and a Cockney hooker. Lilly is house manager. Her job is to flick the lights on and off at the end of intermission.

I was so freaked out by what Mr. Gianini said I couldn't even *say* anything. I just sat there and felt myself turning all red. Maybe that was why later, when Lilly and I went by my locker at lunch, Lana, who was there waiting for Josh, was all, "Oh, hello, *Amelia*," in her snottiest voice, even though nobody has called me Amelia (except Grandmère) since kindergarten, when I asked everybody not to.

Then, as I bent over to get my money out of my backpack, Lana must have got a good look down my blouse, because all of a sudden she goes, "Oh, how sweet. I see we still can't fit into a bra. Might I suggest Band-Aids?"

I would have hauled off and slugged her—well, probably not; the Drs. Moscovitz say I have issues about confrontation—if Josh Richter hadn't walked up AT THAT VERY MOMENT. I knew he totally heard, but all he said was, "Can I get by here?" to Lilly, since she was blocking his path to his locker.

I was ready to go slinking down to the cafeteria and forget the whole thing—God, that's all I need, my lack of chest pointed out *right in front* of Josh Richter!—but Lilly couldn't leave well enough alone. She got all red in the face and said to Lana, "Why don't you do us all a favor and go curl up someplace and die, Weinberger?"

Well, nobody tells Lana Weinberger to go curl up someplace and die. I mean, nobody. Not if she doesn't want her name written up all over the walls of the girls' room. Not that this would be such a heinous thing—I mean, no boys are going to see it in the girls' room—but I sort of like keeping my name off walls, for the most part.

But Lilly doesn't care about things like that. I mean, she's short and sort of round and kind of resembles a pug, but she totally doesn't care how she looks. I mean, she has her own TV show, and guys call in all the time and say how ugly they think she is, and ask her to lift her shirt up (*she* isn't flat-chested; she wears a C cup already), and she just laughs and laughs.

Lilly isn't afraid of anything.

So when Lana Weinberger started in on her for telling her to curl up and die, Lilly just blinked up at her and was like, "Bite me."

The whole thing would have escalated into this giant

girl fight—Lilly has seen every single episode of *Xena: Warrior Princess*, and can kickbox like nobody's business—if Josh Richter hadn't slammed his locker door closed and said "I'm outta here" in a disgusted voice. That was when Lana just dropped it like a hot potato and scooted after him, going, "Josh, wait up. Wait up, Josh!"

Lilly and I just stood there looking at each other like we couldn't believe it. I still can't. Who *are* these people, and why do I have to be incarcerated with them on a daily basis?

HOMEWORK

Algebra: problems 1–12, pg. 79
English: proposal
World Civ: questions at end of Chapter 4
G & T: none
French: use *avoir* in neg. sentence, rd. lessons one to three, *pas de plus*
Biology: none

B = {$x|x$ is an integer}
D = {2,3,4}
4ED
5ED
E = {$x|x$ is an integer greater than 4 but less than 258}

Tuesday, September 30

Something really weird just happened. I got home from school, and my mom was there (she's usually at her studio all day during the week). She had this funny look on her face, and then she went, "I have to talk to you."

She wasn't humming anymore, and she hadn't cooked anything, so I knew it was serious.

I was kind of hoping Grandmère was dead, but I knew it had to be much worse than that, and I was worried something had happened to Fat Louie, like he'd swallowed another sock. The last time he did that, the vet charged us $1,000 to remove the sock from his small intestines, and he walked around with a funny look on his face for about a month.

Fat Louie, I mean. Not the vet.

But it turned out it wasn't about my cat, it was about my dad. The reason my dad kept on calling was because he wanted to tell us that he just found out, because of his cancer, that he can't have any more kids.

Cancer is a scary thing. Fortunately, the kind of cancer my dad had was pretty curable. They just had to cut off the cancerous part, and then he had to have chemo, and after a year, so far, the cancer hasn't come back.

Unfortunately, the part they had to cut off was . . .

Ew, I don't even like writing it.

His *testicle*.

GROSS!

It turns out that when they cut off one of your testicles, and then give you chemo, you have like a really strong chance of becoming sterile. Which is what my dad just found out he is.

Mom says he's really bummed out. She says we have to be very understanding of him right now, because men have needs, and one of them is the need to feel progenitively omnipotent.

What I don't get is, what's the big deal? What does he need more kids for? He already has me! Sure, I only see him summers and at Christmastime, but that's enough, right? I mean, he's pretty busy running Genovia. It's no joke trying to make a whole country, even one that's only a mile long, run smoothly. The only other things he has time for besides me are his girlfriends. He's always got some new girlfriend slinking around. He brings them with him when we go to Grandmère's place in France in the summer. They always drool all over the pools and the stables and the waterfall and the twenty-seven bedrooms and the ballroom and the vineyard and the farm and the airstrip.

And then he dumps them a week later.

I didn't know he wanted to *marry* one of them and have kids.

I mean, he never married my mom. My mom says that's because at the time she rejected the bourgeois mores of a society that didn't even accept women as equals to men and refused to recognize her rights as an individual.

I kind of always thought that maybe my dad just never asked her.

Anyway, my mom says Dad is flying here to New York tomorrow to talk to me about this. I don't know *why*. I mean, it doesn't have anything to do with *me*. But when I said to my mom, "Why does Dad have to fly all the way over here to talk to me about how he can't have kids?" she got this funny look on her face and started to say something, and then she stopped.

Then she just said, "You'll have to ask your father."

This is bad. My mom only says "Ask your father" when I want to know something she doesn't feel like telling me, like why people sometimes kill their own babies and how come Americans eat so much red meat and read so much less than the people of Iceland.

Note to self: Look up the words *progenitive, omnipotent,* and *mores*

distributive law
$5x + 5y - 5$
$5(x + y - 1)$

Distribute WHAT??? FIND OUT BEFORE QUIZ!!!

My dad's here. Well, not here in the loft. He's staying at the Plaza, as usual. I'm supposed to go see him tomorrow, after he's "rested." My dad rests a lot, now that he's had cancer. He stopped playing polo, too. But I think that's because one time a horse stepped on him.

Anyway, I hate the Plaza. Last time my dad stayed there, they wouldn't let me in to see him because I was wearing shorts. The lady who owns the place was there, they said, and she doesn't like to see people in cutoffs in the lobby of her fancy hotel. I had to call my dad from a house phone and ask him to bring down a pair of pants. He just told me to put the concierge on the phone, and the next thing you know, everybody was apologizing to me like crazy. They gave me this big basket filled with fruit and chocolate. It was cool. I didn't want the fruit, though, so I gave it to a homeless man I saw on the subway on my way back down to the Village. I don't think the homeless man wanted the fruit either, since he threw it all in the gutter and just kept the basket to use as a hat.

I told Lilly about what my dad said, about not being able to have kids, and she said that was very telling. She said it revealed that my dad still has unresolved issues with his parents, and I said, "Well, duh. Grandmère is a *huge* pain in the ass."

Lilly said she couldn't comment on the veracity of that statement since she'd never met my grandmother. I've been asking if I could invite Lilly to Miragnac for like years, but Grandmère always says no. She says young people give her migraines.

Lilly says maybe my dad is afraid of losing his youth, which many men equate with losing their virility. I really think they should move Lilly up a grade, but she says she likes being a freshman. She says this way she has four whole years to make observations on the adolescent condition in post–Cold War America.

STARTING TODAY I WILL

1. Be nice to everyone, whether I like him/her or not
2. Stop lying all the time about my feelings
3. Stop forgetting my Algebra notebook
4. Keep my comments to myself
5. Stop writing my Algebra notes in my journal

The 3rd power of x is called cube of x—negative numbers have no sq root

Lilly—I can't stand this. When is she going to go back to the teachers' lounge?

> *Maybe never. I heard they were shampooing the carpet today. God, he is so CUTE.*

Who's cute?

> *BORIS!*

He isn't cute. He's gross. Look what he did to his sweater. Why does he DO that?

> *You're so narrow-minded.*

I am NOT narrow-minded. But someone should tell him that in America we don't tuck in our sweaters.

> *Well, maybe in Russia they do.*

But this isn't Russia. Also, someone should tell him to learn a new song. If I have to hear that requiem for dead King Whoever one more time . . .

> *You're just jealous because Boris is a musical genius and you're flunking Algebra.*

Lilly, just because I am flunking Algebra does NOT mean I'm stupid.

> *OK, OK. What is wrong with you today?*

NOTHING!!!!!

slope: slope of a line denoted m is $m = \dfrac{y^2 - y^1}{x^2 - x^1}$

Find equation of line with slope = 2

Find the degree of slope to Mr. G's nostrils

Well.

I guess now I know why my dad is so concerned about not being able to have more kids.

BECAUSE HE'S A PRINCE!!!

Geez! How long did they think they could keep something like *that* from me?

Although, come to think of it, they managed for a pretty long time. I mean, I've BEEN to Genovia. Miragnac, where I go every summer, and also most Christmases, is the name of my grandmother's house in France. It is actually on the border of France, right near Genovia, which is between France and Italy. I've been going to Miragnac ever since I was born. Never with my mother, though. Only with my dad. My mom and dad have never lived together. Unlike a lot of kids I know, who sit around wishing their parents would get back together after they get divorced, I'm perfectly happy with this arrangement. My parents broke up before I was ever born, although they have always been pretty friendly to one another. Except when my dad is being moody, that is, or my mom is being a flake, which she can be sometimes. Things would majorly suck, I think, if they lived together.

Anyway, Genovia is where my grandmother takes me to shop for clothes at the end of every summer, when she's sick of looking at my overalls. But nobody there ever mentioned anything about my dad's being a PRINCE.

Come to think of it, I did that fact sheet on Genovia two years ago, and I copied down the name of the royal family, which is Renaldo. But even then I didn't connect it with my *dad*. I mean, I know his name is Phillipe Renaldo. But the name of the prince of Genovia was listed in the encyclopedia I used as Artur Christoff Phillipe Gerard Grimaldi Renaldo.

And that picture of him must have been totally old. Dad hasn't had any hair since before I was born (so when he had chemo, you couldn't even tell, since he was practically bald anyway). The picture of the prince of Genovia showed someone with A LOT of hair, sideburns, and a mustache, too.

I guess I can see now how Mom might have gone for him, back when she was in college. He was something of a Baldwin.

But a PRINCE? Of a whole COUNTRY? I mean, I knew he was in politics, and of course I knew he had money—how many kids at my school have summer homes in France? Martha's Vineyard, maybe, but not *France*—but a PRINCE?

So what I want to know is, if my dad's a prince, how come I have to learn Algebra?

I mean, seriously.

I don't think it was such a good idea for Dad to tell me he was a prince in the Palm Court at the Plaza. First of all, we almost had a repeat performance of the shorts incident: The doorman wouldn't even let me in at first. He said, "No minors unaccompanied by an adult," which totally blows that whole *Home Alone II* movie, right?

And I was all, "But I'm supposed to meet my dad—"

"No minors," the doorman said again, "unaccompanied by an adult."

This seemed totally unfair. I wasn't even wearing shorts. I was wearing my uniform from Albert Einstein. I mean, pleated skirt, kneesocks, the whole thing. Okay, maybe I was wearing Doc Martens, but come on! I practically WAS that kid Eloise, and she supposedly ruled the Plaza.

Finally, after standing there for like half an hour, saying, "But my dad . . . but my dad . . . but my dad . . ." the concierge came over and asked, "Just who *is* your father, young lady?"

As soon as I said his name they let me in. I realize now that's because even THEY knew he was a prince. But his own daughter, his own daughter nobody tells!

Dad was waiting at a table. High tea at the Plaza is supposed to be this very big deal. You should *see* all the German tourists snapping pictures of themselves eating chocolate chip scones. Anyway, I used to get a kick out of it when I was a little girl, and since my dad refuses to believe fourteen is not little anymore, we still meet there when he's in town. Oh, we go other places, too. Like we always go to see *Beauty and the Beast*, my all-time favorite Broadway musical, I don't care what Lilly says about Walt Disney and his misogynistic undertones. I've seen it seven times.

So has my dad. His favorite part is when the dancing forks come out.

Anyway, we're sitting there drinking tea and he starts telling me in this very serious voice that he's the prince of Genovia, and then this terrible thing happens:

I get the hiccups.

This only happens when I drink something hot and then eat bread. I don't know why. It had never happened at the Plaza before, but all of a sudden my dad is like, "Mia, I want you to know the truth. I think you're old enough now, and the fact is, now that I can't have any more children, this will have a tremendous impact on your life, and it's only fair I tell you. I am the prince of Genovia."

And I was all, "Really, Dad?" *Hiccup*.

"Your mother has always felt very strongly that there

wasn't any reason for you to know, and I agreed with her. I had a very . . . well, *unsatisfactory* childhood—"

He's not kidding. Life with Grandmère couldn't have been any *picque-nicque. Hiccup.*

"I agreed with your mother that a palace is no place to raise a child." Then he started muttering to himself, which he always does whenever I tell him I'm a vegetarian, or the subject of Mom comes up. "Of course, at the time I didn't think she intended to raise you in a *bohemian artist's loft* in *Greenwich Village,* but I will admit that it doesn't seem to have done you any harm. In fact, I think growing up in New York City instilled you with a healthy amount of skepticism about the human race at large—"

Hiccup. And he had never even *met* Lana Weinberger.

"—which is something I didn't gain until college, and I believe is partly responsible for the fact that I have such a difficult time establishing close interpersonal relationships with women—"

Hiccup.

"What I'm trying to say is, your mother and I thought by not telling you we were doing you a favor. The fact was, we never envisioned that an occasion might arise in which you might succeed the throne. I was only twenty-five when you were born. I felt certain I would meet another woman, marry her, and have more children. But now, unfortunately, that will never be. So, the fact is, you, Mia, are the heir to the throne of Genovia."

I hiccuped again. This was getting embarrassing. These weren't little ladylike hiccups, either. They were huge, and made my whole body go sproinging up out of my chair like I was some kind of five-foot-nine frog. They were loud, too. I mean *really* loud. The German tourists kept looking over, all giggly and stuff. I knew what my dad was saying was superserious, but I couldn't help it, I just kept hiccuping! I tried holding my breath and counting to thirty—I only got to ten before I hiccuped again. I put a sugar cube on my tongue and let it dissolve. No go. I even tried to scare myself, thinking about my mom and Mr. Gianini French-kissing—even *that* didn't work.

Finally, my dad was like, "Mia? Mia, are you listening? Have you heard a word I said?"

I said, "Dad, can I be excused for a minute?"

He looked sort of pained, like his stomach hurt him, and he slumped back in his chair in this defeated way, but he said, "Go ahead," and gave me five dollars to give to the washroom attendant, which I of course put in my pocket. Five bucks for the washroom attendant! Geez, my whole allowance is ten bucks a week!

I don't know if you've ever been to the ladies' room at the Plaza, but it's like totally the nicest one in Manhattan. It's all pink, and there are mirrors and little couches every-where, in case you look at yourself and feel the urge to faint from your beauty or something. Anyway, I banged in there, hiccuping like a maniac, and all these women in these fancy hairdos looked up, annoyed at the interrup-tion. I guess I made them mess up their lip liner or some-thing.

I went into one of the stalls, each of which, besides a toilet, has its own private sink with a huge mirror and a dressing table with a little stool with tassels hanging off it. I sat on the stool and concentrated on not hiccuping any-more. Instead, I concentrated on what my dad had said:

He's the prince of Genovia.

A lot of things are beginning to make sense now. Like how when I fly to France I just walk onto the plane from the terminal, but when I get there I'm escorted off the plane before everyone else and get taken away by limo to meet my dad at Miragnac.

I always thought that was because he had frequent flyer privileges.

I guess it's because he's a prince.

And then there's that fact that whenever Grandmère takes me shopping in Genovia she always takes me either before the stores are officially open or after they are officially closed. She calls ahead to ensure we will be let in, and no one has ever said no. In Manhattan, if my mother had tried to do this, the clerks at the Gap would have fallen over from laughing so hard.

And when I'm at Miragnac, I notice that we never go out to eat anywhere. We always have our meals there, or sometimes we go to the neighboring chateau, Mirabeau, which is owned by these nasty British people who have a lot of snotty kids who say things like "That's rot" and "You're a wanker" to one another. One of the younger girls, Nicole, is sort of my friend, but then one night she told me this story about how she was Frenching a boy and I didn't know what Frenching was. I was only eleven at the time, which is no excuse, because so was she. I just thought Frenching was some weird British thing, like toad-in-the-hole, or air raids, or something. So then I mentioned it at the dinner table in front of Nicole's parents, and after that all those kids stopped talking to me.

I wonder if the Brits know that my dad is the prince of Genovia. I bet they do. God, they must have thought I was mentally retarded or something.

Most people have never heard of Genovia. I know when we had to do our fact sheets, none of the other kids ever had. Neither had my mother, she says, before she met my dad. Nobody famous ever came from there. Nobody who was born there ever invented anything, or wrote anything, or became a movie star. A lot of Genovians, like my grandpa, fought against the Nazis in World War II, but other than that, they aren't really known for anything.

Still, people who *have* heard of Genovia like to go there because it's so beautiful. It's very sunny nearly all the time, with the snow-capped Alps in the background and the crystal-blue Mediterranean in front of it. It has a lot of hills, some of which are as steep as the ones in San Francisco, and most of which have olive trees growing on them. The main export of Genovia, I remember from my fact sheet, is olive oil, the really expensive kind my mom says only to use for salad dressing.

There's a palace there, too. It's kind of famous because they filmed a movie there once, a movie about the three Musketeers. I've never been inside, but we've driven by it before, me and Grandmère. It's got all these turrets and flying buttresses and stuff.

Funny how Grandmère never mentioned having *lived* there all those times we drove past it.

My hiccups are gone. I think it's safe to go back to the Palm Court.

I'm going to give the washroom attendant a dollar, even though she didn't attend me.

Hey, I can afford it: My dad's a prince!

I'm so freaked out I can barely write, plus people keep bumping my elbow, and it's dark in here, but whatever. I have to get this down exactly the way it happened. Otherwise, when I wake up tomorrow I might think it was just a nightmare.

But it wasn't a nightmare. It was REAL.

I'm not going to tell anybody, not even Lilly. Lilly would NOT understand. NOBODY would understand. Because nobody I know has ever been in this situation before. Nobody ever went to bed one night as one person and then woke up the next morning to find out that she was somebody completely different.

When I got back to our table after hiccuping in the ladies' room at the Plaza, I saw that the German tourists had been replaced by some Japanese tourists. This was an improvement. They were much quieter. My dad was on his cellular phone when I sat back down. He was talking to my mom, I realized right away. He had on the expression he wears only when he is talking to her. He was saying, "Yes, I told her. No, she doesn't seem upset." He looked at me. "Are you upset?"

I said, "No," because I wasn't upset—not THEN.

He said, into the phone, "She says no." He listened for a minute, then he looked at me again. "Do you want your mother to come up here and help to explain things?"

I shook my head. "No. She has to finish that mixed-media piece for the Kelly Tate Gallery. They want it by next Tuesday."

My dad repeated this to my mom. I heard her grumble back. She is always very grumbly when I remind her that she has paintings due by a certain time. My mom likes to work when the muses move her. Since my dad pays most of our bills, this is not usually a problem, but it is not a very responsible way for an adult to behave, even if she is an artist. I swear, if I ever met my mom's muses, I'd give 'em such swift kicks in the toga they wouldn't know what hit them.

Finally my dad hung up and then he looked at me. "Better?" he asked.

So I guess he had noticed the hiccups after all. "Better," I said.

"Do you really understand what I'm telling you, Mia?"

I nodded. "You are the prince of Genovia."

"Yes . . ." he said, like there was more.

I didn't know what else to say. So I tried, "Grandpère was the prince of Genovia before you?"

He said, "Yes . . ."

"So Grandmère is . . . what?"

"The dowager princess."

I winced. Ew. That explained a whole lot about Grandmère.

Dad could tell he had me stumped. He kept on looking at me all hopeful like. Finally, after I tried just smiling at him innocently for a while, and that didn't work, I slumped over and said, "Okay. What?"

He looked disappointed. "Mia, don't you know?"

I had my head on the table. You aren't supposed to do that at the Plaza, but I hadn't noticed Ivana Trump looking our way. "No . . ." I said. "I guess not. Know what?"

"You're not Mia Thermopolis anymore, honey," he said. Because I was born out of wedlock, and my mom doesn't believe in what she calls the cult of the patriarchy, she gave me her last name instead of my dad's.

I raised my head at that. "I'm not?" I said, blinking a

34

few times. "Then who am I?"

And he went, kind of sadly, "You're Amelia Mignonette Grimaldi Thermopolis Renaldo, Princess of Genovia."

Okay.

WHAT? A PRINCESS?? ME???

Yeah. Right.

This is how NOT a princess I am. I am so NOT a princess that when my dad started telling me that I was one I totally started crying. I could see my reflection in this big gold mirror across the room, and my face had gotten all splotchy, like it does in PE whenever we play dodge ball and I get hit. I looked at my face in that big mirror and I was like, *This* is the face of a princess?

You should see what I look like. You never saw anyone who looked LESS like a princess than I do. I mean, I have really bad hair that isn't curly or straight; it's sort of triangular, so I have to wear it really short or I look like a Yield sign. And it isn't blond or brunette, it's in the middle, the sort of color they call mouse brown, or dishwater blond. Attractive, huh? And I have a really big mouth and no breasts and feet that look like skis. Lilly says my only attractive feature is my eyes, which are gray, but right then they were all squinty and red-looking since I was trying not to cry.

I mean, princesses don't cry, right?

Then my dad reached out and started patting my hand. Okay, I love my dad, but he just has no clue. He kept saying how sorry he was. I couldn't say anything in reply because I was afraid if I talked I'd cry harder. He kept on saying how it wasn't that bad, that I'd like living at the palace in Genovia with him, and that I could come back to visit my little friends as often as I wanted.

That's when I lost it.

Not only am I a princess, but I have to MOVE???

I stopped crying almost right away. Because then I got mad. Really mad. I don't get mad all that often, because of my fear of confrontation and all, but when I *do* get mad, look out.

"I am NOT moving to Genovia," I said in this really loud voice. I know it was loud because all the Japanese tourists turned around and looked at me, and then started whispering to one another.

My dad looked kind of shocked. The last time I yelled at him had been years ago, when he agreed with Grandmère that I ought to eat some foie gras. I don't care if it *is* a delicacy in France; I'm not eating anything that once walked around and quacked.

"But Mia," my dad said in his Now-let's-be-reasonable voice, "I thought you understood—"

"All I understand," I said, "is that you *lied* to me my whole life. Why should I come live with *you?*"

I realize this was a completely teen prime-time drama kind of thing to say, and I'm sorry to say that I followed it up with some pretty teen drama-queen kind of behavior. I stood up real fast, knocking over my big gold chair, and rushed out of there, nearly bowling over the snobby doorman.

I think my dad tried to chase me, but I can run pretty fast when I want to. Mr. Wheeton is always trying to get me to go out for track, but that's like such a joke, because I hate running for no reason. A letter on a stupid jacket is no reason to run, as far as I'm concerned.

Anyway, I ran down the street, past the stupid touristy horses and carriages, past the big fountain with the gold statues in it, past all the traffic outside of F.A.O. Schwarz, right into Central Park, where it was getting kind of dark and cold and spooky and stuff, but I didn't care. Nobody was going to attack me because I was this five-foot-nine girl running in combat boots, with a big backpack with bumper stickers on it that said stuff like SUPPORT GREEN-PEACE and I BRAKE FOR ANIMALS. Nobody messes with a girl in combat boots, particularly when she's also a vegetarian.

After a while I got tired of running, and then I tried to figure out where I could go, since I wasn't ready to go home yet. I knew I couldn't go to Lilly's. She is vehemently opposed to any form of government that is not by the people, exercised either directly or through elected representatives. She's always said that when sovereignty is vested in a single person whose right to rule is hereditary, the principles of social equality and respect for the individual within a community are irrevocably lost. This is why, today, real power has passed from reigning monarchs to constitutional assemblies, making royals such as Queen Elizabeth mere symbols of national unity.

At least, that's what she said in her oral report in World Civ the other day.

And I guess I kind of agree with Lilly, especially about Prince Charles—he did treat Diana like dirt—but my dad isn't like that. Yeah, he plays polo and all, but he would never dream of subjecting anyone to taxation without representation.

Still, I was pretty sure the fact that the people of Genovia don't have to pay taxes wasn't going to make any difference to Lilly.

I knew the first thing my dad would do was call Mom, and she'd be all worried. I hate making my mom worry. Even though she can be very irresponsible at times, it's only with things like bills and the groceries. She's never irresponsible about *me*. Like, I have friends whose parents don't even remember sometimes to give them subway fare. I have friends who tell their parents they're going to So-and-So's apartment and then instead they go out drinking, and their parents never find out because they don't even check with the other kid's parents.

My mom's not like that. She ALWAYS checks.

So I knew it wasn't fair to run off like that and make her worry. I didn't care much then about what my dad thought. I was pretty much hating him by then. But I just had to be alone for a little while. I mean, it takes some getting used to, finding out you're a princess. I guess some girls might like it, but not me. I've never been good at girly stuff, you know, like putting on makeup and wearing panty hose and stuff. I mean, I can *do* it, if I have to, but I'd rather not.

Much rather not.

Anyway, I don't know how, but my feet sort of knew where they were going, and before I knew it I was at the zoo.

I love the Central Park Zoo. I always have, since I was a little kid. It's way better than the Bronx Zoo, because it's really small and cozy, and the animals are much friendlier, especially the seals and the polar bears. I love polar bears. At the Central Park Zoo, they have this one polar bear, and all he does all day long is the backstroke. I swear! He was on the news once because this animal psychologist was worried he was under too much stress. It must suck to have people looking at you all day. But then they bought him some toys, and after that he was all right. He just kicks back in his enclosure—they don't have cages at the Central Park Zoo, they have enclosures—and watches you watching him. Sometimes he holds a ball while he does it. I love that bear.

So after I forked over a couple of dollars to get in— that's the other good thing about the zoo: it's cheap—I paid a little call on the polar bear. He appeared to be doing fine. Much better than I was, at the moment. I mean, *his* dad hadn't told him he was the heir to the throne of any-where. I wondered where that polar bear had come from.

I hoped he was from Iceland.

After a while it got too crowded at the polar bear enclosure, so then I went into the penguin house. It smells kind of bad in here, but it's fun. There are these windows that look underwater, so you can see the penguins swimming around, sliding on the rocks and having a good penguin time. Little kids put their hands on the glass, and when a penguin swims toward them, they start screaming. It totally cracks me up. There's a bench you can sit on, too, and that's where I'm sitting now, writing this. You get used to the smell after a while. I guess you can get used to anything.

Oh, my God, I can't believe I just wrote that! I will NEVER get used to being Princess Amelia Renaldo! I don't even know who that is! It sounds like the name of some stupid line of makeup, or of somebody from a Disney movie who's been missing and just recovered her memory, or something.

What am I going to do? I CAN'T move to Genovia, I just CAN'T!! Who would look after Fat Louie? My mom can't. She forgets to feed *herself*, let alone a *CAT*.

I'm sure they won't let me have a cat in the palace. At least, not a cat like Louie, who weighs twenty-five pounds and eats socks. He'd scare all the ladies-in-waiting.

Oh, God. *What am I going to do?*

If Lana Weinberger finds out about this, I'm dead.

Of course, I couldn't hide out in the penguin house forever. Eventually, they flicked the lights and said the zoo was closing. I put my journal away and filed out with everybody else. I grabbed a downtown bus and went home, where I was sure I was going to get it BIG TIME from my mom.

What I didn't count on was getting it from BOTH my parents at the same time. This was a first.

"Where have you been, young lady?" my mom wanted to know. She was sitting at the kitchen table with my dad, the telephone between them.

My dad said, at the exact same time, "We were worried sick!"

I thought I was in for the grounding of a lifetime, but all they wanted to know was whether I was all right. I assured them that I was and apologized for going all Jennifer Love Hewitt on them. I just needed to be alone, I said.

I was really worried they'd start in on me, but they totally didn't. My mom did try to make me eat some ramen, but I wouldn't, because it was beef flavored. And then my dad offered to send his driver to Nobu to pick up some blackened sea bass, but I was like, "Really, Dad, I just want to go to bed." Then my mom started feeling my head and stuff, thinking I was sick. This nearly made me start crying again. I guess my dad recognized my expression from the Plaza, since all of a sudden he was like, "Helen, just leave her alone."

To my surprise, she did. And so I went into my bathroom and closed the door and took a long, hot bath, then got into my favorite pajamas, the cool red flannel ones, found Fat Louie where he was trying to hide under the futon couch (he doesn't like my dad so much), and went to bed.

Before I fell asleep, I could hear my dad talking to my mom in the kitchen for a long, long time. His voice was rumbly, like thunder. It sort of reminded me of Captain Picard's voice on *Star Trek: The Next Generation*.

My dad actually has a lot in common with Captain Picard. You know, he's white and bald and has to rule over a small populace.

Except that Captain Picard always makes everything okay by the end of the episode, and I sincerely doubt everything will be okay for me.

Today when I woke up, the pigeons that live on the fire escape outside my window were cooing away (Fat Louie was on the windowsill—well, as much of him as could fit on the windowsill, anyway—watching them), and the sun was shining, and I actually got up on time and didn't hit the snooze button seven thousand times. I took a shower and didn't cut my legs shaving them, found a fairly unwrinkled blouse at the bottom of my closet, and even got my hair to look sort of halfway passable. I was in a good mood. It was *Friday*. Friday is my favorite day, besides Saturday and Sunday. Fridays always mean two days—two glorious, relaxing days—of NO Algebra are coming my way.

And then I walked out into the kitchen and there was all this pink light coming down through the skylight right on my mom, who was wearing her best kimono and making French toast using Egg Beaters instead of real eggs, even though I'm no longer ovo-lacto since I realized eggs aren't fertilized so they could never have been baby chicks anyway.

And I was all set to thank her for thinking of me, and then I heard this rustle.

And there was my DAD sitting at the dining room table (well, really it's just a table, since we don't have a dining room, but whatever), reading *The New York Times* and wearing a suit.

A *suit*. At seven o'clock in the morning.

And then I remembered. I couldn't believe I'd forgotten it:

I'm a *princess*.

Oh, my God. Everything good about my day just went right out the window after that.

As soon as he saw me, my dad was all, "Ah, Mia."

I knew I was in for it. He only says *"Ah, Mia"* when he's about to give me a big lecture.

He folded his paper all carefully and laid it down. My dad always folds papers carefully, making the edges all neat. My mom never does this. She usually crumples the pages up and leaves them, out of order, on the futon couch or next to the toilet. This kind of thing drives my father insane and is probably the real reason why they never got married.

My mom, I saw, had set the table with our best Kmart plates, the ones with the blue stripes on them, and the green plastic cactus-shaped margarita glasses from Ikea. She had even put a bunch of fake sunflowers in the middle of the table in a yellow vase. She had done all that to cheer me up, I know, and she'd probably gotten up really early to do it, too. But instead of cheering me up, it just made me sadder.

Because I bet they don't use green plastic cactus-shaped margarita glasses for breakfast at the palace in Genovia.

"We need to talk, Mia," my dad said. This is how his worst lectures always start. Except this time he looked at me kind of funny before he started. "What's wrong with your hair?"

I put my hand up to my head. "Why?" I thought my hair looked good, for a change.

"Nothing is wrong with her hair, Phillipe," my mom said. She usually tries to ward off my dad's lectures, if she can. "Come and sit down, Mia, and have some breakfast. I even heated up the syrup for the French toast, the way you like it."

I appreciated this gesture on my mom's part. I really did. But I was not going to sit down and talk about my future in Genovia. I mean, come on. So I was all, "Uh, I'd love to, really, but I gotta go. I have a test in World Civ today, and I

43

promised Lilly I'd meet her to go over our notes together—"

"*Sit down.*"

Boy, my dad can really sound like a starship captain in the Federation when he wants to.

I sat. My mom shoveled some French toast onto my plate. I poured syrup over it and took a bite, just to be polite. It tasted like cardboard.

"Mia," my mom said. She was still trying to ward off my dad's lecture. "I know how upset you must be about all of this. But really, it isn't as bad as you're making it out to be."

Oh, right. All of a sudden you tell me I'm a princess, and I'm supposed to be happy about it?

"I mean," my mom went on, "most girls would probably be delighted to find out their father is a prince!"

No girls I know. Actually, that's not true. Lana Weinberger would probably *love* to be a princess. In fact, she already thinks she is one.

"Just think of all the lovely things you could have if you went to live in Genovia." My mom's face totally lit up as she started listing the lovely things I could have if I went to live in Genovia, but her voice sounded strange, as if she were playing a mom on TV or something. "Like a car! You know how impractical it is to have a car here in the city. But in Genovia, when you turn sixteen, I'm sure Dad will buy you a—"

I pointed out that there are enough problems with pollution in Europe without my contributing to it. Diesel emissions are one of the largest contributors to the destruction of the ozone layer.

"But you've always wanted a horse, haven't you? Well, in Genovia you could have one. A nice gray one with spots on its back—"

That hurt.

"Mom," I said, my eyes all filling up with tears. I

completely couldn't help it. Suddenly, I was bawling all over again. "What are you *doing*? Do you *want* me to go live with Dad? Is that it? Are you tired of me or something? Do you want me to go live with Dad so you and Mr. Gianini can . . . can . . ."

I couldn't go on because I started crying so hard. But by then my mom was crying, too. She jumped up out of her chair and came around the end of the table and started hugging me, saying, "Oh, no, honey! How could you think something like that?" She stopped sounding like a TV mom. "I just want what's best for you!"

"As do I," my dad said, looking annoyed. He had folded his arms across his chest and was leaning back in his chair, watching us in an irritated way.

"Well, what's best for me is to stay right here and finish high school," I told him. "And then I'm going to join Greenpeace and help save the whales."

My dad looked even *more* irritated at that. "You are *not* joining Greenpeace," he said.

"I am, too," I said. It was totally hard to talk, because I was crying and all, but I told him, "I'm going to go to Iceland to save the baby seals, too."

"You most certainly are not." My dad didn't just look annoyed. Now he looked mad. "You are going to go to college. Vassar, I think. Maybe Sarah Lawrence."

That made me cry even more.

But before I could say anything, my mom held up a hand and was like, "Phillipe, don't. We aren't accomplishing anything here. Mia has to get to school, anyway. She's already late—"

I started looking around for my backpack and coat real fast. "Yeah," I said. "I gotta renew my MetroCard."

My dad made this weird French noise he makes sometimes. It's halfway between a snort and a sigh. It kind of

45

sounds like *Pfuit!* Then he said, "Lars will drive you."

I told my dad that this was unnecessary since I meet Lilly every day at Astor Place, where we catch the uptown 6 train together.

"Lars can pick up your little friend, too."

I looked at my mom. She was looking at my dad. Lars is my dad's driver. He goes everywhere my dad goes. For as long as I've known my dad—okay, my whole life—he's always had a driver, usually a big beefy guy who used to work for the president of Israel or somebody like that.

Now that I think about it, of course I realize these guys aren't really drivers at all but bodyguards.

Duh.

Okay, so the last thing I wanted was for my dad's bodyguard to drive me to school. How would I ever explain it to Lilly? *Oh, don't mind him, Lilly. He's just my dad's chauffeur.* Yeah, right. The only person at Albert Einstein High School who gets dropped off by a chauffeur is this totally rich Saudi Arabian girl named Tina Hakim Baba, whose dad owns some big oil company, and everybody makes fun of her because her parents are all worried she'll get kidnapped between Seventy-fifth and Madison, where our school is, and Seventy-fifth and Fifth, where she lives. She even has a bodyguard who follows her around from class to class and talks on a walkie-talkie to the chauffeur. This seems a little extreme, if you ask me.

But Dad was totally rigid on the driver thing. It's like now that I'm an official princess there's all this concern for my welfare. Yesterday, when I was Mia Thermopolis, it was perfectly okay for me to ride the subway. Today, now that I'm Princess Amelia, forget it.

Well, whatever. It didn't seem worth arguing over. I mean, there are way worse things I have to worry about.

Like which country am I going to be living in in the near future.

As I was leaving—my dad made Lars come up to the loft to walk me down to the car; it was totally embarrassing—I overheard my dad say to my mom, "All right, Helen. Who's this Gianini fellow Mia was talking about?"

Oops.

$ab = a + b$
solve for b
$ab - b = a$
$b(a - 1) = a$
$b = \dfrac{a}{a - 1}$

Lilly could tell right away something was up.

Oh, she swallowed the whole story I fed her about Lars: "Oh, my dad's in town, and he's got this driver, and you know . . ."

But I couldn't tell her about the princess thing. I mean, all I kept thinking about was how disgusted Lilly sounded during that part in her oral report when she mentioned how Christian monarchs used to consider themselves appointed agents of divine will and thus were responsible not to the people they governed but to God alone, even though my dad hardly ever even goes to church, except when Grandmère makes him.

Lilly believed me about Lars, but she was still all over me with the crying thing. She was like, "Why are your eyes so red and squinty? You've been crying. Why were you crying? Did something happen? What happened? Did you get another F in something?"

I just shrugged and tried to look out the passenger window at the uninspiring view of the East Village crack-houses, which we had to drive by to get to the FDR. "It's nothing," I said. "PMS."

"It is not PMS. You had your period last week. I remember because you borrowed a pad from me after PE, and then you ate two whole packs of Yodels at lunch." Sometimes I wish Lilly's memory weren't so good. "So spill. Did Louie eat another sock?"

First of all, it was like totally embarrassing to discuss my menstrual cycle in front of my dad's bodyguard. I mean, Lars is kind of a Baldwin. He was concentrating really hard on driving, though, and I don't know if he could hear us from the front seat, but it was embarrassing, just the same.

"It's nothing," I whispered. "Just my dad. *You know.*"

"Oh," Lilly said in her normal voice. Have I mentioned that Lilly's normal voice is really loud? "You mean the infertility thing? Is he still bummed out about that? Gawd, does *he* ever need to self-actualize."

Lilly then went on to describe something she called the Jungian tree of self-actualization. She says my dad is way on the bottom branches, and he won't be able to reach the top of the thing until he accepts himself as he is and stops obsessing over his inability to sire more offspring.

I guess that's part of my problem. I'm way at the bottom of the self-actualization tree. Like, underneath the roots of it, practically.

But now that I'm sitting here in Algebra, things don't seem so bad, really. I mean, I thought about it all through Homeroom, and I finally realized something:

They can't *make* me be a princess.

They really can't. I mean, this is America, for crying out loud. Here, you can be anything you want to be. At least that's what Mrs. Holland was always telling us last year, when we studied U.S. History. So, if I can be whatever I want to be, I can *not* be a princess. Nobody can *make* me be a princess, not even my dad, if I don't want to be one.

Right?

So when I get home tonight, I'll just tell my dad thanks, but no thanks. I'll just be plain old Mia for now.

Geez. Mr. Gianini just called on me, and I totally had no idea what he was talking about, because of course I was writing in this book instead of paying attention. My face feels like it's on fire. Lana is laughing her head off, of course. She is such a wanker.

What does he keep picking on *me* for, anyway? He should know by now that I don't know the quadratic formula from a hole in the ground. He's only picking on me because of my mom. He wants to make it look as if he's treating me the same as everybody else in the class.

Well, I'm *not* the same as everybody else in the class.

What do I need to know Algebra for, anyway? They don't use Algebra in Greenpeace.

And you can bet you don't need it if you're a princess. So however things turn out, I'm covered.

Cool.

solve $x = a + aby$ for y

$x - a = aby$

$$\frac{x - a}{ab} = \frac{aby}{ab}$$

$$\frac{x - a}{ab} = y$$

Really Late on Friday, Lilly Moscovitz's Bedroom

Okay, so I blew off Mr. Gianini's help session after school. I *know* I shouldn't have. Believe me, Lilly let me know I shouldn't have. I know he has these help sessions just for people like me, who are flunking. I know he does it in his own spare time and doesn't even get paid overtime for it or anything. But if I won't ever need Algebra in any foreseeable future career, why do I need to go?

I asked Lilly if it would be okay if I spent the night at her house tonight and she said only if I promised to stop acting like such a head case.

I promised, even though I don't think I'm acting like a head case.

But when I called my mom from the pay phone in the lobby after school to ask her if it was okay if I stayed overnight at the Moscovitzes, she was all, "Um, actually, Mia, your father was really hoping that when you got home tonight we could have another talk."

Oh, great.

I told my mom that although there was nothing I wanted to do more than have another talk, I was very concerned about Lilly, whose stalker was recently released from Bellevue again. Ever since Lilly started her cable access TV show, this guy named Norman has been calling in, asking her to take off her shoes. According to the Drs. Moscovitz, Norman is a fetishist. His fixation is feet—in particular, Lilly's feet. He sends stuff to her care of the show, CDs and stuffed animals and things like that, and writes that there'll be more where that came from if Lilly would just take off her shoes on air. So what Lilly does is, she takes off her shoes, all right, but then she throws a blanket over her legs and kicks her feet around under it and goes, "Look,

Norman, you freak! I took my shoes off! Thanks for the CDs, sucker!"

This angered Norman so much that he started wandering around the Village looking for Lilly. Everyone knows Lilly lives in the Village, since we filmed a very popular episode where Lilly borrowed the pricing gun from Grand Union and stood on the corner of Bleecker and La Guardia and told all the European tourists wandering around NoHo that if they wore a Grand Union price sticker on their foreheads they could get a free latte from Dean & DeLuca (a surprising amount of them believed her).

Anyway, one day a few weeks ago Norman the foot fetishist found us in the park and started chasing us around, waving twenty dollar bills and trying to get us to take off our shoes. This was very entertaining, and hardly scary at all, especially because we just ran right up to the command post on Washington Square South and Thompson Street, where the Sixth Precinct has been parking this enormous trailer so they can secretly spy on the drug dealers. We told the police that this weird guy was trying to assault us, and you should have seen it: About twenty undercover guys (even a guy I thought was an old homeless man asleep on a bench) jumped on Norman and dragged him, screaming, off to the mental ward!

I always have such a good time with Lilly.

Anyway, Lilly's parents told her Norman just got out of Bellevue and that if she sees him she's not to torment him anymore, because he's just a poor obsessive-compulsive with possible schizophrenic tendencies.

Lilly's devoting tomorrow's show to her feet. She's going to model every single pair of shoes she owns, but not once show her bare feet. She hopes that this will drive Norman over the edge and he'll do something weirder than ever, like get a gun and shoot at us.

I'm not scared, though. Norman has kind of thick glasses, and I bet he couldn't actually hit anything, even with a machine gun, which even a lunatic like Norman is allowed to buy in this country thanks to our totally unrestrictive gun laws, which Michael Moscovitz says in his webzine will ultimately result in the demise of democracy as we know it.

My mom was totally not buying this, though. She was all, "Mia, I appreciate the fact that you want to help your friend through this difficult period with her stalker, but I really think you have more pressing responsibilities here at home."

And I was all, "What responsibilities?" thinking she was talking about the litter box, which I had totally cleaned two days ago.

And she was like, "Responsibility toward your father and me."

I just about lost it right there. Responsibilities? *Responsibilities? She's* telling *me* about responsibilities? When is the last time it ever occurred to *her* to drop off the laundry, let alone pick it up again? When is the last time *she* remembered to buy Q-tips or toilet paper or milk?

And did she ever happen to think to mention, in all of my fourteen years, that I might possibly end up being the princess of Genovia someday???

She thinks she needs to tell *me* about my responsibilities? HA!!!!!!

I nearly hung up on her. But Lilly was sort of standing nearby, practicing her house manager duties by switching on and off the lights in the school lobby. Since I had promised not to act like a head case, and hanging up on my mother would definitely fall into the head case category, I said in this really patient voice, "Don't worry, Mom, I won't forget to stop at Genovese on my way home tomorrow and pick up new vacuum cleaner bags."

And *then* I hung up.

HOMEWORK

Algebra: problems 1–12, pg. 119
English: proposal
World Civ: questions at end of Chapter 4
G & T: none
French: use *avoir* in neg. sentence, rd. lessons one to three, *pas de plus*
Biology: none

Saturday, October 4,
Early, Still Lilly's Place

Why do I always have such a good time when I spend the night at Lilly's? I mean, it's not like they've got stuff that I don't have. In fact, my mom and I have better stuff. The Moscovitzes only get a couple of movie channels, and because I took advantage of the last Time Warner Cable bonus offer, we have all of them, Cinemax *and* HBO *and* Showtime, for the low, low rate of $19.99 per month.

Plus we have way better people to spy on through our windows, like Ronnie, who used to be a Ronald but is now called Ronette, and who has a lot of big fancy parties; and that skinny German couple who wear black all the time, even in summer, and never pull down their blinds. On Fifth Avenue, where the Moscovitzes live, there's *nobody* good to look at: Just other rich psychoanalysts and their children. Let me tell you, you don't see anything good through *their* windows.

But it's like every time I spend the night here, even if all Lilly and I do is hang out in the kitchen eating macaroons left over from Rosh Hashanah, I have such a great time. Maybe that's because Maya, the Moscovitzes' Dominican maid, never forgets to buy orange juice, and she always remembers that I don't like the pulpy kind, and sometimes, if she knows I'm staying over, she'll pick up a vegetable lasagna from Balducci's, instead of a meat one, especially for me, like she did last night.

Or maybe it's because I never find moldy old containers of anything in the Moscovitzes' refrigerator. Maya throws away anything that's even one day past its expiration date. Even sour cream that still has the protective plastic around the lid. Even cans of Tab.

And the Drs. Moscovitz never forget to pay the electricity bill. Con Ed has never once shut down *their* power in the middle of a *Star Trek* movie marathon. And Lilly's mom, she always talks about normal stuff, like what a great deal she got on Calvin Klein panty hose at Bergdorf's.

Not that I don't love my mom or anything. I totally do. I just wish she could be more of a mom and less of an artist.

And I wish my dad could be more like Lilly's dad, who always wants to make me an omelet because he thinks I'm too skinny, and who walks around in his old college sweatpants when he doesn't have to go to his office to analyze anybody.

Dr. Moscovitz would *never* wear a suit at seven in the morning.

Not that I don't love my dad. I do, I guess. I just don't understand how he could let something like this happen. He's usually so organized. *How could he have let himself become a prince?*

I just don't understand it.

The best thing, I guess, about going to Lilly's is that while I'm there I don't even have to think about things like how I'm flunking Algebra or how I'm the heir to the throne of a small European principality. I can just relax and enjoy some real homemade Poppin' Fresh Cinnamon Buns and watch Pavlov, Michael's sheltie, try to herd Maya back into the kitchen every time she tries to come out.

Last night was *totally* fun. The Drs. Moscovitz were out—they had to go to a benefit at the Puck Building for the homosexual children of survivors of the Holocaust—so Lilly and I made this huge vat of popcorn smothered in butter and climbed into her parents' giant canopy bed and watched all the James Bond movies in a row. We were able to definitively determine that Pierce Brosnan was the skinniest James

Bond, Sean Connery the hairiest, and Roger Moore the most tan. None of the James Bonds took off their shirts enough for us to decide who had the best chest, but I think probably Timothy Dalton.

I like chest hair. I think.

It was sort of ironic that while I was trying to decide this Lilly's brother came into the room. He had on a shirt, though. He looked kind of annoyed. He said my dad was on the phone. My dad was all mad because he'd been trying to get through for hours, only Michael was on the Internet answering fan mail for his webzine, *Crackhead*, so my dad kept getting a busy signal.

I must have looked like I was going to throw up or something, because after a minute Michael said, "Okay, don't worry about it, Thermopolis. I'll tell him you and Lilly already went to bed," which is a lie my mother would never believe, but it must have gone over pretty well with my dad, since Michael came back and reported that my dad had apologized for calling so late (it was only eleven) and that he'd speak to me in the morning.

Great. I can't wait.

I guess I must have still looked like I was going to throw up, because Michael called his dog and made him get into bed with us, even though pets aren't allowed in the Drs. Moscovitzes' room. Pavlov crawled into my lap and started licking my face, which he'll only do to people he really trusts. Then Michael sat down to watch the movies with us, and in the interest of science, Lilly asked him which Bond girls were most attractive to him, the blondes who always needed James Bond to rescue them or the brunettes who were always pulling guns on him, and Michael said he couldn't resist a girl with a weapon, which got us started on his two favorite TV shows of all time, *Xena: Warrior Princess* and *Buffy the Vampire Slayer*.

So then, not really in the interest of science but more out of plain curiosity, I asked Michael if it was the end of the world and he had to repopulate the planet but he could only choose one life mate, who would it be, Xena or Buffy?

After telling me how weird I was for thinking of something like that, Michael chose Buffy, and then Lilly asked me if I had to choose between Harrison Ford or George Clooney who would it be, and I said Harrison Ford even though he's so old, but the Harrison Ford from *Indiana Jones*, not *Star Wars*, and then Lilly said she'd choose Harrison Ford as Jack Ryan in those Tom Clancy movies, and then Michael goes, "Who would you choose, Harrison Ford or Leonardo DiCaprio?" and we both chose Harrison Ford because Leonardo is so passé, and then he went, "Who would you choose, Harrison Ford or Josh Richter?" and Lilly said Harrison Ford, because he used to be a carpenter, and if it was the end of the world he could build her a house, but I said Josh Richter, because he'd live longer—Harrison is like SIXTY—and be able to give me a hand with the kids.

Then Michael started saying all this totally unfair stuff about Josh Richter, like how in the face of nuclear Armageddon he'd probably show cowardice, but Lilly said fear of new things is not an accurate measure of one's potential for growth, with which I agreed. Then Michael said we were both idiots if we thought Josh Richter would ever give us so much as the time of day, that he only liked girls like Lana Weinberger, who put out, to which Lilly responded that she would put out for Josh Richter if he was able to meet certain conditions, like bathing beforehand in an antibacterial solution and wearing three condoms coated in spermicidal fluid during the act, in case one broke and one slipped off.

Then Michael asked me if I would put out for Josh

Richter, and I had to think about it for a minute. Losing your virginity is a really big step, and you have to do it with the right person or else you could be screwed up for the rest of your life, like the women in Dr. Moscovitz's Over Forty and Still Single group, which meets every other Tuesday. So after I'd thought about it, I said I would put out for Josh Richter, but only if:

1. We'd been dating for at least a year.
2. He pledged his undying love to me.
3. He took me to see *Beauty and the Beast* on Broadway and didn't make fun of it.

Michael said the first two sounded all right, but if the third one was an example of the kind of boyfriend I expected to get, I'd be a virgin for a long, long time. He said he didn't know anyone with an ounce of testosterone who could watch *Beauty and the Beast* on Broadway without projectile vomiting. But he's wrong, because my dad definitely has testosterone—at least one testicle full—and he's never projectile vomited at the show.

Then Lilly asked Michael who he would choose if he had to, me or Lana Weinberger, and he said, "Mia, of course," but I'm sure he was just saying that because I was right there in the room and he didn't want to dis me to my face.

I wish Lilly wouldn't do things like that.

But she kept on doing it, wanting to know who Michael would choose, me or Madonna, and me or Buffy the Vampire Slayer (he chose me over Madonna, but Buffy won, hands down, over me).

And then Lilly wanted to know who I would choose, Michael or Josh Richter. I pretended to be seriously thinking about it, when to my total relief the Drs. Moscovitz came home and started yelling at us for letting Pavlov in their room and eating popcorn in their bed.

So then later after Lilly and I had cleaned up all the popcorn and gone back to her room, she asked me again who I would choose, Josh Richter or her brother, and I had to say Josh Richter, because Josh Richter is the hottest boy in our whole school, maybe the whole world, and I am completely and totally in love with him, and not just because of the way his blond hair sometimes falls into his eyes when he's bent over, looking for stuff in his locker, but because I know that behind that jock facade he maintains he is a deeply sensitive and caring person. I could tell by the way he said hey to me that day in Bigelows.

But I couldn't help thinking if it *really* were the end of the world, it might be better to be with Michael, even if he isn't so hot, because at least he makes me laugh. I think at the end of the world a sense of humor would be important.

Plus, of course, Michael looks really good without a shirt.

And if it really was the end of the world, Lilly would be dead, so she'd never know her brother and I were pro-creating!

I'd *never* want Lilly to know that I feel that way about her brother. She'd think it was weird.

Weirder even than me turning out to be the princess of Genovia.

The whole way home from Lilly's I worried about what my mom and dad were going to say when I got home. I had never disobeyed them before. I mean, really never.

Well, okay, there was that one time Lilly and Shameeka and Ling Su and I went to see that Christian Slater movie, but we ended up going to *The Rocky Horror Picture Show* instead, and I forgot to call until after the movie, which ended at like 2:30 in the morning and we were in Times Square and didn't have enough money left among us for a cab.

But that was just that one time! And I totally learned a lesson from it, without my mom having to ground me or anything. Not that she would ever do something like that—ground me, I mean. Who would go to the cash machine to get money for takeout if I were grounded?

But my dad's another story. He is totally rigid in the discipline department. My mom says that's because Grandmère used to punish him when he was a little boy by locking him into this one really scary room in their house.

Now that I think about it, the house my dad grew up in was probably the castle, and that scary room was probably the dungeon.

Geez, no wonder my dad does every single thing Grandmère says.

Anyway, when my dad gets mad at me he *really* gets mad. Like the time I wouldn't go to church with Grandmère because I refused to pray to a god who would allow rain forests to be destroyed in order to make grazing room for cows who would later become Quarter Pounders for the ignorant masses who worship that symbol of all that is evil, Ronald McDonald. Not only did my dad tell me that if I didn't go to church he'd wear out my behind, he said he wouldn't let me read Michael's webzine, *Crackhead*, again! He refused to let me go online again for the rest of the summer. He crushed my modem with a magnum of Chateauneuf du Pape.

Talk about reactionary!

So I was totally worried about what he was going to do when I got home from Lilly's.

I tried to hang out at the Moscovitzes' as long as possible: I loaded the breakfast dishes in the dishwasher for Maya, since she was busy writing a letter to her congressman asking him to please do something about her son, Manuel, who was wrongfully imprisoned ten years ago for supporting a revolution in their country. I walked Pavlov, since Michael had to go to an astrophysics lecture at Columbia. I even unclogged the jets in the Drs. Moscovitzes' Jacuzzi—boy, does Lilly's dad shed a lot.

Then Lilly had to go and announce that it was time to shoot the one-hour special episode of her show, the one dedicated to her feet. Only it turned out the Drs. Moscovitz had not left, like we thought they had, for their Rolfing sessions. They totally overheard and told me that I had to go home while they analyzed Lilly about her need to taunt her sex-crazed stalker.

Here's the thing:

I am generally a very good daughter. I mean it. I don't smoke. I don't do drugs. I haven't given birth at any proms. I am completely trustworthy, and I do my homework most of the time. Except for one lousy F in a class that will be of no use to me whatsoever in my future life, I'm doing pretty well.

And then they had to spring the princess thing on me.

I decided on my way home that if my dad tried to punish me I was going to call Judge Judy. He'd really be sorry if he landed in front of Judge Judy because of this. She'd let him have it, boy, let me tell you. People trying to make other people be princesses when they don't want to be? Judge Judy wouldn't stand for any of it.

Of course, when I got home, it turned out I didn't have to call Judge Judy at all.

My mom hadn't gone to her studio, which she does every Saturday without fail. She was sitting there waiting for me to come home, reading old copies of the subscription she got me to *Seventeen* magazine before she realized I was too flat-chested to ever be asked out on a date, so all the information provided in that particular periodical was worthless to me.

Then there was my dad, who was sitting in the exact same spot as he'd been when I'd left the day before, only this time he was reading the Sunday *Times*, even though it was Saturday, and Mom and I have this rule that you can't start reading the Sunday sections until Sunday. To my surprise, he wasn't wearing a suit. Today he had on a sweater—cashmere, no doubt given to him by one of his many girlfriends—and corduroy pants.

When I walked in, he folded the paper all carefully, put it down, and gave me this long, intent look, like Captain Picard right before he starts going on to Riker about the Prime Directive. Then he goes, "We need to talk."

I immediately started in about how it wasn't like I hadn't told them where I was, and how I just needed a little time away to think about things, and how I'd been really careful and hadn't taken the subway or anything, and my dad just went, "I know."

Just like that. "*I know.*" He completely gave in without a fight.

My dad.

I looked at my mom to see if she'd noticed that he'd lost his mind. And then she did the craziest thing. She put the magazine down and came over and hugged me and said, "We're so sorry, baby."

Hello? These are my *parents?* Did the body snatchers come while I was gone and replace my parents with pod people? Because that was the only way I could think of that my parents would be so reasonable.

Then my dad goes, "We understand the stress that this has brought you, Mia, and we want you to know that we'll do everything in our power to try to make this transition as smooth for you as possible."

Then my dad asked me if I knew what a compromise was, and I said yes, of course, I'm not in like the third grade anymore, so he pulled out this piece of paper, and on it we all drafted what my mom calls the Thermopolis-Renaldo Compromise. It goes like this:

> I, *the undersigned, Artur Christoff Phillipe*
> *Gerard Grimaldi Renaldo, agree that my sole*
> *offspring and heir, Amelia Mignonette Grimaldi*
> *Thermopolis Renaldo, may finish out her high*
> *school tenure at Albert Einstein School for Boys*
> *(made coeducational circa 1975) without*
> *interruption, save for Christmas and summer*
> *breaks, which she will spend without complaint*
> *in the country of Genovia.*

I asked if that meant no more summers at Miragnac, and he said yes. I couldn't believe it. Christmas and summer, free of Grandmère? That would be like going to the dentist, only instead of having cavities filled I'd just get to read *Teen People* and suck up a lot of laughing gas! I was so happy, I hugged him right there. But unfortunately, it turned out there was more to the agreement:

I, the undersigned, Amelia Mignonette Grimaldi
Thermopolis Renaldo, agree to fulfill the duties of
heir to Artur Christoff Phillipe Gerard Grimaldi
Renaldo, prince of Genovia, and all that such a
role entails, including but not exclusive to,
assuming the throne upon the latter's demise and
attending functions of state at which the presence
of said heir is deemed essential.

All of that sounded pretty good to me, except the last part. Functions of state? What were they?

My dad got all vague: "Oh, you know. Attending the funerals of world leaders, opening balls, that sort of thing."

Hello? Funerals? Balls? Whatever happened to smashing bottles of champagne against ocean liners, and going to Hollywood premieres, and that kind of thing?

"Well," my dad said, "Hollywood premieres aren't really all they're pegged up to be. Flashbulbs going off in your face, that kind of thing. Terribly unpleasant."

Yeah, but *funerals? Balls?* I don't even know how to put on lip liner, let alone curtsy. . . .

"Oh, that's all right," my dad said, putting the cap back on his pen. "Grandmère will take care of that."

Yeah, right. What can *she* do? She's in France!

Ha! Ha! Ha!

Saturday Night

I can't even believe what a loser I am. I mean, Saturday night, alone with my DAD!

He actually tried to talk me into going to see *Beauty and the Beast*, like he felt sorry for me because I didn't have a date!

I finally had to say, "Look, Dad, I am not a child anymore. Even the prince of Genovia can't get tickets to a Broadway show at a minute's notice on a Saturday night."

He was just feeling left out because Mom had taken off on another date with Mr. Gianini. She wanted to cancel on him, given all the upheaval that has occurred in my life over the past twenty-four hours, but I totally made her go because I could see her lips getting smaller and smaller the more time she spent with Dad. Mom's lips only get small when she's trying to keep herself from saying something, and I think what she wanted to say to my dad was *"Get out! Go back to your hotel! You're paying six hundred dollars a night for that suite! Can't you go stay in it?"*

My dad drives my mom completely insane because he's always going around, digging her bank statements out from the big salad bowl where she throws all our mail, and trying to tell her how much she would save in interest if she would just transfer funds out of her checking account and into a Roth IRA.

So even though she felt like she should stay home, I knew if she did she'd explode, so I said go, please go, and that Dad and I would discuss what it's like to govern a small principality in today's economic market. Only when Mom came out in her datewear, which included this totally hot black minidress from Victoria's Secret (my mom hates shopping, so she buys all her clothes from catalogs while she's soaking in the tub after a long day of painting), my dad started to choke on this ice cube. I guess he had never seen my mom in a minidress before—back in college, when they were going out, all she ever wore was overalls, like me—because he drank down his scotch and soda really fast and then said, "*That's* what you're wearing?" which made my mom go, "What's wrong with it?" and look at herself all worriedly in the mirror.

She looked totally fine; in fact, she looked much better than she usually did, which I guess was the problem. I mean, it sounds weird to admit, but my mom can be a total Betty when she puts her mind to it. I can only *wish* that someday I'll be as pretty as my mom. I mean, *she* doesn't have Yield sign hair or a flat chest or size-ten shoes. She is way hot, as far as moms go.

Then the buzzer rang and Mom ran out because she didn't want Mr. Gianini to come up and meet her ex, the prince of Genovia. Which was understandable, since he was still choking and looked sort of funny. I mean, he looked like a red-faced bald man in a cashmere sweater coughing up a lung. I mean, *I* would have been embarrassed to admit I had ever had sex with him, if I were her.

Anyway, it was good for me that she didn't buzz Mr. Gianini up, because I didn't want him asking me in front of my parents why I hadn't gone to his review session on Friday.

So then, after they were gone, I tried to show my dad how much better suited I am for life in Manhattan than in Genovia by ordering some really excellent food. I got us an insalata caprese, ravioli al funghetto, and a pizza margherita, all for under twenty bucks, but I swear, my dad wasn't a bit impressed! He just poured himself another scotch and soda and turned on the TV. He didn't even notice when Fat Louie sat down next to him. He started petting him like it was nothing. And my dad claims to be *allergic* to cats.

And then, to top it all off, he didn't even want to talk about Genovia. All he wanted to do was watch sports. I'm not kidding. Sports. We have seventy-seven channels, and all he would watch were the ones showing men in uniforms chasing after a little ball. Forget the Dirty Harry movie marathon. Forget Pop-Up Videos. He just turned on the sports channel and stared at it, and when I happened to mention that Mom and I usually watch whatever is on HBO on Saturday nights, he just turned up the volume!!!

What a baby.

And you think that's bad? You should have seen him when the food got here. He made Lars frisk the delivery-man before he would let me buzz him up! Can you believe it? I had to give Antonio a whole extra dollar to make up for the indignity of it all. And then my dad sat down and ate, without saying a word, until, after another scotch and soda, he fell asleep, right on the futon, with Fat Louie on his lap!

I guess being a prince and having had testicular cancer can really make a person think he's something special. I mean, God forbid he should share some quality time with his only daughter, the heir to his throne.

So here I am again, home on a Saturday night. Not that I'm ever NOT home on a Saturday night, except when I'm with Lilly. Why am I so unpopular? I mean, I know I look weird and stuff, but I really try to be nice to people, you know? You'd think people would value me as a human being and invite me to their parties just because they like my company. It's not MY fault my hair sticks out the way it does, any more than it's Lilly's fault her face looks sort of squished.

I tried to call Lilly a zillion times, but her phone was busy, which meant Michael was probably home working on his 'zine. The Moscovitzes are trying to have a second line installed so that people who call them can actually get through once in a while, but the phone company says it doesn't have any more 212 numbers to give out. Lilly's mom says she refuses to have two separate area codes in the same apartment and that if she can't have 212 she'll just buy a beeper. Besides, Michael will be leaving for college next fall, and then their phone problems will be solved.

I really wanted to talk to Lilly. I mean, I haven't told her anything about the princess thing, and I'm not going to, *ever*, but sometimes, even without telling her what's bothering me, talking to Lilly makes me feel better. Maybe it's just knowing that somebody else my age is also stuck at home on a Saturday night. I mean, most of the other girls in our class date. Even Shameeka has started dating. She's been quite popular since she developed breasts over the summer. True, her curfew is ten o'clock, even on weekends, and she has to introduce her date to her mom and dad, and her date has to provide a detailed itinerary of exactly where they're going and what they'll be doing, besides showing two pieces of photo ID for Mr. Taylor to photocopy before he'll let Shameeka go out of the house with him.

But still, she's *dating*. Somebody *asked her out*.

Nobody has ever asked me out.

It was pretty boring, watching my dad snore, even though it was fairly comical the way Fat Louie kept glancing at him, all annoyed, every time he inhaled. I had already seen all the Dirty Harry movies, and there was nothing else on. I decided to try instant messaging Michael, telling him I really needed to talk to Lilly and would he please go off-line so I could call her.

CracKing: What do you want, Thermopolis?

FtLouie: I want to talk to Lilly. Please go off-line so I can call her.

CracKing: What do you want to talk to her about?

FtLouie: None of your business. Just go off-line, please. You can't hog all the lines of communication to yourself. It isn't fair.

CracKing: No one ever said life was fair, Thermopolis. What are you doing home, anyway? What's the matter? Dreamboy didn't call?

FtLouie: Who's Dreamboy?

CracKing: You know, your postnuclear Armageddon life-mate of choice, Josh Richter.

Lilly told him! I can't believe she told him! I'm going to kill her.

FtLouie: Would you please go off-line so I can call Lilly????

CracKing: What's the matter, Thermopolis? Did I strike a nerve?

I logged off. He can be such a jerk sometimes.

But then about five minutes later the phone rang, and it was Lilly. So I guess even though Michael's a jerk, he can be a nice jerk when he wants to be.

Lilly's very upset about how her parents are violating

her First Amendment right to free speech by not letting her make the episode of her show dedicated to her feet. She is going to call the ACLU as soon as it opens on Monday morning. Without her parents' financial support, which they have currently revoked, *Lilly Tells It Like It Is* cannot go on. It costs about $200 per episode, if you include the cost of tape and all. Public access is only accessible to people with cash.

Lilly was so upset that I didn't feel like yelling at her about telling Michael that I chose Josh. Now that I think about it, it's probably just better that way.

My life is a convoluted web of lies.

I can't believe Mr. Gianini told her. I can't believe he told my mother I skipped his stupid review session on Friday!!!!

Hello? Do I have no rights here? Can't I skip a review session and not get finked on by my mother's boyfriend?

I mean, it's not like my life isn't bad enough: I'm already deformed, *and* I have to be a princess. Do I have to have my every activity reported upon by my Algebra teacher????

Thanks a lot, Mr. Gianini. Thanks to you, I got to spend my entire Sunday having the quadratic formula drilled into me by my demented father, who kept rubbing his bald head and screaming in frustration when he found out I don't know how to multiply fractions.

Hello? May I remind everyone that I'm supposed to have Saturday and Sunday OFF from school?

AND Mr. Gianini had to go and tell my mother there's going to be a pop quiz tomorrow. I mean, I guess that was kind of nice of him and all, to give me a heads-up, but you're not supposed to study for a pop quiz. The whole point is to test what you've retained.

Then again, since I've apparently retained nothing mathematical since about the second grade, I guess I can't really blame my dad for being so mad. He said if I don't pass Algebra he's going to make me go to summer school. So then I pointed out that summer school was fine by me, since I'd already agreed to spend summers in Genovia. So then he said I'd have to go to summer school in GEN-OVIA!

I am so sure. I met some kids who went to school in Genovia and they didn't even know what a number line was. And they measure everything by kilos and centi-meters. As if metric wasn't so totally over!

But just in case, I'm not taking any chances. I wrote out the quadratic formula on the white rubber sole of my Converse high-top, right where it curves in between my heel and my toes. I'll wear them tomorrow and cross my legs and take a peek if I get stuck.

Monday, October 6, 3 a.m.

I've been up all night, worrying about getting caught cheating. What will happen if someone sees I have the quadratic formula written on my shoe? Will I be expelled? I don't want to be expelled! I mean, even though everybody at Albert Einstein High School thinks I'm a freak, I'm sort of getting used to it. I don't want to have to start over at a whole new school. I'll have to wear the scarlet mark of being a cheater for the rest of my high school career!

And what about college? I might not get into college if it goes down on my permanent record that I'm a cheater.

Not that I want to go to college. But what about Greenpeace? I'm sure Greenpeace doesn't want cheaters. Oh, my God, what am I going to do???

I tried washing the quadratic formula off my shoe, but it won't come off! I must have used indelible ink or something! What if my dad finds out? Do they still behead people in Genovia?

Monday, October 6, 7 a.m.

Decided to wear my Docs and throw my high-tops away on the way to school—but then I broke one of the bootlaces! I can't wear any of my other shoes because they're all size nine and a half, and my foot grew a whole half inch last month! I can barely walk in my loafers, and my heels hang out over the backs of my clogs. I have no choice but to wear my high-tops!

I'm going to get caught for sure, I just know it.

Realized in the car on the way to school that I could have taken the laces out of my high-tops and strung them through my Doc Martens. I am so stupid.

Lilly wants to know how much longer my dad is going to be in town. She doesn't like being driven to school. She likes to ride the subway, because then she can brush up on her Spanish by reading all the health awareness posters. I told her I didn't know how long my dad was going to be in town, but that I had a feeling I wasn't going to be allowed to ride the subway anymore, anywhere.

Lilly observed that my father was taking this infertility thing too far, that just because he can no longer render anyone *embarazada* is no reason to get all overprotective of me. I noticed that, in the driver's seat, Lars was sort of laughing to himself. I hope he doesn't speak Spanish. How embarrassing.

Anyway, Lilly went on to say I should take a stand right away, now, before things get worse, and that she could tell it was already starting to take a toll on me, since I seemed listless and there were circles under my eyes.

Of course I'm listless! I've been up since 3 A.M., trying to wash my shoes!

Went into the girls' room to try to wash them again. Lana Weinberger came in while I was there. She saw me washing my shoes, and she just rolled her eyes and started brushing her long, Marcia Brady hair and staring at herself in the mirror. I half expected her to walk right up to her reflection and kiss it, she is so obviously in love with herself.

The quadratic formula is smeared, but still legible, on my sneaker. But I won't look at it during the test, I swear.

Okay. I admit it. I looked.

Fat lot of good it did me, too. After he'd collected the test, Mr. Gianini went over the problems on the board, and I got every single one of them wrong anyway.

I CAN'T EVEN CHEAT RIGHT!!!

I have got to be the most pathetic human being on the planet.

polynomials
term: variables multiplied by a coefficient
degree of polynomial = the degree of the term with
    the highest degree

Hello? Does ANYONE care??? I mean, really, truly care about polynomials? I mean, besides people like Michael Moscovitz and Mr. Gianini. Anyone? Anyone at all?

When the bell finally rang, Mr. Gianini goes, "Mia, will I have the pleasure of your company this afternoon at the review session?"

I said yes, but I didn't say it loud enough for anyone to hear but him.

Why me? *Why, why, why?* Like I don't have enough to worry about. I'm flunking Algebra, my mom's dating my teacher, and I'm the princess of Genovia.

Something has just *got* to give.

Ode to Algebra

Thrust into this dingy classroom
we die like lampless moths
locked into the desolation of
fluorescent lights and metal desks.
Ten minutes until the bell rings.
What use is the quadratic formula
in our daily lives?
Can we use it to unlock the secrets
in the hearts of those we love?
Five minutes until the bell rings.
Cruel Algebra teacher,
won't you let us go?

HOMEWORK

Algebra: problems 17–30 on handout
English: proposal
World Civ: questions at end of Chapter 7
G & T: none
French: *huit phrases*, ex. A, pg. 31
Biology: worksheet

Oh no.

She's here.

Well, not *here*, exactly. But she's in this country. She's in the city. She's only like fifty-seven blocks away, as a matter of fact. She's staying at the Plaza, with Dad. Thank God. Now I'll only have to see her after school and on the weekends. It would suck so bad if she were staying here.

It's pretty awful, seeing her first thing in the morning. She wears these really fancy negligees to bed, with big lace sections that everything shows through. You know. Stuff you wouldn't want to see. Plus, even though she takes her makeup off to sleep, she still has on eyeliner, because she had it tattooed onto her eyelids back in the eighties when she went through a brief manic phase shortly after Princess Grace died (according to my mom). It looks pretty weird, seeing this little old lady in a lace nightie with big black lines around her eyes first thing in the morning.

Actually, it's scary. Scarier than Freddy Krueger and Jason put together.

No wonder Grandpère died of a heart attack in bed. He probably rolled over one morning and got a real good look at his wife.

Somebody ought to warn the president she's here. I mean it; he really ought to know. Because if anybody could start World War III, it's my grandmother.

Last time I saw Grandmère, she was having this dinner party, and she served everybody foie gras except this one woman. She just had Marie, her cook, leave that lady's plate bare for the foie gras course. And when I tried to give the lady my foie gras, because I thought maybe they had run out—and anyway, I don't eat anything that once was alive—my grandmother was all, "Amelia!" She said it so loud, she scared me. She made me drop my slice of foie gras on the floor. Her horrible miniature poodle pried it up off the parquet before I could even move.

And then later, after everybody left, when I asked her why she wouldn't give that lady any foie gras, Grandmère said it was because the lady had had a child out of wedlock.

Hello? Grandmère, may I point out that your own son had a child out of wedlock, namely me, Mia, *your grand-daughter?*

But when I said that, Grandmère just yelled for her maid to bring her another drink. Oh, so I guess it's okay to have a child out of wedlock if you're a PRINCE. But if you're just a regular person, no foie gras for you.

Oh, no! What if Grandmère comes to the loft? She's never seen the loft before. I don't think she's ever been below Fifty-seventh Street. She's going to hate it here in the Village, I'm telling you right now. People of the same sex kiss and hold hands in our neighborhood all the time. Grandmère has a fit when she sees people of the *opposite* sex holding hands. What's she going to do during the Gay Pride Parade, when everybody is kissing and holding hands and shouting "We're Here, We're Queer, Get Over It"? Grandmère won't get over it. She might have a heart attack. She doesn't even like pierced ears, let alone pierced anything else.

Plus it's against the law to smoke in restaurants here, and Grandmère smokes all the time, even in bed, which is why Grandpère had these weird disposable oxygen masks installed in every single room at Miragnac and had an underground tunnel dug that we could run through in case Grandmère fell asleep with a cigarette in her mouth and the chateau burst into flames.

Also, Grandmère hates cats. She thinks they jump on

81

children while they're sleeping on purpose to suck out their breath. What's she going to say when she sees Fat Louie? He sleeps in bed with me every night. If he ever jumped on my face, he'd kill me instantly. He weighs twenty-five pounds and seven ounces, and that's before he's had his can of Fancy Feast in the morning.

And can you imagine what she'll do when she sees my mom's collection of wooden fertility goddesses?

Why did she have to come NOW? She's going to ruin EVERYTHING. There's no way I'm going to be able to keep this a secret from everyone with HER around.

Why?
　　　　Why??
　　　　　　　WHY???

Thursday, October 9

I found out why.
She's giving me princess lessons.
In too much shock to write. More later.

Friday, October 10

Princess lessons.

I am not kidding. I have to go straight from my Algebra review session every day to princess lessons at the Plaza with my grandmother.

Okay, so if there's a God, how could this have happened?

I mean it. Like, people always talk about how God doesn't ever give you more than you can handle, but I'm telling you right now, I cannot handle this. This is just *too much*! I *cannot* go to princess lessons every day after school. Not with Grandmère. I am seriously considering running away from home.

My dad says I have no choice. Last night, after I left Grandmère's room at the Plaza, I went straight down to his. I banged on the door, and when he answered it I stalked straight in and told him I wasn't doing it. No way. Nobody had told me anything about princess lessons.

And do you know what he said? He says I signed the compromise, so I am obligated to attend princess lessons as part of my duties as his heir.

I said then we are just going to have to revise the compromise, because there was nothing in there about me having to meet with Grandmère every day after school for any princess lessons.

But my dad wouldn't even talk to me about it. He said he was late and could we please talk about it later. And then while I was standing there, going on about how unfair this all was, in walks this reporter from ABC. I guess she was there to interview him, but it was kind of funny, because I've seen her interview people before, and normally she doesn't wear black sleeveless cocktail dresses when she's interviewing the president or somebody like that.

I'm going to have to take a good look at that compromise tonight, because I don't recall it saying anything about princess lessons.

Here is how my first "lesson" went, yesterday after school:

First the doorman won't even let me in (big surprise). Then he sees Lars, who is like six foot seven and must weigh three hundred pounds. Plus, Lars has this bulge sticking out of his jacket, and I only just now figured out that it's a gun and not the stump of an extraneous third arm, which is what originally I thought. I was too embarrassed to ask him about it, in case it dredged up painful memories for him of being teased as a child in Amsterdam, or wherever he is from. I mean, I know what it's like to be a freak: It's just better not to bring that kind of thing up.

But no, it's a gun, and the doorman got all upset about it and called the concierge over. Thank God the concierge recognized Lars, who's staying there, after all, in a room in Dad's suite.

So then the concierge himself escorted me upstairs to the penthouse, which is where Grandmère is staying. Let me tell you about this penthouse: It is very fancy. I thought the ladies' room at the Plaza was fancy? The ladies' room is nothing compared to this penthouse.

First of all, everything is pink. Pink walls, pink carpet, pink curtains, pink furniture. There are pink roses everywhere, and these portraits hanging on the walls that all feature pink-cheeked shepherdesses and stuff.

And just when I thought I was going to drown in pinkness, out came Grandmère, dressed completely in purple, from her silk turban all the way down to her mules with the rhinestone clips on the toes.

At least, I think they're rhinestones.

Grandmère always wears purple. Lilly says people who

wear purple a lot usually have borderline personality disorders, because they have delusions of grandeur. Traditionally, purple has always stood for the aristocracy, since for hundreds of years peasants weren't allowed to dye their clothes with indigo, and therefore couldn't make violet.

Of course, Lilly doesn't know my grandmother IS a member of the aristocracy. So while Grandmère is definitely delusional, it's not because she THINKS she's an aristocrat; she really IS one.

So Grandmère comes in off the terrace, where she was standing, and the first thing she says to me is, "What's that writing on your shoe?"

But I didn't need to worry about getting caught cheating, because Grandmère started in right away about everything else that was wrong with me.

"Why are you wearing tennis shoes with a skirt? Are those tights supposed to be clean? Why can't you stand up straight? What's wrong with your hair? Have you been biting your nails again, Amelia? I thought we agreed you were going to give up that nasty habit. My God, can't you stop growing? Is it your goal to be as tall as your father?"

Only it sounded even worse, because it was all in French.

And then, as if that wasn't bad enough, she goes, in her creaky old cigaretty voice, "Haven't you a kiss for your *grandmère*, then?"

So I go up to her and bend down (my grandmother is like a foot shorter than me) and kiss her on the cheek (which is very soft because she rubs Vaseline on her face every night before she goes to bed), and then when I start to pull away she grabs me and goes, "*Pfuit!* Have you forgotten *everything* I taught you?" and makes me kiss her on the other cheek, too, because in Europe (and SoHo), that's how you say hello to people.

Anyway, I bent down and kissed Grandmère on the other cheek, and as I did so I noticed Rommel peeking out from behind her. Rommel is Grandmère's fifteen-year-old miniature poodle. He is the same shape and size as an iguana, only not as smart. He shakes all the time and has to wear a fleece jacket. Today his jacket was the same purple as Grandmère's dress. Rommel won't let anyone touch him except for Grandmère, and even then he rolls his eyes around as if he were being tortured while she's petting him.

If Noah had ever met Rommel, he might have changed his mind about letting two of *all* of God's creatures on the ark.

"Now," Grandmère said when she felt we'd been affectionate enough, "let's see if I have this right: Your father tells you that you are the princess of Genovia and you burst into tears. Why is this?"

All of a sudden, I got very tired. I had to sit down on one of the pink foofy chairs before I fell down.

"Oh, Grandmère," I said in English. "I don't want to be a princess. I just want to be me, Mia."

Grandmère said, "Don't converse in English with me. It's vulgar. Speak French when you speak to me. Sit up straight in that chair. Do not drape your legs over the arm. And you are not Mia. You are Amelia. In fact, you are Amelia Mignonette Grimaldi Renaldo."

I said, "You forgot Thermopolis," and Grandmère gave me the evil eye. She is very good at this.

"No," she said. "I did not forget Thermopolis."

Then Grandmère sat down in the foofy chair next to mine and said, "Are you telling me you have no wish to assume your rightful place upon the throne?"

Boy, was I tired. "Grandmère, you know as well as I do that I'm not princess material, okay? So why are we even wasting our time?"

Grandmère looked at me out of her twin tattoos of eyeliner. I could tell she wanted to kill me but probably couldn't figure out how to do it without getting blood on the pink carpet.

"You are the heir to the crown of Genovia," she said in this totally serious voice. "And you will take my son's place on the throne when he dies. This is how it is. There is no other way."

Oh, boy.

So I kind of went, "Yeah, whatever, Grandmère. Look, I got a lot of homework. Is this princess thing going to take long?"

Grandmère just looked at me. "It will take," she said, "as long as it takes. I am not afraid to sacrifice my time— or even myself—for the good of my country."

Whoa. This was getting way patriotic. "Um," I said. "Okay."

So then I stared at Grandmère for a while, and she stared back at me, and Rommel laid down on the carpet between our chairs, only he did it really slow, like his legs were too delicate to support all two pounds of him, and then Grandmère broke the silence by saying, "We will begin tomorrow. You will come here directly after school."

"Um, Grandmère. I can't come here directly after school. I'm flunking Algebra. I have to go to a review session every day after school."

"Then after that. No dawdling. You will bring with you a list of the ten women you admire most in the world, and why. That is all."

My mouth fell open. *Homework?* There's going to be *homework?* Nobody said anything about homework!

"And close your mouth," she barked. "It is uncouth to let it hang open like that."

I closed my mouth. Homework???

"Tomorrow you will wear nylons. Not tights. Not kneesocks. You are too old for tights and kneesocks. And you will wear your school shoes, not tennis sneakers. You will style your hair, apply lipstick, and paint your fingernails—what's left of them, anyway." Grandmère stood up. She didn't even have to push up with her hands on the arms of her chair, either. Grandmère's pretty spry for her age. "Now I must dress for dinner with the shah. Goodbye."

I just sat there. Was she insane? Was she completely nuts? Did she have the slightest idea what she was asking me to do?

Evidently she did, since the next thing I knew Lars was standing there, and Grandmère and Rommel were gone.

Geez! Homework!!! Nobody said there was going to be homework.

And that's not the worst of it. Panty hose? To school? I mean, the only girls who wear panty hose to school are girls like Lana Weinberger, and seniors, and people like that. You know. Show-offs. None of *my* friends wear panty hose.

And, I might add, none of my friends wear lipstick or nail polish or do their hair. Not for *school*, anyway.

But what choice did I have? Grandmère totally scared me, with her tattooed eyelids and all. I couldn't NOT do what she said.

So what I did was, I borrowed a pair of my mom's panty hose. She wears them whenever she has an opening—and on dates with Mr. Gianini, I've noticed. I took a pair of her panty hose to school with me in my backpack. I didn't have any fingernails to paint—according to Lilly, I am orally fixated; if it fits in my mouth, I'll put it there—but I did borrow one of my mom's lipsticks, too. And I tried some mousse I found in the medicine cabinet. It must have worked, since when Lilly got into the car this morning, she said, "Wow. Where'd you pick up the Jersey girl, Lars?"

Which I guess meant that my hair looked really big, like girls from New Jersey wear it when they come into Manhattan for a romantic dinner in Little Italy with their boyfriends.

So then, after my review session with Mr. G at the end of the day, I went into the girls' room and put on the panty hose, the lipstick, and my loafers, which are too small and pinch my toes really bad. When I checked myself out in the mirror, I thought I didn't look so bad. I didn't think Grandmère would have any complaints.

I thought I was pretty slick, waiting to change until after school. I figured on a Friday afternoon there wouldn't be anyone hanging around. Who wants to hang around school on a Friday?

I had forgotten, of course, about the Computer Club.

Everybody forgets about the Computer Club, even the people who belong to it. They don't have any friends, except each other, and they never go on dates—only unlike me, I think this is by choice: No one at Albert Einstein is smart enough for them—except, again, for each other.

Anyway, I walked out of the girls' room and ran smack into Lilly's brother, Michael. He's the Computer Club treasurer. He's smart enough to be president, but he says he has no interest in being a figurehead.

"Christ, Thermopolis," he said, as I scrambled around, trying to pick up all the stuff I'd dropped—like my high-tops and socks and stuff—when I bumped into him. "What happened to *you*?"

I thought he meant why was I there so late. "You know I have to meet with Mr. Gianini every day after school because I'm flunking Alge—"

"I know *that*." Michael held up the lipstick that had exploded out of my backpack. "I mean what's with the war paint?"

I took it away from him. "Nothing. Don't tell Lilly."

"Don't tell Lilly what?" I stood up, and he noticed the panty hose. "Jesus, Thermopolis. Where are *you* going?"

"Nowhere." Must I continuously be forced to lie all the time? I really wished he would go away. Plus a bunch of his computer nerd friends were standing there, staring at me like I was some new kind of pixel or something. It was making me pretty uncomfortable.

"Nobody goes *nowhere* looking like that." Michael shifted his laptop from one arm to the other, then got this funny look on his face. "Thermopolis, are you going out on a *date*?"

"*What*? No, I'm not going on a date!" I was completely shocked at the idea. A *date*? *Me*? I'm so sure! "I have to meet my grandmother!"

Michael didn't look as if he believed me. "And do you usually wear lipstick and panty hose to meet your grandmother?"

I heard some discreet coughing, and looked down the hall. Lars was there by the doors, waiting for me.

I guess I could have stood there and explained that my grandmother had threatened me with bodily harm (well, practically) if I didn't wear makeup and nylons to meet her. But I sort of didn't think he'd believe me. So I said, "Look, don't tell Lilly, okay?"

Then I ran away.

I knew I was dead meat. There was no way Michael wasn't going to tell his sister about seeing me coming out of the girls' room after school in lipstick and panty hose. No way.

And Grandmère's was HORRIBLE. She said the lipstick

I had on made me look like a *poulet*. At least that's what I thought she said, and I couldn't figure out why she thought I looked like a chicken. But just now I looked up *poulet* in my English-French dictionary, and it turns out *poulet* can also mean "prostitute"! My grandmother called me a hooker!

Geez! Whatever happened to nice grandmothers, who bake brownies for you and tell you how precious you are? It's just my luck I get one who has tattooed eyeliner and tells me *I* look like a hooker.

And she said that the panty hose I had on were the wrong color. How could they be the wrong color? They're panty hose color! Then she made me practice sitting down so my underwear didn't show between my legs for like two hours!

I'm thinking about calling Amnesty International. This has to constitute torture.

And when I gave her my essay on the ten women I admire most, she read it and then ripped it up into little pieces! I am not even kidding!

I couldn't help screaming, "Grandmère, why'd you do that?" and she went, all calmly, "These are not the sort of women you should be admiring. You should be admiring *real* women."

I asked Grandmère what she meant by "*real women*," because all of the women on my list are real. I mean, Madonna might have had a little plastic surgery, but she's still *real*.

But Grandmère says real women are Princess Grace and Coco Chanel. I pointed out to her that Princess Diana is on my list, and you know what she said? She says she thinks Princess Diana was a "twink"! That's what she called her. A "twink."

Only she pronounced it "tweenk."

Geez!

After we'd rehearsed sitting for an hour, Grandmère said she had to go and take a bath, since she's having dinner tonight with some prime minister. She told me to be at the Plaza tomorrow no later than ten o'clock—A.M. 10 A.M.!

"Grandmère," I said. "Tomorrow is Saturday."

"I know it."

"But Grandmère," I said. "Saturdays are when I help my friend Lilly film her TV show—"

But Grandmère asked me which was more important, Lilly's TV show or the well-being of the people of Genovia, who, in case you didn't know, number in the 50,000 range.

I guess 50,000 people are more important than one episode of *Lilly Tells It Like It Is*. Still, it's going to be tough explaining to Lilly why I won't be there to hold the camera when she confronts Mr. and Mrs. Ho, owners of Ho's Deli, across the street from Albert Einstein, about their unfair pricing policies. Lilly has discovered that Mr. and Mrs. Ho give significant discounts to the Asian students who go to Albert Einstein, but no discounts at all to the Caucasian, African-American, Latino, or Arab students. Lilly discovered this yesterday after play rehearsal when she went to buy ginkgo biloba puffs and Ling Su, in front of her in line, bought the same thing. But Mrs. Ho charged her (Lilly) *five whole cents more* than Ling Su for the same product.

And then when Lilly complained, Mrs. Ho pretended like she couldn't speak English, even though she must speak some English, or why else would her mini-TV behind the counter always be tuned to Judge Judy?

Lilly has decided to secretly videotape the Hos to gather evidence of their blatantly preferential treatment of Asian

Americans. She's calling for a school-wide boycott of Ho's Deli.

The thing is, I think Lilly's making a really big deal about five cents. But Lilly says it's the principle of the thing, and that maybe if people had made a big deal about how the Nazis smashed up Jewish people's store windows on Kristallnacht they wouldn't have ended up putting so many people in ovens.

I don't know. The Hos aren't exactly Nazis. They're very nice to the little cat they've raised from a kitten to chase rats away from the chicken wings in the salad bar.

Maybe I'm not too sorry about missing the taping tomorrow.

But I *am* sorry Grandmère tore up my list of the ten women I admire most. I thought it was *nice*. When I got home, I printed it out again, just because it made me so mad, her tearing it up like that. I put a copy in this book.

And after carefully reviewing my copy of the Renaldo-Thermopolis Compromise, I see *nothing* about princess lessons. Something is going to have to be done about this. I have been leaving messages for Dad all night, but he doesn't answer. Where *is* he?

Lilly isn't home, either. Maya says the Moscovitzes went to Great Shanghai for dinner as a family, in order to grow to understand one another better as human beings.

I wish Lilly would hurry up and get home and call me back. I don't want her to think I'm in any way against her groundbreaking investigation into Ho's Deli. I just want to tell her the reason I won't be able to be there is because I have to spend the day with my grandmother.

I hate my life.

THE TEN WOMEN I ADMIRE MOST
IN THE WHOLE WORLD
by Mia Thermopolis

Madonna. Madonna Ciccone revolutionized the fashion world
with her iconoclastic sense of style, sometimes offending
people who are not very open-minded—for instance, her
rhinestone cross earrings, which made many Christian groups
ban her CDs—or who have no sense of humor—like Pepsi,
which didn't like it when she danced in front of some burning
crosses. It was because she wasn't afraid to make people like
the Pope mad that Madonna became one of the richest female
entertainers in the world, paving the way for women performers
everywhere by showing them that it is possible to be sexy
onstage and smart off it.

Princess Diana. Even though she is dead, Princess Diana is one
of my favorite women of all time. She, too, revolutionized the
fashion world by refusing to wear the ugly old hats that her
mother-in-law told her to wear, and instead wore Halston and Bill
Blass. Also she visited a lot of really sick people, even though
nobody made her do it, and some people, like her husband, even
made fun of her for doing it. The night Princess Diana died I
unplugged the TV and said I would never watch it again, since
media was what killed her. But then I regretted it the next
morning when I couldn't watch Japanese anime on the Sci-Fi
channel, because unplugging the TV scrambled our cable box.

Hillary Rodham Clinton. Hillary Rodham Clinton totally
recognized that her thick ankles were detracting from her image
as a serious politician, and so she started wearing pants. Also,
even though everybody was talking bad about her all the time for
not leaving her husband, who was going around having sex with
people behind her back, she pretended like nothing was going

on and went on running the country, just like she'd always done, which is how a president should behave.

Picabo Street. She won all those gold medals in skiing, all because she just practiced like crazy and never gave up, even when she was crashing into fences and things. Plus she picked her own name, which is cool.

Leola Mae Harmon. I saw a movie about her on the Lifetime channel. Leola was an air force nurse who was in a car accident and the lower part of her face got all mangled, but then Armand Assante, who plays a plastic surgeon, said he could fix her. Leola had to endure hours of painful reconstructive surgery, during which her husband left her because she didn't have any lips (which I guess is why the movie is called *Why Me?*). Armand Assante said he would make her a new pair of lips, only the other air force doctors didn't like the fact that he wanted to make them out of skin from Leola's vagina. But he did it anyway, and then he and Leola got married and worked together to help give other accident victims vagina lips. And the whole thing turned out to have been *based on a true story*.

Joan of Arc. Joan of Arc—or Jeanne d'Arc as they say in France—lived in like the twelfth century and one day when she was my age she heard this angel's voice tell her to take up arms and go help the French army fight against the British (the French were always fighting the British, all the way up until the Nazis attacked, and then they were like, "*Zut alors!* Can you help us?" and the British had to go in and try to save their lazy butts, for which nobody French has ever been properly grateful, as exemplified by their sloppy highway maintenance; see death of Princess Diana, above). Anyway, Joan cut off her hair and got herself a suit of armor, just like Mulan in the Disney movie, and went and led the French forces to victory in a number of battles. But then, like typical politicians, the French government decided Joan was too powerful, so they accused her of being a witch and burned her to death at the stake. And unlike Lilly, I do NOT believe that Joan was suffering from adolescent onset schizophrenia. I think angels really DID talk to her. None of the schizophrenics in our school have ever had their voices tell them to do something cool like lead their country into battle. All Brandon Hertzenbaum's voices told him to do was go into the boys' room and carve "Satan" in the door to the bathroom stall with a protractor. So there you go.

Christy. Christy is not really a person. She is the fictional heroine of my favorite book of all time, which is called *Christy*, by Catherine Marshall. Christy is a young girl who goes to teach school in the Smokey Mountains at the turn of the century because she believes she can make a difference, and all these really hot guys fall in love with her and she learns about God and typhoid and stuff. Only I can't tell anyone, especially Lilly, that this is my favorite book, because it's kind of sappy and religious, and plus it doesn't have any spaceships or serial killers in it.

The Lady Cop I Once Saw give a truck driver a ticket for honking at a woman who was crossing the street (her skirt was kind of short). The lady cop told the truck driver it was a no-honking zone, and then when he argued about it, she wrote him another ticket for arguing with an officer of the law.

Lilly Moscovitz. Lilly Moscovitz isn't really a woman, yet, but she's someone I admire very much. She is very, very smart, but unlike many very smart people, she doesn't rub it in all the time, the fact that she's so much smarter than me. Well, at least, not much. Lilly is always thinking up fun things for us to do, like go to Barnes & Noble and secretly film me asking Dr. Laura, who was signing books there, if she knows so much how come she's divorced, then showing it on her (Lilly's) TV show, including the part where we got thrown out and banned from the Union Square Barnes & Noble forever after. Lilly is my best friend and I tell her everything, except the part about me being a princess, which I don't think she'd understand.

Helen Thermopolis. Helen Thermopolis, besides being my mother, is a very talented artist who was recently featured in *Art in America* magazine as one of the most important painters of the new millennium. Her painting *Woman Waiting for Price Check at the Grand Union* won this big national award and sold for $140,000, only part of which my mom got to keep, since 15 percent of it went to her gallery and half of what was left went to taxes, which sucks, if you ask me. But even though she's such an important artist, my mom always has time for me. I also respect her because she is deeply principled: She says she would never think of inflicting her beliefs on others and would thank others to pay her the same courtesy.

Can you believe Grandmère tore this up? I'm telling you, this is the sort of essay that could bring a country to its knees.

So I was right: Lilly *does* think the reason I'm not participating in the taping today is because I'm against her boycott of the Hos.

I told her that wasn't true, that I had to spend the day with my grandmother. But guess what? She doesn't believe me. The one time I tell the truth, and she doesn't believe me!

Lilly says that if I really wanted to get out of spending the day with Grandmère I could, but because I'm so codependent, I can't say no to anyone. Which doesn't even make sense, since obviously I am saying no to *her*. When I pointed that out to Lilly, though, she just got madder. I can't say no to my grandmother, since she's like sixty-five years old, and she's going to die soon, if there's any justice at all in the world.

Besides, you don't know my grandmother, I said. You don't say no to my grandmother.

Then Lilly went, "No, I don't know your grandmother, do I, Mia? Isn't that curious, considering the fact that you know all *my* grandparents"—the Moscovitzes have me over every year for Passover dinner—"and yet I haven't met any of *yours*?"

Well, of course the reason for *that* is that my mom's parents are like total farmers who live in a place called Versailles, Indiana, only they pronounce it "Ver-sales." My mom's parents are *afraid* to come to New York City because they say there are too many "furinners"—by which they mean foreigners—here, and anything that isn't 100 percent American scares them, which is one of the reasons my mom left home when she was eighteen and has only been back twice, and that was with me. Let me tell you, Versailles is a small, small town. It's so small that there's a sign on the door at the bank that says IF BANK IS

CLOSED, PLEASE SLIDE MONEY UNDER DOOR. I am not lying, either. I took a photo of it and brought it back to show everyone because I knew they wouldn't believe me. It's hanging on our refrigerator.

Anyway, Grandpa and Grandma Thermopolis don't make it out of Indiana much.

And the reason I'd never introduced Lilly to Grandmère Renaldo is because Grandmère Renaldo hates children. And I can't introduce her now because then Lilly will find out I'm the princess of Genovia, and you can bet I'll never hear the end of *that*. She'd probably want to interview me, or something, for her TV show. That's all I need: My name and image plastered all over Manhattan Public Access.

So I was telling Lilly all of this—about how I had to go out with my grandmother, not about my being a princess, of course—and as I was talking I could hear her breathing over the phone in that way she does when she's mad, and finally she just goes, "Oh, come over tonight then, and help me edit," and slammed the phone down.

Geez.

Well, at least Michael didn't tell her about the lipstick and panty hose. *That* would have really made her mad. She never would have believed I was only going to my grand-mother's. No way.

This was all at like nine-thirty, while I was getting ready to go to Grandmère's. Grandmère told me that for today I don't have to wear lipstick or panty hose. She said I could wear anything I wanted. So I wore my overalls. I know she hates them, but hey, she said anything I wanted. Hee hee hee.

Oops, gotta go. Lars just pulled up in front of the Plaza. We're here.

I can never go to school again. I can never go *anywhere* again. I will never leave this loft, ever, ever again.

You won't believe what she did to me. *I* can't believe what she did to me. I can't believe my dad *let* her do this to me.

Well, he's going to pay. He's totally paying for this, and I mean BIG. As soon as I got home (right after my mom went, "Well, hey, Rosemary. Where's your baby?" which I suppose was some kind of joke about my new haircut, but it was NOT funny), I marched right up to him and said, "You are paying for this. Big time."

Who says I have a fear of confrontation?

He totally tried to get out of it, going, "What do you mean? Mia, I think you look beautiful. Don't listen to your mother, what does she know? I like your hair. It's so . . . short."

Gee, I wonder why? Maybe because his mother met Lars and me in the lobby as soon as we'd turned the car over to the valet, and just pointed at the door. Just pointed at the door again, and said, "*On y va,*" which in English means "Let's go."

"Let's go where?" I asked, all innocently (this was this morning, remember, back when I was still innocent).

"Chez Paolo," Grandmère said. *Chez Paolo* means "Paul's house." So I thought we were going to meet one of her friends, maybe for brunch or something, and I thought, huh, cool, field trip. Maybe these princess lessons won't be so bad.

But then we got there, and I saw Chez Paolo wasn't a house at all. At first I couldn't tell what it was. It looked a little like a really fancy hospital—it was all frosted glass and these Japanese-looking trees. And then we got inside;

all of these skinny young people were floating around, dressed all in black. They were all excited to see my grandmother, and took us to this little room where there were these couches and all these magazines. So then I figured Grandmère maybe had some plastic surgery scheduled, and while I am sort of against plastic surgery—unless you're like Leola Mae and you need lips—I was like, Well, at least she'll be off my back for a while.

Boy, was I ever wrong! Paolo isn't a doctor. I doubt he's ever even been to college! Paolo is a *stylist*! Worse, he styles *people*! I'm serious. He takes unfashionable, frumpy people like me, and he makes them stylish—for a *living*. And Grandmère sicced him on *me*! *Me!!* Like it's bad enough I don't have breasts. She has to tell some guy named *Paolo* that?

What kind of name is Paolo, anyway? I mean, this is America, for Pete's sake! YOUR NAME IS PAUL!!!

That's what I wanted to scream at him. But, of course, I couldn't. I mean, it wasn't Paolo's fault my grandmother dragged me there. And as he pointed out to me, he only made time for me in his incredibly busy schedule because Grandmère told him it was this big emergency.

God, how embarrassing. *I'm* a fashion emergency.

Anyway, I was plenty peeved at Grandmère, but I couldn't start yelling at her right there in front of Paolo. She totally knew it, too. She just sat there on this velvet couch, petting Rommel, who was sitting on her lap with his legs crossed—she's even taught her *dog* to sit ladylike, and *he's* a boy—sipping a Sidecar she got somebody to make for her and reading W.

Meanwhile, Paolo was picking up chunks of my hair and making this face and going, all sadly, "It must go. It must *all* go."

And it went. All of it. Well, almost all of it. I still have some like bangs and a little fringe in back.

Did I mention that I'm no longer a dishwater blond? No. I'm just a plain old blond now.

And Paolo didn't stop there. Oh, no. I now have fingernails. I am not kidding. For the first time in my life, I have fingernails. They're completely fake, but I have them. And it looks like I'll have them for a while: I already tried to pull one off, and it HURT. What kind of secret astronaut glue did that manicurist use, anyway?

You might be wondering why, if I didn't want to have all my hair cut off and fake fingernails glued over my real, stumpy fingernails, I let them do all that.

I'm sort of wondering that myself. I mean, I know I have a fear of confrontation. So it wasn't like I was going to throw down my glass of lemonade and say, "Okay, stop making a fuss over me, right now!" I mean, they gave me lemonade! Can you imagine that? At the International House of Hair, which is where my mom and I usually go, over on Sixth Avenue, they sure don't give you lemonade, but it *does* only cost $9.99 for a cut and blow dry.

And it is sort of hard when all these beautiful, fashionable people are telling you how good you'd look in *this* and how much *that* would bring out your cheekbones, to remember you're a feminist and an environmentalist, and don't believe in using makeup or chemicals that might be harmful to the earth. I mean, I didn't want to hurt their feelings, or cause a scene, or anything like that.

And I kept telling myself, She's only doing this because she loves you. My grandmother, I mean. I know she probably wasn't doing it for that reason—I don't think Grandmère loves me any more than I love her—but I *told* myself that, anyway.

I told myself that after we left Paolo's and went to Bergdorf Goodman, where Grandmère bought me four pairs of shoes that cost almost as much as the removal of that sock from Fat Louie's small intestines. I told myself that after she bought me a bunch of clothes I will never wear. I did tell her I would never wear these clothes, but she just waved at me. Like, Go on, go on. You tell such amusing stories.

Well, I for one will not stand for it. There isn't a single inch of me that hasn't been pinched, cut, filed, painted, sloughed, blown dry, or moisturized. I even have fingernails.

But I am not happy. I am not a bit happy. *Grandmère's* happy. *Grandmère's* head over heels happy about how I look. Because I don't look a thing like Mia Thermopolis. Mia Thermopolis never had fingernails. Mia Thermopolis never had blond highlights. Mia Thermopolis never wore makeup or Gucci shoes or Chanel skirts or Christian Dior bras, which, by the way, don't even come in 32A, which is my size. I don't even know who I am anymore. It certainly isn't Mia Thermopolis.

She's turning me into someone else.

So I stood in front of my father, looking like a human Q-tip in my new hair, and I let him have it.

"First she makes me do homework. Then she rips the homework up. Then she gives me sitting lessons. Then she has all my hair dyed a different color and most of it hacked off, makes someone glue tiny surfboards to my fingernails, buys me shoes that cost as much as small animal surgery, and clothes that make me look like Vicki, the captain's daughter in that old seventies series *The Love Boat*.

"Well, Dad, I'm sorry, but I'm not Vicki, and I never will be, no matter how much Grandmère dresses me up like her. I'm not going to do great in school, be supercheerful all the time, or have any shipboard romances. That's Vicki. That's not me!"

My mom was coming out of her bedroom, putting the last touches on her date wear, when I screamed this. She was wearing a new outfit. It was this sort of Spanish skirt in all these different colors, and a sort of off-the-shoulder top. Her long hair was all over the place, and she looked really great. In fact, my dad headed for the liquor cabinet again when he saw her.

"Mia," my mom said as she fastened on an earring, "nobody is asking you to be Vicki, the captain's daughter."

"Grandmère is!"

"Your grandmother is just trying to prepare you, Mia."

"Prepare me for what? I can't go to school looking like this, you know," I yelled.

My mom looked kind of confused. "Why not?"

Oh, my God. Why me?

"Because," I said, as patiently as I could, "I don't want anyone at school finding out I'm the princess of Genovia!"

My mom shook her head. "Mia, honey, they're going to find out sometime."

I don't see how. See, I have it all worked out: I'll only be a princess in Genovia, and since the chances of anybody I know from school ever actually going to Genovia are like none, no one here will ever find out, so I'm totally safe from being branded a freak, like Tina Hakim Baba. Well, at least not the kind of freak who has to ride in a chauffeured limo to school every day and be followed by bodyguards.

"Well," my mom said, after I'd told her all this. "What if it's in the newspaper?"

"Why would it be in the newspaper?"

My mom looked at my dad. My dad looked away and took a sip from his drink.

You wouldn't believe what he did next. He put down his drink, then he reached into his pants pocket, took out his Prada wallet, opened it, and asked, "How much?"

I was shocked. So was my mom.

"Phillipe," she said, but my dad just kept looking at me.

"I'm serious, Helen," he said. "I can see the compromise we drew up is getting us nowhere. The only solution in matters like these is cold, hard cash. So how much do I have to pay you, Mia, to let your grandmother turn you into a princess?"

"Is that what she's doing?" I started yelling some more. "Well, if that's what she's doing, she has it all screwed up. I never saw a princess with hair this short, or feet as big as mine, who didn't have breasts!"

My dad just looked at his watch. I guess he had somewhere to go. I bet it was another "interview" with that blond anchorwoman from ABC News.

"Consider it a job," he said, "this learning how to be a princess business. I will pay your salary. Now, how much do you want?"

I started yelling even more about personal integrity and how I refused to sell my soul to the company store, that kind of thing. Stuff I got from some of my mom's old records. I think she recognized this, since she sort of started slinking away, saying she had to go get ready for her date with Mr. G. My dad shot her the evil eye—he can do it almost as well as Grandmère—and then he sighed and went, "Mia, I will donate one hundred dollars a day, in your name, to—what is it? Oh, yes—Greenpeace, so they can save all the whales they want, if you will make my mother happy by letting her teach you to be a princess."

Well.

That's an entirely different matter. It would be one thing if he were paying *me* to have my hair color chemically altered. But paying one hundred dollars per day to Greenpeace? That's $356,000 per year! In my name! Why,

Greenpeace will *have* to hire me after I graduate. I practically will have donated a million dollars by that time!

Wait, maybe that's only $36,500. Where's my calculator????

Well, I don't know who Lilly Moscovitz thinks she is, but I sure know who she isn't: my friend. I don't think anyone who was my friend would be as mean to me as Lilly was tonight. I couldn't believe it. And all because of my *hair*!

I guess I could understand it if Lilly was mad at me about something that mattered—like missing the taping of the Ho segment. I mean, I'm like the main cameraperson for *Lilly Tells It Like It Is*. I also do a lot of the prop work. When I'm not there, Shameeka has to do my job as well as hers, and Shameeka is already executive producer and location scout.

So I guess I could see how Lilly might kind of resent the fact that I missed today's taping. She thinks Ho-Gate—that's what she's calling it—is the most important story she's ever done. I think it's kind of stupid. Who cares about five cents, anyway? But Lilly's all, "We're going to break the cycle of racism that has been rampant in delis across the five boroughs."

Whatever. All I know is, I walked into the Moscovitzes' apartment tonight, and Lilly took one look at my new hair and was like, "Oh, my God, what happened to you?"

Like I had frostbite all over my face, and my nose had turned black and fallen off, like those people who climbed Mt. Everest.

Okay, I knew people were going to freak and stuff when they saw my hair. I totally washed it before I came over, and got all the mousse and goop out of it. Plus I took off all the makeup Paolo had slathered on me, and put on my overalls and high-tops (you can hardly see the quadratic formula anymore). I really thought, except for my hair, I looked mostly normal. In fact, I kind of thought maybe I looked good—for me, I mean.

But I guess Lilly didn't think so.

I tried to be casual, like it was no big deal. Which it isn't, by the way. It wasn't as if I'd had breast implants or something.

"Yeah," I said, taking off my coat. "Well, my grand-mother made me go see this guy Paolo, and he—"

But Lilly wouldn't even let me finish. She was in this state of shock. She went, "Your hair is the same color as Lana Weinberger's."

"Well," I said. "I know."

"What's on your *fingers*? Are those fake fingernails? Lana has those, too!" She stared at me all bug-eyed. "Oh my God, Mia. You're turning into Lana Weinberger!"

Now, that kind of peeved me off. I mean, in the first place, I am *not* turning into Lana Weinberger. In the second place, even if I am, Lilly's the one who's always going on about how stupid people are for not seeing that it doesn't matter what anybody looks like; what matters is what's going on on the inside.

So I stood there in the Moscovitzes' foyer, which is made out of black marble, with Pavlov jumping up and down against my legs because he was so excited to see me, going, "It wasn't me. It was my grandmother. I had to—"

"What do you mean, you had to?" Lilly got this really crabby look on her face. It was the same look she gets every year when our PE instructor tells us we have to run around the reservoir in Central Park for the Presidential Fitness test. Lilly doesn't like to run anywhere, particularly around the reservoir in Central Park (it's really big).

"What are you?" she wanted to know. "Completely passive? You're mute or something? Unable to say the word *no*? You know, Mia, we really need to work on your assertiveness. You seem to have real issues with your grandmother. I mean, you certainly don't have any trouble saying no to *me*. I could have really used your help today with the Ho segment, and you totally let me down. But you've got no problem letting your grandmother cut off all your hair and dye it yellow—"

Okay, now keep in mind I'd just spent the whole day hearing how bad I looked—at least, until Paolo got ahold of me and made me look like Lana Weinberger. Now I had to hear there was something wrong with my personality, too.

So I cracked. I said, "Lilly, *shut up*."

I have never told Lilly to shut up before. Not ever. I don't think I have ever told anyone to shut up before. It's just not something I do. I don't know what happened, really. Maybe it was the fingernails. I never had fingernails before. They sort of made me feel strong. I mean, really, why was Lilly *always* telling me what to do?

Unfortunately, right as I was telling Lilly to shut up, Michael came out, holding an empty cereal bowl and not wearing a shirt.

"Whoa," he said, backing up. I wasn't sure if he said whoa and backed up because of what I'd said or how I looked.

"What?" Lilly said. "*What* did you just say to me?"

Now she looked more like a pug than *ever*.

I totally wanted to back down. But I didn't, because I knew she was right: I *do* have problems being assertive.

So instead I said, "I'm tired of you putting me down all the time. All day long, my mom and dad and grandmother and teachers are telling me what to do. I don't need my *friends* getting on my case, too."

"Whoa," Michael said again. This time I knew it was because of what I said.

"What," Lilly said, her eyes getting all narrow, "is your *problem*?"

I went, "You know what? I don't have a problem. *You're* the one with the problem. You seem to have a big problem with me. Well, you know what? I'm going to solve your problem for you. I'm leaving. I never wanted to help you with your stupid Ho-Gate story anyway. The Hos are nice people. They haven't done anything wrong. I don't see why you have to pick on them. And"—I said this as I opened the door—"my hair is *not* yellow."

Then I left. I sort of slammed the door behind me, too.

While I was waiting for the elevator, I sort of thought Lilly might come out and apologize to me.

But she didn't.

I came straight home, took a bath, and got into bed with my remote control and Fat Louie, who's the only person who likes me the way I am right now. I was thinking Lilly might call to apologize, but so far she hasn't.

Well, I'm not apologizing until she does.

And you know what? I looked in the mirror a minute ago, and my hair doesn't look that bad.

Past Midnight, Sunday, October 12

She still hasn't called.

Oh, my God. I am so embarrassed. I wish I could disappear. You will never believe what just happened.

I walked out of my room to get breakfast, and there were my mom and Mr. Gianini sitting at the table eating pancakes!

And Mr. Gianini was wearing a T-shirt and boxer shorts!! My mom was in her kimono!!! When she saw me, she choked on her orange juice. Then she went, "Mia, what are you doing here? I thought you spent the night at Lilly's."

I wish I had. I wish I had never chosen to be assertive last night. I could have stayed over at the Moscovitzes' and never had to look at Mr. Gianini in his boxer shorts. I could have lived a full and happy life without ever having seen *that*.

Not to mention him seeing me in my bright red flannel nightie.

How am I ever going to go to a review session again?

This is so horrible. I wish I could call Lilly, but I guess we are fighting.

Oh, okay. According to my mom, who just came into my room, Mr. Gianini spent the night on the futon couch because a train on the line he normally takes to his apartment in Brooklyn derailed, and it was going to be out of service for hours, so she told him to just stay over.

If I were still friends with Lilly, she would probably say that my mother was lying to compensate for having traumatized my perception of her as a strictly maternal, and therefore nonsexual, being. That's what Lilly always says when anybody's mother has a guy over and then lies about it.

I prefer to believe my mom's lie, though. The only way I will ever pass Algebra is to believe my mother's lie, because I could never sit there and concentrate on polynomials knowing that the guy in front of me has not only probably stuck his tongue in my mom's mouth but has also probably seen her naked.

Why do all these bad things keep happening to me? I would think it would be time for something good to happen to me for a change.

After my mom came in and lied to me, I got dressed and went out into the kitchen to make breakfast. I had to, because my mom wouldn't bring me breakfast in my room, like I asked her to. Actually, she went, "Who do you think you are, anyway? The princess of Genovia?"

Which I suppose she thinks is hysterically funny, but really it isn't.

By the time I left my room, Mr. Gianini had gotten dressed, too. He was trying to be all jokey about what had happened, which is the only way you can be about it, I guess.

I wasn't feeling too jokey at first. But then Mr. G started

talking about what it would be like to see certain people from Albert Einstein in their pajamas. Like Principal Gupta. Mr. G thinks Principal Gupta probably wears a football jersey to bed, with her husband's sweatpants. I kind of started to laugh, thinking about Principal Gupta in sweatpants. I said I bet Mrs. Hill wears a negligee, one of those fancy ones with the feathers and stuff. But Mr. G said he thought Mrs. Hill was more into flannel than feathers. I wonder how Mr. G knows. Did he go out with Mrs. Hill, too? For a boring guy with so many pens in his shirt pocket, he sure gets around.

After breakfast, my mom and Mr. Gianini tried to get me to go to Central Park with them, because it was all nice outside and everything, but I said I had too much homework, which wasn't too big of a lie. I *do* have homework—Mr. G should know—but not that much. I just didn't really want to be hanging around with a couple. It's like when Shameeka started going with Aaron Ben-Simon in the seventh grade, and she wanted us to go with her to the movies with him and stuff because her dad wouldn't let her go anywhere with a guy alone (even a totally harmless guy like Aaron Ben-Simon, whose neck was as thick as my upper arm), but when we went with her she sort of ignored us, which I guess is the point. Only for the two weeks they went out, you sort of couldn't talk to Shameeka, because all she could talk about was Aaron.

Not that all my mom can talk about is Mr. Gianini. She's not like that at all. But I had a feeling if I went to Central Park I might have to see kissing. Not that there's anything wrong with kissing, like on TV. When it's your mom and your Algebra teacher, though . . .

You know what I mean, right?

REASONS I SHOULD MAKE UP WITH LILLY

1. We've been best friends since kindergarten.
2. One of us has to be the bigger person and make the first move.
3. She makes me laugh.
4. Who else can I eat lunch with?
5. I miss her.

REASONS I SHOULD NOT MAKE UP WITH LILLY

1. She's always telling me what to do.
2. She thinks she knows everything.
3. Lilly is the one who started it, so she should be the one to apologize.
4. I will never achieve self-actualization if I always back down from my convictions.
5. What if I apologize and she STILL won't talk to me????

Even Later on Sunday

I just turned on my computer to look up some stuff about Afghanistan on the Internet (I have to write a paper for World Civ on a current event), and then I saw that someone was instant messaging me. I hardly ever get instant messages, so I was totally excited.

But then I saw who it was from: CracKing.

Michael Moscovitz? What could *he* want?

Here's what he wrote:

CracKing: Hey, Thermopolis. What happened to you last night? It's like you went mental, or something.

Me? Mental???

FtLouie: For your information, I did not go mental. I just got tired of your sister always telling me what to do. Not that it's any of your business.

CracKing: What are you being so snotty about? Of course it's my business. I have to live with her, don't I?

FtLouie: Why? Is she talking about me?

CracKing: You could say that.

I can't believe she's been talking about me. And you know she can't have been saying anything good.

FtLouie: What's she saying?

CracKing: I thought it wasn't any of my business.

I'm so glad I don't have a brother.

FtLouie: It isn't. What's she saying about me?

CracKing: That she doesn't know what's with you these days, but ever since your dad came to visit you've been acting like a head case.

FtLouie: Me? A head case? What about her? She's the one who's always criticizing me. I'm so sick of it!! If she wants to be my friend, why can't she just accept me the way I am???

CracKing: No need to yell.

FtLouie: I'm not yelling!!!

CracKing: You're using excessive amounts of punctuation, and online, that's like yelling. Besides, she's not the only one criticizing. She says you won't support her boycott of Ho's Deli.

FtLouie: Well, she's right. I won't. It's stupid. Don't you think it's stupid?

CracKing: Sure it's stupid. Are you still flunking Algebra?

That was out of the blue.

FtLouie: I guess so. But considering the fact that Mr. G slept over last night, I'll probably scrape by with a D. Why?

CracKing: What? Mr. G slept over? At your place? What was that like?

Now, why did I tell him that? It'll be all over school by tomorrow morning. Maybe Mr. G will get fired! I don't know if teachers are allowed to date their pupils' mothers. Why did I tell Michael that?

> FtLouie: It was pretty awful. But then he kind of joked around, and made it okay. I don't know. I should probably be more mad, but my mom's so happy, it's hard.

> CracKing: Your mom could do a lot worse than Mr. G. Imagine if she was going out with Mr. Stuart.

Mr. Stuart teaches Health. He thinks he's God's gift to women. I haven't had him yet, since you don't have Health until sophomore year, but even I know that you should never go near Mr. Stuart's desk, because if you do, he'll reach out and rub your shoulders like he's giving you a massage, but everybody says he's really just trying to see whether or not you're wearing a bra.

If my mom ever went out with Mr. Stuart, I would move to Afghanistan.

> FtLouie: Ha ha ha. Why'd you want to know whether or not I'm flunking Algebra?

> CracKing: Oh, because I'm done with this month's issue of Crackhead, and I thought if you wanted, I could tutor you during G & T. If you wanted.

Michael Moscovitz, offering to do something for me? I couldn't believe it. I nearly fell off my computer chair.

> FtLouie: Wow, that would be great! Thanks!

CracKing: Don't mention it. Hang in there, Thermopolis.

Then he signed off.

Can you believe it? Wasn't that nice? I wonder what's got into him.

I should definitely fight with Lilly more often.

Just when I thought things might be looking very slightly up, my dad called. He said he was sending Lars over to pick me up so me and him and Grandmère could have dinner together at the Plaza.

Notice the invitation didn't include Mom.

But I guess that's okay, since Mom didn't want to go anyway. When I told her I was going she got really cheerful, in fact.

"Oh, that's okay," she said. "I'll just stay here and order in some Thai food and watch *Sixty Minutes*."

She's been really cheerful ever since she got back from Central Park. She says she and Mr. G went on one of those dorky carriage rides. I was shocked. Those carriage drivers don't take care of their horses at all. There's always some ancient carriage horse keeling over from lack of water. I had always vowed never to ride in one of those carriages. At least not until they start giving those horses some rights, and I always thought my mom agreed with me.

Love can do strange things to people.

The Plaza wasn't that bad this time. I guess I'm getting used to it. The doormen know who I am now—or at least they know who Lars is—so they don't give me a hard time anymore. Grandmère and my dad were both in kind of bad moods. I don't know why. I guess they're not getting paid to spend time with each other, like I kind of am.

Dinner was *so* boring. Grandmère went on and on about which fork to use with what and why. There were all these courses, and most of them were meat. One was fish, though, so I ate that, plus dessert, which was a big fancy tower of chocolate. Grandmère tried to tell me that when I am representing Genovia at state functions I have to eat whatever is put down in front of me or I will insult my hosts and possibly create an international incident. But I told her I would have my staff explain to my hosts ahead of time that I don't eat meat, so not to serve me any.

Grandmère looked kind of mad. I guess it never occurred to her that I might have watched that made-for-TV movie about Princess Diana. I know all about how to get out of eating stuff at state dinners, and also about barfing up what you did eat afterwards (only I would never do that).

All through dinner, Dad kept asking me these weird questions about Mom. Like was I uncomfortable about her relationship with Mr. Gianini, and did I want him to say something to her. I think he was trying to get me to tell him whether or not I thought it was serious between the two of them—Mr. G and my mom, I mean.

Well, I know it's pretty serious if he's spending the night. My mom only lets guys she really, really likes spend the night. So far, including Mr. G, that's only been three guys in the past fourteen years: Wolfgang, who turned out to be gay; this guy Tim, who turned out to be a Republican; and now my Algebra teacher. That's not so many, really. It's only like one guy every four years.

Or something like that.

But of course I couldn't tell my dad that Mr. G had spent the night, or I know he'd have had an embolism. He is such a chauvinist—he has girlfriends stay over at Miragnac every summer, sometimes a new one every two weeks!—but he expects Mom to stay pure as the driven snow.

If Lilly were still speaking to me, I know she'd say men are such hypocrites.

A part of me wanted to tell my dad about Mr. G, just so he'd stop being so smug. But I didn't want to give my grandmother any more ammunition against my mom—

Grandmère says my mom is "flighty"—so I just pretended like I didn't know anything about it.

Grandmère says we're going to work on my vocabulary tomorrow. She says my French is atrocious but my English is even worse. She says if she ever hears me say "*Whatever*" again, she's going to wash my mouth out with soap.

I said, "Whatever, Grandmère," and she shot me this way dirty look. I wasn't trying to be smart-alecky, though. I really forgot.

To date, I've made $200 for Greenpeace. I'm probably going to go down in history as the girl who saved all the whales.

When I got home, I noticed there were *two* empty containers of pad Thai in the trash. Also *two* sets of plastic chopsticks and *two* bottles of Heineken in the recycling bin. I asked my mom if she'd had Mr. G over for dinner—my God, she'd spent the whole day with him already!—and she said, "Oh, no, honey. I was just really hungry."

That's two lies she's told me in one day. This thing with Mr. G must be pretty serious.

Lilly still hasn't called. I'm starting to think maybe *I* should call *her*. But what would I say? *I* didn't do anything. I mean, I know I told her to shut up, but that was only because she told me I was turning into Lana Weinberger. I had every right to tell her to shut up.

Or did I? Maybe nobody has a right to tell anybody to shut up. Maybe this is how wars get started, because someone tells someone else to shut up, and then no one will apologize.

If this keeps up, who am I going to eat lunch with tomorrow?

When Lars pulled up in front of Lilly's building to pick her up for school, her doorman said she'd already left. Talk about holding a grudge.

This is the longest fight we've ever had.

When I walked into school, the first thing somebody did was shove a petition in my face.

BOYCOTT HO'S DELI!
SIGN BELOW AND TAKE A
STAND AGAINST RACISM!

I said I wouldn't sign it, and Boris, who was the person holding it, told me I was ungrateful, and that in the country he came from voices raised in protest had been crushed for years by the government, and that I should feel lucky I lived in a place where I could sign a petition and not live in fear that the secret police would come after me.

I told Boris that in America we don't tuck our sweaters into our pants.

One thing you have to say for Lilly: She acts fast. The whole school is plastered with Boycott Ho's Deli posters.

The other thing you have to say about Lilly: When she's mad, she stays mad. She is totally not speaking to me.

I wish Mr. G would get off my case. Who *cares* about integers, anyway?

Operations on Real Numbers: negatives or opposites— numbers on opposite sides of the zero but the same distance from zero on the number line are called negatives or opposites

What to Do During Algebra

O *what to do during Algebra!*
The possibilities are limitless:
There's drawing, and yawning,
and portable chess.

There's dozing, and dreaming,
and feeling confused.
There's humming, and strumming,
and looking bemused.

You can stare at the clock.
You can hum a little song.
I've tried just about everything
to pass the time along.

BUT NOTHING WORKS!!!!!

So even if Lilly and I weren't in a fight, I wouldn't have been able to sit with her at lunch today. She's become the queen of the cause célèbre. All these people were clustered around the table where she and I and Shameeka and Ling Su normally eat our dumplings from Big Wong. *Boris Pelkowski* was sitting where I usually sit.

Lilly must be in heaven. She's always wanted to be worshiped by a musical genius.

So I was standing there like a total idiot with my stupid tray of stupid salad, which was the only vegetarian entree today, since they ran out of cans of Sterno for the bean and grain bar, and I was like, Who am *I* going to sit by? There are only about ten tables in our caf, since we have rotating lunch shifts: There's the table where I sit with Lilly, and then the jock table, the cheerleader table, the rich kid table, the hip-hop table, the druggie table, the drama freak table, the National Honor Society table, the foreign exchange students table, and the table where Tina Hakim Baba sits every day with her bodyguard.

I couldn't sit with the jocks or the cheerleaders, because I'm not either. I couldn't sit at the rich kids' table because I don't have a cell phone or a broker. I'm not into hip-hopping or drugs, I didn't get a part in the latest play, and with my F in Algebra the chance of my getting into the National Honor Society is like nil, and I can't understand anything the foreign exchange students say since there are no French ones.

I looked at Tina Hakim Baba. She had a salad in front of her, just like me. Only Tina eats salad because she has a weight problem, not because she's a vegetarian. She was reading a romance novel. It had a photograph on the front of a teenage boy with his arms around a teenage girl. The teenage girl had long blond hair and pretty big breasts for someone with such thin thighs. She looked exactly the way I know my grandmother wants me to look.

I walked over and put my tray down in front of Tina Hakim Baba's.

"Can I sit here?" I asked.

Tina looked up from her book. She had an expression of total shock on her face. She looked at me, and then she looked at her bodyguard. He was a tall, dark-skinned man in a black suit. He had on sunglasses even though we were inside. I think Lars could probably have taken him, if it had come down to a fight between the two of them.

When Tina looked at her bodyguard, he looked at me—at least I think he did; it was hard to tell with those sunglasses—and nodded.

Tina smiled really big at me. "Please," she said, laying down her book. "Sit with me."

I sat down. I felt kind of bad, seeing Tina smile like that. Like maybe I should have asked to sit down with her before. But I used to think she was such a freak because she rode to school in a limo and had a bodyguard.

I don't think she's as much of a freak now.

Tina and I ate our salads and talked about how much school food sucks. She told me about her diet. Her mother put her on it. She wants to lose twenty pounds by the Cultural Diversity Dance. But the Cultural Diversity Dance is this Saturday, so I don't know how that's going to work out for her. I asked Tina if she had a date for the Cultural Diversity Dance or something, and she got all giggly and said yes she did. She's going with a guy from Trinity, which is another private school in Manhattan. The guy's name is Dave Farouq El-Abar.

Hello? It isn't fair. Even Tina Hakim Baba, whose father doesn't allow her to walk two blocks to school, has

127

been asked out by someone.

Well, she's got breasts, so I guess that's why.

Tina is pretty nice. When she got up to go to the jet line to get another diet soda—the bodyguard went with her; God, if Lars ever started shadowing me like that, I'd kill myself—I read the back of her book. The book was called *I Think My Name Is Amanda*, and it was about a girl who woke up from a coma and couldn't remember who she was. This really cute boy comes to visit her in the hospital and tells her that her name is Amanda and that he's her boyfriend. She spends the rest of the book trying to figure out whether or not he's lying.

I am so sure! If some cute boy wants to tell you that he's your boyfriend, why wouldn't you just *let* him? Some girls don't know when they've got it made.

While I was reading the back of the book, this shadow fell over it, and I looked up and there was Lana Weinberger. It must have been a game day, because she had on her cheerleader uniform, a green-and-white pleated miniskirt and a tight white sweater with a giant *A* across the front of it. I think she stuffs her pom-poms down her bra when she isn't using them. Otherwise, I don't see how her chest could stick out so much.

"Nice hair, Amelia," she said in her snotty voice. "Who are you supposed to be? Tank Girl?"

I looked past her. Josh Richter was standing there with some of his dumb jock friends. They weren't paying any attention to me and Lana. They were talking about a party they'd been to over the weekend. They were all "wrecked" from having consumed too much beer.

I wonder if their coach knows.

"What do you call this color, anyway?" Lana wanted to know. She touched the top of my head. "Pus yellow?"

Tina Hakim Baba and her bodyguard came back while

Lana was standing there tormenting me. In addition to her diet soda, Tina had purchased a Nutty Royale ice cream cone, which she gave to me. I thought this was very nice of her, considering the fact that I'd hardly ever spoken to her before.

But Lana didn't see the niceness of this gesture. Instead she asked, all innocently, "Oh, Tina, did you buy that ice cream for Amelia here? Did your daddy give you an extra hundred dollars today so you could buy yourself a new friend?"

Tina's dark eyes filled up with hurt. The bodyguard saw this and opened his mouth.

Then a strange thing happened. I was sitting there, looking at the tears welling up in Tina Hakim Baba's eyes, and then the next thing I knew, I'd taken my Nutty Royale and thrust it with all my might at the front of Lana's sweater.

Lana looked down at the vanilla ice cream, hard chocolate shell, and peanuts that were sticking to her chest. Josh Richter and the other jocks stopped talking and looked at Lana's chest, too. The noise level in the cafeteria plummeted to the quietest I've heard it. *Everyone* was looking at the ice cream cone sticking to Lana's chest. It was so quiet I could hear Boris breathing through the wires of his bionater.

Then Lana started to scream.

"You—you—" I guess she couldn't think of a word bad enough to call me. "You—you . . . Look what you've done! Look what you've done to my sweater!"

I stood up and grabbed my tray. "Come on, Tina," I said. "Let's go somewhere a little bit quieter."

Tina, her big brown eyes on the sugar cone sticking out of the middle of the *A* on Lana's chest, picked up her tray and followed me. The bodyguard followed Tina. I could swear he was laughing.

As Tina and I walked past the table where Lilly and I usually sat, I saw Lilly staring at me with her mouth open. She had obviously seen the whole thing.

Well, I guess she's going to have change her diagnosis: I am *not* unassertive. Not when I don't want to be.

I'm not sure, but as Tina and her bodyguard and I left, I thought I heard some applause coming from the geek table.

I think self-actualization might be right around the corner.

Oh, my God. I am in so much trouble. Nothing like this has ever happened to me before!

I am sitting in the principal's office!

That's right. I got sent to the principal's office for stabbing Lana Weinberger with a Nutty Royale!

I should have known she'd tell on me. She is such a big whiner.

I'm kind of scared. I've never disobeyed a student rule before. I've always been a really good kid. When the student worker came to our G & T class with the pink hall pass, I never thought for a minute it might be for me. I was sitting there with Michael Moscovitz. He was showing me that the way I subtract is all wrong. He says my main problem is that I don't write my numbers neat enough when borrowing. Also that I don't keep track of my notes, and scribble them in whatever notebook I happen to have handy. He says I should keep all my Algebra notes in one notebook.

Also, he says I seem to have trouble concentrating.

But the reason I couldn't concentrate was that I had never sat so close to a boy before! I mean, I realize it was only Michael Moscovitz, and that I see him all the time, and he'd never like me anyway because I'm a freshman and he's a senior, and I'm his little sister's best friend and all—at least, I used to be.

But he's still a boy, a *cute* boy, even if he *is* Lilly's brother. It was really hard to pay attention to subtraction when I could smell this really nice clean boy smell coming from him. Plus every once in a while he would put his hand over mine and take my pencil away and go, "No, like *this*, Mia."

Of course, I was also having trouble concentrating

because I kept feeling like Lilly was looking at us. She wasn't, of course. Now that she's fighting the evil forces of racism in our neighborhood, she doesn't have time for the little people like me. She was sitting at this big table with all of her supporters, plotting their next move in the Ho Offensive. She even let Boris come out of the supply closet to help.

May I point out that he was all over her? How she can stand having his spindly little violin-stroking arm around the back of her chair, I can't imagine. And he *still* hasn't untucked his sweater.

So I really shouldn't have worried that anybody was going to notice me and Michael. I mean, he certainly didn't have his arm around the back of *my* chair. Although once, under the table, his knee touched my knee. I nearly died at the niceness of it all.

Then that stupid hall pass arrived with *my* name on it.

I wonder if I'm going to get expelled. Maybe if I get expelled I could go to a different school, where nobody knows that my hair used to be a different color and that these fingernails aren't really real. That might be kind of nice.

FROM NOW ON I WILL

1. Think before I act.
2. Try to be gracious, no matter how much I am provoked to behave otherwise.
3. Tell the truth, except when doing so would hurt someone's feelings.
4. Stay as far away as possible from Lana Weinberger.

Uh-oh. Principal Gupta is ready to see me now.

Well, I don't know what I'm going to do now. I have detention for a week, *plus* math review with Mr. G, *plus* princess lessons with Grandmère.

I didn't get home until nine o'clock tonight. Something has *got* to give.

My father is furious. He says he is going to sue the school. He says no one can give his daughter detention for defending the weak. I told him that Principal Gupta can. She can do anything. She's the principal.

I can't say I really blame her. I mean, it wasn't like I said I was sorry or anything. Principal Gupta is a nice lady, but what could she do? I admitted I had done it. She told me I'd have to apologize to Lana and pay to have her sweater cleaned. I said I'd pay for the sweater but that I wouldn't apologize. Principal Gupta looked at me over the rims of her bifocals and went, "I beg your pardon, Mia?"

I repeated that I wouldn't apologize. My heart was beating like crazy. I didn't want to make anybody mad, especially Principal Gupta, who can be very scary when she wants to. I tried to picture her in her husband's sweatpants, but it didn't work. She still scared me.

But I won't apologize to Lana. I won't.

Principal Gupta didn't look mad, though. She looked concerned. I guess that's how educators are supposed to look. You know. Concerned about you. She went, "Mia, I must say, when Lana came in here with her complaint, I was extremely surprised. It's usually Lilly Moscovitz I have to pull in here. I never expected I was going to have to pull *you* in. Not for disciplinary reasons. Academic reasons, maybe. I understand you aren't doing very well in Algebra. But I've never known you to be a discipline problem before. I really feel I must ask you, Mia . . . is everything all right?"

For a minute I just stared at her.

Is everything all right? *Is everything all right?*

Hmm, hold on a minute, let me see . . . my mom is going out with my Algebra teacher, a subject I'm flunking, by the way; my best friend hates me; I'm fourteen years old and I've never been asked out; I don't have any breasts; and oh, I just found out I'm the princess of Genovia.

"Oh, sure," I said to Principal Gupta. "Everything is fine."

"Are you certain, Mia? Because I can't help wondering if this isn't all rooted in some problems you might be having . . . maybe at home?"

Who did she think I was, anyway? Lana *Whine*berger? Like I was really going to sit there and tell her my problems. Yeah, Principal Gupta. On top of all that other stuff, my grandmother is in town, and my dad is paying $100 a day for me to get lessons from her in how to be a princess. Oh, and this weekend, I ran into Mr. Gianini in my kitchen, and all he was wearing was a pair of boxer shorts. Anything else you want to know?

"Mia," Principal Gupta said, "I want you to know that you are a very special person. You have many wonderful qualities. There is no reason for you to feel threatened by Lana Weinberger. None at all."

Oh, okay. Just because she's the prettiest, most popular girl in my class, and she's going out with the handsomest, most popular boy in school, you're right, Principal Gupta. There's no reason at all to feel threatened by her. Especially since she puts me down every chance she gets and tries to humiliate me in public. Threatened? *Me?* Nah.

"You know, Mia," Principal Gupta said, "I bet if you

took the time to get to know Lana you'd find that she's really a very nice girl. A girl just like you."

Right. Just like me.

I was so upset, I actually told Grandmère all about it at our vocabulary lesson. She was surprisingly sympathetic.

"When I was a girl your age," Grandmère said, "there was a girl just like this Lana at my school. Her name was Genevieve. She sat behind me in Geography. Genevieve would take the end of my braid and dip it in her inkwell, so that when I stood up I got ink all over my dress. But the teacher would never believe me that Genevieve did it on purpose."

"Really?" I was kind of impressed. That Genevieve had some guts. I never met anyone who'd try to dis my grandmother. "What did you do?"

Grandmère let out this evil laugh. "Oh, nothing."

There is no way she did *nothing* to Genevieve. Not with a laugh like that. But no matter how hard I pestered her, Grandmère wouldn't tell me what she did to get back at Genevieve. I'm kind of thinking maybe she killed her.

Well? It could happen.

But I guess I shouldn't have pestered Grandmère so hard, because to shut me up she gave me a quiz! I'm not kidding!

It was really hard, too. I've stapled it in here, since I got a 98. Grandmère says I've really come a long way since we started.

Grandmère's Test

In a restaurant, what does one do with one's napkin when one rises to go to the powder room?

If it's a four-star restaurant, hand it to the waiter who rushes over to help you with your chair. If it's a normal place, and no waiter rushes over, leave your napkin on your empty chair.

Under what circumstances is it acceptable to apply lipstick in public?

Never.

What are the characteristics of capitalism?

Private ownership of the means of production and distribution, and the exchange of goods based on the operations of the market.

What is the appropriate reply to make to a man who says he loves you?

Thank you. You are very kind.

What did Marx consider to be the contradiction in capitalism?

The value of any commodity is determined by the amount of labor needed to produce it. In denying workers the value of what they have produced, the capitalists are undermining their own economic system.

White shoes are unacceptable . . .

At funerals, after Labor Day, before Memorial Day, and anywhere there might be horses.

Describe an oligarchy.
Small group exercises control for generally
corrupt purposes.

Describe a Sidecar.
⅓ lemon juice, ⅓ Cointreau, ⅓ brandy
shaken well with ice, strained before serving.

The only one I missed was the one about what to say
to a man when he tells you he loves you. It turns out you
aren't supposed to say thank you.

Not, of course, that this will ever happen to me. But
Grandmère says I might be surprised someday.

I wish!

No Lilly again this morning. Not that I expected there to be. But I made Lars stop at her place anyway, just in case maybe she wanted to be friends again. I mean, she could have seen how assertive I was with Lana and decided she was wrong to criticize me so much.

But I guess not.

The funny thing is, when Lars was dropping me off at school, Tina Hakim Baba's chauffeur was dropping her off, too. We sort of smiled at each other, then walked into school together, her bodyguard behind us. Tina said she wanted to thank me for what I had done yesterday. She said she told her parents about it, and that they want me to come over for dinner Friday night.

"And maybe," Tina asked, all shyly, "you could spend the night after, if you wanted."

I said, "Okay." I mostly said it because I feel sorry for Tina, since she doesn't have any other friends, because everybody thinks she's so weird, with the bodyguard and all. I also said it because I heard she has a fountain in her house, just like Donald Trump, and I wanted to see if that was true.

And I kind of like her, too. She's *nice* to me.

It's nice to have somebody be nice to you.

I HAVE <u>GOT</u> TO

1. Stop waiting for the phone to ring (Lilly is NOT going to call; neither is Josh Richter)
2. Make more friends
3. Have more self-confidence
4. Stop biting my fake fingernails
5. Start acting more:
   - A. Responsible
   - B. Adult
   - C. Mature
6. Be happier
7. Achieve self-actualization
8. Buy:
   - trash bags
   - napkins
   - conditioner
   - tuna
   - toilet paper!!!!

Oh, my God. I can't even believe this. But it must be true, since Shameeka just told me.

Lilly has a date to the Cultural Diversity Dance this weekend.

Lilly has a date. Even *Lilly* has a date. I thought all the boys in our school were terrified of Lilly.

But there's one boy who's not:

Boris Pelkowski.

AAAAHHHHHHHHHHHHHHHHH!

No boy will ever ask me out. Ever. EVERYONE has a date to the Cultural Diversity Dance: Shameeka, Lilly, Ling Su, Tina Hakim Baba. I'm the only one not going. The ONLY ONE.

Why was I born under such an unlucky star? Why did *I* have to be cursed with such freakishness? Why? WHY???

I would give anything if, instead of being a five-foot-nine flat-chested princess, I could be a five-foot-six normal person with breasts.

ANYTHING.

Satire—employs humor systematically for the purpose of persuasion

Irony—counter to expectation

Parody—close imitation that exaggerates ridiculous or objectionable features

More Tuesday, French

Today in G & T, in between showing me how to carry over, Michael Moscovitz complimented me on my handling of what he called the Weinberger Incident. I was surprised he'd heard about it. He said it was all over school, about how I'd decimated Lana in front of Josh. He said, "Your locker is right next to Josh's, isn't it?"

I said yes it was.

He said, "That must be awkward," but I told him actually it wasn't, since Lana seems to be avoiding that area lately, and Josh never talks to me at all, except to say, "Can I get by here?" once in a while.

I asked him if Lilly was still saying mean things about me, and he said, all taken aback, "She's never said mean things about you. She just doesn't understand why you blew up at her like that."

I said, "Michael, she's always putting me down! I just couldn't take it anymore. I have too many other problems without having friends who aren't supportive of me."

He laughed. "What kind of problems could *you* have?"

Like I was too much of a kid or something to have problems!

Boy, did I straighten him out. I couldn't exactly tell him about being the princess of Genovia, or about not having any breasts or anything, but I did remind him that I'm flunking Algebra, I have detention for a week, and I had recently woken up to find Mr. Gianini in his boxer shorts eating breakfast with my mom.

He said he guessed I did have some problems after all.

The whole time Michael and I were talking, I saw Lilly shooting us these looks from behind the poster board she was writing Ho-Gate slogans on with a big black Magic Marker. So I guess because I'm fighting with her I'm not allowed to be friends with her brother.

Or maybe she's just sore because her boycott of Ho's Deli is creating serious turmoil within the school. First of all, all the Asian kids have started doing their shopping exclusively at Ho's. And why not? Because of Lilly's campaign, now they know they can get a five-cent discount on just about anything. The other problem is that there is no other deli within walking distance. This has caused some serious division within the ranks of the protesters. The nonsmokers want to continue the boycott, but the smokers are all for writing the Hos a stern letter and then forgetting about it. And since all the popular kids in school smoke, they aren't honoring the boycott at all. They're going to Ho's just like they always did to get their Camel Lights.

When you can't get the popular kids on your side, you have to realize it's hopeless: Without celebrity supporters, no cause stands a chance. I mean, where would all those starving kids be without Sally Struthers?

Anyway, then Michael asked me a strange question. He went, "So, are you grounded?"

I looked at him kind of funny. "You mean for getting detention? No, of course not. My mom is totally on my side. My dad wants to sue the school."

Michael said, "Oh. Well, I was wondering because, if you aren't busy Saturday, I thought maybe we could—"

But then Mrs. Hill came in and made us all fill out questionnaires for the Ph.D. she's doing on urban youth violence, even though Lilly complained that we're hardly qualified to comment, seeing as how the only youth violence any of us had ever experienced was when there was a sale on relaxed fit jeans at the Gap on Madison Avenue.

Then the bell rang, and I ran out as fast as I could. I knew what Michael was going to ask me, see. He was going to suggest we meet to go over my long division, which he says is a human tragedy. And I just didn't think I could take it. Math? On the weekend? After spending almost every waking moment on it all week?

No, thank you.

But I didn't want to be rude, so I left before he could ask me. Was that terrible of me?

Really, a girl can only take so much criticism on her remainders.

ma	*mon*	*mes*
ta	*ton*	*tes*
sa	*son*	*ses*
notre	*notre*	*nos*
votre	*votre*	*vos*
leur	*leur*	*leurs*

HOMEWORK

Algebra: pg. 121, 1–57 odd only
English: ??? Ask Shameeka
World Civ: questions at end of Chapter 9
G & T: none
French: *pour demain, une vignette culturelle*
Biology: none

Grandmère says Tina Hakim Baba sounds like a much better friend for me than Lilly Moscovitz. But I think she is only saying that because Lilly's parents are psychoanalysts, and it turns out Tina's dad is this Arabian sheikh and her mom is related to the king of Sweden, so they are more appropriate for the heir to the throne of Genovia to hang out with.

The Hakim Babas are also superrich, according to my grandmother. They own about a gazillion oil wells. Grandmère told me when I go have dinner with them on Friday night, I have to bring a gift and wear my Gucci loafers. I asked Grandmère what kind of gift, and she said breakfast. She's special-ordering it from Balducci's and having it delivered Saturday morning.

Being a princess is hard work.

I just remembered: At lunch today Tina had a new book with her. It had a cover just like the last one, only this time the heroine was a brunette. This one was called *My Secret Love*, and it was about a girl from the wrong side of the tracks who falls in love with a rich boy who never notices her. Then the girl's uncle kidnaps the boy and holds him for ransom, and she has to bathe his wounds and help him to escape and stuff, and of course he falls madly in love with her. Tina said she already read the end, and the girl gets to go and live with the rich boy's parents after her uncle goes to jail and can no longer support her.

How come things like that don't ever happen to *me*?

No Lilly again today. Lars suggested we'd make better time if we just drove straight to school and didn't stop by her place every day. I guess he's right.

It was really weird when we pulled up to Albert Einstein. All the people who normally hang around outside before school starts, smoking and sitting on Joe, the stone lion, were all clustered into these groups looking at something. I suppose somebody's dad has been accused of money laundering again. Parents can be so self-centered: Before they do something illegal, they should totally stop and think about how their kids are going to feel if they get caught.

I just walked right on by to show I wasn't going to have any part in gossip. A bunch of people stared at me. I guess Michael's right: It really *has* gotten around, about me stabbing Lana with that Nutty Royale. Either that or my hair was sticking up in some weird way. But I checked in the mirror in the girls' room and it wasn't.

A bunch of girls ran out of the bathroom giggling like crazy when I went in, though.

Sometimes I wish I lived on a desert island. Really. With nobody else around for hundreds of miles. Just me, the ocean, the sand, and a coconut tree.

And maybe a high-definition 37-inch TV with a satellite dish and a Sony PlayStation with Bandicoot, for when I get bored.

LITTLE KNOWN FACTS

1. The most commonly asked question at Albert Einstein High School is "Do you have any gum?"
2. Bees and bulls are attracted to the color red.
3. In my homeroom, it sometimes takes up to half an hour just to take attendance.
4. I miss being best friends with Lilly Moscovitz.

Later on Wednesday, Before Algebra

This totally weird thing happened. Josh Richter came up to his locker to put his Trig book away, and he said, "How you doin'?" to me as I was getting out my Algebra notebook.

I swear to God I am not making this up.

I was in such total shock, I nearly dropped my backpack. I don't have any idea what I said to him. I think I said I was fine. I *hope* I said I was fine.

Why is Josh Richter speaking to me?

It must have been another one of those synaptic breakdowns, like the one he had at Bigelow's.

Then Josh slammed his locker closed, *looked right down into my face*—he's really tall—and said, "See you later."

Then he walked away.

It took me five minutes to stop hyperventilating.

His eyes are so blue they hurt to look at.

It's over.

I'm dead.

That's it.

Now I know what everyone was looking at outside. I know why they were whispering and giggling. I know why those girls ran out of the bathroom. I know why Josh Richter talked to me.

My picture is on the cover of the *Post*.

That's right. The *New York Post*. Read by millions of New Yorkers daily.

Oh, yeah. I'm dead.

It's a pretty good picture of me, actually. I guess somebody took it as I was leaving the Plaza Sunday night, after dinner with Grandmère and my dad. I'm going down the steps just outside the revolving door. I'm sort of smiling, only not at the camera. I don't remember anybody taking my picture, but I guess somebody did.

Superimposed over the photo are the words *Princess Amelia*, and then in smaller letters *New York's Very Own Royal*.

Great. Just great.

Mr. Gianini was the one who figured it out. He said he was walking to catch the subway to work and he saw it on the newsstand. He called my mother. My mom was taking a shower, though, and didn't hear the phone. Mr. G left a message. But my mom never checks the machine in the morning, because everyone who knows her knows she is not a morning person, so nobody ever calls before noon. When Mr. G called again, she had already left for her studio, where she never answers the phone, because she wears an iPod when she paints so she can listen to Howard Stern.

So then Mr. G had no choice but to call my dad at the Plaza, which was pretty nervy of him, if you think about it. According to Mr. G, my dad blew a gasket. He told Mr. G that until he could get there, I should be sent to the principal's office, where I would be "safe."

My dad has obviously never met Principal Gupta.

Actually, I shouldn't say that. She hasn't been so bad. She showed me the paper and said, kind of sarcastically, but in a nice way, "You might have shared this with me, Mia, when I asked you the other day if everything was all right at home."

I blushed. "Well," I said, "I didn't think anybody would believe me."

"It is," Principal Gupta said, "a bit unbelievable."

That's what the story on page 2 of the *Post* said, too. Fairy Tale Comes True for One Lucky New York Kid was how the reporter, one Ms. Carol Fernandez, put it. Like I had won the lottery, or something. Like I should be *happy* about it.

Ms. Carol Fernandez went on at length about my mom, "the raven-haired avant-garde painter Helen Thermopolis," and about my dad, "the handsome Prince Phillipe of Genovia," who'd "successfully battled his way back from a bout of testicular cancer." Oh, thanks, Carol Fernandez, for letting all of New York know my dad's only got one you-know-what.

Then she went on to describe me as "the statuesque beauty who is the product of Helen and Phillipe's tempestuous whirlwind college romance."

HELLO??? CAROL FERNANDEZ, ARE YOU ON CRACK????

I am NOT a statuesque beauty. Yeah, I'm TALL. I'm way TALL. But I am no beauty. I want what Carol Fernandez has been smoking, if she thinks *I'M* beautiful.

No wonder everybody was laughing at me. This is SO embarrassing. I mean, really.

Oh, here comes my dad. Boy, does *he* look mad. . . .

It isn't fair.

This is totally, completely unfair.

I mean, anybody else's dad would have let them come home. Anybody else's dad, if his kid's picture was on the front of the *Post*, would say, "Maybe you should skip school for a few days until things calm down."

Anybody else's dad would have been like, "Maybe you should change schools. How do you feel about Iowa? Would you like to go to school in Iowa?"

But oh, no. Not *my* dad. Because *he's* a prince. And he says members of the royal family of Genovia do not "go home" when there is a crisis. No, they stay where they are and slug it out.

Slug it out. I think my dad has something in common with Carol Fernandez: They're BOTH on crack.

Then my dad reminded me that it's not like I'm not getting paid for this. Right! One hundred lousy bucks! One hundred lousy bucks a day to be publicly ridiculed and humiliated.

Those baby seals better be grateful, that's all I have to say.

So here I am in English, and everybody is whispering about me and pointing at me like I'm a victim of alien abduction or something, and my dad expects me to sit here and let them, because I'm a princess and that's what princesses do.

But these kids are *brutal*.

I tried to tell my dad that. I was like, "Dad, you don't understand. They're all laughing at me."

And all he said was, "I'm sorry, honey. You're just going to have to tough it out. You knew this was going to happen eventually. I'd hoped it wouldn't be quite this soon, but it's probably just as well to get it over with. . . ."

Um, hello? I did *not* know this was going to happen eventually. I thought I was going to be able to keep this whole princess thing a secret. My lovely plan about only being a princess in Genovia is falling apart. I have to be a princess right here in Manhattan, and believe me, that is no picnic.

I was so mad at my dad for telling me I had to go back to class, I accused him of having ratted me out to Carol Fernandez himself.

He got all offended. "*Me?* I don't know any Carol Fernandez." He shot this funny look at Mr. Gianini, who was standing there with his hands in his pockets, looking all concerned.

"What?" Mr. G said, going from concerned to surprised real fast. "*Me?* I'd never even *heard* of Genovia until this morning."

"Geez, Dad," I said. "Don't blame Mr. G. *He* had nothing to do with it."

My dad didn't look very convinced. "Well, *somebody* leaked the story to the press. . . ." He said it in this mean way, too. You could totally tell he thought Mr. G had done it. But it couldn't have been Mr. Gianini. Carol Fernandez wrote about stuff in her story that there's no way Mr. G could know, because even *Mom* doesn't know about it. Like how Miragnac has a private airstrip. I never told her about that.

But when I told my dad that, he just shot Mr. G a suspicious look. "Well," he said again. "I'm just going to give this Carol Fernandez a call and see who her source is."

And while my dad was doing that, I got stuck with Lars. I'm not kidding. Just like Tina Hakim Baba, I now have a bodyguard trailing around after me from class to class. Like I'm not enough of a laughingstock already.

I now have an armed escort.

I totally tried to get out of it. I was like, "Dad, I can seriously take care of myself," but he was completely rigid and said that even though Genovia is a small country, it is a very wealthy country, and he cannot take the risk of my being kidnapped and held for ransom like the boy in *My Secret Love*, only my dad didn't say that because he's never read *My Secret Love*.

I said, "Dad, no one is going to kidnap me. This is *school*," but he wouldn't go for it. He asked Principal Gupta if it was all right, and she said, "Of course, Your Highness."

Your Highness! Principal Gupta called my dad Your Highness! If it hadn't been all serious and stuff, I would have wet my pants laughing.

The only good thing that has come out of this is that Principal Gupta let me off detention for the rest of the week, claiming that having my picture in the *Post* is punishment enough.

But really the only reason is that she is totally charmed by my father. He pulled such a Jean-Luc Picard on her, you wouldn't believe it, calling her Madam Principal and apologizing for all the fuss. I practically expected him to kiss her hand, he was flirting so hard with her. And Principal Gupta has been married a million years, and has this big black mole on the side of her nose. And she totally fell for it! She was eating it up!

I wonder if Tina Hakim Baba will still sit with me at lunch. Well, if she does, at least our bodyguards will have something to do: They can compare civilian defense tactics.

I guess I should have my picture on the front of the *Post* more often.

Suddenly I am very popular.

I walked into the cafeteria (I told Lars to keep five paces behind me at all times; he kept stepping on the backs of my combat boots), and Lana Weinberger, of all people, came up to me while I was in the jet line getting my tray, and said, "Hey, Mia. Why don't you come and sit with us?"

I am not even kidding. That lousy hypocrite wants to be friends with me now that I'm a princess.

Tina was right behind me in line (well, Lars was behind me; Tina was behind Lars, and Tina's bodyguard was behind her). But did Lana invite Tina to join her? Of course not. The *New York Post* hadn't called *Tina* a "statuesque beauty." Short, heavyset girls—even one whose father is an Arab sheikh—aren't good enough to sit by *Lana*. Oh, no. Only purebred Genovian princesses are good enough to sit by *Lana*.

I nearly threw up all over my lunch tray.

"No, thanks, Lana," I said. "I already have someone to sit with."

You should have seen Lana's face. The last time I saw her look that shocked, a sugar cone had been stuck to her chest.

Later, when we were sitting down, Tina could only nibble at her salad. She hadn't said a word about the princess thing. Meanwhile, though, everybody in the whole cafeteria—including the geeks, who never notice anything—were staring at our table. Let me tell you, it was way uncomfortable. I could feel Lilly's eyes boring into me. She hadn't said anything to me yet, but I think she had to have known. Nothing much escapes Lilly.

Anyway, after a while I couldn't stand it anymore. I put down a forkful of rice and beans and said, "Look, Tina. If you don't want to sit with me anymore, I understand."

Tina's big eyes filled up with tears. I mean it. She shook her head, and her long black braid swayed. "What do you mean?" she asked. "You don't like me anymore, Mia?"

It was my turn to be shocked. "What? Of course I like you. I thought maybe you might not like *me*. I mean, everyone is staring at us. I could see why you might not want to sit with me."

Tina smiled sadly. "Everyone always stares at me," she said. "Because of Wahim, you see."

Wahim is her bodyguard. Wahim and Lars were sitting next to us, arguing over whose gun had the most firepower, Wahim's 357 Magnum or Lars's 9mm Glock. It was kind of a disturbing topic, but they both seemed happy as could be. In a minute or two, I expected they'd start to arm wrestle.

"So you see," Tina said, "*I'm* used to people thinking I'm weird. It's *you* I feel sorry for, Mia. You could be sitting with anyone—anyone in this whole cafeteria—and yet you're stuck with me. I don't want you to feel you have to be nice to me just because no one else is."

I got really mad then. Not at Tina. But at everybody else at Albert Einstein. I mean, Tina Hakim Baba is really, really nice, and no one knows it because no one ever talks to her, because she isn't very thin and she's kind of quiet and she's stuck with a stupid bodyguard. While people are worrying about things like the fact that a deli is overcharging some people by five cents for gingko biloba rings, there are human beings walking around our school in abject misery because no one will even say Good morning to them, or How was your weekend?

And then I felt guilty, because a week ago *I* had been one of those people. I had always thought Tina Hakim Baba was a freak. The whole reason I hadn't wanted anyone to find out I was a princess was that I was afraid they'd treat *me* the way they treated Tina Hakim Baba. And now that I know Tina, I know just how wrong I'd been to think badly of her.

So I told Tina I didn't want to sit with anybody but her. I told her I thought we needed to stick together, and not just for the obvious reason (Wahim and Lars). I told her we needed to stick together because everyone else at this stupid school is completely NUTS.

Tina looked a lot happier then, and started filling me in on the new book she's reading. This one is called *Love Only Once*, and it's about a girl who falls in love with a boy who has terminal cancer. I told Tina it seemed like kind of a bummer thing to read, but she told me she'd already read the end, and that the boy's terminal cancer goes away. So I guess that's okay then.

As we cleared our trays, I saw Lilly staring in my direction. It wasn't the kind of stare someone who was about to apologize would use. So I wasn't too surprised when later, after I got to G & T, Lilly sat there and stared at me some more. Boris kept on trying to talk to her, but she obviously wasn't listening. Finally he gave up and picked up his violin and went back into the supply closet, where he belongs.

Meanwhile, this is how my tutoring session with Lilly's brother went:

Me: Hi, Michael. I did all those problems you gave me. But I still don't see why you couldn't just look at the train schedule to find out what time a train traveling at 67 miles per hour will arrive in Fargo, North Dakota, if it leaves

157

Salt Lake City at 7 A.M.

Michael: So. Princess of Genovia, huh? Were you ever going to share that little piece of info with the group, or were we all supposed to guess?

Me: I was kind of hoping no one would ever find out.

Michael: Well, that's obvious. I don't see why, though. It's not like it's a bad thing.

Me: Are you kidding me? Of course it's bad!

Michael: Did you *read* the article in today's *Post*, Thermopolis?

Me: No way. I'm not going to read that trash. I don't know who this Carol Fernandez thinks she is, but—

Then Lilly got into the act. It was like she couldn't stand not to get involved.

Lilly: So you're not aware that the crown prince of Genovia—namely, your father—has a total personal worth which, including real estate property and the palace's art collection, is estimated at over three hundred million dollars?

Well, I guess it's pretty obvious that *Lilly* read the article in today's *Post*.

Me: Um . . .

Hello? Three hundred million dollars?? And I get a lousy $100 a day???

Lilly: I wonder how much of that fortune was amassed by taking advantage of the sweat of the common laborer.

Michael: Considering that the people of Genovia have traditionally never paid income or property taxes, I would say none of it. What is *with* you, anyway, Lil?

Lilly: Well, if *you* want to tolerate the excesses of the monarchy, you can be my guest, Michael. But I happen to think that it's disgusting, with the world economy in the state it's in today, for anyone to have a total worth of three hundred million dollars . . . especially someone who never did a day's work for it!

Michael: Pardon me, Lilly, but it's my understanding that Mia's father works extremely hard for his country. His father's historic pledge, after Mussolini's forces invaded in 1939, to exercise the rights of sovereignty in accordance with the political and economic interests of neighboring France in exchange for military and naval protection in the event of war might have tied the hands of a lesser politician, but Mia's father has managed to work around that agreement. His efforts have resulted in a nation that has the highest literacy rate in Europe, some of the best educational attainment rates, and the lowest infant mortality, inflation, and unemployment rates in the Western Hemisphere.

I could only stare at Michael after that. *Wow.* Why doesn't Grandmère teach me stuff like *that* at our princess lessons? I mean, this is information I could actually use. I don't exactly need to know which direction to tip my soup bowl. I need to know how to defend myself from virulent antiroyalists like my ex–best friend Lilly.

Lilly: (to Michael) Shut up. (to me) I see they already have you spouting off their populist propaganda like a good little girl.

Me: Me? Michael's the one who—

Michael: Aw, Lilly, you're just jealous.

Lilly: I am not!

Michael: Yes, you are. You're jealous because she got her hair cut without consulting you. You're jealous because you stopped talking to her and she went out and got a new friend. And you're jealous because all this time Mia's had this secret she didn't tell you.

Lilly: Michael, SHUT UP!

Boris: (leaning out of the supply closet door) Lilly? Did you say something?

Lilly: I WASN'T TALKING TO YOU, BORIS!

159

Boris: Sorry. (goes back into closet)

Lilly: (really mad now) Gosh, Michael, you sure are quick to come to Mia's defense all of a sudden. I wonder if maybe it ever occurred to you that your argument, while ostensibly based on logic, might have less intellectual than libidinous roots.

Michael: (turning red for some reason) Well, what about your persecution of the Hos? Is that rooted in intellectual reasoning? Or is it more an example of vanity run amok?

Lilly: That's a circular argument.

Michael: It isn't. It's empirical.

Wow. Michael and Lilly are so smart. Grandmère's right: I need to improve my vocabulary.

Michael: (to me) So does this guy (he pointed at Lars) have to follow you around everywhere from now on?

Me: Yes.

Michael: Really? *Everywhere?*

Me: Everywhere except the ladies' room. Then he waits outside.

Michael: What if you were to go on a date? Like to the Cultural Diversity Dance this weekend?

Me: That hasn't exactly been an issue, considering that no one's asked me.

Boris: (leaning out of the supply closet) Excuse me. I accidentally knocked over a bottle of rubber cement with my bow, and it's getting hard to breathe. Can I come out now?

Everyone in the G & T room: NO!!!

Mrs. Hill: (poking her head in from the hallway) What's all this noise in here? We can hardly hear ourselves think in the teachers' lounge. Boris, why are you in the supply closet? Come out now. Everybody else, get back to work!

I need to take a closer look at that article in today's *Post*. Three hundred million dollars?? That's as much as Oprah made last year!

So if we're so rich, how come the TV in my room is only black and white?

Note to self: Look up the words *empirical* and *libidinous*

Wednesday Night

No wonder my dad was so mad about Carol Fernandez's article! When Lars and I walked out of Albert Einstein after my review session there were reporters all over the place. I am not even kidding. It was just like I was a murderer, or a celebrity, or something.

According to Mr. Gianini, who walked out with us, reporters have been arriving all day. There were vans there from New York One, Fox News, CNN, *Entertainment Tonight*—you name it. They've been trying to interview all the kids who go to Albert Einstein, asking them if they know me (for once, being unpopular pays off; I can't imagine they were able to find anybody who could actually remember who I was—at least, not with my new nontriangular hair). Mr. G says Principal Gupta finally had to call the police, because Albert Einstein High is private property and the reporters were trespassing all over, dropping cigarette butts on the steps and blocking the sidewalk and leaning on Joe and stuff.

Which, if you think about it, is exactly what all the popular kids do when they hang around the school grounds after the last bell rings, and Principal Gupta never calls the cops on *them* . . . but then again, I guess their parents are paying tuition.

I have to say, I sort of know now how Princess Diana must have felt. I mean, when Lars and Mr. G and I came out, the reporters started trying to swarm all over, waving microphones at us and yelling stuff like, "Amelia, how about a smile?" and "Amelia, what's it like to wake up one morning the product of a single-parent family and go to bed the next night a royal princess worth over three hundred million dollars?"

I was kind of scared. Even if I'd wanted to, I couldn't

have answered their questions, because I didn't know which microphone to talk into. Plus I was practically rendered blind by all the flashbulbs going off in front of my face.

Then Lars went into action. You should have seen it. First, he told me not to say anything. Then he put his arm around me. He told Mr. G to put his arm around my other side. Then, I don't know how, but we ducked our heads and barreled through all the cameras and microphones and the people attached to them, until the next thing I knew, Lars was pushing me into the backseat of my dad's car and jumping in after me.

Hello! I guess all that training in the Israeli army paid off. (I overheard Lars telling Wahim that's where he'd learned how to work an Uzi. Wahim and Lars actually have some mutual friends, it turns out. I guess all bodyguards go to the same training school out in the Gobi Desert.)

Anyway, as soon as Lars slammed the back door shut, he said "Drive," and the guy behind the wheel hit the gas. I didn't recognize him, but sitting in the passenger seat beside him was my dad. And while we're pulling away, brakes squealing, flashbulbs going off, reporters jumping onto the windshield to get a better shot, my dad goes, all casual, "So. How was your day, Mia?"

Geez!

I decided to ignore my dad. Instead, I turned around in my seat to wave good-bye to Mr. G. Only Mr. G had been swallowed up in a sea of microphones! He wouldn't talk to them, though. He just kept waving his hands at them and trying to head for the subway, so he could take the E train home.

I felt sorry for poor Mr. Gianini then. True, he had probably stuck his tongue in my mom's mouth, but he's a really nice guy and doesn't deserve to be harassed by the media.

I said so to my dad, also that we should have given Mr. G a ride home, and he just got huffy and tugged on his seat belt. He said, "Damn these things. They always choke me."

So then I asked my dad where I was going to go to school now.

My dad looked at me like I was nuts. "You said you wanted to stay at Albert Einstein!" he kind of yelled.

I said, well, yes, but that was before Carol Fernandez outed me.

Then my dad wanted to know what outing was, so I explained to him that outing is when somebody reveals your sexual orientation on national TV, or in the newspaper, or in some other large public forum. Only in this case, I explained, instead of my sexual orientation, my royal status had been revealed.

So then my dad said I couldn't go to a new school just because I'd been outed as being a princess. He said I have to stay at Albert Einstein, and Lars will go to class with me and protect me from reporters.

So then I asked him who'll drive him around, and he pointed to the new guy, Hans.

The new guy nodded to me in the rearview mirror and said, "Hi."

So then I said, "Lars is going to go with me everywhere I go?" Like how about if I just wanted to walk over to Lilly's? I mean, if Lilly and I were still friends. Which is certainly never going to happen now.

And my dad said, "Lars would go with you."

So basically, I am never going anywhere alone again.

This made me kind of mad. I sat in the backseat with red from a traffic light flashing down on my face, and I said, "Okay, well, that's it. I don't want to be a princess anymore. You can take back your one hundred dollars a day and send Grandmère back to France. I quit."

And my dad said, in this tired voice, "You can't quit, Mia. The article today closed the deal. Tomorrow your face will be in every newspaper in America—maybe even the world. Everyone will know that you are the princess Amelia of Genovia. And you cannot quit being who you are."

I guess it wasn't a very princessy thing to do, but I cried all the way to the Plaza. Lars gave me his handkerchief, which I thought was very nice of him.

My mom thinks the person who tipped off Carol Fernandez is Grandmère.

But I really can't believe Grandmère would do something like that—you know, give the *Post* the inside scoop on me. Especially when I'm so far behind in my princess lessons. You know? It's almost guaranteed that now I'm going to have to start acting like a princess—I mean, *really* acting like one—but Grandmère hasn't even gotten to all the really important stuff yet, the stuff like how to argue knowledgeably with virulent antiroyalists like Lilly. So far all Grandmère has taught me is how to sit; how to dress; how to use a fish fork; how to address senior members of the royal household staff; how to say thank you so much and no, I don't care for that, in seven languages; how to make a Sidecar; and some Marxist theory.

What good is any of THAT going to do me?

But my mom is convinced. Nothing will change her mind. My dad got really mad at her, but she still wouldn't budge. She says Grandmère is the one who tipped off Carol Fernandez and that all my dad has to do is ask her and he'll find out the truth.

My dad did ask her—not Grandmère. Mom. He asked her why she never bothered to consider that her boyfriend might be the one who spilled the beans to Carol Fernandez.

The minute he said it, I think my dad probably regretted it. Because my mom's eyes got the way they do when she's really mad—I mean *really* mad, like the time I told her about the guy in Washington Square Park who flashed his you-know-what at me and Lilly one day when we were filming for her show. Her eyes got narrower and narrower, until they were nothing more than little slits. Then, next thing I knew, she was putting on her coat and going out to kick some flasher butt.

Only she didn't put on her coat when my dad said that about Mr. Gianini. Instead, her eyes got very narrow, and her lips almost disappeared, she pressed them together so hard, and then she went, "Get . . . out," in a voice that kind of sounded like the poltergeist in that movie *Amityville Horror*.

But my dad wouldn't get out, even though technically the loft belongs to my mom (thank God Carol Fernandez didn't put the loft's address in the paper; and thank God my mom is so paranoid about Jesse Helms siccing the CIA on sociopolitical artists like herself, in order to yank their NEA grants, that she keeps our phone number unlisted; no reporters have discovered the loft, so we can at least order in Chinese without fear of hearing a story on *Extra* on how much the princess Amelia likes moo shu vegetable).

Instead, my dad went, "Really, Helen. I think you're letting your dislike of my mother blind you to the real truth."

"The real truth?" my mom yelled. "The real truth, Phillipe, is that your mother is—"

At this point, I decided it might be best to retire to my room. I put my headphones on so I wouldn't have to listen to them fight. This is a trick I learned from watching kids on made-for-TV movies whose parents are divorcing. My favorite CD right now is the latest Hilary Duff, which I know is really dorky, and I could never tell Lilly, but secretly I sort of want to be Hilary Duff. Once I had a dream I *was* Hilary, and I was performing in the auditorium at Albert Einstein, and I had this little pink minidress on, and Josh Richter complimented me on it right before I went onstage.

Isn't that an embarrassing thing to admit? The funny thing is, while I know I could never tell Lilly about that dream without her going all Freudian on me and telling me how the pink dress is a phallic symbol and being Britney signifies my low self-esteem or something, I know I could tell Tina Hakim Baba, and she would totally get into it and just want to know whether or not Josh was wearing leather pants.

I don't think I've ever mentioned this, but it's really hard to write with my new fake fingernails.

The more I think about it, the more I wonder whether or not Grandmère really is the one who tipped off Carol Fernandez. I mean, when I went to my princess lesson today I was still crying, and Grandmère was totally unsympathetic about it. She was all, "And these tears are because . . . ?" And when I told her, she just raised her painted-on eyebrows—she plucks hers all out and draws on new ones every day, which kind of defeats the purpose, if you ask me, but whatever—and went, "*C'est la vie,*" which means "Well, that's life" in French.

Only in life, I don't think a whole lot of girls get their faces plastered across the cover of the *Post,* unless they've won the lottery or had sex with the president or something. *I* didn't do anything except get born.

I don't think "that's life" at all. I think that sucks, is what I think.

Then Grandmère started talking about how she'd been fielding calls all day from representatives of the media, and how all these people want to interview me, like Leeza Gibbons and Barbara Walters and stuff, and she said I ought to have a press conference, and that she'd already talked to the Plaza people about it, and they'd set aside this special room with a podium and a pitcher of ice water and some potted palms and stuff.

I couldn't believe it! I was like, "Grandmère! I don't want to talk to Barbara Walters! God! Like I really want everyone knowing my business!"

And Grandmère said, all prissy, "Well, if you don't try to accommodate the media, they're just going to try to get the story any way they can, which means they'll keep showing up at your school. And at your friends' houses, and at your grocery store, and at the place where you rent those movie videos you like so much."

Grandmère doesn't believe in VCRs. She says if God meant for us to watch movies at home He wouldn't have invented coming attractions.

Then Grandmère wanted to know where my sense of civic duty was. She said it would greatly promote tourism in Genovia if I just went on *Dateline*.

I really want to do what's best for Genovia. I really do. But I also have to do what's best for Mia Thermopolis. And going on *Dateline* would definitely not be good for me.

But Grandmère seems really gung-ho on the whole promoting Genovia thing. So I sort of started to wonder if maybe, just maybe, my mom is right. Maybe Grandmère *did* talk to Carol Fernandez.

But would Grandmère do something like that?

Well. Yeah.

I just lifted up my headphones. They're still at it.

Looks like it's going to be a long night.

Well, this morning my face was on the covers of the *Daily News* and *New York Newsday*. My picture was also in the Metro Section of *The New York Times*. They used my school photo, and let me tell you, my mom wasn't too happy about that, since that meant either somebody in our family, to whom she sent copies of that photo—which looks bad for Grandmère—or someone at Albert Einstein must have leaked it, which looks bad for Mr. Gianini. I wasn't too happy about it because my school photo was taken before Paolo fixed my hair and I look like one of those girls who are always going on TV to talk about their bad experience being in a cult or escaping from an abusive husband or something.

There were more reporters than ever in front of Albert Einstein when Hans pulled up in front of it this morning. I guess all the morning news shows needed something they could report live. Usually it's an overturned chicken truck on the Palisades Parkway or a crackhead holding his wife and kids hostage in Queens. But today it was me.

I had sort of anticipated that this might happen, and I was a little more prepared today than I was yesterday. So, in flagrant violation of my grandmother's fashion dictums, I wore my newly relaced combat boots (in case I had to kick anybody holding a microphone who got too close), and I also wore all of my Greenpeace and antifur buttons, so at least my celebrity status will be put to good use.

It was the same drill as the day before. Lars took me by the arm and the two of us sprinted through a sea of TV cameras and microphones into the school. As we ran, people shouted stuff at me like, "Amelia, do you intend to follow the example of Princess Diana and become the queen of people's hearts?" and "Amelia, who do you like better,

Leonardo DiCaprio or Prince William?" and "Amelia, what are your feelings on the meat industry?"

They almost got me on that one. I started to turn around, but Lars dragged me on into the school.

HERE'S WHAT I NEED TO DO

1. Think of some way to get Lilly to like me again
2. Stop being such a wimp
3. Stop lying
   and/or
   Think of better lies
4. Stop being so dramatic
5. Start being more
   A. Independent
   B. Self-reliant
   C. Mature
6. Stop thinking about Josh Richter
7. Stop thinking about Michael Moscovitz
8. Get better grades
9. Achieve self-actualization

Thursday, Algebra

Today in Algebra Mr. Gianini was totally trying to teach us about the Cartesian plane, but nobody could pay attention because of all the news vans outside. People kept jumping up to lean out the windows and yell at the reporters: "You killed Princess Di! Bring back Princess Di!"

Mr. Gianini kept trying to bring people to order, but it was impossible. Lilly was getting all burned up because everyone was coming together against the reporters but no one had wanted to stand outside Ho's Deli and do her chant, which was "We oppose the racist Hos."

That's kind of harder to say than "You killed Princess Di! Bring back Princess Di!" so maybe that's why. Lilly's chant has too many big words.

So then Mr. Gianini had to have a talk with us about whether the media was really to blame for killing Princess Diana, or if maybe it was the fact that the guy driving the car she was in might have been drunk. And then somebody tried to say the driver hadn't been drunk, that he'd been poisoned and that it was all a plot by the British secret service, but Mr. Gianini said could we please come back to reality now.

And then Lana Weinberger wanted to know how long I'd known I was a princess, and I couldn't believe she was actually asking me a question without being snotty about it, and I was like, well, I don't know, a couple of weeks or something, and then Lana said if she found out she was a princess she would go straight to DisneyWorld, and I said, no, you wouldn't, because you'd miss cheerleading practice, and then she said she didn't see why I didn't go to DisneyWorld since I'm not even that involved in extracurricular activities, and then Lilly started in about the Disneyfication of America and how Walt Disney was actually a fascist, and then everybody started wondering if it

172

was really true about his body being cryogenically frozen under the castle in Anaheim, and then Mr. Gianini was like, could we please return to the Cartesian plane?

Which is probably a safer plane to be on, if you think about it, than the one we live on, since there aren't any reporters there.

Cartesian coordinate system divides the plane into 4 parts called quadrants

So I was eating lunch with Tina Hakim Baba and Lars and Wahim, and Tina was telling me about how in Saudi Arabia, where her father comes from, girls have to wear this thing called a chadrah, which is like a huge blanket that covers them from head to foot with just a slit for them to see out of. It's supposed to protect them from the lustful eyes of men, but Tina says her cousins wear Gap jeans underneath their chadrahs, and as soon as there aren't any adults around they take their chadrahs off and hang out with boys just like we do.

Well, like we *would* do if any boys liked us.

I take that back. I forgot that Tina has a boy to hang out with, her Cultural Diversity date, Dave Farouq El-Abar.

Geez. What is *wrong* with me, anyway? How come no boys like *me*?

So Tina was telling me all about chadrahs when all of a sudden Lana Weinberger set her tray down next to ours.

I am not even kidding. *Lana Weinberger.*

I, of course, thought she was going to whip out the receipt for the Nutty Royaled sweater's dry cleaning or start shaking Tabasco sauce all over our salads or something, but instead she just went, all breezy, "You guys don't mind if we join you, do you?"

And then I saw this tray sliding over next to mine. It was loaded down with two double cheeseburgers, large fries, two chocolate milks, a bowl of chili, a bag of Doritos, a salad with French dressing, a pack of Yodels, an apple, and a large Coke. When I looked up to see who could possibly be ingesting that many saturated fats, I saw Josh Richter pulling out the chair next to mine.

I am not even kidding. *Josh Richter.*

He went, "Hey," to me and sat down and started eating.

I looked at Tina, and Tina looked at me, and then both of us looked at our bodyguards. But they were busy arguing over whether rubber-tipped bullets really did hurt rioters or if it was better just to use hoses.

Tina and I looked back at Lana and Josh.

Really attractive people, like Lana and Josh, don't ever go anywhere alone. They always have this sort of entourage that follows them around. Lana's entourage consists of a bunch of other girls, most of whom are junior varsity cheerleaders like she is. They are all really pretty, with long hair and breasts and stuff, like Lana.

Josh's entourage consists of a bunch of senior boys who are all on the crew team with him. They are all really large and handsome, and they were all eating excessive amounts of animal by-products, just like Josh.

Josh's entourage put their trays down beside Josh's. Lana's entourage put their trays beside Lana's. And soon, our table, which had consisted only of two geeky girls and their bodyguards, was being graced by the most beautiful people in Albert Einstein—maybe even in all of Manhattan.

I got a good look at Lilly, and her eyes were bugging out the way they do when she sees something she thinks would make a good episode of her show.

"So," Lana said, all chatty-like, while she picked at her salad—no dressing, and only water on the side. "What are you up to this weekend, Mia? Are you going to the Cultural Diversity Dance?"

It was the first time she'd ever called me Mia and not Amelia.

"Uh," I said brilliantly. "Let me see . . ."

"Because Josh's parents are going away, and we were thinking about having a thing at his place on Saturday night, after the dance, and all. You should come."

"Huh," I said. "Well, I don't—"

"She should totally come," Lana said, stabbing at a cherry tomato with her fork. "Shouldn't she, Josh?"

Josh was shoveling chili into his mouth using Doritos instead of a spoon. "Sure," he said with his mouth full. "She should come."

"It's going to be so *cool*," Lana said. "Josh's place is like *great*. It's got six bedrooms. On Park Avenue. And there's a Jacuzzi in the master bedroom. Isn't there a Jacuzzi, Josh?"

Josh said, "Yeah, there's—"

Pierce, a member of Josh's entourage, and a six-foot-two-inch rower, interrupted. "Hey, Richter, remember after the last dance? When Bonham-Allen passed out in your mom's Jacuzzi? That was *rad*."

Lana giggled. "Oh, God! She chugged that whole bottle of Bailey's Irish Cream. Remember, Josh? She drank practically the whole thing herself—what a hog!—and then she wouldn't stop throwing up."

"Major vomitage," Pierce agreed.

"She had to have her stomach pumped," Lana said to Tina and me. "The paramedics said if Josh hadn't phoned them when he did she'd have died."

We all turned to look at Josh. He said, modestly, "It was *way* uncool."

Lana stopped giggling. "It was," she said, all solemn now that Josh Richter had declared the incident uncool.

I didn't know what I was supposed to say about that, so I just said, "Wow."

"So," Lana said. She ate a shred of lettuce and swished some water around in her mouth. "Are you coming, or not?"

"I'm sorry," I said. "I can't."

A lot of Lana's friends, who'd been talking among

themselves, stopped talking and looked at me. Josh's friends, however, went right on eating.

"You *can't?*" Lana said, making this very astonished face.

"No," I said. "I can't."

"What do you mean, you *can't?*"

I thought about lying. I could have said something like, Lana, I can't go because I have to have dinner with the prime minister of Iceland. I could have said, I can't go because I have to go christen a cruise ship. There were all sorts of excuses I could have made up. But for once, for once in my stupid life, I went and told the truth.

"I can't go," I said, "because my mom wouldn't let me go to a party like that."

Oh, my God. Why did I say that? Why, why, why? I should have lied. I totally should have lied. Because how did I sound, saying something like that? Uh, like a total freak. Worse than a freak. A dork. A grade A nerd.

I don't know what compelled me to tell the truth in the first place. It wasn't even the *real* truth. I mean, it was *a* truth, but it wasn't the *real* reason I was saying no. I mean, it's true there was no way my mom was going to *let* me go to a party in a boy's apartment when his parents are out of town. Even with a bodyguard. But the real reason, of course, is that I wouldn't know how to *act* at a party like that. I mean, I've heard about these kinds of parties. There are like *whole rooms* reserved for people to go into to make out. We're talking major French kissing. Maybe even MORE than French kissing. Maybe even like above-the-waist touching. Maybe even below-the-waist touching. I don't know for sure, because no one I know has ever been to one of those parties. No one I know is popular enough to get invited.

Plus everybody drinks. But I don't drink, and I don't

have anybody to make out with. So what would I *do* there?

Lana looked at me, and then she looked at her friends, and then she burst out laughing. Loud. I mean, REALLY loud.

Well, I guess I can't really blame her.

"Oh, my God," Lana said when she had gotten over laughing so hard that she couldn't talk. "You can't be serious."

I knew right then Lana had just latched upon a whole new thing to torture me about. I didn't really care so much about me, but I felt bad for Tina Hakim Baba, who'd managed to keep such a low profile for so long. Suddenly, because of me, she was being sucked into the middle of the popular girl torture zone.

"Oh, my God," Lana said. "Are you kidding me?"

"Um," I said. "No."

"Well, you're not supposed to tell her the *truth*," Lana said, all snotty again.

I didn't know what she was talking about.

"Your mom. *Nobody* tells their mom the *truth*. You tell her you're spending the night at a girlfriend's house. *Duh*."

Oh.

She meant lie. To my mom. Lana had obviously never met my mom. *Nobody* lies to my mom. You just can't. Not about something like that. No way.

So I said, "Look, it's not like I don't appreciate being asked, and all, but I really don't think I can come. Besides, I don't even drink. . . ."

Okay, *that* was another big mistake.

Lana looked at me like I'd just said I'd never watched *Bring It On*, or something. She went: "You don't *drink*?"

I just looked at her. The truth is, at Miragnac I do drink. We drink wine with dinner every night. That's just what you do in France. You don't drink it for *fun*, though. You drink it because it goes with the food. It's supposed to make the foie gras taste better. I wouldn't know about that, since I don't eat foie gras, but I can tell you from experience that wine goes better with goat cheese than Dr Pepper does.

I certainly wouldn't chug a whole bottle of it, though, not even on a dare. Not even for Josh Richter.

So I just shrugged and went, "No. I try to be respectful of my body and not put a whole lot of toxins into it."

Lana snorted at that, but across from her—beside me—Josh Richter swallowed the mouthful of burger he was chewing and said, "I can respect that."

Lana's mouth dropped open. So, I'm sorry to say, did mine. Josh Richter respected something *I* had said? Are you *kidding* me?

But he looked perfectly serious. More than serious. He looked the way he had that day at Bigelows, like he could see into my soul with those electric blue eyes of his. . . . Like he already *had* seen into my soul. . . .

I guess Lana didn't notice her boyfriend looking into my soul, though. Because she said, "God, Josh. You drink more'n anybody else in this whole *school*."

Josh turned his head and looked at her with those hypnotic eyes. He said, without smiling, "Well, maybe I should quit, then."

Lana started laughing. She said, "Oh, right! That'll happen!"

Josh didn't laugh, though. He just went on looking at her.

That's when I started to get the heebie-jeebies. Josh just kept staring at Lana. I was glad he wasn't staring at *me* like that; those blue eyes of his are no joke.

I got up real fast and grabbed my tray. Tina, seeing

what I was doing, did the same.

"Well," I said, "bye."

Then we booked out of there.

On the way to drop off our trays, Tina was like, "What was *that* all about?" and I said I didn't know. But I know one thing for sure:

For once, I'm kind of glad I'm not Lana Weinberger.

More Thursday, French

When I went to my locker after lunch to get my books for French, Josh was there. He was sort of leaning on his closed locker door, looking around. When he saw me coming, he straightened up and went, "Hey."

And then he smiled. A big smile that showed all of his white teeth. His perfectly straight white teeth. I had to look away, those teeth were so perfect and so blindingly white.

I said, "Hey," back. I was really embarrassed and all, since I had sort of seen him fighting with Lana a few minutes before. I figured he was probably waiting for her, and that the two of them would make up and probably French kiss all over the place, so I tried to work my combination as quickly as possible and get the heck out of there so I wouldn't have to watch.

But Josh started *talking* to me. He said, "I really agree with what you said in the caf just now. You know, about respecting your body and everything. I think that's really, you know, a cool attitude."

I could feel my face start to burn. It was sort of like I was on fire. I concentrated on not dropping anything as I moved books around in my locker. It's too bad my hair is so short now. I couldn't duck my head to hide the fact that I was blushing. "Huh," I said, real intelligently.

"So," Josh said, "are you going to the dance with anyone, or not?"

I dropped my Algebra book. It went skittering across the hall. I stooped down to pick it up.

"Um," I said, by way of answering his question.

I was down on my hands and knees, picking up old worksheets that had slid out of my Algebra book, when I saw these knees covered in gray flannel bend. Then Josh's face was right next to mine.

"Here," he said, and handed me my favorite pencil, the one with the feathery pom-pom on the end.

"Thanks," I said. Then I made the mistake of looking into his too-blue eyes.

"No," I said, real faintly, because that's how his eyes made me feel: faint. "I'm not going to the dance with anyone."

Then the bell rang.

Josh said, "Well, see you." And then he left.

I am still in shock.

Josh Richter *spoke* to me. He actually *spoke* to me. *Twice.*

For the first time in like a month, I don't care that I'm flunking Algebra. I don't care that my mom is dating one of my teachers. I don't care that I'm the heir to the throne of Genovia. I don't even care that my best friend and I aren't speaking.

I think Josh Richter might *like* me.

HOMEWORK

Algebra: ??? Can't remember!!!
English: ??? Ask Shameeka
World Civ: ??? Ask Lilly. Forgot. Can't ask Lilly. She's not speaking to me.
G & T: none
French: ???
Biology: ???

God, just because a boy might like me, I completely lose my head. I disgust myself.

Grandmère says: "Well, of course the boy likes you. What wouldn't he like? You are turning out very well, thanks to Paolo's handiwork and my tutelage."

Geez, Grandmère, thanks. Like it would be impossible for any guy to like me for *me*, and not because all of a sudden I'm a princess with a $200 haircut.

I think I sort of hate her.

I mean it. I know it's wrong to hate people, but I really do sort of hate my grandmother. At least, I strongly dislike her. I mean, besides the fact that she's totally vain and thinks only about herself, she's also kind of mean to people.

Like tonight, for instance:

Grandmère decided that for my lesson today we would go to dinner somewhere outside of the hotel so she could teach me how to deal with the press. Only there wasn't a whole lot of press around when we went outside, just some kid reporter from *Tiger Beat*, or something. I guess all the real reporters had gone home to get their dinner. (Plus it's no fun for the press to stalk you when you're ready for them. It's only when you least expect them that they come around. This is how they get their kicks, at least as far as I can figure out.)

Anyway, I was pretty happy about this, because who needs the press around, yelling questions and setting off flashbulbs in your face? Believe me, as it is, I see big purple splotches everywhere I go.

But then as I was getting into the car Hans had brought around, Grandmère said, "Wait one moment," and went back inside. I thought maybe she'd forgotten her tiara or something, but she came back out a minute later looking no different than before.

But then, when we pulled up in front of the restaurant,

which was the Four Seasons, there were all these reporters there! At first I thought somebody important had to be inside, like Shaquille O'Neal or Madonna, but then they all started taking pictures of me and yelling "Princess Amelia, how does it feel to grow up in a single-parent household, then find out your mom's ex has three hundred million dollars?" and "Princess, what kind of running shoes do you wear?"

I totally forgot my whole fear of confrontation thing. I was mad. I turned to Grandmère in the car, and I said, "How did they know we were coming here?"

Grandmère just dug around in her purse for her cigarettes. "Now, what did I do with that lighter?" she asked.

"You called them, didn't you?" I was so mad, I could hardly even see straight. "You called and told them we were coming here."

"Don't be ridiculous," Grandmère said. "I had no time to call all these people."

"You didn't have to. You'd just have to call one, and they'd all follow. Grandmère, *why*?"

Grandmère lit her cigarette. I hate when she smokes in the car. "This is an important part of being a royal, Amelia," she said between puffs. "You must learn to handle the press. Why are you taking on so?"

"You're the one who told all that stuff to Carol Fernandez." I said it totally calm.

"Of course I did," Grandmère said, with a kind of *So, what?* shrug.

"Grandma," I yelled. "How could you?"

She looked totally taken aback. She said, "Don't call me Grandma."

"Seriously," I yelled. "Dad thinks Mr. Gianini did it! He and Mom had this totally big fight about it. She said it was you, but he wouldn't believe her!"

Grandmère blew cigarette smoke out of her nostrils. "Phillipe," she said, "always was incredibly naïve."

"Well," I said, "I'm telling him. I'm telling him the truth."

Grandmère just waved a hand, as if to say *Whatever*.

"Seriously," I said. "I'm telling him. He's going to be really mad at you, Grandmère."

"He won't. You needed the practice, darling. That piece in the *Post* was only the beginning. Soon you'll be on the cover of *Vogue*, and then—"

"Grandmère!" I yelled. "I DO NOT WANT TO BE ON THE COVER OF *VOGUE*! DON'T YOU UNDERSTAND? I JUST WANT TO PASS THE NINTH GRADE!"

Grandmère looked a little startled. "Well, all right, darling, all right. You needn't *shout*."

I don't know how much of that sank in, but after dinner I noticed the reporters had all gone home. So maybe she heard me.

When I got home, Mr. Gianini was here, AGAIN. I had to go into my room to call my dad. I said, "Dad, it was Grandma, not Mr. Gianini, who told Carol Fernandez everything," and he said, "I know," in this miserable way.

"You *know*?" I could hardly believe it. "You *know*, and you haven't said anything?"

He went, "Mia, your grandmother and I have a very complicated relationship."

He means he's scared of her. I guess I can't really blame him, considering the fact that she used to lock him in the dungeon and everything.

"Well," I said, "you could still apologize to Mom for what you said about Mr. Gianini."

He went, still sounding all miserable, "I know."

So I said, "Well? Are you going to?"

And he said, "Mia . . . " Only now he sounded all exasperated. I figured I'd done enough good deeds for one day, and hung up.

After that, I sat around while Mr. Gianini helped me with my homework. I was too distracted by Josh Richter's talking to me today to pay attention while Michael was trying to help me in G & T.

I guess I can sort of see how my mom likes Mr. G. He's okay to just hang out with, you know, like in front of the TV. He doesn't hog the remote, like some of my mom's past boyfriends. And he doesn't seem to care about sports at all.

About a half hour before I went to bed, my dad called back and asked to speak to my mother. She went into the room to talk to him, and when she came out again she looked all smug, in an I-told-you-so sort of way.

I wish I could tell Lilly about Josh Richter talking to me.

OH, MY GOD!!!
JOSH AND LANA BROKE UP!!!!

I am not even kidding. It's all over school. Josh broke up with her last night after crew practice. They were having dinner together at the Hard Rock Cafe, and he asked for his class ring back!!! Lana was completely humiliated under the pointy cone bra Gaultier made for Madonna!

I wouldn't wish that on my worst enemy.

Lana wasn't hanging around Josh's locker this morning, like usual. And then when I saw her in Algebra, her eyes were all red and squinty, and her hair looked like it hadn't been brushed, let alone washed, and her thigh-highs had come unglued and were all baggy around her knees. I never thought I'd see Lana Weinberger looking like a mess!!! Before class started, she was on her cell phone with Bergdorf's, trying to convince them to take her Cultural Diversity Dance dress back even though she'd already removed the tags. Then, during class, she sat there with a big black marker crossing out "*Mrs. Josh Richter*" from where she'd written it all over her book covers.

It was so depressing. I could hardly factor my integers, I was so distracted.

I WISH I WERE

1. A size 36 double D
2. Good at math
3. A member of a world-famous rock band
4. Still friends with Lilly Moscovitz
5. Josh Richter's new girlfriend

You will not even believe what just happened. I was putting my Algebra book away in my locker, and Josh Richter was there getting his Trig notes, and he goes, in this totally casual way, "Hey, Mia, who you going to the dance with tomorrow?"

Needless to say, the fact that he actually spoke to me at all practically caused me to pass out. And then the fact that he was actually saying something that sounded like it might be a prelude to asking me out—well, I nearly threw up. I mean it. I felt really sick, but in a good way.

I think.

Somehow, I managed to stammer out, "Uh, no one," and he goes, and I kid you not:

"Well, why don't we go together?"

OH MY GOD!!!!! JOSH RICHTER ASKED ME OUT!!!!!

I was so shocked I couldn't say anything at all for like a minute. I thought I was going to hyperventilate, like I did the time I saw that documentary about how cows become hamburgers. I could only stand there and look up at him. (He's so tall!)

Then a funny thing happened. This tiny part of my brain—the only part that wasn't completely stunned by his asking me out—went: He's only asking you out because you're the princess of Genovia.

Seriously. That's what I thought, for just a second.

Then this other part of my brain, a much bigger part, went: SO WHAT???

I mean, maybe he asked me to the dance because he respects me as a human being and wants to get to know me better and maybe, just maybe, likes me, sort of.

It could happen.

So the part of my brain that was rationalizing all this made me go, all nonchalantly, "Yeah, okay. That might be fun."

Then Josh said a bunch of stuff about how he'd pick me up and we'd have dinner beforehand or something. But I barely heard him. Because inside my head, this voice was going:

Josh Richter just asked you out. Josh Richter just asked YOU out. JOSH RICHTER JUST ASKED YOU OUT!!!!

I think I must have died and gone to heaven. Because it had happened. It had finally happened: Josh Richter had finally looked into my soul. He had looked into my soul, and had seen the real me, the one beneath the flat chest. AND THEN HE'D ASKED ME OUT.

Then the bell rang, and Josh went away, and I just kept standing there until Lars poked me in the arm.

I don't know what Lars's problem is. I *know* he's not my personal secretary.

But thank God he was there, or I'd never have known Josh was picking me up tomorrow night at seven. I'm going to have to learn not to be so shocked the next time he asks me out, or I'll never get the hang of this dating thing.

THINGS TO DO (I THINK, NEVER HAVING BEEN ON A DATE BEFORE, I AM NOT EXACTLY SURE WHAT TO DO)

1. Get a dress
2. Get hair done
3. Get nails redone (stop biting fake ones off)

189

Okay, so I don't know who Lilly Moscovitz thinks she is. First she stops talking to me. Then, when she finally does deign to speak to me, it's only to criticize me some more. What right has she got, I ask you, to dump all over my Cultural Diversity Dance date? I mean, *she's* going with Boris Pelkowski. *Boris Pelkowski.* Yeah, he might be a musical genius and all, but he's still *Boris Pelkowski.*

Lilly goes: "Well, at least I know Boris isn't on the rebound."

Excuse me. Josh Richter is *not* on the rebound. He and Lana had been broken up for sixteen whole hours before he asked me out.

Lilly goes: "Plus Boris doesn't do *drugs.*"

I swear, for someone so smart, Lilly sure does go for the whole rumor and innuendo thing in a major way. I asked her if she'd ever *seen* Josh do drugs, and she looked at me all sarcastically.

But really, if you think about it, there isn't any *proof* Josh does drugs. He definitely hangs out with people who do drugs, but hey, Tina Hakim Baba hangs out with a princess, and that doesn't make *her* one.

Lilly didn't like that argument, though. She went: "You're overrationalizing. Whenever you overrationalize, Mia, I know you're worried."

I am *not* worried. I am going to the biggest dance of the fall semester with the cutest, most sensitive boy in school, and nothing anyone can do or say will make me feel bad about that.

Except that it does kind of make me feel weird, seeing Lana looking so sad and Josh looking like he doesn't care at all. Today at lunch, he and his entourage sat with Tina and me, and Lana and her entourage sat back with the other cheerleaders. It was just so *strange*. Plus neither Josh nor any of his friends talked to me or to Tina. They just talked to each other. Which didn't bother Tina any, but it kind of bothered me. Especially since Lana kept trying so hard not to look over at our table.

Tina didn't say anything bad about Josh when I told her the news. She just got very excited and said tonight, when I spend the night, we can try on different outfits and experiment with our hair to see what will look best for tomorrow night. Well, I have no hair to experiment with, but we can experiment with her hair. Actually, Tina's almost more excited than I am. She is a much more supportive friend than Lilly, who went, all sarcastically, when she heard: "Where's he taking you to dinner? The Harley-Davidson Cafe?"

I said, "No," very sarcastically. "Tavern on the Green."

Lilly went, "Oh, how imaginative."

I suppose superartsy Boris is taking *her* somewhere in the Village.

Then Michael, who had been pretty quiet (for him) all through class, looked at Lars and went, "You're going, too, right?"

And Lars went, "Oh, yes." And the two of them looked at each other in that infuriating way guys look at each other sometimes, like they have this secret. You know in sixth grade, when they made all of us girls go into this other room and watch a video about getting our periods and stuff? I bet while we were gone, the boys were watching a video about how to look at each other in that infuriating way.

Or maybe a cartoon or something.

But now that I think of it, Josh *is* kind of dissing Lana. I mean, he probably shouldn't have asked out another girl so soon after breaking up with her—at least, not to something he was going to go to with her. Know what I mean? I kind of feel bad about the whole thing.

But not bad enough not to go.

FROM NOW ON I WILL

1. Be nicer to everyone, even Lana Weinberger.
2. Never ever bite my fingernails, even the fake ones.
3. Write faithfully in this journal every day.
4. Stop watching old *Baywatch* reruns and use my time wisely, like to study Algebra, or maybe improve the environment, or something.

Friday Night

Abbreviated lesson with Grandmère today because of my spending the night at Tina's. Grandmère had pretty much gotten over my yelling at her yesterday about the press. She was totally into helping me figure out what I'm going to wear tomorrow night, just like I knew she would. She got on the phone with Chanel and set up an appointment for tomorrow to pick something out. It will have to be a rush job, and will cost a fortune, but she says she doesn't care. It will be my first formal event as a representative of Genovia, and I have to "sparkle" (her word, not mine).

I pointed out to her that it was a school dance, not an inauguration ball or anything, and that it wasn't even a prom, just a stupid dance to celebrate the diversity of the various racial and cultural groups that attend Albert Einstein High School. But Grandmère went ape anyway, and kept on worrying there wouldn't be time to dye shoes to match my gown.

There's a lot of stuff about being a girl I never realized. Like having your shoes match your gown. I didn't know that was so important.

But Tina Hakim Baba sure knows. You should see her room. She must have every women's magazine ever printed. They are in order on shelves all around her room, which, by the way, is huge and pink, much like the rest of her apartment, which takes up the entire top floor of her building. You hit PH on the elevator buttons, and the elevator opens in the Hakim Babas' marble foyer, which really does have a fountain, only you're not supposed to throw pennies in it, I found out.

And then there's just room after room after room. They have a maid, a cook, a nanny, and a driver, all of whom live in. So you can imagine how many rooms there are, on top of the fact that Tina has three little sisters and a baby brother, and all of *them* have their own rooms, too.

Tina's room has its own 37-inch TV with a Sony PlayStation. I can see now that I have been living a life of monastic simplicity compared to Tina.

Some people have all the luck.

Anyway, Tina is a lot different at home than she is at school. At home, she's totally bubbly and outgoing. Her parents are pretty nice, too. Mr. Hakim Baba is really funny. He had a heart attack last year and isn't allowed to eat practically anything but vegetables and rice. He has to lose twenty more pounds. He kept pinching my arm and going, "How do you stay so skinny?" I told him about my strict vegetarianism, and he went, "Oh," and shuddered really hard. The Hakim Babas' cook has orders to prepare only vegetarian meals, which was good for me. We had couscous and vegetable goulash. It was all quite delicious.

Mrs. Hakim Baba is beautiful, but in a different way than my mom. Mrs. Hakim Baba is British and very blond. I think she's pretty bored, living here in America and not having a job and all. Mrs. Hakim Baba used to be a model, but she quit when she got married. Now she doesn't get to meet all the interesting people she used to meet when she was modeling. She once stayed in the same hotel as Prince Charles and Princess Diana. She says they slept in separate bedrooms. And that was on their honeymoon!

No wonder things didn't work out between them.

Mrs. Hakim Baba is as tall as me, which makes her about five inches taller than Mr. Hakim Baba. But I don't think Mr. Hakim Baba minds.

Tina's little sisters and brother are really cute. After we messed around with the fashion magazines, looking up hairstyles, we tried some of them out on Tina's sisters.

They looked pretty funny. Then we put butterfly clips in Tina's little brother's hair and gave him a French manicure like mine, and he got very excited and changed into his Batman suit and ran around the apartment, screaming. I thought it was cute, but Mr. and Mrs. Hakim Baba didn't think so. They made the nanny put little Bobby Hakim Baba to bed right after dinner.

Then Tina showed me her dress for tomorrow. It's a Nicole Miller. It's so pretty, like sea foam. Tina Hakim Baba looks much more like a princess than I ever could.

Then it was time for *Lilly Tells It Like It Is*, which comes on on Friday nights at nine. This was the episode dedicated to exposing the unjust racism at Ho's Deli. It was filmed before Lilly called off the boycott due to lack of interest. It was a very hard-hitting piece of television news journalism, and I can say that without bragging, since I wasn't involved in its creation. If *Lilly Tells It Like It Is* ever went network, I bet it would be as highly rated as *60 Minutes*.

At the end, Lilly came on and did a segment she must have shot the night before, with a tripod in her bedroom. She sat on her bed and said that racism is a powerful force of evil that all of us must work to combat. She said that even though paying five cents more for a bag of gingko biloba rings might not seem like much to some of us, victims of real racism, like the Armenians and the Rwandans and the Ugandans and the Bosnians, would recognize that that five cents was only the first step on the road to genocide. Lilly went on to say that because of her daring stand against the Hos there was a little bit more justice on the side of right today.

I don't know about that, but I did sort of start to miss her when she waggled her feet, in their furry bear claw slippers, into the camera as a tribute to Norman. Tina is a fun friend and everything, but I've known Lilly since kindergarten. It's kind of hard to forget that.

We stayed up really late reading Tina's teenage love novels. I swear, there wasn't a single one where the boy broke up with a snotty girl and started going out with the heroine right away. Usually he waited a tactful amount of time, like a summer or at least a weekend, before asking her out. The only ones with a guy who started going out with the heroine right away turned out to be ones where the guy was just using the girl to get revenge or something.

But then Tina said even though she loves reading those books, she never takes them as a guide to real life. Because how many times in real life does anybody ever get amnesia? And when do cute young European terrorists ever take anybody hostage in the girls' locker room? And if they did, wouldn't it be on the day when you're wearing your worst underwear, the kind with the holes and loose elastic, and a bra that doesn't match, and not a pink silk camisole and tap pants, like the heroine of that particular book?

She has a point.

Tina's turning out the light now, because she's tired. I'm glad. It's been a long day.

When I got home, the first thing I did was check to make sure Josh hadn't called to cancel.

He hadn't.

Mr. Gianini was there, though (of course). This time he had pants on, thank God. When he heard me ask my mom if a boy named Josh had called, he was all, "You don't mean Josh Richter, do you?"

I got kind of mad, because he sounded . . . I don't know. Shocked or something.

I said, "Yes, I mean Josh Richter. He and I are going to the Cultural Diversity Dance tonight."

Mr. Gianini raised his eyebrows. "What about that Weinberger girl?"

It kind of sucks to have a parent who's dating a teacher in your school. I went, "They broke up."

My mom was watching us pretty closely, which is unusual for her, since most of the time she's in her own world. She went, "Who's Josh Richter?"

And I went, "Only the cutest, most sensitive boy in school."

Mr. Gianini snorted and said, "Well, most popular, anyway."

To which my mom replied, with a lot of surprise, "And he asked *Mia* to the dance?"

Needless to say, this was not very flattering. When your own mother knows it's weird for the cutest, most popular boy in school to ask you to the dance, you know you're in trouble.

"Yes," I said, all defensively.

"I don't like this," Mr. Gianini said. And when my mom asked him why, he said, "Because I know Josh Richter."

My mom went, "Uh oh. I don't like the sound of that," and before I could say anything in Josh's defense, Mr. Gianini went, "That boy is going one hundred miles per hour," which doesn't even make any sense.

At least it didn't until my mom pointed out that since I'm only going five miles per hour (FIVE!) she was going to have to consult my father "about this."

Hello? Consult him about what? What am I, a car with a faulty fan belt? What's this five-miles-per-hour stuff?

"He's fast, Mia," Mr. Gianini translated.

Fast? FAST? What is this, the fifties? Josh Richter is a rebel without a cause all of a sudden?

My mom went, as she was dialing my dad's phone number over at the Plaza, "You're just a freshman. You shouldn't be going out with seniors anyway."

How unfair is THAT? I finally get a date, and all of a sudden my parents turn into Mike and Carol Brady? I mean, come on!

So I was standing there, listening to my mom and dad over the speakerphone go on about how they both think I'm too young to date and that I SHOULDN'T date, since this has been a very confusing time for me, what with finding out I'm a princess and all. They were planning out the rest of my life for me (no dating until I'm eighteen, all-girls dorm when I get to college, etc.) when the buzzer to the loft went off, and Mr. G went to answer it. When he asked who it was, this all-too-familiar voice went, "This is Clarisse Marie Grimaldi Renaldo. Who is *this*?"

Across the room, my mom nearly dropped the phone. It was Grandmère. Grandmère had come to the loft!

I never in my life thought I'd be grateful to Grandmère for something. I never thought I'd be glad to see her. But when she showed up at the loft to take me shopping for my dress, I could have kissed her—on both cheeks, even—I really could have. Because when I met her at the door, I was like, "Grandmère, they won't let me go!"

I forgot Grandmère had never even been to the loft before. I forgot Mr. Gianini was there. All I could think about was the fact that my parents were trying to low-ball me about Josh. Grandmère would take care of it, I knew.

And boy, did she ever.

Grandmère came bursting in, giving Mr. Gianini a very dirty look—"This is *he*?" she stopped long enough to ask, and when I said yes, she made this sniffing sound and walked right by him—and heard Dad on the speaker-phone. She shouted, "Give me that phone," at my mother, who looked like a kid who'd just gotten caught jumping a turnstile by the Transit Authority.

"Mother?" my dad's voice shouted over the speaker-phone. You could tell he was in almost as much shock as Mom. "Is that you? What are *you* doing there?"

For someone who claims to have no use for modern technology, Grandmère sure knew' how to work that speakerphone. She took Dad right off it, snatched the receiver out of my mother's hand, and went, "Listen here, Phillipe," into it. "Your daughter is going to the dance with her beau. I traveled fifty-seven blocks by limo to take her shopping for a new dress, and if you think I'm not going to watch her dance in it, then you can just—"

Then my grandmother used some pretty strong language. Only since she said it all in French, only my dad and I understood. My mom and Mr. Gianini just stood there. My mom looked mad. Mr. G looked nervous.

After my grandmother had finished telling my dad just where he could get off, she slammed the phone down, then looked around the loft. Let's just say Grandmère has never been one for hiding her feelings, so I wasn't too surprised when the next thing she said was, "*This* is where the princess of Genovia is being brought up? In this . . . *ware-house?*"

Well, if she had lit a firecracker under my mom, she couldn't have made her madder.

"Now look here, Clarisse," my mother said, stomping around in her Birkenstocks. "Don't you dare try to tell me how to raise my child! Phillipe and I have already decided she isn't going out with this boy. You can't just come in here and—"

"Amelia," my grandmother said, "go and get your coat."

I went. When I got back, my mom's face was really red, and Mr. Gianini was looking at the floor. But neither of them said anything as Grandmère and I left the loft.

Once we were outside, I was so excited I could hardly stand it. "Grandmère!" I yelled. "What'd you *say* to them? What'd you say to convince them to let me go?"

But Grandmère just laughed in this scary way and said, "I have my ways."

Boy, did I ever not hate her then.

More Saturday

Well, I'm sitting here in my new dress, my new shoes, my new nails, and my new panty hose, with my newly waxed legs and underarms, my newly touched-up hair, my professionally made-up face, and it's seven o'clock, and there's no sign of Josh, and I'm wondering if maybe this whole thing was a joke, like in the movie *Carrie*, which is too scary for me to watch but Michael Moscovitz rented it once, and then he told Lilly and me what it was about: This homely girl gets asked to a dance by the most popular boy in school just so he and his popular friends can pour pig blood on her. Only he doesn't know Carrie has psychic powers, and at the end of the night she kills everyone in the whole town, including Steven Spielberg's first wife and the mom from *Eight Is Enough*.

The problem is, of course, I don't have psychic powers, so if it turns out that Josh and his friends pour pig blood on me I won't be able to kill them all. I mean, unless I call in the Genovian national guard or something. But that would be difficult, since Genovia doesn't have an air force or navy, so how would the guards get here? They'd have to fly commercially, and it costs A LOT to buy tickets at the last minute. I doubt my dad would approve such an exorbitant expenditure of government funds—especially for what he'd be bound to consider a frivolous reason.

But if Josh Richter stands me up, I can assure you, I will *not* have a frivolous reaction. I got my LEGS waxed for him. Okay? And if you think that doesn't hurt, think about having your UNDERARMS waxed, which I also had done for him. Okay? That waxing stuff HURTS. I practically started to cry, it hurt so bad. So don't be telling ME we can't call out the Genovian national guard if I get stood up.

I know my dad thinks Josh has stood me up. He's sitting at the kitchen table right now, pretending to read *TV Guide*. But I see him sneaking peeks at his watch all the time. Mom, too. Only she never wears a watch, so she keeps sneaking peeks at the blinking-eye cat clock on the wall.

Lars is here, too. He isn't checking the clock, though. He keeps checking his ammunition clip to make sure he has enough bullets. I suppose my dad told him to shoot Josh if he makes a move on me.

Oh, yes. My dad said I can go out with Josh, but only if Lars goes, too. This is no big thing since I always expected Lars would go, anyway. But I pretended to be all mad about it so my dad wouldn't think I was getting off too easy. I mean, HE's in BIG trouble with Grandmère. She told me while I was being fitted for my dress that my dad has always had a problem with commitment and that the reason he doesn't want me to go out with Josh is that he can't stand to see me dumped the way my dad has dumped countless models all over the world.

God! Assume the worst, why don't you, Dad.

Josh can't dump me. He's never even been out with me yet.

And if he doesn't show up soon, well, all I can say is HIS LOSS. I look better than I have ever looked in my whole entire life. Old Coco Chanel really outdid herself; my dress is HOT, pale, pale blue silk, all scrunched up on top like an accordion, so my being flat-chested doesn't even show, then straight and skinny the rest of the way down, all the way to my matching pale, pale blue silk high heels. I think I kind of resemble an icicle, but according to the ladies at Chanel, this is the look of the new millennium. Icicles are *in*.

The only problem is I can't pet Fat Louie or I'll get

orange cat hair on myself. I should have got one of those masking tape roller thingies last time I was at Rite Aid, but I forgot. Anyway, he's sitting beside me on the futon, looking all sad because I won't pet him. I picked up all my socks, just in case he got it into his head to punish me or something by eating one.

My dad just looked at his watch and went, "Hmm. Seven-fifteen. I can't say much for this boy's promptness."

I tried to remain calm. "I'm sure there's a lot of traffic," I said, in as princessy a voice as I could.

"I'm sure," said my dad. He didn't sound very sad, though. "Well, Mia, we can still make it to *Beauty and the Beast*, if you want to go. I'm sure I can get—"

"Dad!" I was horrified. "I am NOT going to *Beauty and the Beast* with you tonight."

Now he sounded sad. "But you used to love *Beauty and the Beast*. . . ."

THANK GOD the intercom just rang. It's him. My mom just buzzed him up. The other stipulation, before my dad would let me go, is that besides Lars going, Josh has to meet both my parents—and probably submit proof of ID, though I'm not sure Dad's thought of that yet.

I'm going to have to leave this book here, because there's no room for it in my "clutch," which is what my skinny, flat purse is called.

Oh my God, my hands are sweating so hard! I should have listened when Grandmère suggested those elbow-length gloves—

Okay, so I lied. I brought this book anyway. I made Lars carry it. Well, it's not like he doesn't have room in that briefcase he carries around. I know it's filled with silencers and grenades and stuff, but I knew he could fit one measly journal into it.

And I was right.

So I'm in the bathroom at the Tavern on the Green. The ladies' room here isn't as nice as the one at the Plaza. There isn't a little stool to sit on in my stall, so I'm sitting on the toilet with the lid down. I can see a lot of fat ladies' feet moving around outside my stall door. There are a whole lot of fat ladies here, mostly for this wedding between a very Italian-looking dark-haired girl who needs a good eyebrow waxing and a skinny redheaded boy named Fergus. Fergus gave me the old eyeball when I walked into the dining room. I am not kidding. My first married man, even if he has only been married about an hour and looks my age. This dress is the BOMB!

Dinner's not so great as I thought it would be, though. I mean, I know from Grandmère which fork to use and all that, and to tilt my soup bowl away from me, but that's not it.

It's Josh.

Don't get me wrong. He looks totally hot in his tux. He told me he owns it. Last year, he escorted his girlfriend before Lana to all the debutante events in the city, his girlfriend before Lana having been related to the guy who invented those plastic bags you put vegetables in when you go to the grocery store. Only his were the first to say OPEN HERE so you knew which end was the one you were supposed to try to open. Those two little words earned the guy half a billion dollars, Josh says.

I don't know why he told me this. Am I supposed to be impressed by something his ex-girlfriend's dad did? He isn't acting very sensitive, to tell you the truth.

Still, he was really good with my parents. He came in, gave me a corsage (tiny white roses tied together with pink ribbon, totally gorgeous; it must have cost him ten dollars *at least*—I couldn't help thinking, though, that he'd originally picked it out for another girl, with a different color dress), and shook my dad's hand. He said, "It's a pleasure to meet you, Your Highness," which made my mom start laughing really loud. She can be so embarrassing sometimes.

Then he turned to my mom and said, "You're Mia's mother? Oh my gosh, I thought you must be her college-age sister," which is a totally foolish thing to say, but my mom actually fell for it, I think. She BLUSHED as he was shaking her hand. I guess I am not the only Thermopolis woman to fall under the spell of Josh Richter's blue eyes.

Then my dad cleared his throat and started asking Josh a whole lot of questions about what kind of car he was driving (his dad's BMW), where we're going (duh), and what time we would be back (in time for breakfast, Josh said). My dad didn't like that, though, and Josh said, "What time would you like her back, sir?"

SIR! Josh Richter called my dad SIR!

And my dad looked at Lars and said, "One o'clock at the latest," which I thought was pretty decent of him, since my normal curfew is eleven on weekends. Of course, considering that Lars was going to be there, and there wasn't anything that could actually happen to me, it was kind of bogus that I couldn't stay out as late as I wanted, but Grandmère told me a princess should always be prepared to compromise, so I didn't say anything.

Then my dad asked Josh some more questions, like where was he going to college in the fall (he hasn't decided yet, but he's applying to all the Ivy Leagues) and what does he plan on studying (business), and then my mom asked him what was wrong with a liberal arts education, and Josh said he was really looking for a degree that would guarantee him a minimum salary of eighty thousand a year, to which my mom replied that there are more important things than money, and then I said, "Gosh, look at the time," and grabbed Josh and headed out the door.

Josh and Lars and I went down to Josh's dad's car, and Josh held the door to the front seat open for me, and then Lars said why didn't he drive so Josh and I could sit in the back and get to know each other. I thought this was way nice of Lars, but when Josh and I got in the back, we didn't have a whole lot to say to each other. I mean, Josh was like, "You look really nice in that dress," and I said I liked his tux and thanked him for my corsage. And then we didn't say anything for like twenty blocks.

I am not even kidding. I was so embarrassed! I mean, I don't hang around with boys that much, but I've never had that problem with the ones I HAVE hung around with. I mean, Michael Moscovitz practically never shuts up. I couldn't understand why Josh wasn't SAYING anything. I thought about asking him who he'd rather spend eternity with if it was the end of the world and he had to choose, Winona Ryder or Nicole Kidman, but I didn't feel like I knew him well enough. . . .

But finally Josh broke the silence by asking if it was true my mom was dating Mr. Gianini. Well, I should have expected *that* to get around. Maybe not as fast as my being a princess, but it had gotten around, all right.

So I said, yes, it was true, and then Josh wanted to know what that was like.

But then for some reason I couldn't tell him about seeing Mr. G in his underwear at my kitchen table. It just didn't seem . . . I don't know. I just couldn't tell him. Isn't that funny? I had told Michael Moscovitz without even having been asked. But I couldn't tell Josh, even though he had looked into my soul and everything. Weird, huh?

Then after like a zillion more blocks of silence we pulled up in front of the restaurant, and Lars surrendered the car to the valet and Josh and I went in (Lars promised he wouldn't eat with us; he said he'd just stand by the door and look at everybody who arrived in a mean way, like Arnold Schwarzenegger), and it turned out all of Josh's entourage was meeting us here, which I didn't know but was kind of relieved to see. I mean, I'd sort of been dreading sitting there for another hour or so with nothing to say. . . .

But thank God, all the guys on the crew team were at this big long table with their cheerleader girlfriends, and at the head of this table were these two empty places, one for Josh and one for me.

I have to say, everyone has been pretty nice. The girls all complimented me on my dress and asked me questions about being a princess, like how weird was it to wake up and see your picture on the front of the *Post*, and do you ever wear a crown, and stuff like that. They're all much older than me—some of them are seniors—so they're pretty mature. None of them have made any comments about how I have no chest or anything, like Lana would have if she'd been here.

But then, if Lana were here I wouldn't be.

The thing that most surprised me is that Josh ordered champagne, and nobody even questioned his ID, which, of course, was totally fake. The table's been through three bottles already, and Josh just keeps ordering more, since his dad gave him his platinum American Express card for the occasion. I just don't get it. Can't the waiters tell he's only eighteen and that most of his guests are even younger than that?

And how can Josh sit there and drink so much? What if Lars hadn't been here to drive? Josh would be driving his dad's BMW half sloshed. How irresponsible can you get? And Josh is class valedictorian!

And then, without even asking me, Josh ordered dinner for the whole table: filet mignon for everyone. I guess that's very nice and all, but I won't eat meat, not even for the most sensitive boy in the world.

And he hasn't even noticed I haven't touched my food! I totally had to fill up on salad and bread rolls to keep from starving to death.

Maybe I could sneak out of here and get Lars to pick up a veggie wrap for me from Emerald Planet.

And the funny thing is, the more champagne Josh has to drink, the more he keeps on touching me. Like he keeps on putting his hand on my leg under the table. At first I thought it was a mistake, but he's done it four times now. The last time, he squeezed!

I don't think he's drunk, exactly, but he's certainly friendlier than he was in the car on the way up. Maybe he's just feeling less inhibited, with Lars not hovering around, two feet away.

Well, I guess I should go back out there. I just wish Josh had told me we were meeting his friends. Then maybe I could have invited Tina Hakim Baba and her date—or even Lilly and Boris. Then at least I'd have someone fun to talk to.

Oh, well. Here goes nothing.

Why?

Why??

Why???

I can't even believe this is happening. I can't believe it's happening to ME!

WHY? WHY ME? WHY IS IT ALWAYS ME these things have to happen to????

I'm trying to remember what Grandmère told me about how to act under duress. Because I am definitely under duress. I keep trying to breathe in through my nose, out through my mouth, like Grandmère said. In through my nose, out through my mouth. In through my nose, out through my—

HOW COULD HE DO THIS TO ME???? HOW, HOW, HOW?????!!!

I could rip his stupid face off, I really could. I mean, who does he think he is? Do you know what he did? Do you know what he did? Well, let me tell you what he did.

After polishing off NINE bottles of champagne—that's practically one bottle per person, except I only had a couple of sips, so somebody drank my bottle as well as his—Josh and his friends finally decided it was time to go to the dance. Oh, gee, let me see, the dance had only started an HOUR earlier. It was only about TIME we left.

So we go and wait for the valet to bring the car around, and I was thinking maybe everything would be all right, since while we were waiting Josh had his arm around my shoulders, which was really nice, since my dress is sleeveless, and even though I have a wrap it's just this shimmery see-through veil thing. So I'm appreciative of this arm, since it's keeping me warm. It's a nice arm, really, very

209

muscular from all that rowing. The only problem is, Josh doesn't smell that good, not a bit like Michael Moscovitz, who always smells like soap. No, I think Josh must have taken a bath in Drakkar Noir, which in large doses actually smells pretty vile. I could hardly breathe, but whatever. In spite of that, I'm thinking, okay, things aren't so bad. Yes, he didn't respect my rights as a vegetarian, but you know, everybody makes mistakes. We'll go to the dance and he'll look into my soul again with those electric blue eyes and everything will be all right.

Boy, was I ever wrong.

First of all, we can barely pull up to the school, there's so much traffic. At first I couldn't figure it out. Yes, it was Saturday night, but there shouldn't be THAT much traffic in front of Albert Einstein's, right? I mean, it's just a school dance. Most kids in New York City don't even have access to cars, right? We're probably like the only people who go to Albert Einstein's who drove.

And then I realize why there's so much congestion. There are news vans parked all over the place. They're shining these big bright lights all over the steps to Albert Einstein's. There are reporters swarming around all over the place, smoking cigarettes, talking on cell phones, waiting.

Waiting for what?

Waiting for me, it turns out.

As soon as Lars saw the lights, he started to swear very colorfully in some language that wasn't English or French. But you could tell they were swear words by his voice. I leaned forward and was like, "How could they have known? How could they have known? Could Grandmère have told them?"

But you know, I really don't think Grandmère would have done this. I really don't. Not after our talk. I laid it on the line for Grandmère. I came down on her like a New

York cop on a game of three-card monte. Grandmère would not, I'm sure, EVER call the press on me again, without my permission.

But there they all were, and SOMEBODY called them, all right, and if it wasn't Grandmère, then who was it?

Josh was totally unconcerned by all the lights and cameras and everything. He goes, "So what? You ought to be used to it by now."

Oh, right. Let me tell you how used to it I am by now. So used to it that the thought of getting out of that car, even with the arm of the cutest boy in the school around me, made me feel like I was going to barf up all of that salad and bread.

"Come on," Josh said. "You and I can make a run for it while Lars goes and parks the car."

Lars totally did not like that idea. He went, "I think not. *You* will park the car, and the princess and *I* will make a run for it."

But Josh was already opening his door. He had hold of my hand. He said, "Come on. You only live once," and started dragging me out of the car.

And like the really stupid chump that I am, I let him.

That's right. I let him drag me out of the car. Because his hand felt so nice over mine, so big and protective, so warm and secure, I thought, Oh, what could happen? So a bunch of flashbulbs will go off. So what? We'll just make a run for it, like he said. Everything will be fine.

So I said to Lars, "That's okay, Lars. You park the car. Josh and I'll go on inside."

Lars said, "No, Princess, wait—"

Which were the last words I heard out of him—for a while, anyway—since by that time Josh and I were out of the car and he had slammed the door shut behind us.

And then, instantly, the press was on us, everyone

throwing down their cigarettes and pulling the lens caps off their cameras, yelling, "It's her! It's her!"

And then Josh was pulling me up the steps, and I was sort of laughing, since for the first time it *was* sort of fun. Flashbulbs were going off everywhere, blinding me, so that all I could see were the steps underneath us as we ran up them. I was totally concentrating on holding up the hem of my dress so I didn't trip on it, and had put all my faith in those fingers wrapped around my other hand. I was completely dependent on Josh to lead the way, since I couldn't see a blessed thing.

So when he suddenly stopped, I thought it was because we were at the school doors. I thought we'd stopped because Josh was opening the doors for me. I know it's stupid, but that's what I thought. I could see the doors. We were standing right in front of them. Below us, on the stairs, the reporters were screaming questions and taking pictures. Some moron was yelling, "Kiss her! Kiss her!" which I don't need to tell you was way embarrassing.

And so I just stood there, like a complete IDIOT, waiting for Josh to open the doors, instead of doing the smart thing, which was open the doors myself and get inside where it was safe, where there weren't any cameras or reporters or people yelling "*Kiss her, Kiss her!*"

And then, I don't know how, the next thing I knew Josh had put his arm around me again, dragged me to him, and smashed his mouth against mine.

I swear, that's exactly what it felt like. He just smashed his mouth up against mine, and all these flashes started going off, but believe me, it wasn't like in those books Tina is always reading, where the boy kisses the girl and she sees like fireworks and stuff behind her eyelids. I really WAS seeing lights go off, but they weren't fireworks, they were flashes from cameras. EVERYONE was taking a picture of

Princess Mia getting her first kiss.

I am not even kidding. Like it wasn't bad enough that this was my first kiss.

It was my first kiss and *Teen People* was photographing it.

And another thing about those books Tina reads: In those books, when the girl gets her first kiss, she gets this warm gushy feeling inside. She feels like the guy is drawing her soul up from deep within her. I didn't get that feeling. I didn't get that feeling at all. All I got was embarrassed. It didn't feel especially good, having Josh Richter kiss me. All it felt, really, was strange. It felt strange, having this guy stand there and smash his mouth against mine. And you would think that after I'd spent so much time thinking this guy was the greatest thing on earth I'd have felt SOME-THING when he kissed me.

But all I felt was embarrassed.

And like our car ride to the restaurant, I just kept wishing it would end. All I could think was, When is he going to stop doing this? Am I even doing this right? In the movies they move their heads around a lot. Should I move my head around? What am I going to do if he tries to stick his tongue in there, like I used to see him do to Lana? I can't let *Teen People* take a picture of me with some guy's tongue in my mouth; my dad will kill me.

Then, just when I thought I couldn't stand it another minute, that I was going to DIE of embarrassment right there on the steps of Albert Einstein High School, Josh lifted up his head, waved to the reporters, opened the doors to the school, and pushed me inside.

Where, I swear to God, every single person I knew was standing, looking at us.

I am not kidding. There were Tina and her date from Trinity, Dave, looking at me in a sort of shocked way.

There were Lilly and Boris, and for once Boris hadn't tucked in anything that wasn't supposed to be tucked. In fact, he almost looked handsome, in a geeky, musical genius kind of way. And Lilly, in a beautiful white dress with spangles all over it, and white roses in her hair. And there were Shameeka and Ling Su with their dates, and a bunch of other people I probably knew but didn't recognize out of their school uniforms, all looking at me with the same sort of expression Tina was wearing, one of total and complete astonishment.

And there was Mr. G, standing by the ticket booth in front of the doors to the cafeteria, where the dance was being held, looking more astonished than anybody.

Except maybe me. I would have to say, out of everybody there, I was the person in the most shock. I mean, Josh Richter HAD just kissed me. JOSH RICHTER had just KISSED me. Josh Richter had just kissed ME.

Did I mention that he'd kissed me ON THE LIPS?

Oh, and that he did it in front of reporters from *TEEN PEOPLE*?

So I'm standing there, and everybody is looking at me, and I could still hear the reporters yelling outside, and inside the cafeteria I could hear the *thump, thump, thump* of the sound system as it ground out some hip-hop, a tribute to our Latino student population, and these thoughts are moving really sluggishly through my head, these thoughts that are saying:

He set you up.

He only asked you out so he could get his picture in the paper.

He's the one who notified the press that you'd be here tonight.

He probably only broke up with Lana just so he could tell his friends he's dating a girl worth three hundred million dollars. He never even noticed you until your picture was on the cover of the *Post*. Lilly was right: That day in Bigelows, he WAS only suffering from a synaptic breakdown when he smiled at you. He probably thinks his chances of getting into Harvard or whatever are way enhanced by the fact that he's the princess of Genovia's boyfriend.

And like a big idiot, I fell for it.

Great. Just great.

Lilly says I'm not assertive enough. Her parents say I have a tendency to internalize everything and fear confrontation.

My mom says the same thing. That's why she gave me this book, in the hopes that what I won't tell her, I'll at least get out into the open somehow.

If it hadn't turned out that I'm a princess, maybe I might still be all that stuff. You know, unassertive, fearful of confrontation, an internalizer. I probably wouldn't have done what I did next.

Which was turn to Josh and ask, "Why did you do that?"

He was busy patting himself down, trying to find the dance tickets to hand to the sophomores who were manning the ticket table. "Do what?"

"Kiss me like that, in front of everybody."

He found the tickets in his wallet. "I don't know," he said. "Didn't you hear them? They were yelling at me to kiss you. So I did. Why?"

"Because I didn't appreciate it."

"You didn't appreciate it?" Josh looked confused. "You mean you didn't like it?"

"Yes," I said. "That's exactly what I mean. I didn't like it. I didn't like it at all. Because I know you didn't kiss me because you like me. You just kissed me because I'm

215

the princess of Genovia."

Josh looked at me like he thought I was crazy.

"That's crazy," he said. "I like you. I like you a lot."

I said, "You can't like me a lot. You don't even *know* me. That's why I thought you asked me out. So you could get to know me better. But you haven't tried to get to know me at all. You just wanted to get your picture on *Extra*."

He laughed at that, but I noticed he didn't look me in the eye when he said, "What do you mean, I don't even know you? Of course I know you."

"No, you don't. Because if you did, you wouldn't have ordered me a steak for dinner."

I heard a murmur go around through all of my friends. I guess they recognized the seriousness of Josh's mistake, even if he didn't. He heard them, too, so when he replied, he was talking to them, too. "So I ordered the girl a steak," he said, with his arms open in a so-sue-me sort of way. "That's a crime? It was *filet mignon*, for God's sake."

Lilly said, in her meanest voice, "She's a vegetarian, you sociopath."

This information didn't seem to bother Josh very much. He just shrugged and went, "Oops, my bad."

Then he turned to me and said, "Ready to slide?"

But I had no intention of sliding with Josh. I had no intention of doing anything with Josh, ever again. I couldn't believe, after what I'd just said to him, he thought I'd still *want* to. The guy really *was* a sociopath. How could I ever have thought he'd seen into my soul? How???

Disgusted, I did the only thing a girl can be expected to do under those circumstances:

I turned my back on him and walked out.

Only, since of course I couldn't go back outside—not if I didn't want *Teen People* to get a nice close-up of me crying—my only recourse was to walk out into the girls' room.

It finally registered on Josh that I was ditching him. By that time, all of his friends had shown up, and they came tumbling through the doors just as Josh said, sounding totally peeved, "Jesus! It was just a kiss!"

I whirled around. "It wasn't just a kiss," I said. I was getting really mad. "Maybe that's how you wanted it to look, like it was just a kiss. But you and I both know what it really was: A media event. And one that you've been planning since you saw me in the *Post*. Well, thank you, Josh, but I can get my own publicity. I don't need *you*."

Then, after holding out my hand to Lars for my journal, I took it and stalked into the girls' room. Which is where I am now, writing this.

God! Can you BELIEVE that? I mean, I ask you: My first kiss—my first kiss ever—and next week it's going to be in every teen magazine in the country. Probably even some international magazines will pick it up, like *Majesty* magazine, which follows the lives of all the young royals in Great Britain and Monaco. They ran a whole article on the wardrobe of Prince Edward's wife, Sophie, once, rating each one of her outfits on a scale of one to ten. They called it "*Out of the Closet.*" I don't suppose it will be too long before *Majesty* magazine starts following me around, rating my wardrobe—and boyfriends—too. I wonder what the caption under the picture of me and Josh will be. "*Young Royal in Love*"?

Excuse me, but *ew*.

And the kicker of it all is that I am totally NOT in love with Josh Richter. I mean, it would have been nice—Who am I kidding? It would have been GREAT—to have a boyfriend. Sometimes I think there really is something wrong with me, that I don't have one.

But the thing is, I would rather not have a boyfriend at all than have one who is only using me for my money or the fact that my father is a prince or for any reason, really, except that he likes me for *me*, and nothing else.

Of course, now that everyone knows I'm a princess, it's going to be kind of hard to tell which guys like me for me and which guys like me for my tiara. But at least I realized the truth about Josh before things went on too long.

How could I have ever liked him? He's such a user. He totally used me! He purposefully hurt Lana and then tried to use me. And I played right into his hands like the stupid sap that I am.

What am I going to do? When my dad sees that photograph, he is going to FLIP OUT. There is no way I will ever be able to explain that it wasn't my fault. Maybe if I'd punched Josh in the stomach in front of all those cameras, maybe then my dad would believe I was an innocent bystander. . . .

But probably not.

I will never be allowed out of the house with a boy again, ever, for the rest of my natural life.

Uh-oh. I see shoes outside my stall. Somebody is talking to me.

It's Tina. Tina wants to know if I'm all right. Somebody is with her.

Oh my God, I recognize those feet! It's Lilly! Lilly and Tina both want to know if I'm all right!

Lilly is actually speaking to me again. Not criticizing me or complaining about my behavior. She is actually speaking to me in a friendly manner. She's saying through the stall door that she's sorry for laughing at my hair and that she knows she's controlling and that she suffers from a borderline authoritarian personality disorder, and she says she's going to make a concerted effort to stop telling everyone, especially me, what to do.

Wow! Lilly is admitting she did something wrong! I

can't believe it! I CAN'T BELIEVE IT!

She and Tina want me to come out and hang out with them. But I told them I don't want to. It would be too awkward, all of them with dates and me by myself like a big dope.

And then Lilly goes, "Oh, that's okay. Michael's here. He's been hanging around by himself like a big dope all night."

Michael Moscovitz came to a school event??? I can't believe it!! He never goes anywhere, except to like lectures in quantum physics and stuff!!

I have got to see this for myself. I am going out there right now.

More later.

I just woke up from the strangest dream.

In my dream, Lilly and I weren't fighting anymore; she and Tina had become friends; Boris Pelkowski actually turned out to be not so bad when you got him away from his violin; Mr. Gianini said he was raising my nine week grade from an F to a D; I slow-danced with Michael Moscovitz; and Iran bombed Afghanistan, so there wasn't a single picture of me and Josh kissing in any newspaper on the newsstand, since all the papers were filled with photos of war carnage.

But it wasn't a dream. It wasn't a dream at all, none of it! It had all really happened!

Because I woke up this morning with something wet on my face, and when I opened my eyes, I saw that I was lying in the spare bed in Lilly's room, and her brother's sheltie was licking me all over my face. I mean it. I have dog spit all over me.

And I don't even care! Pavlov can drool all over me if he wants to! I have my best friend back! I'm not going to flunk out of ninth grade! My dad isn't going to kill me for kissing Josh Richter!

Oh, and I think Michael Moscovitz might like me!

I can hardly write for happiness.

Little did I know when I came out of the girls' room last night with Lilly and Tina that all this happiness lay in store for me. I was morbidly depressed—yes, *morbidly*. Isn't that a good word? I learned it from Lilly—over what had happened with Josh.

But when I came out of the girls' room, Josh was gone. Lilly told me later that after I publicly humiliated him and then went storming off into the bathroom, Josh went on into the dance, not looking as if he cared too much. Lilly isn't sure what happened after that, because Mr. G asked her and Tina to go and check on me (wasn't that sweet of him?), but I have a feeling Lars might have used one of his special nerve-paralyzing holds on Josh, because the next time I saw him, Josh was slumped over at the Pacific Islander display table with his forehead resting on a model of Krakatoa. He didn't move all night, either, but I just thought that was because of all the champagne he'd had to drink.

Anyway, Lilly and Tina and I joined Boris and Dave—who is really nice, even if he does go to Trinity—and Shameeka and her boyfriend, Allan, and Ling Su and her date, Clifford, at this table they had snagged. It was the Pakistani table, with a display sponsored by the Economics Club, detailing how the market for maunds (a Pakistani unit of measurement) of rice was falling. We moved some of the maunds and sat there anyway, right on the tabletop, so we could see everything.

And then Michael suddenly appeared out of nowhere, looking crescent fresh—isn't that a funny expression? I learned it from Michael—in the tux his mom made him get for his cousin Steve's bar mitzvah. Michael really didn't have anyone else to hang out with, since Principal Gupta ruled that the Internet is not a culture and therefore cannot have its own table, and so the Computer Club boycotted the Cultural Diversity Dance on principle.

But Michael didn't seem to care what the Computer Club thought, and he's the treasurer! He sat down next to me and asked if I was all right, and then we had fun for a while cracking jokes about how all the cheerleaders sure don't practice any cultural diversity, since they were all dressed in practically the same gown, a slinky black number by Donna Karan. Then somebody started talking about *Star Trek: Deep Space Nine* and whether or not there's caffeine in replicator coffee, and Michael insisted that the matter used to make the things that come out of the replicator is from refuse, which means maybe when you order an ice cream sundae it might be made out of urine, but with the germs and impurities extracted. And we were all getting kind of grossed out when the music changed, and a slow song came on, and everybody left the table to go and dance.

Except for me and Michael, of course. We just sat there amid the maunds of rice.

Which wasn't too bad, actually, since Michael and I never run out of things to talk about—unlike me and Josh. We kept on arguing about the replicator, and then we moved on to who was the more effective leader, Captain Kirk or Captain Picard, when Mr. Gianini came over and asked me if I was okay.

I said of course, and that was when Mr. G told me he was glad to hear it, and, by the way, based on my latest scores on the practice sheets he'd been giving me evey day, I had brought my F in Algebra up to a D, for which he congratulated me, and he urged me to keep up the hard work.

But I credited my improved math performance to Michael, who taught me to stop writing my Algebra notes in my journal, not be so messy with my columns, and to cross things out when I borrow during subtraction. Michael got all embarrassed and claimed not to have had anything to do with it, but Mr. G didn't hear him since he had to hurry off and dissuade a group of Goths from embarking upon a demonstration over the unfair exclusion of a table dedicated to Satan worshipers by the event organizers.

Then a fast song came on and everybody came back, and we sat around and talked about Lilly's show, which Tina Hakim Baba is now going to be producer of, since we found out she gets $50 a week in allowance (she is going to start borrowing teen romances from the library instead of buying them new so that she can use all of her funds for promoting *Lilly Tells It Like It Is*). Lilly asked if I'd mind being the topic for next week's show, titled "The New Monarchy: Royals Who Make a Difference." I gave her exclusive rights to my first public interview if she'd promise to ask me about my feelings on the meat industry.

Then another slow song came on, and everybody went to go and dance to it. Michael and I were left sitting amid the rice again, and I was about to ask him who he'd choose to spend eternity with if nuclear Armageddon wiped out the rest of the population, Buffy the Vampire Slayer or Storm from the *X-Men* comics, when he asked me if I wanted to dance!

I was so surprised, I said sure without even thinking about it. And then the next thing I knew, I was dancing my first dance with a boy who wasn't my dad!

And it was a *slow* one!

Slow dancing is *strange*. It isn't even dancing, really. It's more like standing there with your arms around the other person, moving from one foot to the other in time to the music. And I guess you aren't supposed to talk—at least, nobody else around us was talking. I guess I could sort of see why, since you're so busy *feeling* stuff it's hard to think of anything to say. I mean, Michael *smelled* so good—like Ivory soap—and *felt* so good—the dress Grandmère picked out for me was pretty and everything, but I was kind of cold in it, so it was nice to stand close to Michael, who was so warm—that it was next to impossible to *say* anything.

I guess Michael felt the same way, because even though when we were sitting there on the table with all the rice neither of us ever shut up, we had so much to talk about,

223

when we were dancing together neither of us said a word.

But the minute the song was over Michael started talking again, asking me if I wanted some Thai iced tea from the Thai Culture table, or maybe some edamame from the Japanese Anime Club's table. For somebody who'd never been to a single school event—aside from Computer Club meetings—Michael sure was making up for lost time in his enthusiasm over being at this one.

And that was how the rest of the night went: We sat around and talked during the fast songs and danced during the slow ones.

And you know, to tell the truth, I couldn't say which I liked better, talking to Michael or dancing with him. They were both so . . . interesting.

In different ways, of course.

When the dance was over we all piled into the limo Mr. Hakim Baba sent to pick up Tina and Dave (the news vans had all left by then, since the story about the bombing had broken; I suppose they went to go stake out the Iranian embassy). I called my mom on the limo cell phone and told her where I was and asked if I could spend the night at Lilly's, since that's where we were all headed. She said yes without asking any questions, which led me to believe that she'd already talked to Mr. G and that he'd filled her in on the night's events. I wonder if he told her he'd raised my F to a D.

You know, he could have given me a D plus. I have been nothing but supportive of his relationship with my mother. That kind of loyalty ought to be rewarded.

Dr. and Dr. Moscovitz seemed kind of surprised when all ten of us—twelve, if you count Lars and Wahim— showed up at their door. They were especially surprised to see Michael; they hadn't realized he'd left his room. But they let us take over the living room, where we played End of the World until Lilly and Michael's dad finally came out in his pajamas and said everybody had to go home, he had an early appointment with his tai chi instructor.

Everybody said good-bye and piled into the elevator, except for me and the Moscovitzes. Even Lars hitched a ride back to the Plaza—once I had been locked down for the night, his responsibilities were over. I made him promise not to tell my dad about the kiss. He said he wouldn't, but you can never tell with guys; they have this weird code of their own, you know? I was reminded of it when I saw Lars and Michael giving each other high fives right before he left.

The strangest thing out of everything that happened last night is that I found out what Michael does in his room all the time. He showed me, but he made me swear never to tell anyone, including Lilly. I probably shouldn't even write it down here, in case someone ever finds this book and reads it. All I can say is Lilly's been wasting her time worshiping Boris Pelkowski; there's a musical genius in her very own family.

And to think, he's never had one lesson! He taught himself how to play the guitar—and he writes all his own songs! The one he played for me is called "Tall Drink of Water." It's about this very tall pretty girl who doesn't know this boy is in love with her. I predict that one day it will be number one on the *Billboard* chart. Michael Moscovitz could one day be as famous as Kanye West.

It wasn't until everyone was gone that I realized how tired I was. It had been a really long day. I had broken up with a boy I had only been out on half a date with. That can be very emotionally wearing.

Still, I woke up way early, like I always do when I spend the night at Lilly's. I lay there with Pavlov in my arms and listened to the sound of the morning traffic on

Fifth Avenue, which isn't really very loud, since the Moscovitzes had their windows soundproofed. As I lay there, I thought, Really, I am a very lucky girl. Things had looked pretty bad there for a while. But isn't it funny how everything kind of works itself out in the end?

I hear stirrings in the kitchen. Maya must be there, pouring out glasses of pulpless orange juice for breakfast. I'm going to go see if she needs any help.

I don't know why, but I AM SO HAPPY!

I guess it doesn't take much, does it?

Grandmère showed up at the loft today with Dad in tow. Dad wanted to find out how things went at the dance. Lars didn't tell him! God, I *love* my bodyguard. And Grandmère wanted to let me know that she has to go away for a week, so our princess lessons are suspended for the time being. She says it's time to pay her yearly visit to somebody named Baden-Baden. I suppose he's friends with that other guy she used to hang around with, Boutros-Boutros Something-or-other.

Even *my grandmother* has a boyfriend.

Anyway, she and Dad just showed up out of the blue, and you should have seen my mom's face. She looked about ready to heave. Especially when Grandmère started bossing her around about how messy the loft is (I've been too busy lately to clean).

To distract Grandmère from my mom, I told her I'd walk her back to her limo, and on the way I told her all about Josh, and she was way interested, since the story had everything in it that she likes, reporters and cute boys and people getting their hearts totally stomped on and stuff like that.

Anyway, while we were standing on the corner saying good-bye until next week (*YES!* No princess lessons for a whole week! She shoots; she scores!) the Blind Guy walked by, tapping his cane. He stopped at the corner and stood there, waiting for his next victim to come along and help him cross the street. Grandmère saw this and totally fell for it. She was like, "Amelia, go and help that poor young man."

But, of course, I knew better. I said, "No way."

"Amelia!" Grandmère was shocked. "One of the most important traits in a princess is her unfailing kindness to strangers. Now, go and help that young man cross the street."

I said, "No way, Grandmère. If you think he needs help so much, *you* do it."

So Grandmère, all bent out of shape—and I guess intent on showing me how unfailingly kind she is—went up to the Blind Guy and said in this fakey voice, "Let me help you, young man. . . ."

The Blind Guy grabbed Grandmère by the arm. I guess he liked what he felt, because the next thing I knew, he was going, "Oh, thank you so much, ma'am," and he and Grandmère were crossing Spring Street.

I didn't think the Blind Guy was going to try to feel up my grandmother. I really didn't, or I wouldn't have let her help him. I mean, Grandmère is no spring chicken, if you know what I mean. I couldn't imagine any guy, even a blind one, feeling her up.

But next thing I knew, Grandmère was yelling her head off, and both her driver and our neighbor who used to be a man came running out to help her.

But Grandmère didn't need any help. She whacked the Blind Guy across the face with her purse so hard his sunglasses went flying off. After that there was no doubt about it: The Blind Guy can see.

And let me tell you something: I don't think he'll be taking any more trips down our street for a while.

After all that yelling, it was almost a blessing to go inside and work on my Algebra homework for the rest of the day. I needed some peace and quiet.

MEG CABOT

Princess

in the spotlight

HARPER TEEN

AN IMPRINT OF HARPERCOLLINSPUBLISHERS

For my grandparents,
Bruce and Patsy Mounsey,
who are nothing like any
of the grandparents in this book.

ACKNOWLEDGMENTS

Many thanks to Barb Cabot, Debra Martin Chase, Bill Contardi, Sarah Davies, Laura Langlie, Abby McAden, Alison Donalty, and the usual suspects: Beth Ader, Jennifer Brown, Dave Walton, and especially, Benjamin Egnatz.

When things are horrible—just horrible—
I think as hard as ever I can of being a princess.
I say to myself,
"I am a princess."
You don't know how it makes you forget.

A LITTLE PRINCESS
Frances Hodgson Burnett

Okay. So I was just in the kitchen, eating cereal, you know, the usual Monday morning routine, when my mom comes out of the bathroom with this funny look on her face. I mean, she was all pale and her hair was kind of sticking out and she had on her terry cloth robe instead of her kimono, which usually means she's premenstrual.

So I said, "Mom, you want some Midol? Because, no offense, you look like you could use some."

Which is sort of a dangerous thing to say to a premenstrual woman, but you know, she's my mom, and all. It's not like she was going to karate chop me, the way she would if anybody else said that to her.

But she just said, "No. No, thanks," in this dazed voice.

So then I assumed something really horrible had happened. You know, like Fat Louie had eaten another sock, or they were cutting off our electricity again because I'd forgotten to fish the bill out of the salad bowl where Mom keeps stuffing them.

So I grabbed her and I was like, "Mom? Mom, what is it? What's wrong?"

She sort of shook her head, like she does when she's confused over the microwave instructions on a frozen pizza. "Mia," she said, in this shocked but happy way, "Mia. I'm pregnant."

Oh, my God. OH, MY GOD.

My mom is having my Algebra teacher's baby.

I am really trying to take this calmly, you know? Because there isn't any point in getting upset about it.

But how can I *NOT* be upset? My mother is about to become a single parent. *AGAIN.*

You would think she'd have learned a lesson with me and all, but apparently not.

As if I don't have enough problems. As if my life isn't over already. I just don't see how much more I can be expected to take. I mean, apparently, it is not enough that

1. I am the tallest girl in the freshman class.
2. I am also the least endowed in the chest area.
3. Last month, I found out my mother has been dating my Algebra teacher.
4. Also last month, I found out that I am the sole heir to the throne of a small European country.
5. I have to take princess lessons from my paternal grandmother. *Every day.*
6. In December, I am supposed to be introduced to my new countrymen and women on national television (in Genovia, population 50,000, but still).
7. I don't have a boyfriend.

Oh, no. You see, all of that isn't enough of a burden, apparently. Now my mother has to get pregnant out of wedlock. *AGAIN.*

Thanks, Mom. Thanks a whole lot.

And what *about* that? Why weren't she and Mr. Gianini using birth control? Could someone please explain that to me? Whatever happened to her diaphragm? I know she has one. I found it once in the shower when I was a little kid. I took it and used it as a birdbath for my Barbie townhouse for a few weeks, until my mom finally found out and took it away.

And what about condoms??? Do people my mother's age think they are immune to sexually transmitted diseases? They are obviously not immune to pregnancy, so what gives?

This is *so* like my mother. She can't even remember to buy toilet paper. How is she going to remember to use birth control????????

I can't believe this. I really can't believe this.

She hasn't told him. My mother is having my Algebra teacher's baby, *and she hasn't even told him.*

I can tell she hasn't told him, because when I walked in this morning, all Mr. Gianini said was, "Oh, hi, Mia. How are you doing?"

Oh, hi, Mia. How are you doing?????

That is not what you say to someone whose mother is having your baby. You say something like, "Excuse me, Mia, may I see you a moment?"

Then you take the daughter of the woman with whom you have committed this heinous indiscretion out into the hallway, where you fall on bended knee to grovel and beg for her approval and forgiveness. That is what you do.

I can't help staring at Mr. G and wondering what my new baby brother or sister is going to look like. My mom is totally hot, like Carmen Sandiego, only without the trench coat—further proof that I am a biological anomaly, since I inherited neither my mother's thick curly black mane of hair nor her C cup. So there's nothing to worry about there.

But Mr. G, I just don't know. Not that Mr. G isn't good-looking, I guess. I mean, he's tall and has all his hair (score one for Mr. G, since my dad's as bald as a parking meter). But what is with his nostrils? I totally can't figure it out. They are just so . . . big.

I sincerely hope the kid gets my mom's nostrils and Mr. G's ability to divide fractions in his head.

The sad thing is, Mr. Gianini doesn't have the slightest

idea what is about to befall him. I would feel sorry for him if it weren't for the fact that it is all his fault. I know it takes two to tango, but please, my mother is a painter. He is an Algebra teacher.

You tell me who is supposed to be the responsible one.

Great. Just great.

As if things aren't bad enough, now our English teacher says we have to complete a *journal* this semester. I am not kidding. A *journal*. Like I don't already keep one.

And get this: At the end of every week, we're supposed to *turn our journals in*. For Mrs. Spears to *read*. Because she wants to get to know us. We are supposed to begin by introducing ourselves, and listing our pertinent stats. Later, we are supposed to move on to recording our innermost thoughts and emotions.

She has got to be joking. Like I am going to allow Mrs. Spears to be privy to my innermost thoughts and emotions. I won't even tell my innermost thoughts and emotions to my *mother*. Would I tell them to my *English teacher*?

And I can't possibly turn *this* journal in. There's all sorts of stuff in here I don't want anyone to know. Like how my mother is pregnant by my Algebra teacher, for instance.

Well, I will just have to start a new journal. A *fake* journal. Instead of recording my innermost emotions and feelings in it, I'll just write a bunch of lies, and hand that in instead.

I am such an accomplished liar, I very highly doubt Mrs. Spears will know the difference.

ENGLISH JOURNAL
by Mia Thermopolis

KEEP OUT!!!
THIS MEANS YOU,
UNLESS YOU ARE MRS. SPEARS!!!!!!

An Introduction

NAME:

Amelia Mignonette Grimaldi Thermopolis Renaldo
Known as Mia for short.
Her Royal Highness the princess of Genovia or just
Princess Mia in some circles.

AGE:

Fourteen

YR IN SCHOOL:

Freshman

SEX:

Haven't had it yet. Ha, ha, just kidding, Mrs. Spears!
Ostensibly female, but lack of breast size lends disturbing androgyny.

DESCRIPTION:

Five foot nine
Short mouse-brown hair (new blond highlights)
Gray eyes
Size ten shoe
The rest is not worth remarking on.

PARENTS:

Mother: Helen Thermopolis

OCCUPATION:
    Painter
FATHER:
    Artur Christoff Phillipe Gerard Grimaldi Renaldo
OCCUPATION:
    Prince of Genovia
PARENTS' MARITAL STATUS:
    Because I am the result of a fling my mother and father had in college, they never married (each other) and are both currently single. It is probably better this way, since all they ever do is fight.

    With each other, I mean.
PETS:
    One cat, Fat Louie. Orange and white, Louie weighs twenty-five pounds. Louie is eight years old, and has been on a diet for approximately six of those years. When Louie is upset with us for, say, forgetting to feed him, he eats any socks he might find lying around. Also, he is attracted to small glittery things, and has quite a collection of beer bottle caps and tweezers which he thinks I don't know about, hidden behind the toilet in my bathroom.
BEST FRIEND:
    My best friend is Lilly Moscovitz. Lilly has been my best friend since kindergarten. She is fun to hang out with because she is very very smart and has her own public access television show, *Lilly Tells It Like It Is*. She is always thinking up fun things to do, like steal the foamboard sculpture of the Parthenon that the Greek and Latin Derivatives class made for Parents'

Night and hold it for a ransom of ten pounds of lime Starbursts.

Not that that was us, Mrs. Spears. I am just using that as an example of the type of crazy thing Lilly *might* do.

BOYFRIEND:

Ha! I wish.

ADDRESS:

I have lived all of my life in New York City with my mother, except for summers, which I have traditionally spent with my father at his mother's chateau in France. My father's primary residence is Genovia, a small country in Europe located on the Mediterranean between the Italian and French border. For a long time I was led to believe that my father was an important politician in Genovia, like the mayor, or something. Nobody told me that he was actually a member of the Genovian royal family—that he was, in fact, the reigning monarch, Genovia being a principality. I guess nobody ever would have told me, either, if my dad hadn't gotten testicular cancer and become sterile, making me, his illegitimate daughter, the only heir he'll ever have to his throne. Ever since he finally let me in on this *slightly* important little secret (a month ago) Dad has been living at the Plaza Hotel here in New York, while his mother, my grandmère, the dowager princess, teaches me what I need to know in order to be his heir.

For which I can only say: Thanks. Thanks a *whole* lot.

And do you want to know what the *really* sad part is? None of that was lies.

Okay, Lilly knows.

All right, maybe she doesn't *KNOW*, but she knows something is wrong. I mean, come on: she's been my best friend since like kindergarten. She can totally tell when something is bothering me. We totally bonded in first grade, the day Orville Lockhead dropped trou in front of us in the line to the music room. I was appalled, having never seen male genitalia before. Lilly, however, was unimpressed. She has a brother, you see, so it was no big surprise to her. She just looked Orville straight in the eye and said, "I've seen bigger."

And you know what? Orville never did it again.

So you can see that Lilly and I share a bond that is stronger than mere friendship.

Which was why she took just one look at my face when she sat down at our lunch table today and said, "What's wrong? Something's wrong. It's not Louie, is it? Did Louie eat another sock?"

As if. This is so much more serious. Not that it isn't totally scary when Louie eats a sock. I mean, we have to rush him to the animal hospital and all, and right away, or he could die. A thousand bucks later, we get an old half-digested sock as a souvenir.

But at least the cat is back to normal.

But this? A thousand bucks won't cure *this*. And nothing will ever be back to normal again.

It is so incredibly embarrassing. I mean, that my mom and Mr. Gianini—you know, DID IT.

Worse, that they DID IT without using anything. I mean, please. Who DOES that anymore?

I told Lilly there wasn't anything wrong, that it was just PMS. It was totally embarrassing to admit this in front of my bodyguard, Lars, who was sitting there eating a gyro that Tina Hakim Baba's bodyguard Wahim—Tina has a bodyguard because her father is a sheik who fears that she will be kidnapped by executives from a rival oil company; I have one because . . . well, just because I'm a princess, I guess—had bought from the vendor in front of Ho's Deli across the street from the school.

The thing is, who announces the vagaries of her menstrual cycle in front of her bodyguard?

But what else was I supposed to say?

I noticed Lars totally didn't finish his gyro, though. I think I completely grossed him out.

Could this day get any worse?

Anyway, even then, Lilly didn't drop it. Sometimes she really does remind me of one of those little pug dogs you always see old ladies walking in the park. I mean, not only is her face kind of small and squashed in (in a nice way), but sometimes when she gets hold of something she simply will not let it go.

Like this thing at lunch, for instance. She was all, "If the only thing bothering you is PMS, then why are you writing in your journal so much? I thought you were mad at your mom for giving that to you. I thought you weren't even going to use it."

Which reminds me that I *was* mad at my mom for giving it to me. She gave me this journal because she says I have a lot of pent-up anger and hostility, and I have to get it out somehow, since I'm not in touch with my inner child and have an inherent inability to verbalize my feelings.

I think my mom must have been talking to Lilly's parents, who are both psychoanalysts, at the time.

But then I found out I was the princess of Genovia, and I started using this journal to record my feelings about that, which, looking back at what I wrote, really were pretty hostile.

But that's nothing compared with how I feel now.

Not that I feel *hostile* toward Mr. Gianini and my mother. I mean, they're adults, and all. They can make their own decisions. But don't they see that this is one decision that is going to affect not just them, but everyone around them? I mean, Grandmère is NOT going to like it when she finds out my mother is having ANOTHER child out of wedlock.

And what about my father? He's already had testicular cancer this year. Finding out that the mother of his only child is giving birth to another man's baby just might kill him. Not that he's still in love with my mom, or anything like that. I don't think.

And what about Fat Louie? How is he going to react to having a baby in the house? He is starved enough for affection as it is, considering I'm the only person who remembers to feed him. He might try to run away, or maybe move up from eating just socks to eating the remote control or something.

I guess I wouldn't mind, though, having a little sister or brother. It might be cool, actually. If it's a girl, I'd share my room with her. I could give her bubble baths and dress her up the way Tina Hakim Baba and I dressed up her little sisters—and her little brother, too, now that I think of it.

I don't think I want a little brother. Tina Hakim Baba told me that baby boys pee in your face when you try to change them. That is so disgusting I don't even want to think about it.

You would think my mother might have considered things like this before deciding to have sex with Mr. Gianini.

And what about that, anyway? How many dates has my mom even been on with Mr. G, anyway? Not many. I mean, like eight, maybe. Eight dates, and it turns out she's already slept with him? And probably a couple of times, because thirty-six-year-old women do not get pregnant just like that. I know, because I can't pick up a copy of *New York* magazine without seeing about a gazillion ads from victims of early menopause who are looking for egg donations from younger women.

But not my mom. Oh, no. Ripe as a mango, that's my mom.

I should have known, of course. I mean, what about that morning I walked out into the kitchen and Mr. Gianini was standing there in his boxer shorts?

I was trying to repress that memory, but I guess it didn't work.

Also, has she even thought about her folic acid intake? I know for a fact she has not. And may I just point out that alfalfa sprouts can be deadly for a newly developing fetus? We have alfalfa sprouts in our refrigerator. Our refrigerator is a deathtrap for a gestating child. There is BEER in the vegetable crisper.

My mother may think she is a fit parent, but she has a lot to learn. When I get home, I fully intend to show her all this information I've printed out off the Web. If she thinks she can put the health of my future baby sister at risk by eating alfalfa sprouts in her sandwiches and drinking coffee and stuff, she is in for a big surprise.

14

Lilly caught me looking up stuff about pregnancy on the Internet.

She said, "Oh, my God! Is there something about your date with Josh Richter that you didn't tell me?"

Which I really didn't appreciate, since she said it right in front of her brother Michael—not to mention Lars, Boris Pelkowski, and the rest of the class. She said it really loud, too.

You know, these kinds of things wouldn't happen if the teachers at this school would do their jobs and actually teach once in a while. I mean, except for Mr. Gianini, every teacher in this school seems to think it is perfectly acceptable to toss out an assignment and then leave the room to go have a smoke in the teachers' lounge.

Which is probably a health violation, you know.

And Mrs. Hill is the worst of all. I mean, I know Gifted and Talented isn't a real class at all. It's more like study hall for the socially impaired. But if Mrs. Hill would be in here once in a while to supervise, people like me who are neither gifted nor talented and only ended up in this class because they happen to be flunking Algebra and need the extra study time might not get picked on all the time by the resident geniuses.

Because the truth is, Lilly knows perfectly well that the only thing that went on during my date with Josh Richter was that I found out that Josh Richter was totally using me, just because I happen to be a princess and he thought he could get his picture on the cover of *Teen Beat*. I mean, it wasn't like we were ever even alone with each other, unless you count when we were in the car, which I don't, since Lars was there, too, looking out for Euro-trash terrorists who might feel compelled to kidnap me.

Anyway, I exited really fast from the You and Your Pregnancy site I had been looking at, but not fast enough for Lilly. She kept going, "Oh, my God, Mia, why didn't you tell me?"

It was getting kind of embarrassing, even though I explained that I was doing an extra-credit report for Biology, which isn't really a lie, since my lab partner, Kenny Showalter, and I are ethically opposed to dissecting frogs—which the class would be doing next—and Mrs. Sing said we could do a term paper instead.

Only the term paper is supposed to be on the life cycle of the mealworm. But Lilly doesn't know that.

I tried to change the subject by asking Lilly if she knew the truth about alfalfa sprouts, but she just kept blabbing on and on about me and Josh Richter. I really wouldn't have minded so much if it hadn't been for her brother Michael sitting right there, listening instead of working on his webzine, *Crackhead*, like he was supposed to be doing. I mean, it's not like I haven't had a crush on him since forever.

Not that he's noticed, of course. To him, I'm just his kid sister's best friend, that's all. He has to be nice to me, or Lilly will tell everyone in school how she once caught him getting teary-eyed over an old *7th Heaven* rerun.

Besides which, I'm just a lowly freshman. Michael Moscovitz is a senior and has the best grade point average in the whole school (after Lilly) and is covaledictorian of his

16

class. And he didn't inherit the squashed-in-face gene, like his sister. Michael could go out with any girl at Albert Einstein High School that he wanted to.

Well, except for the cheerleaders. They only date jocks.

Not that Michael isn't athletic. I mean, he doesn't believe in organized sports, but he has excellent quadriceps. All his ceps are nice, actually. I noticed last time he came into Lilly's room to yell at us for screaming obscenities too loudly during a Christina Aguilera video, and he didn't happen to be wearing a shirt.

So I really didn't appreciate Lilly standing there talking about how I might be pregnant, right in front of her brother.

TOP FIVE REASONS WHY IT'S HARD BEING BEST FRIENDS WITH A CERTIFIED GENIUS

1. She uses a lot of words I don't understand.
2. She is often incapable of admitting that I might make a meaningful contribution to any conversation or activity.
3. In group situations, she has trouble relinquishing control.
4. Unlike normal people, when solving a problem, she does not go from A to B, but from A to D, making it difficult for us lower human life forms to follow along.
5. You can't tell her anything without her analyzing it half to death.

HOMEWORK

Algebra: problems on pg. 133
English: write a brief family history
World Civ: find an example of negative stereotyping of
Arabs (film, television, literature) and submit with
explanatory essay
G&T: N/A
French: écrivez une vignette parisienne
Biology: reproductive system (get answers from Kenny)

ENGLISH JOURNAL

My Family History

The ancestry of my family on my father's side can be traced back to A.D. 568. That is the year when a Visigothic warlord named Albion, who appeared to be suffering from what today would be called an authoritarian personality disorder, killed the king of Italy and all these other people, then made himself king. And after he made himself king, he decided to marry Rosagunde, the daughter of one of the old king's generals.

Only Rosagunde didn't much like Albion after he made her drink wine out of her dead dad's skull, and so she got back at him the night of their wedding by strangling him with her braids while he slept.

With Albion dead, the old king of Italy's son took over. He was so grateful to Rosagunde that he made her princess of an area that is today known as the country of Genovia. According to the only existing records of that time, Rosagunde was a kind and thoughtful ruler. She is my great-grandmother times about sixty. She is one of the primary reasons why today Genovia has some of the best literacy, infant mortality, and employment rates in all of Europe: Rosagunde implemented a highly sophisticated (for its time) system of governmental checks and balances, and did away entirely with the death penalty.

On my mom's side of the family, the Thermopolises were goat herders on the island of Crete until the year 1904, when Dionysius Thermopolis, my mom's great-grandfather, couldn't take it anymore, and ran away to

America. He eventually settled in Versailles, Indiana, where he opened an appliance store. His offspring have been running the Handy Dandy Hardware store on the Versailles, Indiana, courthouse square ever since. My mom says her upbringing would have been much less oppressive, not to mention more liberal, back in Crete.

A Suggested Daily Diet for Pregnancy

• Two to four protein servings of meat, fish, poultry, cheese, tofu, eggs, or nut-grain-bean-dairy combinations
• One quart of milk (whole, skim, buttermilk) or milk equivalents (cheese, yogurt, cottage cheese)
• One or two vitamin C–rich foods: whole potato, grapefruit, orange, melon, green pepper, cabbage, strawberries, fruit, orange juice
• A yellow or orange fruit or vegetable
• Four to five slices of whole-grain bread, pancakes, tortillas, cornbread, or a serving of whole-grain cereal or pasta. Use wheat germ and brewers' yeast to fortify other foods.
• Butter, fortified margarine, vegetable oil
• Six to eight glasses of liquid: fruit and vegetable juices, water, and herb teas. Avoid sugar-sweetened juices and colas, alcohol, and caffeine.
• For snacks: dried fruits, nuts, pumpkin and sunflower seeds, popcorn

My mom is so not going to go for this. Unless she can smother it in hoisin sauce from Number One Noodle Son, she is just not interested.

TO DO BEFORE MOM GETS HOME

Throw out:
Heineken
cooking sherry
alfalfa sprouts
Colombian roast
chocolate chips
salami
Don't forget the
bottle of Absolut
in the freezer!

Buy:
multivitamins
fresh fruit
wheat germ
yogurt

Just when I thought things couldn't get any worse, suddenly, they did.

Grandmère called.

This is so unfair. I thought she was supposed to have gone to Baden-Baden for a little R and R. I was fully looking forward to a respite from her torture sessions—also known as princess lessons, which I am forced by my father, the despot, to attend. I mean, I could use a little vacation myself. Do they really think anyone in Genovia cares whether I know how to use a fish fork? Or if I can sit down without getting wrinkles in the back of my skirt? Or if I know how to say thank you in Swahili? Shouldn't my future countrymen and women be more concerned with my views on the environment? And gun control? And overpopulation?

But according to Grandmère, the people of Genovia don't care about any of that. They just want to know that I won't embarrass them at any state dinners.

As if. Grandmère's the one they should be worried about. I mean, *I* didn't have eyeliner permanently tatooed onto *my* eyelids. *I* don't dress up *my* pet in chinchilla bolero jackets. *I* was never a close personal friend of Richard Nixon.

But oh, no, it's *me* everyone is supposedly so worried about. Like *I* might commit some huge social gaffe at my introduction to the Genovian people in December.

Right.

But whatever. It turns out she didn't go after all, on account of the Baden-Baden baggage handlers being on strike.

I wish I knew the head of the baggage handlers' union in Baden-Baden. If I did, I would totally offer him the one hundred dollars per day my dad has been donating in my name to Greenpeace for performing my duties as princess of Genovia, just so he and the other baggage handlers would go back to work, and get Grandmère out of my hair for a while.

Anyway, Grandmère left a very scary message on the answering machine. She says she has a "surprise" for me. I'm supposed to call her right away.

I wonder what her surprise is. Knowing Grandmère, it's probably something totally horrible, like a coat made out of the skin of baby poodles.

Hey, I wouldn't put it past her.

I'm going to pretend I didn't get the message.

Just got off the phone with Grandmère. She wanted to know why I hadn't returned her call. I told her I didn't get the message.

Why am I such a liar? I mean, I can't even tell the truth about the simplest things. And I'm supposed to be a princess, for crying out loud. What kind of princess goes around lying all the time?

Anyway, Grandmère says she is sending a limo to pick me up. She and my dad and I are going to have dinner in her suite at the Plaza. Grandmère says she is going to tell me all about my surprise then.

Tell me all about it. Not *show me*. Which hopefully rules out the puppy-skin coat.

I guess it's just as well I'm having dinner with Grandmère tonight. My mom invited Mr. Gianini over to the loft tonight so they can "talk." She's not very happy with me for throwing out the coffee and beer (I didn't actually throw it away. I gave it to our neighbor Ronnie). Now my mom is stomping around complaining that she has nothing to offer Mr. G when he comes over.

I pointed out that it's for her own good, and that if Mr. Gianini is any sort of gentleman he'll give up beer and coffee anyway, to support her in her time of need. I know I would expect the father of my unborn child to pay me that courtesy.

That is, in the unlikely event that I were ever actually to have sex.

Monday, October 20, 11 p.m.

Some surprise *that* was.

Somebody really needs to tell Grandmère that surprises are supposed to be pleasant. There is nothing pleasant about the fact that she has managed to wrangle a prime-time interview for me with Beverly Bellerieve on *TwentyFour/Seven.*

I don't care if it *is* the most highly rated television news show in America. I told Grandmère a million times I don't want to have my picture taken, let alone be on TV. I mean, it's bad enough that everyone I know is aware that I look like a walking Q-tip, what with my lack of breasts and my Yield-sign–shaped hair. I don't need all of America finding it out.

But now Grandmère says it's my duty as a member of the Genovian royal family. And this time she got my dad into the act. He was all, "Your grandmother's right, Mia."

So I get to spend next Saturday afternoon being interviewed by Beverly Bellerieve.

I told Grandmère I thought this interview thing was a really bad idea. I told her I wasn't ready for anything this big yet. I said maybe we could start small, and have Carson Daly or somebody like that interview me.

But Grandmère didn't go for it. I never met anybody who needed to go to Baden-Baden so badly for a little rest and relaxation. Grandmère looks about as relaxed as Fat Louie right after the vet sticks his thermometer you know where in order to take his temperature.

Of course, this might have had something to do with the fact that Grandmère shaves off her eyebrows and draws on

new ones every morning. Don't ask me why. I mean, she has perfectly good eyebrows. I've seen the stubble. But lately I've noticed those eyebrows are getting drawn on higher and higher up her forehead, which gives her this look of perpetual surprise. I think that's because of all her plastic surgeries. If she doesn't watch it, one of these days her eyelids are going to be up in the vicinity of her frontal lobes.

And my dad was no help at all. He was asking all these questions about Beverly Bellerieve, like was it true she was Miss America in 1991 and did Grandmère happen to know if she (Beverly) was still going out with Ted Turner, or was that over?

I swear, for a guy who only has one testicle, my dad sure spends a lot of time thinking about sex.

We argued about it all through dinner. Like were they going to shoot the interview at the hotel, or back in the loft? If they shot it at the hotel, people would be given a false impression about my lifestyle. But if they shot it at the loft, Grandmère insisted, people would be horrified by the squalor in which my mother has brought me up.

Which is totally unfair. The loft is not squalid. It just has that nice, lived-in look.

"Never-been-cleaned look, you mean," Grandmère said, correcting me. But that isn't true, because just the other day I Lemon Pledged the whole place.

"With that animal living there, I don't know how you can ever get the place really clean," Grandmère said.

But Fat Louie isn't responsible for the mess. Dust, as everyone knows, is 95 percent human skin tissue.

The only good thing that I can see about all this is that

at least the film crew isn't going to follow me around at school and stuff. That's one thing to be thankful for, anyway. I mean, could you imagine them filming me being tortured by Lana Weinberger during Algebra? She would so totally start flipping her cheerleading pom-poms in my face, or something, just to show the producers what a wimp I can be sometimes. People all over America would be, like, What is wrong with that girl? Why isn't she self-actualized?

And what about G and T? In addition to there being absolutely no teacher supervision in that class, there's the whole thing with us locking Boris Pelkowski in the supply closet so we don't have to listen to him practice his violin. That has to be some kind of violation of Haz-mat codes.

Anyway, the whole time we were arguing about it, a part of my brain was going, *Right now, as we're sitting here arguing over this whole interview thing, fifty-seven blocks away, my mother is breaking the news to her lover—my Algebra teacher— that she is pregnant with his child.*

What was Mr. G going to say? I wondered. If he expressed anything but joy, I was going to sic Lars on him. I really was. Lars would beat up Mr. G for me, and he probably wouldn't charge me very much for it, either. He has three ex-wives he's paying alimony to, so he can always use an extra ten bucks, which is all I can afford to pay a hired thug.

I really need to see about getting more of an allowance. I mean, who ever heard of a princess who only gets ten bucks a week spending money? You can't even go to the movies on that.

Well, you can, but you can't get popcorn.

The thing is, though, now that I'm back at the loft, I can't tell whether I will need Lars to beat up my Algebra teacher or not. Mr. G and my mom are talking in hushed voices in her room.

I can't hear anything going on in there, even when I press my ear to the door.

I hope Mr. G takes it well. He's the nicest guy my mom's ever dated, despite that F he almost gave me. I don't think he'll do anything stupid, like dump her, or try to sue for full custody.

Then again, he's a man, so who knows?

It's funny, because as I'm writing this, an instant message comes over my computer. It's from Michael! He writes:

CracKing: What was with you at school today? It was like you were off in this whole other world or something.

I write back:

FtLouie: I don't have the slightest idea what you are talking about. Nothing is wrong with me. I'm totally fine.

I am such a liar.

CracKing: Well, I got the impression that you didn't hear a word that I said about negative slopes.

Since I found out my destiny is to rule a small European principality someday, I have been trying really hard to understand Algebra, as I know I will need it to balance the budget of Genovia, and all. So I have been attending review sessions every day after school, and during Gifted and Talented, Michael has been helping me a little, too.

It's very hard to pay attention when Michael tutors me. This is because he smells really, really good.

How can I think about negative slopes when this guy I've had a major crush on since, oh, I don't know—forever practically, is sitting there right next to me, smelling like soap and sometimes brushing my knee with his?

I reply:

FTLOUIE: I heard everything you said about negative slopes. Given slope m, +y-intercept (0,b) equation y+mx+b Slope-intercept.
CRACKING: WHAT???
FTLOUIE: Isn't that right?
CRACKING: Did you copy that out of the back of the book?

Of course.
Uh-oh, my mom is at the door.

My mom came in. I thought Mr. G had left, so I went, "How'd it go?"

Then I saw she had tears in her eyes, so I went over and gave her this big hug.

"It's okay, Mom," I said. "You'll always have me. I'll help with everything, the midnight feedings, the diaper changing, everything. Even if it turns out to be a boy."

My mom hugged me back, but it turned out she wasn't crying because she was sad. She was crying because she was so happy.

"Oh, Mia," she said. "We want you to be the first to know."

Then she pulled me out into the living room. Mr. Gianini was standing there with this really dopey look on his face. Dopey happy.

I knew before she said it, but I pretended to be surprised anyway.

"We're getting married!"

My mom pulled me into this big group hug between her and Mr. G.

It's sort of weird to be hugged by your Algebra teacher. That's all I have to say.

Hey, I thought my mom was a feminist who didn't believe in the male hierarchy and was against the subjugation and obfuscation of the female identity that marriage necessarily entails.

At least, that's what she always used to say when I asked her why she and my dad didn't ever get married.

I always thought it's because he just never asked her.

Maybe that's why she told me not to tell anyone just yet. She wants to let my dad know in her own way, she says.

All of this excitement has given me a headache.

Tuesday, October 21, 2 a.m.

Oh, my God. I just realized that if my mom marries Mr. Gianini, it means he'll be living here. I mean, my mom would never move to Brooklyn, where he lives. She always says the subway aggravates her antipathy toward the corporate hordes.

I can't believe it. I'm going to have to eat breakfast every morning with my *Algebra teacher*.

And what happens if I accidentally see him naked, or something? My mind could be permanently scarred.

I'd better make sure the lock on the bathroom door is fixed before he moves in.

Now my throat hurts, in addition to my head.

When I woke up this morning, my throat hurt so much, I couldn't even talk. I could only croak.

I tried croaking for my mom for a while, but she couldn't hear me. So then I tried banging on the wall, but all that did was make my Greenpeace poster fall down.

Finally I had no choice but to get up. I wrapped my comforter around me so I wouldn't get a chill and get even sicker, and went down the hall to my mom's room.

To my horror, there was not one lump in my mom's bed, but TWO!!!! Mr. Gianini stayed over!!!!

Oh, well. It's not like he hasn't already promised to make an honest woman of her.

Still, it's a little embarrassing to stumble into your mom's bedroom at six in the morning and find your *Algebra teacher* in there with her. I mean, that kind of thing might warp a lesser person than myself.

But whatever. I stood there croaking in the doorway, totally too freaked out to go in, and finally my mom cracked an eye open. Then I whispered to her that I was sick, and told her that she'd have to call the attendance office and explain that I wouldn't be in school today.

I also asked her to call and cancel my limo, and to let Lilly know we wouldn't be stopping by to pick her up.

I also told her that if she was going to go to the studio, she'd have to get my dad or Lars (please not Grandmère) to come to the loft and make sure no one tried to kidnap or assassinate me while she was gone and I was in my weakened physical state.

I think she understood me, but it was hard to tell.

I tell you, this princess business is no joke.

My mom stayed home from the studio today.

I croaked to her that she shouldn't. She has a show at the Mary Boone Gallery in about a month, and I know she only has about half the paintings done that she's supposed to have. If she should happen to succumb to morning sickness, she is one dead realist.

But she stayed home anyway. I think she feels guilty. I think she thinks my getting sick is her fault. Like all my anxiety over the state of her womb weakened my autoimmune system, or something.

Which totally isn't true. I'm sure whatever it is I have, I picked it up at school. Albert Einstein High School is one giant petri dish of bacteria, if you ask me, what with the astonishing number of mouth-breathers who go there.

Anyway, about every ten minutes, my guilt-ridden mother comes in and asks me if I want anything. I forgot she has a Florence Nightingale complex. She keeps making me tea, and cinnamon toast with the crusts cut off. This is very nice, I must say.

Except then she tried to get me to let some zinc dissolve on my tongue, as one of her friends told her this is supposedly a good way to combat the common cold.

That was not so nice.

She felt bad about it when the zinc made me gag a whole bunch. She even ran down to the deli and bought me one of those king-size Crunch bars to make up for it.

Later she tried to make me bacon and eggs in order to build up my strength, but there I drew the line: Just because

I'm on my deathbed does not mean it's okay to abandon all of my vegetarian principles.

My mother just took my temperature. Ninety-nine point six.

If this were medieval times, I would probably be dead.

TEMPERATURE CHART
11:45 a.m.—99.2
12:14 p.m.—99.1
1:27 p.m.—98.6

This stupid thermometer must be broken!

2:05 p.m.—99.0
3:35 p.m.—99.1

Clearly, if this keeps up, I will be unable to be interviewed by Beverly Bellerieve on Saturday.

YIPPEE!!!

Lilly just stopped by. She brought me all of my homework. She says I look wretched, and that I sound like Linda Blair in *The Exorcist*. I've never seen *The Exorcist*, so I don't know if this is true or not. I don't like movies where people's heads spin around, or where things come bursting out of their stomachs. I like movies with beauty makeovers and dancing.

Anyway, Lilly says that the big news at school is that the "It Couple," Josh Richter and Lana Weinberger, got back together, after having been broken up one whole entire week (a personal record for the both of them: Last time they broke up, it was for only three days). Lilly says when she went by my locker to get my books, Lana was standing there in her cheerleader uniform, waiting for Josh, whose locker is next to mine.

Then, when Josh showed up, he laid a big wet one on Lana that Lilly swears was the equivalent to an F5 on the Fujimoto scale of tornado suck zone intensity, making it impossible for Lilly to close my locker door again (how well I know that problem). Lilly resolved the situation pretty quickly, however, by accidentally-on-purpose stabbing Josh in the spine with the tip of her number two pencil.

I thought about telling Lilly my own Big News: you know, about my mom and Mr. G. I mean, she's going to find out about it anyway.

Maybe it was the infection coursing through my body, but I just couldn't bring myself to do it. I just couldn't bear the thought of what Lilly might say regarding the potential size of my future brother's or sister's nostrils.

Anyway, I have about a ton of homework. Even the father of my unborn sibling, who you would think would feel an iota of sympathy toward me, loaded me down with it. I tell you, there isn't a single perk to having your mother engaged to your Algebra teacher. Not a single one.

Well, except when he comes over for dinner and helps me with the assignment. He doesn't give me the answers, though, so I mostly get sixty-eights. And that's still a D.

And I am really sick now! My temperature has gone up to ninety-nine point eight! Soon it will reach one hundred.

If this were an episode of *ER*, they'd have practically put me on a respirator already.

There is no way I'll be able to be interviewed by Beverly Bellerieve now. NO WAY.

Tee hee.

My mom has her humidifier in here, going on full blast. Lilly says my room is just like Vietnam, and why don't I at least crack the window, for God's sake.

I never thought of it before, but Lilly and Grandmère sort of have a lot in common. For instance, Grandmère called a little while ago. When I told her how sick I was, and how I probably wouldn't be able to make it to the interview on Saturday, she actually *chastised* me.

That's right. Chastised me, like it was *my* fault I got sick. Then she starts going on about how on her wedding day she had a fever of one hundred and two, but did she let that stop her from standing through a two-hour wedding ceremony, then riding in an open coach through the streets of Genovia waving to the populace, and then dining on prosciutto and melon at her reception and waltzing until four in the morning?

No, you might not be too surprised to learn. It did not.

That, Grandmère said, is because a princess does not use poor health as an excuse to shirk her duties to her people.

As if the people of Genovia care about my doing some lousy interview for *Twenty-Four/Seven*. They don't even get that show there. I mean, except for the people who have satellite dishes, maybe.

Lilly is just about as unsympathetic as Grandmère. In fact, Lilly isn't really a very soothing visitor to have at all when you are sick. She suggested that it was possible that I have consumption, just like Elizabeth Barrett Browning. I said I thought it was probably only bronchitis, and Lilly said that's probably what Elizabeth Barrett Browning thought, too, before she died.

HOMEWORK

Algebra: problems at the end of Chapter 10
English: in your journal, list your favorite TV show, movie, book, food, etc.
World Civ: one thousand word essay explaining the conflict between Iran and Afghanistan
G&T: as if
French: écrivez une vignette amusante (Oh, right)
Biology: endocrine system (get answers from Kenny)

God! What are they trying to do over there, anyway? Kill me?

Wednesday, October 22

This morning my mom called my dad where he's staying at the Plaza, and made him bring the limo over so I could go to the doctor. This is because when she took my temperature after I woke up, it was one hundred and two, just like Grandmère's on her wedding day.

Only I can tell you, I didn't feel much like waltzing. I could hardly even get dressed. I was so feverish I actually put on one of the outfits Grandmère bought me. So there I was in Chanel from head to toe, with my eyes all glassy and this sheen of sweat all over me. My dad jumped about a foot and a half when he saw me, I think because he thought for a minute that I *was* Grandmère.

Only of course I am much taller than Grandmère. Though my hair isn't as big.

It turns out that Dr. Fung is one of the few people in America who hadn't heard yet that I'm a princess, so we had to sit in the waiting room for like ten minutes before he could see me. My dad spent the ten minutes talking to the receptionist. That's because she was wearing an outfit that showed her navel, even though it is practically winter.

And even though my dad is completely bald and wears suits all the time instead of khakis like a normal dad, you could tell the receptionist was completely into him. That's because in spite of his incipient European-ness, my dad is still something of a hottie.

Lars, who is also a hottie in a different sort of way (being extremely large and hairy), sat next to me, reading *Parenting* magazine. I could tell he would have preferred the latest

41

copy of *Soldier of Fortune*, but they don't have a subscription to that at the SoHo Family Medical Practice.

Finally Dr. Fung saw me. He took my temperature (101.7) and felt my glands to see if they were swollen (they were). Then he tried to take a throat culture to check for strep.

Only when he jabbed that thing into my throat, it made me gag so hard, I started coughing uncontrollably. I couldn't stop coughing, so I told him between coughs that I was going to get a drink of water. I think I must have been delusional because of my fever and all, since what I did instead of getting water was walk right out of the doctor's office. I got back into the limo and told the chauffeur to take me to Emerald Planet right away, so I could get a smoothie.

Fortunately the chauffeur knew better than to take me somewhere without my bodyguard. He got on the radio and said some stuff, and then Lars came out to the limo with my dad, who asked me what on earth I thought I was doing.

I thought about asking him the exact same thing, only about the receptionist with the pierced belly button. But my throat hurt too much to talk.

Dr. Fung was pretty nice about it in the end. He gave up on the throat culture and just prescribed some antibiotics and this cough syrup with codeine in it—but not until he had one of his nurses take a picture of us shaking hands together inside the limo so he could hang it on his wall of celebrity photos. He has pictures of himself up there shaking hands with other famous patients of his, like Robert Goulet and Lou Reed.

Now that my raging fever has gone down, I can see that

I was behaving completely irrationally. I would have to say that that trip to the doctor's office was probably one of the most embarrassing moments of my life. Of course, there've been so many, it's hard to tell where this one ranks. I think I would chalk it up there with the time I accidentally dropped my dinner plate in the buffet line at Lilly's bat mitzvah, and everybody kept stepping in gefiltefish for the rest of the night.

MIA THERMOPOLIS'S TOP FIVE
MOST EMBARRASSING MOMENTS

1. Josh Richter kissing me in front of the whole school while everyone looked at me.
2. The time when I was six and Grandmère ordered me to hug her sister, Tante Jean Marie, and I started to cry because I was afraid of Jean Marie's mustache, and hurt Jean Marie's feelings.
3. The time when I was seven and Grandmère forced me to attend a boring cocktail party she gave for all her friends, and I was so bored I picked up this little ivory coaster holder which was shaped like a rickshaw, and then I wheeled it around the coffee table, making noises like I was speaking Chinese, until all the coasters fell out the back of the rickshaw and rolled around on the floor very noisily, and everyone looked at me. (This is even more embarrassing when I think of it now, because imitating Chinese people is very rude, not to mention politically incorrect.)
4. The time when I was ten and Grandmère took me

and some of my cousins to the beach and I forgot my bikini top and Grandmère wouldn't let me go back to the chateau to get it, she said this was France for God's sake and I should just go topless like everybody else, and even though I didn't have anything more up there to show than I do now, I was mortified and wouldn't take my shirt off and everyone looked at me because they thought I had a rash or disfiguring birthmark or a shriveled-up Siamese-twin fetus hanging off me.

5. The time when I was twelve and I got my first period, and I was at Grandmère's house and I had to tell her about it because I didn't have any pads or anything, and later that night as I walked in for dinner I overheard Grandmère telling all her friends about it, and then for the rest of the night all they did was make jokes about the wonder of womanhood.

Now that I think about it, almost all of the most embarrassing moments of my life have something to do with Grandmère.

I wonder what Lilly's parents, who are both psychoanalysts, would have to say about this.

TEMPERATURE CHART

5:20 p.m.—99.3
6:45 p.m.—99.2
7:52 p.m.—99.1

Is it possible I am getting better *already*? This is horrible. If I get better, I'll have to go on that stupid interview. . . .

This calls for drastic measures: Tonight I fully intend to take a shower and stick my head out the window with my hair wet.

That will show them.

Thursday, October 23

Oh, my God. Something so exciting just happened, I can hardly write.

This morning as I was lying in my sickbed, my mom handed me a letter that she said had come in the mail yesterday, only she forgot to give it to me.

This wasn't like the electricity or cable bills my mom usually forgets about after they have arrived. This was a personal letter to me.

Still, since the address on the front of it was typed, I didn't suspect anything out of the ordinary. I thought it was a letter from school, or something. Like maybe I'd made honor roll (HA HA). Except that there was no return address, and usually mail from Albert Einstein High School has Albert's thoughtful face in the left-hand corner, along with the school's address.

So you can imagine my surprise when I opened the letter and found not a flier asking me to show my school spirit by making rice krispy treats to help raise money for the crew team but the following . . . which, for want of a better word, I can only call a love letter:

Dear Mia (the letter went)
I know you will think it's strange, receiving a letter like this. I feel strange writing it. And yet I am too shy to tell you face-to-face what I'm about to tell you now: And that's that I think you are the Josiest girl I've ever met.

I just want to make sure you know that there's one

person, anyway, who liked you long before he found out
you were a princess . . .
And will keep on liking you, no matter what.

Sincerely,
A Friend

Oh, my God!

I couldn't believe it! I'd never gotten a letter like this before. Who could it be from? I seriously couldn't figure it out. The letter was typed, like the address on the envelope. Not by a typewriter, either, but obviously on a computer.

So even if I wanted to compare keystrokes, say, on a suspect's typewriter (like Jan did on *The Brady Bunch* when she suspected Alice of sending her that locket), I couldn't. You can't compare the type on laser printers, for God's sake. It's always the same.

But who could have sent me such a thing?

Of course, I know who I *want* to have sent it.

But the chances of a guy like Michael Moscovitz ever actually liking me as more than just a friend are like zero. I mean, if he liked me, he had a perfect opportunity to say something about it the night of the Cultural Diversity dance, when he was so nice to step in and ask me to dance, after Josh Richter dogged me so hard. And we didn't just dance once, either. We danced a few times. Slow dances, too. And after the dance, we hung out in his room at the Moscovitzes' apartment. He could have said something then, if he'd wanted to.

But he didn't. He didn't say a thing about liking me.

And why would he? I mean, I am a complete freak, what with my noticeable lack of mammary glands, my gigantism,

47

and my utter inability ever to mold my hair into something remotely resembling a style.

We just got through studying people like me in Bio, as a matter of fact. Biological sports, we are called. A biological sport occurs when an organism shows a marked change from the normal type or parent stock, typically as a result of mutation.

That is me. That is so totally me. I mean, if you looked at me, and then you looked at my parents, who are both very attractive people, you would be all, What *happened*?

Seriously. I should go live with the X-men, I am such a mutant.

Besides, is Michael Moscovitz really the type of guy who'd say I was the *Josiest* girl in school? I mean, I am assuming the author is referring to Josie, the lead singer of Josie and the Pussycats, played by Rachael Leigh Cook in the movie. Except that in no way do I resemble Rachael Leigh Cook. I wish. *Josie and the Pussycats* started out as a cartoon about a girl band that solves crimes, like on *Scooby Doo*, and Michael doesn't even watch the Cartoon Network, as far as I know.

Michael generally only watches PBS, the Sci Fi Channel, and *Buffy the Vampire Slayer*. Maybe if the letter had said *I think you are the* Buffiest *girl I've ever met.* . . .

But if it isn't from Michael, who could it be from?

This is all so exciting, I want to call someone and tell them. Only who? Everyone I know is in school.

WHY DID I HAVE TO GET SICK????

Forget sticking my wet head out the window. I have to get better right away so I can go back to school and figure out who my secret admirer is!

TEMPERATURE CHART:
10:45 a.m.—99.2
11:15 a.m.—99.1
12:27 p.m.—98.6

Yes! YES! I am getting better! Thank you, Selman Waksman, inventor of the antibiotic.

2:05 p.m.—99.0

No. Oh, no.

3:35 p.m.—99.1

Why is this happening to me?

This afternoon while I was lying around with icepacks under the covers, trying to bring my fever down so I can go to school tomorrow and find out who my secret admirer is, I happened to see the best episode of *Baywatch* ever.

Really.

See, Mitch met this girl with this very fake French accent during a boat race, and they totally fell in love and ran around in the waves to this excellent soundtrack, and then it turned out the girl was engaged to Mitch's opponent in the boat race—and not only that—she was actually the *princess of this small European country Mitch had never heard of.* Her fiancé was this prince her father had betrothed her to at birth!

While I was watching this, Lilly came over with my new homework assignments, and she started watching with me, and she totally missed the deep philosophical importance of the episode. All she said was, "Boy, does that royal chick need an eyebrow waxing."

I was appalled.

"Lilly," I croaked. "Can't you see that this episode of *Baywatch* is prophetic? It is entirely possible that I have been betrothed since birth to some prince I've never even met, and my dad just hasn't told me yet. And I could very likely meet some lifeguard on a beach and fall madly in love with him, but it won't matter, because I will have to do my duty and marry the man my people have picked out for me."

Lilly said, "Hello, exactly how much of that cough medicine have you had today? It says one *tea*spoon every four hours, not *table*spoon, dorkus."

I was annoyed at Lilly for failing to see the bigger picture. I couldn't, of course, tell her about the letter I'd gotten. Because what if her brother was the one who wrote it? I wouldn't want him thinking I'd gone blabbing about it to everyone I knew. A love letter is a very private thing.

But still, you would think she'd be able to see it from my perspective.

"Don't you understand?" I rasped. "What is the point of me liking anybody, when it's entirely possible that my dad has arranged a marriage for me with some prince I've never met? Some guy who lives in, like, Dubai, or somewhere, and who gazes daily at my picture and longs for the day when he can finally make me his own?"

Lilly said she thought I'd been reading too many of my friend Tina Hakim Baba's teen romances. I will admit, that is sort of where I got the idea. But that is not the point.

"Seriously, Lilly," I said. "I have to guard diligently against falling in love with somebody like David Hasselhoff or your brother, because in the end I might have to marry Prince William." Not that that would be such a great sacrifice, and all.

Lilly got up off my bed and stomped out into the loft's living room. My dad was the only one around, because when he'd come over to check on me, my mom had suddenly remembered an errand she had to get done and dashed off.

Only of course there was no errand. My mom still hasn't told my dad about Mr. G and her pregnancy, and how they're getting married, and all. I think she's afraid that he might start yelling at her for being so irresponsible (which I could totally see him doing).

So instead she flees from Dad in guilt every time she sees him. It would almost be funny, if it wasn't such a pathetic way for a thirty-six-year-old woman to behave. When I am thirty-six, I fully intend to be self-actualized, so you will not catch me doing any of the things my mother is always doing.

"Mr. Renaldo," I heard Lilly say, as she went out into the living room. She calls my dad Mr. Renaldo even though she knows perfectly well he is the prince of Genovia. She doesn't care though, because she says this is America and she isn't calling anybody "Your Highness." She is fundamentally opposed to monarchies—and principalities, like Genovia, fall under that heading. Lilly believes that sovereignty rests with the people. In colonial times, she'd probably have been branded a Whig.

"Mr. Renaldo," I heard her ask my dad. "Is Mia secretly betrothed to some prince somewhere?"

My dad lowered his newspaper. I could hear it crinkling all the way from my bedroom. "Good God, no," he said.

"Moron," she said to me, when she came stomping back into my room. "And while I can see why you might want to guard diligently against falling in love with David Hasselhoff, who is, by the way, old enough to be your father, and hardly a hottie, what does my *brother* have to do with any of this?"

Too late, I realized what I'd said. Lilly has no idea how I feel about her brother Michael. Actually, *I* don't really have any idea about how I feel about him either. Except that he looks extremely Casper Van Dien with his shirt off.

I *so* want him to be the one who'd written that letter. I really, really do.

But I'm not about to mention this to his sister.

Instead, I told her I think it unfair of her to demand explanations for stuff I said under the influence of codeine cough syrup.

Lilly just got that expression she gets sometimes when teachers ask a question and she knows the answer, only she wants to give someone else in the class a chance to answer for a change.

It really can be exhausting sometimes, having a best friend with an IQ of 170.

HOMEWORK

Algebra: problems 1–20, pg. 115
English: Chapter 4 of Strunk and White
World Civ: two-hundred–word essay on the conflict between India and Pakistan
G&T: Yeah, right
French: Chaptre huit
Biology: pituitary gland (ask Kenny!)

LILLY MOSCOVITZ AND MIA THERMOPOLIS'S
LIST OF CELEBRITIES AND THEIR BREASTS

CELEBRITY	LILLY	MIA
Britney Spears	Fake	Real
Lindsay Lohan	Fake	Real
Angelina Jolie	Fake	Real
Gwen Stefani	Fake	Fake
Jennifer Aniston	Fake	Real
Paris Hilton	Fake	Fake
Beyoncé	Fake	Real
Scarlett Johansson	Fake	Real
Sarah Michelle Gellar	Real	Real
Christina Aguilera	Fake	Real
Sienna Miller	Real	Real
Ashlee Simpson	Fake	Real
Mariah Carey	Fake	Fake

After dinner I felt well enough to get out of bed, and so I did.

I checked my e-mail. I was hoping there might be something from my mysterious "friend." If he knew my "snail mail" address, I figured he'd know my e-mail address, too. Both are listed in the school directory.

Tina Hakim Baba was one of the people who e-mailed me. She sent get-well wishes. So did Shameeka. Shameeka mentioned that she was trying to talk her father into letting her have a Halloween party, and that if she succeeded, would I come? I wrote back to say of course, if I wasn't too weak from coughing.

There was also a message from Michael. It was a get-well message, too, but it was animated, like a little film. It showed a cat that looked a lot like Fat Louie doing a little get-well dance. It was very cute. Michael signed it "Love, Michael."

Not Sincerely.

Not Yours Truly.

Love.

I played it four times, but I still couldn't tell whether he was the one who'd sent me that letter. The letter, I noticed, never once mentioned the word *love*. It said the sender *liked* me. And he signed it "sincerely."

But there was no love. Not a hint of love.

Then I saw a message from someone whose e-mail address I didn't recognize. Oh, my God! Could it be my anonymous liker? My fingers were trembling on my mouse. . . .

And then I opened it and saw the following message from JoCrox:

JoCrox: Just a note to say hope you are feeling better. Missed you in school today! Did you get my letter? Hope it made you feel at least a little better, knowing there's someone out there who thinks you rock. Get well soon.
Your Friend

Oh, my God! It's *him*! My anonymous admirer!

But who is Jo Crox? I don't know anyone named Jo Crox. He says he missed me in school today, which means we might be in a class together. But there are no Jo's in any of my classes.

Maybe Jo Crox isn't really his name. In fact, Jo Crox doesn't sound like a name at all. Maybe that actually stands for Joc Rox.

But I don't know any jocks, either. I mean, not personally.

Oh, no, wait, I get it:

Jo-C-rox.

Josie Rocks! Oh, my God! Josie from *Josie and the Pussycats*!

That is just so *cute*.

But who? *Who is it*?

I figured there was only one way to find out, so I wrote back right away:

FtLouie: Dear Friend, I got your letter. Thank you very much. Thanks also for the get-well wishes.

56

WHO ARE YOU? (I swear I won't tell anyone.)
Mia

I sat around for half an hour, hoping he would write back, but he never did.

WHO IS IT??? WHO IS IT??

I have GOT to get well by tomorrow so I can go to school and figure out who Jo-C-rox is. Otherwise, I will go mental, just like Mel Gibson's girlfriend in *Hamlet*, and I'll end up floating in my Lanz of Salzburg nightie in the Hudson with the rest of the medical waste.

I AM BETTER!!!!!

Well, actually, I don't feel all that great, but I don't care. I don't have a temperature, so my mother had no choice but to let me go to school. There was no way I was going to lie in bed another day. Not with Jo-C-rox out there somewhere, possibly loving me.

But so far, nothing. I mean, we swung by Lilly's in the limo and picked her up, as usual, and Michael was with her and all, but by the casual way he said hello to me you would hardly have known that he'd ever sent me a get-well e-mail signed "Love, Michael," let alone ever called me the Josiest girl he's ever met. It is so very clear that he isn't Jo-C-rox.

And that *Love* at the end of his e-mail was just a platonic *Love*. I mean, Michael's *Love* obviously didn't mean he actually *loves* me.

Not that I ever thought he did. Or might. Love me, I mean.

He did walk me to my locker, though. This was extremely nice of him. Granted, we were in the middle of a heated discussion about Tuesday's episode of *Buffy the Vampire Slayer*, but still, no boy has ever walked me to my locker before. Boris Pelkowski meets Lilly at the front doors to the school and walks her to her locker *every single morning*, and has done so ever since the day she agreed to be his girlfriend.

Okay, I admit that Boris Pelkowski is a mouth-breather who continues to tuck his sweaters into his pants despite my frequent hints that in America, this is considered a *Glamour*

"Don't." But still, he is a boy. And it is always cool to have a boy—even one who wears a retainer—walk you to your locker. I know I have Lars, but it's different having your *bodyguard* walk you to your locker, as opposed to an actual *boy*.

I just noticed that Lana Weinberger has purchased all new notebook binders. I guess she threw away the old ones. She had written "Mrs. Josh Richter" all over them, then crossed it out when she and Josh broke up. They are back together now. I guess she's willing once again to have her identity obfuscated by taking her "husband's" name, since she's already got three *I Love Josh*es and seven *Mrs. Josh Richter*s on her Algebra notebook alone.

Before class started, Lana was telling everyone who would listen about some party she is going to tonight. None of us are invited, of course. It's a party given by one of Josh's friends.

I never get invited to parties like that. You know, like the ones in movies about teenagers, where somebody's parents go out of town, so everybody in the school comes over with kegs of beer and trashes the house?

I do not actually know anybody who lives in a house. Just apartment buildings. And if you start trashing an apartment, you can bet the people next door will call the doorman to complain. That could get you in major trouble with the co-op board.

I don't suppose Lana has ever considered these things, however.

The 3rd power of *x* is called cube of *x*
The 2nd power of *x* is squared

Ode to the View from the
Window in My Algebra Class

Sun-warmed concrete benches
next to tables with built-in checkerboards
and the graffiti left by hundreds
before us in
Day-Glo spray paint:

Joanne Loves Richie
Punx Rule
Nuke Fags and Lesbos
And
Amber Is a Slut.

The dead leaves and plastic bags scatter
in the breeze from the park
and men in business suits try to keep the
last few remaining strands of hair covering
their pink bald spots.
Cigarette packets and used-up chewing gum
coat the gray sidewalk.

And I think
What does it matter
that it is not a linear equation if any variable is raised to
a power?
We're all just going to die anyway.

LIST FIVE BASIC TYPES OF GOVERNMENT

anarchy
monarchy
aristocracy
dictatorship
oligarchy
democracy

LIST FIVE PEOPLE WHO COULD CONCEIVABLY BE JO-C-ROX

Michael Moscovitz (I wish)
Boris Pelkowski (please no)
Mr. Gianini (in a misguided attempt to cheer me up)
My dad (ditto)
That weird boy I see sometimes in the cafeteria who gets so upset whenever they serve chili and there's corn in it (please please no)

AAAAARRRRRGGGGGGGHHHHHH!!!!!!!!!!!!

It turns out that since I've been gone, Boris has started learning some new music on his violin. Right now he is playing a concerto by someone named Bartok.

And let me tell you, that's exactly how it sounds. Even though we locked him and his violin into the supply closet, it isn't doing any good. You can't even hear yourself think. Michael had to go to the nurse's office for ibuprofen.

But before he left, I tried to steer the conversation in the direction of mail. You know, casually, and all.

Just in case.

Anyway, Lilly was talking about her show, *Lilly Tells It Like It Is*, and I asked her if she's still getting a lot of fan mail—one of her biggest fans, her stalker Norman, sends her free stuff all the time, with the understanding that he wants her to show her bare feet on the air: Norman is a foot fetishist.

Then I mentioned that I'd received some *intriguing* mail lately. . . .

Then I looked at Michael real fast, to see how he responded.

But he didn't even glance up from his laptop.

And now he is back from the nurse's office. She wouldn't give him any ibuprofen because it is a violation of the school drug code. So I gave him some of my codeine cough syrup. He says it cleared his headache right up.

But that might also have been because Boris knocked over a can of paint thinner with his bow and we had to let him out of the supply closet.

HERE IS WHAT I HAVE TO DO

1. Stop thinking so much about Jo-C-rox
2. Ditto Michael Moscovitz
3. Ditto my mother and her reproductive issues
4. Ditto my interview tomorrow with Beverly Bellerieve
5. Ditto Grandmère
6. Have more self-confidence
7. Stop biting off fake fingernails
8. Self-actualize
9. Pay more attention in Algebra
10. Wash PE shorts

Talk about embarrassing! Principal Gupta somehow found out about my giving Michael some of my codeine cough syrup, and I got called out of Bio and sent to her office to discuss my trafficking of controlled substances on school grounds!

Oh, my God! I really and truly thought I was going to get expelled then and there.

I explained to her about the ibuprofen and the Bartok, but Principal Gupta was totally unsympathetic. Even when I brought up all the kids who stand outside the school and smoke. Do they get in trouble for bumming cigarettes off one another?

And what about the cheerleaders and their Dexatrim?

But Principal Gupta said cigarettes and Dexatrim are different from narcotics. She took my codeine cough syrup away and told me I could have it back after school. She also told me not to bring it to school on Monday.

She doesn't have to worry. I was so embarrassed about the whole thing, I am seriously considering never coming back to school at all, let alone on Monday.

I don't see why I can't be home-schooled, like the boys from Hanson. Look how they turned out.

HOMEWORK

Algebra: problems on pg. 129
English: describe an experience that moved you profoundly
World Civ: two hundred words on the rise of the Taliban in Afghanistan
G&T: *Please*
French: devoirs—les notes grammaticals: 141–143
Biology: central nervous system

My Favorite Things

FOOD

Vegetarian lasagna

MOVIE

My favorite movie of all time is one I first saw on HBO when I was twelve. It has remained my favorite movie in spite of my friends' and family's efforts to introduce me to so-called finer examples of cinematic art. Quite frankly, I think that *Dirty Dancing*, starring Patrick Swayze and a pre–nose-job Jennifer Grey, has everything films like *Breathless* and *September*, created by supposed "auteurs" of the medium, lack. For instance, *Dirty Dancing* takes place at a summer resort. Movies that take place in resorts (other good examples include *Cocktail* and *Aspen Extreme*) are just plain better, I've noticed, than other movies. Also, *Dirty Dancing* has dancing. Dancing in movies is always good. Think how much better Oscar Award–winning films, like *The English Patient*, would be if they had dancing in them. I am always so much less bored at the movies when there are people dancing on the screen. So all I have to say to the many, many people who disagree with me about *Dirty Dancing* is: "Nobody puts Baby in the corner."

TV SHOW

My favorite TV show is *Baywatch*. I know people think it is very lame and sexist, but actually it isn't. The boys are as scantily clad as the girls, and in the later episodes at least, a woman is in charge of the whole life-guarding operation. And the truth of the matter is, whenever I watch this show, I feel happy. That is because I know whatever jam Hobie gets into, whether it is giant electric eels or emerald smugglers, Mitch will get him out of it, and everything will be done to an excellent soundtrack, and with stunning shots of the ocean. I wish there was a Mitch in my life to make everything all right at the end of the day.

Also that my breasts were as big as Carmen Electra's.

BOOK

My favorite book is called *IQ 83*. It is by the best-selling author of *The Swarm*, Arthur Herzog. *IQ 83* is about a bunch of doctors who mess around with DNA, and they unwittingly cause an accident that makes everyone in the world lose a bunch of IQ points and start acting dumb. Seriously! Even the president of the United States. He ends up drooling like an idiot! And it's up to Dr. James Healey to save the country from being populated by a bunch of overweight morons who do nothing but watch Jerry Springer and eat Ho Hos all day. This book has never gotten the attention it should receive. It hasn't even been made into a movie!

This is a literary travesty.

What am I supposed to do about this stupid English journal assignment, *Describe an experience that moved you profoundly?* I am so sure. What do I write about? The time I walked into the kitchen and found my Algebra teacher standing there in his underwear? That didn't move me, exactly, but it was certainly an experience.

Or should I talk about the time my dad spilled his guts about how it turns out I am the heir to the throne of the principality of Genovia? That was an experience, although I don't know if it was profound, and even though I was crying, I don't think it was because I was moved. I was just mad nobody had told me before. I mean, I guess I can understand that it might be embarrassing for him to have to admit to the Genovian people that he had a child out of wedlock, but to hide that fact for fourteen years? Talk about denial.

My Bio partner Kenny, who also has Mrs. Spears for English, says he is going to write about his family's trip to India last summer. He contracted cholera there, and nearly died. As he lay in his hospital bed in that far-off foreign land, he realized that we are only on this planet for a short while, and that it is vital we use every moment we have left as if it were our last. That is why Kenny is devoting his life to finding a cure for cancer, and promoting Japanese anime.

Kenny is so lucky. If only I could contract a potentially fatal disease.

I am beginning to realize that the only thing profound about my life so far is its complete and utter lack of profundity.

Jefferson Market
The freshest produce—guaranteed
Fast, Free Delivery

Order no. 2764

1 package soybean curd
1 bottle wheat germ
1 loaf whole-grain bread
5 grapefruits
12 oranges
1 bunch bananas
1 package brewer's yeast
1 quart skim milk
1 quart orange juice (not from concentrate)
1 pound butter
1 dozen eggs
1 bag unsalted sunflower seeds
1 box whole-grain cereal
Toilet paper
Q-tips

Deliver to:
Mia Thermopolis, 1005 Thompson Street, #4A

I am sitting here waiting for my interview. In addition to my throat hurting, I feel like I am going to throw up. Maybe my bronchitis has turned into the flu, or something. Maybe the falafel I ordered in for dinner last night was made from rotten chickpeas, or something.

Or maybe I'm just totally nervous, since this interview is going to be broadcast to an estimated 22 million homes on Monday night.

Although I find it very hard to believe that 22 million families could possibly be interested in anything *I* have to say.

I read that when Prince William gets interviewed, he gets the questions about a week before, so he has time to think up really smart and incisive answers. Apparently, members of the Genovian royal family are not extended that same courtesy. Not that even with a week's worth of notice I could ever think of anything smart and incisive. Well, okay, maybe smart, but definitely not incisive.

Well, probably not even smart, either, depending on what they ask.

So I am sitting here and I really do feel like I am going to throw up, and I wish I could hurry up and get this over with. It was supposed to start two hours ago.

But Grandmère isn't satisfied with the way the cosmetic technician (makeup lady) did my eyes. She says I look like a *poulet*. That means "hooker" in French. Or chicken. But when my Grandmère says it, it always means hooker.

Why can't I have a nice, normal grandma, who makes

rugelach and thinks I look wonderful no matter what I have on? Lilly's grandma has never said the word *hooker* in her life, even in Yiddish. I know that for a fact.

So the makeup lady had to go down to the hotel gift shop to see if they have any blue eyeshadow. Grandmère wants blue, because she says it matches my eyes. Except that my eyes are gray. I wonder if Grandmère is color-blind.

That would explain a lot.

I met Beverly Bellerieve. The one good thing about all this is that she actually seems semi-human. She told me that if she asked anything that I felt was too personal or embarrassing, that I could just say I don't want to answer. Isn't that nice?

Plus she is very beautiful. You should see my dad. I can already tell that Beverly is going to be this week's girlfriend. Well, she's better than the women he usually hangs around with. At least Beverly looks as if she probably isn't wearing a thong. And as if her brainstem is fully functional.

So, considering that Beverly Bellerieve turns out to be so nice and all, you'd think I wouldn't be so nervous.

And truthfully, I'm not so sure it's just the interview that's making me feel like I'm going to hurl. It's actually something my dad said to me, when I came in. It was the first time I'd seen him since the time he spent at the loft while I was sick. Anyway, he asked me how I was feeling and all, and I lied and said fine, and then he said, "Mia, is your Algebra teacher—"

And I was all, "Is my Algebra teacher what?" thinking he was going to ask me if Mr. Gianini was teaching me about parallel numbers.

But that is so totally NOT what he asked me. Instead, he asked me, "Is your Algebra teacher living in the loft?"

Well, I was so shocked, I didn't know what to say. Because of course Mr. Gianini isn't living there. Not really.

But he will be. And probably pretty shortly, too.

So I just went, "Um, no."

And my dad looked relieved! He actually looked relieved!

So how is he going to look when he finds out the *truth*?

It is very hard to concentrate on the fact that I am about to be interviewed by this world-renowned television news journalist, when all I can think about is how my poor dad is going to feel when he finds out my mother is marrying my Algebra teacher and also having his baby. Not that I think my dad still loves my mom, or anything. It's just that, as Lilly once pointed out, his chronic bed-hopping is a clear indication that he has some serious intimacy issues.

And with Grandmère as a mother, you can see why that might be.

I think he really would like to have what my mom has with Mr. Gianini. Who knows how he is going to take the news about their impending marriage, when my mom finally works up the guts to tell him? He might completely freak out. He might even want me to come live with him in Genovia, to comfort him in his grief!

And of course I will have to say yes, because he is my dad and I love him, and all.

Except that I really don't want to live in Genovia. I mean, I would miss Lilly and Tina Hakim Baba and all my other friends. And what about Jo-C-rox? How would I ever find out who he is? And what about Fat Louie? Would I get to keep him, or what? He is very well behaved (except when it comes to ingesting socks, and that whole thing with the sparkly objects) and if there was a rodent problem in the castle, he would totally solve it. But what if they don't let cats in the palace? I mean, he hasn't had his claws removed, so if there's any sort of valuable furniture or tapestries or whatever, you can pretty much kiss them good-bye. . . .

Mr. G and my mom are already talking about where his stuff is going to go when he moves into the loft. And Mr. G has some really cool-sounding stuff. Like a foozball table, a drum set (who knew Mr. Gianini was *musical*?), a pinball machine, AND a 36-inch flat-screen TV.

I am not even kidding. He is *way* cooler than I ever thought.

If I move to Genovia, I will totally miss out on having my own foozball table.

But if I don't move to Genovia, who will comfort my poor dad in his chronic loneliness?

Oops, the cosmetic technician is back with the blue eyeshadow.

I swear I am going to heave. Good thing I was too nervous to eat anything all day.

Oh, God, oh, God, oh, God, oh, God, oh, God, OH, GOD.

I screwed up. I REALLY screwed up.

I don't know what happened. I honestly don't. Everything was going along fine. I mean, that Beverly Bellerieve, she's so . . . *nice*. I was really, really nervous, and she did her very best to try to calm me down.

Still, I think I did some major babbling.

Think??? I KNOW I did.

I didn't mean for it to happen. I really didn't. I don't even know how it slipped out. I was just so nervous and hyper, and there were those lights and that microphone and everything. I felt like . . . I don't know. Like I was back in Principal Gupta's office, living through that whole codeine cough-syrup thing again.

So when Beverly Bellerieve said, "Mia, didn't you have some exciting news recently?" I totally freaked out. Part of me was like, How did she know? And another part of me was like, Millions of people are going to see this. Act happy.

So I went, "Oh. Yes. Well, I'm pretty excited. I've always wanted to be a big sister. But they don't really want to make a big deal out of it, you know. It's just going to be a very small ceremony at City Hall, with me as their witness—"

That's when my dad dropped the glass of Perrier he'd been drinking. Then Grandmère started hyperventilating and had to breathe into a paper bag.

And I sat there going, Oh, my God. Oh, my God, what have I done?

Of course it turned out that Beverly Bellerieve hadn't been referring to my mother's pregnancy at all. Of course not. How could she have known about it?

What she'd actually been referring to, of course, was my F in Algebra being raised to a D.

I tried to get up and go to my dad to comfort him, since I could see he'd sunk into a chair and had his head in his hands. But I was all tangled up in my microphone wires. It had taken about half an hour for the sound guys to get the wires right, and I didn't want to mess them up or anything, but I could see that my dad's shoulders were shaking, and I was sure he was crying, just like he always does at the end of *Free Willy*, though he tries to pretend it's just allergies.

Beverly, seeing this, made a slashing motion with her hand to the camera guys, and very nicely helped me get untangled.

But when I finally got to my dad, I saw he wasn't crying. . . . But he certainly didn't look too good. He didn't sound very good, either, when he croaked for someone to bring him a whiskey.

After three or four gulps, though, he got a little of his color back. Which is more than I can say for Grandmère. I don't think she will ever recover. Last time I saw her, she was downing a Sidecar that someone had dropped some Alka-Seltzer tablets into.

I don't even want to think about what my mom is going to say when she finds out what I've done. I mean, even though my dad said not to worry, that he'll explain to Mom what happened, I don't know. He had kind of a weird look on his face. I hope he doesn't plan on popping Mr. G one in the piehole.

Me and my big mouth. My HUGE, GROTESQUE, DISPROPORTIONATELY MASSIVE mouth.

There's no telling what else I said, once the interview got underway again. I was so completely freaked out by that first thing, I can't remember a single other thing Beverly Bellerieve might have asked me.

My dad has assured me that he's not the least bit jealous of Mr. Gianini, that he is very happy for my mother, and that he thinks she and Mr. G make a great couple. I think he means it. He seemed pretty unfazed, after the initial shock. Once the interview was over, I noticed that he and Beverly Bellerieve were yukking it up quite a bit.

All I can say is, thank goodness I am going straight from the hotel to Lilly's. She is having us all over to film next week's episode of her show. I think I'll see if I can spend the night. Maybe this way, by the time my mom sees me tomorrow, she'll have had time to process the whole thing, and will have forgiven me.

I hope.

Okay, I just have one question: Why does it always have to go from bad to worse for me?

I mean, apparently it is not enough that

1. I was born lacking any sort of mammary growth gland
2. My feet are as long as a normal person's thigh
3. I'm the sole heir to the throne of a European principality
4. My grade point average is still slipping in spite of everything
5. I have a secret admirer who will not declare himself
6. My mother is pregnant with my Algebra teacher's baby, and
7. All of America is going to know it after Monday night's broadcast of my exclusive interview on *Twenty-Four/Seven*

No, in addition to all of that, I happen to be the only one of my friends who still has yet to be French-kissed.

Seriously. For next week's show, Lilly insisted on shooting what she calls a Scorsesian confessional, in which she hopes to illustrate the degenerate lows to which today's youth have sunk. So she made us all confess to the camera our worst sins, and it turns out Shameeka, Tina Hakim Baba, Ling Su, and Lilly have ALL had boys' tongues in their mouths. *All of them.*

Except for me.

Okay, I'm not so surprised about Shameeka. Ever since she grew breasts over the summer, boys have been buzzing around her like she was the newest version of Tomb Raider, or something. And Ling Su and that Clifford guy she has been seeing are way into each other.

But Tina? I mean, she has a bodyguard, just like me. When has *she* ever been alone long enough with a boy for him to French her?

And Lilly? Excuse me, but Lilly, MY BEST FRIEND? Who I thought tells me everything (even though I don't necessarily always return the favor)? She has known the touch of a boy's tongue upon her own, and she never thought to tell me until NOW?

Boris Pelkowski is apparently a much smoother operator than you would suspect, considering that whole sweater thing.

I am sorry, but that is just sick. Sick, sick, sick, sick. I would rather die a dried-up, never-been-kissed old maid than be French-kissed by Boris Pelkowski. I mean, he always has FOOD in his retainer. And not just any food, either, but usually weird, multicolored foods like Gummi Bears and Jelly Bellies.

Lilly says he takes his retainer out when they kiss, though.

God, I am such a reject. The only boy who has ever kissed me did it just so he could get his picture in the paper.

Yeah, there was some tongue action, but believe me, I kept my lips way closed.

And since I have never been French-kissed, and had nothing good to confess on the show, Lilly decided to punish me by giving me a Dare. She didn't even ask me if I would prefer a Truth.

Lilly dared me I wouldn't drop an eggplant onto the sidewalk from her sixteenth-story bedroom window.

I said I most certainly would, even though of course, I totally didn't want to. I mean, how stupid. Somebody could seriously get hurt. I am all for illustrating the degenerate lows to which America's teens have sunk, but I wouldn't want anybody to get their head bashed in.

But what could I do? It was a Dare. I had to go along with it. I mean, it's bad enough I've never been Frenched. I don't want to be branded a wimp, too.

And I couldn't exactly stand there and go, well, all right, I may never have been French-kissed by a boy, but I have been the recipient of a love letter that was written by one. A boy, I mean.

Because what if Michael is Jo-C-rox? I mean, I know he probably isn't, but . . . well, what if he is? I don't want Lilly to know—any more than I want her to know about my inter-view with Beverly Bellerieve, or the fact that my mom and Mr. G are getting married. I am trying very hard to be a normal girl, and frankly, none of the aforementioned can be even remotely construed as normal.

I guess the knowledge that somewhere in the world there is a boy who likes me gave me a sense of empowerment—something I certainly could have used during my interview with Beverly Bellerieve, but whatever. I may not be able to form a coherent sentence when there is a television camera aimed in my direction, but I am at least capable, I decided, of throwing an eggplant out the window.

Lilly was shocked. I had never accepted a Dare like that before.

I can't really explain why I did it. Maybe I was just trying to live up to my new reputation as a very Josie-ish type of girl.

Or maybe I was more scared of what Lilly would try to make me do if I said no. Once she made me run up and down the hallway naked. Not the hallway in the Moscovitzes' apartment, either. The hallway *outside* of it.

Whatever my reasons, I soon found myself sneaking past the Drs. Moscovitz—who were lounging around in sweatpants in the living room, with stacks of important medical journals all around their chairs—though Lilly's father was reading a copy of *Sports Illustrated* and Lilly's mom was reading *Cosmo*—and creeping into the kitchen.

"Hello, Mia," Lilly's father called from behind his magazine. "How are you doing?"

"Um," I said, nervously. "Fine."

"And how is your mother?" Lilly's mother asked.

"She's fine," I said.

"Is she still seeing your Algebra teacher in a social capacity?"

"Um, yes, Dr. Moscovitz," I said. More than you know.

"And are you still amenable to the relationship?" Lilly's father wanted to know.

"Um," I said. "Yes, Dr. Moscovitz." I didn't think it would be appropriate to mention the whole thing about how my mom is having Mr. G's baby. I mean, I was supposed to be on a Dare, after all. You aren't supposed to stop for psychoanalysis when you are on a Dare.

"Well, tell her hello from me," Lilly's mother said. "We can't wait until her next show. It's at the Mary Boone Gallery, right?"

"Yes, ma'am," I said. The Moscovitzes are big fans of my mother's work. One of her best paintings, *Woman Enjoying a Quick Snack at Starbucks*, is hanging in their dining room.

"We'll be there," Lilly's father said.

Then he and his wife turned back to their magazines, so I hurried into the kitchen.

I found an eggplant in the vegetable crisper. I hid it under my shirt so the Drs. Moscovitz wouldn't see me sneaking back into their daughter's room holding a giant ovoid fruit, something sure to cause unwanted questions. While I carried it, I thought, *This is how my mother is going to look in a few months.* It wasn't a very comforting thought. I don't think my mother is going to dress any more conservatively while pregnant than she did not pregnant.

Which is to say, not very.

Then, while Lilly narrated gravely into the microphone about how Mia Thermopolis was about to strike a blow for good girls everywhere, and Shameeka filmed, I opened the window, made sure no innocent bystanders were below, and then. . . .

"Bomb's away," I said, like in the movies.

It *was* kind of cool seeing this huge purple eggplant—it was the size of a football—tumbling over and over in the air as it fell. There are enough streetlamps on Fifth Avenue, where the Moscovitzes live, for us to see it as it plummeted downward, even though it was night. Down and down the eggplant went, past the windows of all the psychoanalysts and investment bankers (the only people who can afford apartments in Lilly's building) until suddenly—

SPLAT!

The eggplant hit the sidewalk.

Only it didn't just hit the sidewalk. It *exploded* on the sidewalk, sending bits of eggplant flying everywhere— mostly all over an M1 city bus that was driving by at the time, but quite a lot all over a Jaguar that had been idling nearby.

While I was leaning out the window, admiring the splatter pattern the eggplant's pulp had made all over the street and sidewalk, the driver-side door of the Jaguar opened up, and a man got out from behind the wheel, just as the doorman to Lilly's building stepped out from beneath the awning over the front doors, and looked up—

Suddenly, someone threw an arm around my waist and yanked me backward, right off my feet.

"Get down!" Michael hissed, pulling me down to the parquet.

We all ducked. Well, Lilly, Michael, Shameeka, Ling Su, and Tina ducked. I was already on the floor.

Where had Michael come from? I hadn't even known he was home—and I'd asked, believe me, on account of the whole running-down-the-hallway-naked thing. Just in case, and all.

But Lilly had said he was at a lecture on quasars over at Columbia and wouldn't be home for hours.

"Are you guys stupid, or what?" Michael wanted to know. "Don't you know, besides the fact that it's a good way to kill someone, it's also against the law to drop things out a window in New York City?"

"Oh, Michael," Lilly said, disgustedly. "Grow up. It was just a common garden vegetable."

"I'm serious." Michael looked mad. "If anyone saw Mia do that just now, she could be arrested."

"No, she couldn't," Lilly said. "She's a minor."

"She could still go to juvenile court. You'd better not be planning on airing that footage on your show," Michael said.

Oh, my God, Michael was defending my honor! Or at least trying to make sure I didn't end up in juvenile court. It was just so sweet. So . . . well, Jo-C-rox of him.

Lilly went, "I most certainly am."

"Well, you'd better edit out the parts that show Mia's face."

Lilly stuck her chin out. "No way."

"Lilly, everybody knows who Mia is. If you air that segment, it will be all over the news that the princess of Genovia was caught on tape dropping projectiles out the window of her friend's high-rise apartment. Get a clue, will you?"

Michael had let go of my waist, I noticed, with regret.

"Lilly, Michael's right," Tina Hakim Baba said. "We better edit that part out. Mia doesn't need any more publicity than she has already."

And Tina didn't even *know* about the *TwentyFour/Seven* thing.

Lilly got up and stomped back toward the window. She started to lean out—checking, I guess, to see whether the doorman and the owner of the Jaguar were still there—but Michael jerked her back.

"Rule Number One," he said. "If you insist on dropping something out the window, never, ever check to see if anybody is standing down there, looking up. They will see you look out and figure out what apartment you are in. Then you will be blamed for dropping whatever it was. Because no one but the guilty party would be looking out the window under such circumstances."

"Wow, Michael," Shameeka said admiringly. "You sound like you've done this before."

Not only that. He sounded like Dirty Harry.

Which was just how I felt when I dropped that eggplant out the window. Like Dirty Harry.

And it had felt good—but not quite so good as having Michael rush to my defense like that.

Michael said, "Let's just say I used to have a very keen interest in experimenting with the earth's gravitational pull."

Wow. There is so much I don't know about Lilly's brother. Like he used to be a juvenile delinquent!

Could a computer genius-slash-juvenile delinquent ever be interested in a flat-chested princess like myself? He did save my life tonight (well, okay: he saved me from possible community service).

It's not a French kiss, or a slow dance, or even an admission he's the author of that anonymous letter.

But it's a start.

I know what yer thinkin':
Did he fire six shots, or only five?
Frankly, in all the confusion,
I kinda lost track myself.
But you gotta ask yourself one question:

(*beat*)

Do I feel lucky?

(*long pause*)

Well?

(*long pause*)

Do ya, punk?

THINGS TO DO

1. English journal
2. Stop thinking about that stupid letter
3. Ditto Michael Moscovitz
4. Ditto the interview
5. Ditto Mom
6. Change cat litter
7. Drop off laundry
8. Get super to put lock on bathroom door
9. Buy: Dishwashing liquid
   Q-tips
   Canvas stretchers (for Mom)
   That stuff you put on your fingernails that
   makes them taste bad
   Something nice for Mr. Gianini, to say
   welcome to the family
   Something nice for Dad, to say don't worry,
   someday you, too, will find true love

I was really afraid that when I got home my mom was going to be disappointed in me.

Not *yell* at me. My mom is really not a yelling kind of person.

But she does get disappointed in me, like when I do something stupid like not call and tell her where I am if I am out late (which, given my social life, or lack thereof, hardly ever happens).

But I did screw up this time, and big time. It was really, really hard to leave the Moscovitzes' apartment this morning and come home, knowing the potential for disappointment that awaited me there.

Of course, it's always hard to leave Lilly's. Every time I go there, it's like taking a vacation from my real life. Lilly has such a nice, normal family. Well, as normal as two psychoanalysts whose son has his own webzine and whose daughter has her own cable-access television show can be. At the Moscovitzes', the biggest problem is always whose turn is it to walk Pavlov, their sheltie, or whether to order Chinese or Thai take-out.

At my house, the problems always seem to be a little more complicated.

But of course when I finally did work up the courage to come home, my mom was totally happy to see me. She gave me a big hug, and told me not to worry about what had happened at the interview taping. She said Dad had talked to her, and that she completely understood. She even tried to get me to believe that it was *her* fault for not having said anything to him right away.

Which I know isn't true—it's still my fault, me and my idiot mouth—but it was nice to hear, just the same.

So then we had a nice, fun time sitting around planning her and Mr. G's wedding. My mom decided Halloween would be an excellent day to get married, because the idea of marriage is so scary. Since it was going to be at City Hall, that meant I'd probably have to skip school, but that was okay by me!

Since it would be Halloween, my mom decided that instead of a wedding dress, she would go to the courthouse dressed as King Kong. She wants me to dress up as the Empire State Building (God knows I am tall enough). She was trying to convince Mr. G to dress as Fay Ray when the phone rang, and she said it was Lilly, for me.

I was surprised, since I had just left Lilly's, but I figured I must have left my toothbrush there, or something.

But that wasn't why she was calling. That wasn't why she was calling at all—as I found out when she demanded tartly, "What's this I hear about you being interviewed on *TwentyFour/Seven* this week?"

I was stunned. I actually thought Lilly had ESP or something, and had been hiding it from me all these years. I said, "How did you know?"

"Because there are commercials announcing it every five minutes, dorkus."

I switched on the TV. Lilly was right! No matter what station you put it on, there were ads urging viewers to "tune in tomorrow night" to see Beverly Bellerieve's exclusive interview with "America's royal, Princess Mia."

Oh, my God. My life is so over.

"So why didn't you tell me you are going to be on TV?" Lilly wanted to know.

"I don't know," I said, feeling like I was going to throw up all over again. "It just happened yesterday. It's no big deal."

Lilly started yelling so loud I had to hold the phone away from my ear.

"NO BIG DEAL??? You were interviewed by Beverly Bellerieve and it was NO BIG DEAL??? Don't you realize that BEVERLY BELLERIEVE IS ONE OF AMERICA'S MOST POPULAR AND HARDEST-HITTING JOURNALISTS, and that she is my all-time ROLE MODEL and HERO???"

When she finally calmed down enough to let me talk, I tried to explain to Lilly that I had no idea about Beverly's journalistic merits, much less that she was Lilly's all-time role model and hero. She just seemed, I said, like a very nice lady.

By that time, Lilly was totally fed up with me. She said, "The only reason I'm not mad at you is that tomorrow you are going to tell me every single little detail about it."

"I am?"

Then I asked a more important question. "Why should you be mad at me?" I really wanted to know.

"Because you gave me exclusive first rights to interview you," Lilly pointed out. "For *Lilly Tells It Like It Is.*"

I have no memory of this, but I guess it must be true.

Grandmère, I could see from the ads, had been right about the blue eyeshadow. Which was surprising, because she's never been right about much else.

TOP FIVE THINGS GRANDMÈRE HAS BEEN WRONG ABOUT

1. That my dad would settle down when he met the right woman.
2. That Fat Louie would suck out my breath and suffocate me as I slept.
3. That if I didn't attend an all-girls school, I would contract a social disease.
4. That if I got my ears pierced, they would get infected and I would die of blood poisoning.
5. That my figure would fill out by the time I hit my teens.

Sunday, October 26, 8 p.m.

You will not believe what got delivered to our house while I was gone. I was sure it was a mistake, until I saw the following attached. I am going to kill my mother.

Jefferson Market
The freshest produce—guaranteed
Fast, Free Delivery

Order no. 2803

1 package microwave cheese popcorn
1 case Yoo Hoo chocolate drink
1 jar cocktail olives
1 bag Oreos
1 container fudge ripple ice cream
1 package all-beef hot dogs
1 package hot-dog buns
1 package string cheese
1 bag milk chocolate chips
1 bag barbecue potato chips
1 container beer nuts
1 bag Milano cookies
1 jar sweet gherkins
Toilet paper
6-pound ham

Deliver to:
Helen Thermopolis, 1005 Thompson Street, #4A

Hasn't she the slightest idea how adversely all this saturated fat and sodium will affect her unborn child? I can see that Mr. Gianini and I will have to be hypervigilant for the next seven months. I have given everything except the toilet paper to Ronnie, next door. Ronnie says she is going to hand out the junkiest stuff to any trick-or-treaters who might come by. She has to watch her figure since her sex-change operation. Now that she's taking all those estrogen injections, everything goes right to her hips.

Sunday, October 26, 9 p.m.

Another e-mail from Jo-C-rox!
This one went:

JoCrox: Hi, Mia. I just saw the ad for your interview. You
look great.
Sorry I can't tell you who I am. I'm surprised you haven't
guessed by now. Now stop checking your e-mail and get to
work on your Algebra homework. I know how you are about
that. It's one of the things I like best about you.
Your Friend

Okay, this is going to drive me insane. Who could it be?
Who????
I wrote back right away:

FtLouie: WHO ARE YOU???????????????????????????
??
?????????????????????????????????????

I was hoping that would get the point across, but he so
totally did not write back. I was trying to figure out who I
know who knows that I always wait until the last minute to
do my Algebra homework. Unfortunately, though, I think
everyone knows it.

But the person who knows it best of all is Michael. I mean,
doesn't he help me every day with my Algebra homework in
G and T? And he is always chastising me for not putting my
carry-overs in straight enough lines and all of that.

If ONLY Jo-C-rox were Michael Moscovitz. If only, if only, if ONLY.

But I'm sure it isn't. That would simply be too good to be true. And really excellent things like that only happen to girls like Lana Weinberger, never to girls like me. Knowing my luck, it will totally be that weird chili guy. Or some guy who breathes through his mouth, like Boris.

WHY ME?

Unfortunately, it appears that Lilly is not the only one who noticed the ads for tonight's broadcast.

Everybody is talking about it. I mean, EVERYBODY.

And everybody says they are going to watch it.

Which means by tomorrow, everyone will know about my mom and Mr. Gianini.

Not that I care. There is nothing to be ashamed of. Nothing at all. Pregnancy is a beautiful and natural thing.

Still, I wish I could remember more about what Beverly and I talked about. Because I am sure my mom's impending marriage is not all we discussed. And I am totally worried I said other stuff that will come off sounding stupid.

I have decided that I should look more closely into that home-schooling idea, just in case. . . .

Tina Hakim Baba told me that her mother, who was a supermodel in England before she married Mr. Hakim Baba, used to get interviewed all the time. Mrs. Hakim Baba says that as a courtesy the interviewers would send her a copy of the tape before it aired, so if she had any objections, she could straighten them out before the thing was broadcast.

This sounded like a good idea, so at lunch I called my dad in his hotel suite and asked him if he could get Beverly to do that for me.

He said, "Hold on," and asked her. It turns out Beverly was right there! In my dad's hotel room! On a Monday afternoon!

Then, to my utter mortification, Beverly Bellerieve actually got on the phone and said, "What's the matter, Mia?"

I told her I was still pretty nervous about the interview, and was there any chance I could see a copy of it before it aired?

Beverly said a bunch of stuff about how adorable I was and how that wouldn't be necessary. Now that I think about it, I can't remember exactly what she said, but I just got this overwhelming feeling that everything would be just fine.

Beverly is just one of those people who make you feel good about yourself. I don't know how she does it.

No wonder my dad hasn't let her out of his hotel room since Saturday.

Two cars, one going north at 40 mph and one going south at 50 mph, leave town at the same time. In how many hours will they be 360 miles apart?

Why does it matter? I mean, really.

Mrs. Sing, our Biology teacher, says it is physiologically impossible to die of either boredom or embarrassment, but I know that isn't true, because I am experiencing heart failure right now.

That is because after G and T, Michael and Lilly and I were walking down the hall together, since Lilly was going to Psych and I was going to Bio and Michael was going to Calc, which are all right across the hall from one another, and Lana Weinberger walked right up to us—RIGHT UP TO MICHAEL AND ME—and held up two of her fingers and waggled them at us, and went, "Are you two going out?"

I could seriously die right now. I mean, you should have seen Michael's face. It was like his head was about to explode, he turned that red.

And I'm sure I wasn't all that pale myself.

Lilly didn't help by letting out this giant horse laugh and going, "As if!"

Which caused Lana and her cronies to burst out laughing, too.

I don't see what's so funny about it. Those girls obviously haven't seen Michael Moscovitz with his shirt off. Believe me, I have.

I guess because the whole thing was so ridiculous and everything, Michael just kind of ignored it. But I'm telling you, it's getting harder and harder for me not to ask him if he is Jo-C-rox. Like I keep trying to find ways to work *Josie and the Pussycats* into the conversation. I know I shouldn't, but I just can't help it!

97

I don't know how much longer I can stand being the only girl in the ninth grade who doesn't have a boyfriend.

HOMEWORK

Algebra: problems on pg. 135
English: "Make the most of yourself, for that is all there is of you." —Ralph Waldo Emerson
Write feelings about this quote in journal
World Civ: questions at the end of Chapter 9
G&T: N/A
French: plan an itinerary for a make-believe trip to Paris
Biology: Kenny's doing it

Remind Mom to make appointment with licensed geneticist. Could she or Mr. G be a carrier for the genetic mutation Tay-Sachs? It is common in Jews of Eastern European origin and in French Canadians. Are there any French Canadians in our family? FIND OUT!

I never thought I would say this, but I am worried about Grandmère.

I am serious. I think she has officially lost it.

I walked into her hotel suite for my princess lesson today—since I am scheduled to have my official introduction to the Genovian people sometime in December, and Grandmère wants to be sure I don't insult any dignitaries or whatever during it—and guess what Grandmère was doing?

Consulting with the royal Genovian event planner about my mother's wedding.

I am totally serious. Grandmère had the guy flown in. All the way from Genovia! There they sat at the dining table with this huge sheet of paper stretched in front of them, on which were drawn all these circles, and to which Grandmère was attaching these tiny slips of paper. She looked up when I came in and said, in French, "Oh, Amelia. Very nice. Come and sit down. We have much to discuss, you and Vigo and I."

I think my eyes must have been bulging out of my head. I couldn't believe what I was seeing. I was totally hoping what I was seeing was, you know . . . not what I was seeing.

"Grandmère," I said. "What are you *doing*?"

"Isn't it obvious?" Grandmère looked at me with her drawn-on eyebrows raised higher than ever. "Planning a wedding, of course."

I swallowed. This was bad. WAY bad.

"Um," I said. "Whose wedding, Grandmère?"

She looked at me very sarcastically. "Guess," she said.

I swallowed some more. "Uh, Grandmère?" I said. "Can I talk to you a minute? In private?"

But Grandmère just waved her hand and said, "Anything you have to say to me, you can say in front of Vigo. He has been dying to meet you. Vigo, Her Royal Highness, the Princess Amelia Mignonette Grimaldi Renaldo."

She left out the Thermopolis. She always does.

Vigo jumped up from the table and came rushing over to me. He was way shorter than me, about my mom's age, and had on a gray suit. He seemed to share my grandmother's penchant for purple, since he was wearing a lavender shirt in some kind of very shiny material, along with an equally shiny dark purple tie.

"Your Highness," he gushed. "The pleasure is all mine. So delightful finally to meet you." To Grandmère, he said, "You're right, madame, she has the Renaldo nose."

"I told you, did I not?" Grandmère sounded smug. "Uncanny."

"Positively." Vigo made a little picture frame out of his index fingers and thumbs and squinted at me through it.

"Pink," he said, decidedly. "Absolutely pink. I do so love a pink maid of honor. But the other attendants will be in ivory, I think. *So* Diana. But then, Diana was always so *right*."

"It's really nice to meet you," I said to Vigo. "But the thing is, I think my mom and Mr. Gianini were kind of planning on having a private ceremony down at—"

"City Hall." Grandmère rolled her eyes. It is very scary when she does this, because a long time ago, she had black eyeliner tattooed all around her eyelids so she wouldn't have to waste valuable time putting on makeup when she could be, you know, terrorizing someone. "Yes, I heard all about it. It is ridiculous, of course. They will be married in the White and Gold Room at the Plaza, with a reception directly afterward in the Grand Ballroom, as befits the mother of the future regent of Genovia."

"Um," I said. "I really don't think that's what they want."

Grandmère looked incredulous. "Whyever not? Your father is paying for it, of course. And I have been very generous. They are each allowed to invite twenty-five guests."

I looked down at the sheet of paper in front of her. There were way more than fifty slips of paper in front of her.

Grandmère must have noticed the direction of my gaze, since she went, "Well, I, of course, require at least three hundred."

I stared at her. "Three hundred what?"

"Guests, of course."

I could see that I was way out of my depth. I was going to have to call in for reinforcements if I hoped to get anywhere with her.

"Maybe," I said, "I should just give Dad a call and run this by him. . . . "

"Good luck," Grandmère said with a snort. "He went off with that Bellerieve woman, and I haven't heard from him since. If he is not careful, he is going to end up in the same situation as your Algebra teacher over there."

Except it's totally unlikely Dad would be getting anybody pregnant, since the whole reason I was his heir, instead of some legitimately produced offspring, is that he is no longer

101

fertile, due to the massive doses of chemotherapy that cured his testicular cancer. But I suppose Grandmère is still in denial about this, considering what a disappointing heir I've turned out to be.

It was at this point that a strange moaning noise came out from under Grandmère's chair. We both looked down. Rommel, Grandmère's miniature poodle, was cowering in fright at the sight of me.

I know I am hideous and all of that, but really, it's ridiculous how scared that dog is of me. And I love animals!

But even St. Francis of Assisi would have a hard time appreciating Rommel. I mean, first of all, he recently has developed a nervous disorder (if you ask me, it's from living in such close proximity to my grandmother) that made all his fur fall out, so Grandmère dresses him up in little sweaters and coats so he won't catch cold.

Today Rommel had on a mink bolero jacket. I am not even joking. It was dyed lavender to match the one slung across Grandmère's shoulders. It is horrifying enough to see a person wearing fur, but it is a thousand times worse to see an animal wearing another animal's fur.

"Rommel," Grandmère yelled at the dog. "Stop that growling."

Except that Rommel wasn't growling. He was moaning. Moaning with fright. At the sight of me. ME!

How many times in one day must I be humiliated?

"Oh, you stupid dog." Grandmère reached down and picked Rommel up, much to his unhappiness. You could tell her diamond brooches were poking him in the spine (there is no fat on him at all, and since he doesn't have any fur, he is especially sensitive to pointy objects), but even though he wriggled to be free, she wouldn't let go of him.

"Now, Amelia," Grandmère said. "I need your mother and whatever-his-name-is to write their guests' names and addresses down tonight so I can have the invitations messengered tomorrow. I know your mother is going to want to invite some of those more, ahem, free-spirited friends of hers, Mia, but I think it would be better if perhaps if they just stood outside with the reporters and tourists and waved as she climbed in and out of the limo. That way they'll still have a feeling of belonging, but they won't make anyone uncomfortable with their unattractive hairstyles and ill-fitting attire."

"Grandmère," I said. "I really think—"

"And what do you think about this dress?" Grandmère held up a picture of a Vera Wang wedding gown with a big poofy skirt that my mom wouldn't be caught dead in.

Vigo went, "No, no, Your Highness. I really think this is more the thing." Then he held up a photo of a slinky Armani number that my mom similarly wouldn't be caught dead in.

"Uh, Grandmère," I said. "This is all really nice of you, but my mom definitely doesn't want a big wedding. Really. Definitely."

"*Pfuit*," Grandmère said. *Pfuit* is French for "No," duh. "She will when she sees the luscious hors d'œuvres they'll be serving at the reception. Tell her about them, Vigo."

Vigo said with relish: "Truffle-filled mushroom caps, asparagus tips wrapped in salmon slivers, pea pods stuffed with goat cheese, endive with crumbles of blue cheese inside each gently furled leaf. . . ."

I said, "Uh, Grandmère? No, she won't. Believe me."

Grandmère went, "Nonsense. Trust me, Mia, your mother is going to appreciate this someday. Vigo and I will make her wedding day an event she will never forget."

I had no doubt about that.

I said, "Grandmère, Mom and Mr. G were really planning on something very casual and simple—"

But then Grandmère threw me one of those looks of hers—they are really very scary—and said, in this deadly serious voice, "For three years, while your grandfather was off having the time of his life fighting the Germans, I held those Nazis—not to mention Mussolini—at bay. They lobbed mortars at the palace doors. They tried to drive tanks across my moat. And yet I persevered, through sheer willpower alone. Are you telling me, Amelia, that I cannot convince one pregnant woman to see things my way?"

Well, I'm not saying my mom has anything in common with Mussolini or Nazis, but as far as putting up a resistance to Grandmère? I'd place my money on my mom over a fascist foreign dictator any day.

I could see that reasoning wasn't going to be effective in this particular case. So I went along with it, listening to Vigo gush over the menu he had picked out, the music he had selected for the ceremony and later, for the reception—even admiring the portfolio of the photographer he had chosen.

It wasn't until they actually showed me one of the invitations that I realized something.

"The wedding's this Friday?" I squeaked.

"Yes," Grandmère said.

"That's Halloween!" The same day as my mom's courthouse wedding. Also, incidentally, the same night as Shameeka's party.

Grandmère looked bored. "What of it?"

"Well, it's just . . . you know. Halloween."

Vigo looked at my grandmother. "What is this Halloween?" he asked. Then I remembered they don't go in for Halloween much in Genovia.

"A pagan holiday," Grandmère replied, with a shudder. "Children dress up in costumes and demand candy from strangers. Horrible American tradition."

"It's in a *week*," I pointed out.

Grandmère raised her drawn-on eyebrows. "And so?"

"Well, that's so . . . you know. Soon. People—" like me "—might have other plans already."

"Not to be indelicate, Your Highness," Vigo said. "But we do want to get the ceremony out of the way before your mother begins to . . . well, *show*."

Great. So even the royal Genovian event organizer knows my mother is expecting. Why doesn't Grandmère just rent the Goodyear blimp and broadcast it all over the tristate area?

Then Grandmère started telling me that, since we were on the topic of weddings and all, it might be a good opportunity for me to start learning what will be expected out of any future consorts I might have.

Wait a minute. "Future *what*?"

"Consorts," Vigo said, excitedly. "The spouse of the reigning monarch. Prince Philip is Queen Elizabeth's *consort.* Whomever you choose to marry, Your Highness, will be *your* consort."

I blinked at him. "I thought you were the royal Genovian event organizer," I said.

"Vigo not only serves as our event organizer, but also the royal protocol expert," Grandmère explained.

"Protocol? I thought that was something to do with the army. . . ."

Grandmère rolled her eyes. "Protocol is the form of ceremony and etiquette observed by foreign dignitaries at state functions. In your case, Vigo can explain the expectations of your future consort. Just so there won't be any unpleasant surprises later."

Then Grandmère made me get out a piece of paper and write down exactly what Vigo said, so that, she informed me, in four years, when I am in college, and I take it into my head to enter into a romantic liaison with someone completely inappropriate, I will know why she is so mad.

College? Grandmère obviously does not know that I am being actively pursued by would-be consorts at this very moment.

Of course, I don't even know Jo-C-rox's real name, but hey, it's something, at least.

Then I found out what, exactly, consorts have to do. And now I sort of doubt I'll be French-kissing anyone soon. In fact, I can totally see why my mother didn't want to marry my dad—that is, if he ever asked her.

I have glued the piece of paper here:

Expectations of any
Royal Consort of the Princess of Genovia

The consort will ask the princess's permission before he leaves the room.

The consort will wait for the princess to finish speaking before speaking himself.

The consort will wait for the princess to lift her fork before lifting his own at mealtimes.

The consort will not sit until the princess has been seated.

The consort will rise the moment the princess rises.

The consort will not engage in any sort of risk-taking behavior, such as racing—either car or boat—mountain-climbing, sky-diving, et cetera—until such time as an heir has been provided.

The consort will give up his right, in the event of annulment or divorce, to custody of any children born during the marriage.

The consort will give up the citizenship of his native country in favor of citizenship of Genovia.

Okay. Seriously. What kind of dweeb am I going to end up with?

Actually, I'll be lucky if I can get anybody to marry me at all. What schmuck would want to marry a girl he can't interrupt? Or can't walk out on during an argument? Or has to give up citizenship of his own country for?

I shudder to think of the total loser I will one day be forced to marry. I am already in mourning for the cool race car–driving, mountain-climbing, sky-diving guy I could have had, if it weren't for this whole crummy princess thing.

TOP FIVE WORST THINGS ABOUT BEING A PRINCESS

1. Can't marry Michael Moscovitz (he would never renounce his American citizenship in favor of Genovian).
2. Can't go anywhere without a bodyguard (I like Lars, but come on: Even the Pope gets to pray by himself sometimes).
3. Must maintain neutral opinion on important topics such as the meat industry and smoking.
4. Princess lessons with Grandmère.
5. Still forced to learn Algebra even though there is no reason why I will ever have to use it in my future career as ruler of small European principality.

I figured as soon as I got home, I would tell my mom that she and Mr. G need to elope, and right away. Grandmère had brought in a professional! I knew it would be a pain, what with Mom's latest show opening being so soon and all, but it was either that, or a royal wedding the likes of which this city hasn't seen since . . .

Well, ever.

But when I got home, my mom had her head in the toilet.

It turns out her morning sickness has begun, and isn't at all exclusive. She'll throw up just about any time, not just in the a.m.

She was so sick, I didn't have the heart to make her feel worse by telling her what Grandmère had planned.

"Be sure to put a video in," my mom kept calling from the bathroom. I didn't know what she was talking about, but Mr. G did.

She meant to be sure to tape my interview. My interview with Beverly Bellerieve!

I had completely forgotten about it, in light of what had happened at Grandmère's. But my mom hadn't.

Since my mom was incapacitated, Mr. G and I settled in to watch my interview together—well, in between running into the bathroom to offer my mom seltzer and saltines.

I figured I would tell Mr. G about Grandmère and the wedding at the first commercial break—but I sort of forgot, in the unbelievable horror of what followed.

Beverly Bellerieve—undoubtedly in an effort to impress

my father—actually did messenger over both a videotape and a written transcript of the interview. I will enclose parts of the written transcript here, so if I am ever asked to do another interview again, I can look at it and know exactly why I should never allow myself to appear on television ever again.

TWENTYFOUR/SEVEN for Monday 27 October

America's Princess
B. Bellerieve int. w/M. Renaldo

Ext. Thompson Street, south of Houston (SoHo). World Trade in background.

Beverly Bellerieve (BB):

Imagine if you will, an ordinary teenage girl. Well, as ordinary as a teenage girl who lives in New York City's Greenwich Village with her single mom, acclaimed painter Helen Thermopolis, can be.

Mia's life was filled with the normal things most teenagers' lives are full of—homework, friends, and the occasional F in Algebra . . . until one day, it all changed.

Int. penthouse suite, Plaza Hotel.

BB: Mia—may I call you Mia? Or would you prefer that I call you Your Highness? Or Amelia?

Mia Renaldo (MR):

Um, no, you can call me Mia.

BB: Mia. Tell us about that day. The day life as you know it changed completely.

MR: Well, um, what happened was, my dad and I were here

at the Plaza, you know, and I was drinking tea, and I got the hiccups, and everyone was looking at me, and my dad was, you know, trying to tell me I was the heir to the throne of Genovia, the country where he lives, and I was like, Look, I gotta go to the bathroom, and so I did, and I waited there until my hiccups stopped and then I came back to my chair and he told me that I was a princess and I completely flipped out and I ran to the zoo and I sat and looked at the penguins for a while and I totally couldn't believe it because in the seventh grade they made us do fact sheets on all the countries in Europe, but I totally missed the part about my dad being prince of it. And all I could think was that I was going to die if people in school found out, because I didn't want to end up being a freak like my friend Tina, who has to go around school with a body-guard. But that's exactly what happened. I am a freak, a huge freak.

[This is the part where she tries to salvage the situation:]

BB: Oh, Mia, I can't believe that's true. I'm sure you're quite popular.

MR: No, I'm not. I'm not popular at all. Only jocks are popular in my school. And cheerleaders. But I'm not popular. I mean, I don't hang out with the popular people. I never get invited to parties, or anything. I mean, the cool parties, where there is beer and making out and stuff. I mean, I'm not a jock, or a cheerleader, or one of the smart kids—

BB: Oh, but aren't you one of the smart kids, though? I understand one of your classes is called Gifted and Talented.

MR: Yes, but see, G and T is just like study hall. We don't

actually do anything in this class. Except goof around because the teacher is never there, she's always in the teachers' lounge across the hall so she has no idea what we're doing. Which is goofing off.

[Obviously still thinking she can make something out of this interview:]

BB: But I don't imagine you have much time for goofing off, do you, Mia? For instance, we are sitting here in the penthouse suite that belongs to your grandmother, the celebrated dowager princess of Genovia, who is, I understand, instructing you in royal decorum.

MR: Oh, yes. She's giving me princess lessons after school. Well, after my Algebra review sessions, which are after school.

BB: Mia, didn't you have some exciting news recently?

MR: Oh. Yes. Well, I'm pretty excited. I've always wanted to be a big sister. But they don't really want to make a big deal out of it, you know. It's just going to be a very small ceremony at City Hall—

There's more. A lot more, actually. It's too excruciating to go into. Basically, I just babbled like an idiot for about another ten minutes, while Beverly Bellerieve frantically attempted to steer me back toward something resembling the actual question she'd asked me.

But it was completely beyond even her impressive journalistic abilities. I was gone. A combination of nerves and, I'm afraid to say, codeine cough syrup, put me over the edge.

Ms. Bellerieve tried, though. I have to give her that. The interview ended with this:

Ext. Thompson Street, SoHo.

BB: She's not a jock, nor is she a cheerleader. What Amelia Mignonette Grimaldi Thermopolis Renaldo is, ladies and gentlemen, defies the societal stereotypes that exist in today's modern educational institutions. She's a princess. An American princess.

Yet she faces the same problems and pressures that teenagers all over this country face every day. . . with a twist: One day, she'll grow up to govern a nation.

And come spring, she'll be a big sister. Yes, *TwentyFour/Seven* has discovered that Helen Thermopolis and Mia's Algebra teacher, Frank Gianini—who are unmarried— are expecting their first child in May. When we come back, an exclusive interview with Mia's father, the prince of Genovia . . . next on *TwentyFour/Seven.*

What it all boiled down to is that, basically, I'm moving to Genovia.

My mom, who finally came out toward the end of the tape, and Mr. G tried to convince me that it wasn't that bad.

But it was. Oh, believe me, it was.

And I knew I was in for it the minute the phone started ringing, right after the segment aired.

"Oh God," my mother said, suddenly remembering something. "Don't pick it up! It's my mother! Frank, I forgot to tell my mother about us!"

Actually, I was kind of hoping it was Grandma

113

Thermopolis. Grandma Thermopolis was infinitely preferable, in my opinion, to who it actually turned out to be: Lilly.

And boy, was she mad.

"What do you mean, calling us a bunch of freaks?" she
screamed into the phone.

I said, "Lilly, what are you talking about? I didn't call
you a freak."

"You basically informed the entire nation that the population of Albert Einstein High School is divided into various socioeconomic cliques, and that you and your friends
are too uncool to be in any of them!"

"Well," I said. "We are."

"Speak for yourself! And what about G and T?"

"What *about* G and T?"

"You just told the entire country that we sit in there and
goof off because Mrs. Hill is always in the teachers' lounge!
What are you, stupid? You've probably gotten her into
trouble!"

I felt something inside of me clench, as if someone was
squeezing my intestines very, very tightly.

"Oh, no," I breathed. "Do you really think so?"

Lilly just let out a frustrated scream, then snarled, "My
parents say to tell your mother mazel tov."

Then she slammed the phone down.

I felt worse than ever. Poor Mrs. Hill!

Then the phone rang again. It was Shameeka.

"Mia," she said. "Remember how I invited you to my
Halloween party this Friday?"

"Yes," I said.

"Well, my dad won't let me have it now."

"*What?* Why?"

"Because thanks to you he is under the impression that Albert Einstein High School is filled with sex addicts and alcoholics."

"But I didn't say that!" Not in those exact words, anyway.

"Well, that's what he heard. He is currently in the next room surfing the Internet for a girls' school in New Hampshire he can send me to next semester. And he says he's not letting me go out with a boy again until I'm thirty."

"Oh, Shameeka," I said. "I'm so sorry."

Shameeka didn't say anything. In fact, she had to hang up, because she was sobbing too hard to speak.

The phone rang again. I didn't want to answer it, but I had no choice: Mr. Gianini was holding my mom's hair back while she threw up some more.

"Hello?"

It was Tina Hakim Baba.

"Oh, my gosh!" she shouted.

"I'm sorry, Tina," I said, figuring I better just start apologizing to every single person who called, right off the bat.

"Sorry? What are you sorry for?" Tina was practically hyperventilating. "You said my name on TV!"

"Um . . . I know." I had also called her a freak.

"I can't believe it!" Tina yelled. "That was so cool!"

"You aren't . . . you aren't mad at me?"

"Why should I be mad at you? This is the most exciting thing that has ever happened to me. I've never had my name said on television before!"

I was filled with love and appreciation for Tina Hakim Baba.

"Um," I asked, carefully, "did your parents see it?"

"Yes! They're excited, too. My mom said to tell you that the blue eyeshadow was a stroke of genius. Not too much, just enough to catch the light. She was very impressed. Also she said to tell your mother she has some excellent stretch mark cream that she got in Sweden. You know, for when she starts getting big. I'll bring it to school tomorrow, and you can give it to your mother."

"What about your dad?" I asked, carefully. "He's not planning on sending you to girls' school or anything?"

"What are you talking about? He's delighted that you mentioned my bodyguard. Now he thinks anyone who'd had plans to kidnap me will definitely think twice. Oops, there's another call. It's probably my grandmother in Dubai. They have a satellite dish. I'm sure she heard you mention me! 'Bye!"

Tina hung up. Great. Even people in Dubai saw my interview. I don't even know where Dubai is.

The phone rang again. It was Grandmère.

"Well," she said. "That was just terrible, wasn't it?"

I said, "Is there any way I can demand a retraction? Because I didn't mean to say that my Gifted and Talented teacher doesn't do anything and that my school was full of sex addicts. It's not, you know."

"I cannot imagine what that woman was thinking," Grandmère said. I was pleased she was on my side for once. Then she went on, and I saw that she wasn't talking about anything to do with me. "She failed to show a single picture of the palace! And it is at its most beautiful in the autumn. The palm trees look magnificent. This is a travesty, I tell you.

A travesty. Do you realize the promotional opportunities that have been wasted here? Absolutely wasted?"

"Grandmère, you have to do something," I wailed. "I don't know if I'm going to be able to show my face at school tomorrow."

"Tourism has been down in Genovia," Grandmère reminded me, "ever since we banned cruise ships from docking in the bay. But who needs day-trippers? With their sticky-film cameras and their awful Bermuda shorts. If that woman had only shown a few shots of the casinos. And the beaches! Why, we have the only naturally white sand along the Riviera. Are you aware of that, Amelia? Monaco has to import their sand."

"Maybe I could transfer to another school. Do you think there's a school in Manhattan that will take someone with a one point zero in Algebra?"

"Wait—" Grandmère's voice became muffled. "Oh, no, there we are. It's back on, and they're showing some simply lovely shots of the palace. Oh, and there's the beach. And the bay. Oh, and the olive groves. Lovely. Simply lovely. That woman might have a few redeeming qualities after all. I suppose I will have to allow your father to continue seeing her."

She hung up. My own grandmother hung up on me. What kind of a reject am I, anyway?

I went into my mom's bathroom. She was sitting on the floor, looking unhappy. Mr. Gianini was sitting on the edge of the bathtub. He looked confused.

Well, who can blame him? A couple of months ago, he was just an Algebra teacher. Now he's the father of the future sibling of the princess of Genovia.

117

"I need to find another school to go to from now on," I informed them. "Do you think you could help me out with that, Mr. G? I mean, do you have any pull with the teachers' association, or anything?"

My mother went, "Oh, Mia. It wasn't that bad."

"Yes, it was," I said. "You didn't even see most of it. You were in here throwing up."

"Yes," my mother said. "But I could hear it. And what did you say that wasn't true? People who excel at sports have traditionally been treated like gods in our society, while people whose brilliance is cerebral are routinely ignored, or worse, mocked as nerds or geeks. Frankly, I believe scientists working on cures for cancer should be paid the salaries professional athletes are receiving. Professional athletes aren't out there saving lives, for God's sake. They entertain. And actors. Don't tell me acting is art. Teaching. Now there's an art. Frank should be making what Tom Cruise does, for teaching you how to multiply fractions the way he did."

I realized my mother was probably delusional with nausea. I said, "Well, I think I'll just be going to bed now."

Instead of replying, my mother leaned over the toilet and threw up some more. I could see that in spite of all my warnings about the potential lethality of shellfish for a developing fetus, she'd ordered jumbo prawns in garlic sauce from Number One Noodle Son.

I went to my room and went online. Maybe, I thought, I could transfer to the same school Shameeka's father is shipping her off to. At least then I'd already have one friend—if Shameeka would even speak to me after what I'd done, which I doubted. No one at Albert Einstein High, with the exception of Tina Hakim Baba, who was obviously clueless, was ever going to speak to me again.

Then an instant message flashed across my computer screen. Someone wanted to talk to me.

But who? Jo-C-rox??? Was it Jo-C-rox?????

No. Even better! It was Michael. Michael, at least, still wanted to talk to me.

I have printed out our conversation and stuck it here:

CRACKING: Hey. Just saw you on TV. You were good.

FTLOUIE: What are you talking about? I made a complete and utter fool of myself. And what about Mrs. Hill? They're probably going to fire her now.

CRACKING: Well, at least you told the truth.

FTLOUIE: But all these people are mad at me now! Lilly's furious!

CRACKING: She's just jealous because you had more people watching you in that one fifteen-minute segment than all the people who've ever watched all of her shows put together.

FTLOUIE: No, that's not why. She thinks I've betrayed our generation, or something, by revealing that cliques exist at Albert Einstein High School.

CRACKING: Well, that, and the fact that you claimed you don't belong to any of them.

FTLOUIE: Well, I don't.

CRACKING: Yes, you do. Lilly likes to think you belong to the exclusive and highly selective Lilly Moscovitz clique. Only you neglected to mention this, and that has upset her.

FTLOUIE: Really? Did she say that?

CRACKING: She didn't say it, but she's my sister. I know

the way she thinks.

FtLouie: Maybe. I don't know, Michael.

CracKing: Look, are you all right? You were a mess at school today ... although now it's clear why. That's pretty cool about your mom and Mr. Gianini. You must be excited.

FtLouie: I guess so. I mean, it's kind of embarrassing. But at least this time my mom's getting married, like a normal person.

CracKing: Now you won't need my help with your Algebra homework anymore. You'll have your own personal tutor right there at home.

I had never thought of this. How awful! I don't want my own personal tutor. I want Michael to keep helping me during G and T! Mr. Gianini is all right, and everything, but he's certainly not *Michael*.

I wrote really fast:

FtLouie: Well, I don't know. I mean, he's going to be awfully busy for a while, moving in, and then there'll be the baby and everything.

CracKing: God. A baby. I can't believe it. No wonder you were wigging out so badly today.

FtLouie: Yeah, I really was. Wigging out, I mean.

CracKing: And what about that thing this afternoon with Lana? That couldn't have helped much. Though it was pretty funny, her thinking we were going out, huh?

Actually, I didn't see anything particularly funny about it. But what was I supposed to say? Gee, Michael, why don't we give it a try?

As if.

Instead I said:

FtLouie: Yeah, she's such a headcase. I guess it's never occurred to her that two people of the opposite sex can just be friends, with no romantic involvement.

Although I have to admit the way I feel about Michael—particularly when I'm over at Lilly's and he comes out of his room with no shirt on—is quite romantic.

CracKing: Yeah. Listen, what are you doing Friday night?

Was he asking me out? Was Michael Moscovitz finally asking me OUT?

No. It wasn't possible. Not after the way I'd made a fool of myself on national television.

Just to be safe, though, I figured I'd try for a neutral reply, in case what he wanted to know was whether I could come over and walk Pavlov because the Moscovitzes were going to be out of town, or something.

FtLouie: I don't know. Why?

CracKing: Because it's Halloween, you know. I thought a bunch of us could get together and go see *The Rocky Horror Picture Show* over at the Village Cinema. . . .

Okay. Not a date.

But we'd be sitting beside each other in a darkened

room! That counted for something. And *Rocky Horror* is sort of scary, so if I reached over and grabbed him, it might be okay.

FtLouie: Sure, that sounds . . .

Then I remembered. Friday night was Halloween, all right. But it was also the night of my mom's royal wedding! I mean, if Grandmère gets her way.

FtLouie: Can I get back to you? I may have a family obligation that evening.
CracKing: Sure. Just let me know. Well, see you tomorrow.
FtLouie: Yeah. I can't wait.
CracKing: Don't worry. You were telling the truth. You can't get in trouble for telling the truth.

Ha! That's what he thinks. There's a reason I lie all the time, you know.

TOP FIVE BEST THINGS ABOUT BEING IN LOVE WITH YOUR BEST FRIEND'S BROTHER

1. Get to see him in his natural environment, not just at school, thus allowing you access to vital information, like difference between his "school" personality and real personality.
2. Get to see him without a shirt on.
3. Get to see him all the time.
4. Get to see how he treats his mother/sister/ housekeeper (critical clues as to how he will treat any prospective girlfriend).
5. Convenient: You can hang out with your friend and spy on the object of your affections at the same time.

TOP FIVE WORST THINGS ABOUT BEING IN LOVE WITH YOUR BEST FRIEND'S BROTHER

1. Can't tell her.
2. Can't tell him, because he might tell her.
3. Can't tell anyone else, because they might tell him, or worse, her.
4. He will never admit to his true feelings because you are his little sister's best friend.
5. You are continuously thrust into his presence, knowing that he will never think of you as anything but his little sister's best friend for as long as you live, and yet you continue to pine for him until every fiber of your being cries out for him and you think you are probably going to die even though your Biology teacher says it is physiologically impossible to die from a broken heart.

Oh, God! No sooner had I set foot in Homeroom today than I was summoned to the principal's office!

I was hoping it was so that she could make sure I'm not carrying any contraband cough syrup, but it's more likely because of what I said last night on TV. Particularly, I would guess, the part about how divisive and clique-ridden it is around here.

Meanwhile, all the other people in this school who have never been invited to a party given by a popular kid have rallied around me. It's like I've struck a blow for dweebs everywhere, or something. The minute I walked into school today, the hip-hoppers, the brainiacs, the drama freaks, they were all, "Hey! Tell it like it is, sistah."

No one's ever called me sistah before. It is somewhat invigorating.

Only the cheerleaders treat me the way they always have. As I walk down the hall, their eyes flick over me, from the top of my head all the way down to my shoes. And then they whisper to each other and laugh.

Well, I suppose it is amusing to see a five-foot-nine, flat-chested amazon like myself roaming loose in the halls. I'm surprised no one has thrown a net over me and hauled me off to the Natural History Museum.

Of my own friends, only Lilly—and Shameeka, of course—aren't entirely thrilled with last night's performance. Lilly's still unhappy about my spilling the beans about the socioeconomic division of our school population. Not unhappy enough to turn down a ride to school in my limo this morning, however.

Interestingly, Lilly's chilly treatment of me has only served to bring her brother and I closer. This morning in the limo on the way to school, Michael offered to go over my Algebra homework with me, and make sure my equations were all right.

I was touched by his offer, and the warm feeling I had when he pronounced all my problems correct didn't have anything to do with pride, but everything to do with the way his fingers brushed against mine as he handed the piece of paper back to me. Could he be Jo-C-rox? *Could he?*

Uh-oh. Principal Gupta is ready to see me now.

Principal Gupta is way concerned about my mental health.

"Mia, are you really so unhappy here at Albert Einstein?"

I didn't want to hurt her feelings or anything, so I said no. I mean, the truth is, it probably wouldn't matter what school somebody stuck me in. I will always be a five-foot-nine freak with no breasts, no matter where I go.

Then Principal Gupta said something surprising: "I only ask because last night during your interview, you said you weren't popular."

I wasn't quite sure where she was going with this. So I just said, "Well, I'm not," with a shrug.

"That isn't true," Principal Gupta said. "Everyone in the school knows who you are."

I still didn't want her to feel bad, like it was her fault I'm a biological sport, so I explained very gently, "Yes, but that's only because I'm a princess. Before that, I was pretty much invisible."

Principal Gupta said, "That simply isn't true."

But all I could think was, *How would you even know? You aren't out there. You don't know what it's like.*

And then I felt even worse for her, because she is so obviously living in principal fantasy world.

"Perhaps," Principal Gupta said, "if you took part in more extracurricular activities, you'd feel a better sense of belonging."

This caused my jaw to drop.

"Principal Gupta," I couldn't help exclaiming. "I am

barely passing Algebra. All of my free time is spent attending review sessions so that I can scrape by with a D."

"Well," Principal Gupta said, "I am aware of that—"

"Also, after my review sessions, I have princess lessons with my grandmother, so that when I go to Genovia in December for my introduction to the people I will one day rule, I do not make a complete idiot of myself, like I did last night on TV."

"I think the word *idiot* might be a little strong."

"I really don't have time," I went on, feeling more sorry for her than ever, "for extracurricular activities."

"The yearbook committee meets only once a week," Principal Gupta said. "Or perhaps you could join the track team. They won't begin training until the spring, and by that time, hopefully, you won't be having princess lessons anymore."

I just blinked at her, I was so surprised. *Me? Track?* I can barely walk without tripping over my own gargantuan feet. God knows what would happen if I tried running.

And the yearbook committee? Did I really look like someone who wants to remember one single thing about my high school experience?

"Well," Principal Gupta said, I guess realizing from my facial expression that I was not enthused by either of these suggestions. "It was just an idea. I do think you would be much happier here at Albert Einstein if you joined a club. I am aware, of course, of your friendship with Lilly Moscovitz, and I sometimes wonder if she might not be . . . well, a negative influence on you. That television show of hers is quite acerbic."

I was shocked by this. Poor Principal Gupta is more deluded than I thought!

"Oh, no," I said. "Lilly's show is actually quite positive. Didn't you see the episode dedicated to fighting racism in Korean delis? Or the one about how a lot of clothing stores that cater to teens are prejudiced against larger-size girls, since they don't carry enough things in size twelve, the size of the average American woman? Or the one where we tried to hand-deliver a pound of Vaniero cookies to Freddie Prinz Jr.'s apartment because he'd been looking a little thin?"

Principal Gupta held up her hand. "I see that you feel very passionately about this," she said. "And I must say, I am pleased. It is good to know you feel passionate about something, Mia, other than your antipathy toward athletes and cheerleaders."

Then I felt worse than ever. I said, "I don't feel antipathy toward them. I'm just saying that sometimes . . . well, sometimes it feels like they run this school, Principal Gupta."

"Well, I can assure you," Principal Gupta said. "That is not true."

Poor, poor Principal Gupta.

Still, I did feel that I had to intrude upon the fantasy world in which she so obviously lives, just a little.

"Um," I said. "Principal Gupta. About Mrs. Hill . . ."

"What about her?" Principal Gupta asked.

"I didn't mean it when I said she's always in the teachers' lounge during my Gifted and Talented class. That was an exaggeration."

Principal Gupta smiled at me in this very brittle way.

"Don't worry, Mia," she said. "Mrs. Hill has been taken care of."

Taken care of! What does *that* mean?

I am almost scared to find out.

Well, Mrs. Hill didn't get fired.

Instead, I guess they gave her a warning, or something. The upshot of it is, Mrs. Hill won't budge from behind her desk here in the G and T lab.

Which means we have to sit at our desks and actually do our work. And we can't lock Boris in the supply closet. We actually have to sit here and listen to him play.

Play *Bartok*.

And we can't talk to one another, because we are supposed to be working on our individual projects.

Boy, is everyone mad at me.

But no one is madder than Lilly.

It turns out Lilly's been secretly writing a book about the socioeconomic divisions that exist within the walls of Albert Einstein High School. Really! She didn't want to tell me, but finally Boris blurted it out at lunch today. Lilly threw a fry at him and got ketchup all over his sweater.

I can't believe Lilly has told Boris things that she hasn't told me. I'm supposed to be her best friend. Boris is just her boyfriend. Why is she telling him cool things, like about how she's writing a book, and not telling me?

"Can I read it?" I begged.

"No." Lilly was really mad. She wouldn't even look at Boris. He had already totally forgiven her about the ketchup, even though he will probably have to get that sweater dry-cleaned.

"Can I read just one page?" I asked.

"No."

"Just one sentence?"

"No."

Michael didn't know about the book either. He told me right before Mrs. Hill came in that he offered to publish it in his webzine, *Crackhead*, but Lilly said, in quite a snotty voice, that she was holding out for a "legitimate" publisher.

"Am I in it?" I wanted to know. "Your book? Am I in it?"

Lilly said if people don't stop bothering her about it, she is going to fling herself off the top of the school water tower. She is exaggerating, of course. You can't even get up to the water tower anymore, since the seniors, as a prank a few years ago, poured a bunch of tadpoles into it.

I can't believe Lilly's been working on a book and never told me. I mean, I always knew she was going to write a book about the adolescent experience in post–Cold War America. But I didn't think she was going to start it before we had graduated. If you ask me, this book can't be very balanced. Because I hear things get way better sophomore year.

Still, I guess it does make sense that you would tell someone whose tongue has been in your mouth things you wouldn't necessarily tell your best friend. But it makes me mad Boris knows things about Lilly that I don't know. I tell Lilly everything.

Well, everything except how I feel about her brother.

Oh, and about my secret admirer.

And about my mom and Mr. Gianini.

But I tell her practically everything else.

DON'T FORGET:

1. Stop thinking about M.M.
2. English journal! Profound moment!
3. Cat food
4. Q-tips
5. Toothpaste
6. TOILET PAPER!

I am winning friends and influencing people everywhere I go today. Kenny just asked me what I'm doing for Halloween. I said I might have a family obligation to attend, and he said if I could get out of it, he and a bunch of his friends from the Computer Club are going to *Rocky Horror*, and that I should come along.

I asked him if one of his friends was Michael Moscovitz, because Michael is treasurer of the Computer Club, and he said yes.

I thought about asking Kenny if he's heard Michael mention whether or not he likes me, you know, in any special way, but I decided not to.

Because then Kenny might think I like him. Michael, I mean. And how pathetic would I look *then*?

Ode to M

Oh, M,
why can't you see
that x = you
and y = me?
And that
you + me
 = ecstasy,
and together we'd B
4ever happy?

What with all the backlash about my interview on *TwentyFour/Seven*, I completely forgot about Grandmère and Vigo, the Genovian event organizer!

I mean it. I swear I didn't remember a thing about Vigo and the asparagus tips, not until I walked into Grandmère's suite tonight for my princess lesson, and there were all these people scurrying around, doing things like barking into the phone: "No, that's four *thousand* long-stemmed pink roses, not four *hundred*," and calligraphy-ing place cards.

I found Grandmère sitting in the midst of all this activity, sampling truffles with Rommel—stylishly dressed in a chinchilla cape, dyed mauve—in her lap.

I'm not kidding. Truffles.

"No," Grandmère said, putting a gooey half-eaten chocolate ball back into the box Vigo was holding out to her. "Not that one, I think. Cherries are so *vulgar*."

"Grandmère." I couldn't believe this. I was practically hyperventilating, the way Grandmère had when she'd found out my mom was pregnant. "What are you *doing*? Who are all these people?"

"Ah, Mia," Grandmère said, looking pleased to see me. Even though, judging from the remains in the box Vigo was holding, she'd been eating a lot of stuff with nougat in it, none of it got onto her teeth. This is one of the many royal tricks Grandmère had yet to teach me. "Lovely. Sit down and help me decide which of these truffles we should put in the gift box the wedding guests are getting as party favors."

"Wedding guests?" I sank onto the chair Vigo had pulled up for me, and dropped my backpack. "Grandmère, I told you. My mom is never going to go along with this. She wouldn't *want* something like this."

Grandmère just shook her head and said, "Pregnant women are never the most rational creatures."

I pointed out that, judging from my research into the matter, while it was true that hormonal imbalances often cause pregnant women discomfort, I saw no reason to suppose that these imbalances in any way invalidated my mother's feelings on the matter—especially since I knew that they'd have been exactly the same if she weren't pregnant. My mom is not a royal wedding type of gal. I mean, she gets together with her girlfriends for margarita-poker night once a month.

"She," Vigo pointed out, "is the mother of the future reigning monarch of Genovia, Your Highness. As such, it is vital that she be extended every privilege and courtesy the palace can offer."

"Then how about offering her the privilege of planning her wedding for herself?" I said.

Grandmère had a good laugh at that one. She practically choked on the swig of Sidecar she was taking after each bite of truffle in order to cleanse her palate.

"Amelia," she said, when she was through coughing—something Rommel had found extremely alarming, if the way he rolled his eyes back up into his head was any indication. "Your mother will be eternally grateful to us for all the work we are doing on her behalf. You'll see."

I realized it was no good arguing with them. I knew what

I was going to have to do.

And I would do it right after my lesson, which was how to write a royal thank-you note. You would not believe all the wedding presents and baby stuff that people have started sending my mother, care of the Genovian royal family at the Plaza Hotel. Seriously. It is unreal. The place is jam-packed with electric woks, waffle irons, tablecloths, baby shoes, baby hats, baby clothes, baby diapers, baby toys, baby swings, baby changing tables, baby you-name-it. I had no idea so much stuff was necessary for raising a baby. But I have a pretty good idea my mom isn't going to want any of it. She's not really into pastels.

I marched up to the door to my father's hotel suite, and banged on it.

He wasn't there! And when I asked the concierge down in the lobby if she knew where my dad had gone, she said she wasn't sure.

One thing she was quite certain of, however, was that Beverly Bellerieve had been with my dad when he'd left.

Well, I'm glad my dad's found a new friend, I guess, but hello? Is he not aware of the impending disaster growing under his own royal nose?

Tuesday, October 28, 10 p.m., the loft

Well, it happened. The impending disaster is now officially a *real* disaster.

Because Grandmère has gotten completely out of hand.
I didn't even realize how badly, either, until I got home
tonight from my lesson and saw this *family* sitting at our
dining-room table.

That's right. An entire *family*. Well, a mom and a dad
and a kid, anyway.

I am not kidding. At first I thought they were tourists
that had maybe taken a wrong turn—our neighborhood is
very touristy. Like maybe they thought they were going to
Washington Square Park, but ended up following a Chinese
food delivery guy to our loft instead.

But then the woman who was wearing pink jogging
pants—a clear indication that she was from out of town—
looked at me and said, "Oh, my Lord! Are you telling me
that you actually wear your hair like that in real life? I was
sure it was just that way for TV."

My jaw dropped. I went, "*Grandmother Thermopolis?*"

"Grandmother Thermopolis?" The woman squinted at
me. "I guess all this royal stuff really *has* gone to your head.
Don't you remember me, honey? I'm *Mamaw.*"

Mamaw! My grandmother from my mother's side!

And there, sitting beside her—roughly half her size and
wearing a baseball cap—was my mother's father, Papaw!
The hulking boy in a flannel shirt and overalls I didn't
recognize, but that hardly mattered. What were my
mother's estranged parents, who had never left Versailles,

Indiana, before in their lives, doing in our downtown Village loft?

A quick consultation with my mother explained it. I was able to find her by following the phone cord first into her bedroom, then into her walk-in closet, where she was huddled behind her shoe rack (empty—all her shoes were on the floor) in whispered conspiracy with my father.

"I don't care how you do it, Phillipe," she was hissing into the phone. "You tell that mother of yours she's gone too far this time. My *parents*, Phillipe? *You know how I feel about my parents.* If you don't get them out of here, Mia is going to end up paying visits to me through a slot in the door up at Bellevue."

I could hear my father murmuring reassurances through the phone. My mom noticed me and whispered, "Are they still out there?"

I said, "Um, yes. You mean you didn't invite them?"

"Of course not!" My mother's eyes were as wide as Calamata olives. "Your grandmother invited them for some cockamamie wedding she thinks she's throwing for me and Frank on Friday!"

I gulped guiltily. Oops.

Well, all I can say in my own defense is that things have been very very hectic lately. I mean, what with finding out my mother is pregnant, and then getting sick, and the whole thing with Jo-C-rox, and then the interview. . . .

Oh, all right. There's no excuse. I am a horrible daughter.

My mom held out the phone to me. "He wants to talk to you," she said.

I took the phone and went, "Dad? Where are you?"

"I'm in the car," he said. "Listen, Mia, I got the concierge to arrange for rooms for your grandparents at a hotel near your place—the SoHo Grand. Okay? Just put them in the limo and send them there."

"Okay, Dad," I said. "What about Grandmère and this whole wedding thing? I mean, it's sort of out of control." Understatement of the year.

"I'll take care of Grandmère," my dad said, sounding very Captain Picardish. You know, from *Star Trek: The Next Generation*. I got the feeling Beverly Bellerieve was there in the car with him, and he was trying to sound all princely in front of her.

"Okay," I said. "But . . ."

It's not that I didn't trust my dad, or anything, to take care of the situation. It's just—well, we are talking about Grandmère. She can be very scary, when she wants to be. Even, I am sure, to her own son.

I guess he must have known what I was thinking, since he said, "Don't worry, Mia. I'll take care of it."

"Okay," I said, feeling bad for doubting him.

"And Mia?"

I'd been about to hang up. "Yeah, Dad?"

"Assure your mother I didn't know anything about this. I *swear* it."

"Okay, Dad."

I hung up the phone. "Don't worry," I said to my mom. "I'll take care of this."

Then, my shoulders back, I returned to the living room. My grandparents were still sitting at the table. Their farmer friend, however, had gotten up. He was in the kitchen,

139

peering into the refrigerator.

"This all you got to eat around here?" he asked, pointing to the carton of soy milk and the bowl of edamame on the first shelf.

"Um," I said. "Well, yes. We are trying to keep our refrigerator free from any sort of contaminants that might harm a developing fetus."

When the guy looked blank, I said, "We usually order in."

He brightened at once, and closed the refrigerator door. "Oh, Dominos?" he said. "Great!"

"Um," I said. "Well, you can order Dominos, if you want, from your hotel room—"

"Hotel room?"

I spun around. Mamaw had snuck up behind me.

"Um, yes," I said. "You see, my father thought you might be more comfortable at a nice hotel than here in the loft—"

"Well, if that doesn't beat all," Mamaw said. "Here your Papaw and Hank and I come all the way to see you, and you stick us in a hotel?"

I looked at the guy in the overalls with renewed interest. *Hank*? As in my *cousin* Hank? Why, the last time I'd seen Hank had been during my second—and ultimately final—trip to Versailles, back when I'd been about ten or so. Hank had been dropped off at the Thermopolis homestead the year before by his globe-trotting mother—my aunt Marie, who my mom can't stand, primarily because, as my mother puts it, she exists in an intellectual and spiritual vacuum (meaning that Marie is a Republican).

Back then, Hank had been a skinny, whiny thing with a

milk allergy. He wasn't as skinny as he'd once been, but he still looked a little lactose intolerant, if you ask me.

"Nobody said anything about us being hauled off to an expensive New York City hotel when that French woman called." Mamaw had followed me into the kitchen, and now she stood with her hands on her generous hips. "She said she'd pay for everything," Mamaw said, "free and clear."

I realized at once where Mamaw's concern lay.

"Oh, um, Mamaw," I said. "My father will take care of the bill, of course."

"Well, that's different." Mamaw beamed. "Let's go!"

I figured I'd better go with them, just to make sure they got there all right. As soon as we got into the limo, Hank forgot all about how hungry he was, in his delight over all the buttons there were to push. He had a swell time sticking his head in and out of the sun roof. At one point he stuck his whole body through the sun roof, spread his arms out wide, and yelled, "I'm the king of the world!"

Fortunately the limo's windows are tinted, so I don't think anyone from school could have recognized me, but I couldn't help feeling mortified.

So you can understand why, after I got them all checked into the hotel and everything, and Mamaw asked me if I would take Hank to school with me in the morning, I nearly passed out.

"Oh, you don't want to go to school with me, Hank," I said, quickly. "I mean, you're on vacation. You could go do something really fun." I tried to think of something that might seem really fun to Hank. "Like go to the Harley Davidson Cafe."

But Hank said, "Heck, no. I want to go to school with you, Mia. I always wanted to see what it was like at a real New York City high school." He lowered his voice, so Mamaw and Papaw wouldn't hear. "I hear the girls in New York City have all got their belly buttons pierced."

Hank was in for a real big disappointment if he thought he'd see any pierced navels in my school—we wear uniforms, and you aren't even allowed to tie the ends of your shirt into a halter top, a la Britney Spears.

But I couldn't see a way to get out of having him accompany me for the day. Grandmère was always going on about how princesses have to be gracious. Well, I guess this is my big test.

So I said, "Okay." Which didn't sound very gracious, but what else could I say?

Then Mamaw surprised me by grabbing me and giving me a hug good-bye. I don't know why I was so surprised. This was a very grandmotherly thing to do, of course. But I guess, seeing as how the grandmother I spend the most time with is Grandmère, I wasn't expecting it.

As she hugged me, Mamaw said, "Why, you aren't anything but skin and bones, are you?" Yes, thank you, Mamaw. It is true, I am mammarily challenged. But must you shout it out in the lobby of the SoHo Grand? "And when are you going to stop shooting up so high? I swear, you're almost taller than Hank!"

Which was, unfortunately, true.

Then Mamaw made Papaw give me a hug good-bye, too. Mamaw had been very soft when I hugged her. Papaw was the exact opposite, very bony. It was sort of amazing to me that these two people had managed to turn my strong-willed, independent-minded mother into such a gibbering mess. I mean, Grandmère used to lock my dad in the castle dungeon when he was a kid, and he wasn't half as resentful toward her as my mom was toward her parents.

On the other hand, my dad is in deep denial and suffers from classic Oedipal issues. At least according to Lilly.

When I got home, my mom had moved from the closet to her bed, where she lay covered with Victoria's Secret and J. Crew catalogs. I knew she must be feeling a little better. Ordering things is one of her favorite hobbies.

I said, "Hi, Mom."

She looked out from behind the Spring Bathing Suit edition. Her face was all bloated and splotchy. I was glad Mr. Gianini wasn't around. He might have had second thoughts about marrying her if he'd gotten a good look at her just then.

"Oh, Mia," she said when she saw me. "Come here and let me give you a hug. Was it horrible? I'm sorry I'm such a bad mother."

I sat down on the bed beside her. "You aren't a bad mother," I said. "You're a good mother. You just aren't feeling well."

"No," my mother said. She was sniffling, so I knew the reason she looked bloated and horrible was that she'd been crying. "I'm a terrible person. My parents came all the way from Indiana to see me, and I sent them to a hotel."

I could tell my mom was having a hormonal imbalance and wasn't herself. If she'd been herself, she wouldn't have thought twice about sending her parents to a hotel. She has never forgiven them for

a) not supporting her decision to have me,
b) not approving of the way she was raising me, and
c) voting for George Bush Sr., as well as his son.

Hormonal imbalance or not, though, the truth is, my mother does not need this kind of stress. This should be a really happy time for her. It says in all the stuff I've read about pregnancy that preparing for the birth of your child should be a time of joy and celebration.

And it would be, if Grandmère hadn't come around and ruined it all by sticking her nose where no one wants it.

She has *got* to be stopped.

And I'm not just saying that on account of how much I really, really want to go to *Rocky Horror* on Friday with Michael.

Another e-mail from Jo-C-rox!
This one said:

JoCRox: Dear Mia,
Just a note to tell you I saw you last night on TV. You looked
beautiful, as always. I know some people at school have been
giving you a hard time. Don't let them get you down. The
majority of us think you rock the world.
Your Friend

Isn't that the sweetest? I wrote back right away:

FtLouie: Dear Friend,
Thank you so much. PLEASE won't you tell me who you
are? I swear I won't tell a soul!!!!!!!!!!!!
Mia

He hasn't written back yet, but I think my sincerity really
shows, considering all the exclamation points.
I am slowly wearing him down, I just know it.

ENGLISH JOURNAL

My most profound moment was

ENGLISH JOURNAL

Make the most of yourself, for that is all there is of you.
—Ralph Waldo Emerson

I believe that Mr. Emerson was talking about the fact that you are only given one life to live, and so you had better make the best of it. This idea is best illustrated by a movie I saw on the Lifetime Channel while I was sick. The movie was called *Who Is Julia?* In this movie, Mare Winningham portrays Julia, a woman who wakes up one day after an accident to discover that her body has been completely destroyed and her brain transplanted into someone whose body was okay but whose brain had ceased functioning. Since Julia formerly was a fashion model and now her brain is in a housewife's body (Mare Winningham's), she is understandably upset. She goes around banging her head against things because she is no longer blond, five foot ten, and a hundred and ten pounds.

But finally, through Julia's husband's undying devotion to her—despite her iffy new looks and a brief kidnapping by the housewife's psychotic husband, who wants her to come back home to do his laundry—Julia realizes that looking like a model isn't as important as not being dead.

This movie raises the inevitable question, If your body was destroyed in an accident, and they had to transplant your brain into someone else's body, whose body would you want it to be? After considerable thought, I have decided that I would most want to be in the body of Michelle Kwan, the Olympic ice skater, since she is very pretty and has a marketable skill. And as everyone knows, it is quite stylish these days to be Asian.

Either Michelle or Britney Spears, so I could finally have bigger breasts.

Well, one thing is for sure:

Having a guy like my cousin Hank follow you around from class to class certainly keeps people's minds off the idiot you made of yourself on TV the other night.

Seriously. Not that the cheerleaders have forgotten all about the whole *TwentyFour/Seven* thing—I'm still getting the evil eye in the hallway every once in a while. But as soon as their gazes flicked over me and settled on Hank, something seemed to happen to them.

I couldn't figure out what it was, at first. I thought it was just that they were so stunned to see a guy in a flannel shirt and overalls in the middle of Manhattan.

Then I slowly started realizing it was something else. I guess Hank is sort of buff, and he does have sort of nice blond hair that kind of hangs in his pretty-boy-blue eyes.

But I think it's something even more than that. It's like Hank is giving off those pheromones we studied in Bio, or something.

Only I can't sense them, because I am related to him.

As soon as girls notice Hank, they sidle up to me and whisper "Who is *that*?" while gazing longingly at Hank's biceps, which are actually quite pronounced beneath all that plaid.

Take Lana Weinberger, for instance. There she was, hanging around my locker, waiting for Josh to show up so the two of them could take part in their morning face-suckage ritual, when Hank and I appeared. Lana's eyes—heavily circled in Bobbi Brown—widened, and she went, "Who's your friend?" in this voice I had never heard her use before. And I've known her a while.

I said, "He's not my friend, he's my cousin."

Lana said to Hank, in the same strange voice, "You can be *my* friend."

To which Hank replied, with a big smile, "Gee, thanks, ma'am."

And don't think in Algebra Lana wasn't doing everything she could to get Hank to notice her. She swished her long blond hair all over my desk. She dropped her pencil like four times. She kept crossing and recrossing her legs. Finally Mr. Gianini was like, "Miss Weinberger, do you need a bathroom pass?" That calmed her down, but only for like five minutes.

Even Miss Molina, the school secretary, was strangely giggly when she was making out a guest pass for Hank.

But that's nothing compared to Lilly's reaction as she climbed into the limo this morning, when we swung by to pick up her and Michael. She looked across the seat and her jaw dropped open and this piece of Pop Tart she'd been chewing fell right out onto the floor. I'd never seen her do anything like that before in my life. Lilly is generally very good at keeping things in her mouth.

Hormones are very powerful things. We are helpless in their wake.

Which would certainly explain the whole Michael thing.

I mean, about my being so deeply besotted by him and all.

T. Hardy—buried his heart in Wessex, body in Westminster

Um, excuse me, but *gross*.

I don't believe this. I really don't.

Lilly and Hank are missing.

That's right. *Missing.*

Nobody knows where they are. Boris is beside himself. He won't stop playing Mahler. Even Mrs. Hill now agrees that shutting him into the supply closet is the best way to maintain our sanity. She let us sneak into the gymnasium and steal some exercise mats and lean them up against the supply closet door to muffle the sound.

It isn't working, though.

I guess I can understand Boris's despair. I mean, when you're a musical genius and the girl you've been French-kissing on a fairly regular basis suddenly disappears with a guy like Hank, it has to be demoralizing.

I should have seen it coming. Lilly was excessively flirty at lunch. She kept asking Hank all these questions about life back in Indiana. Like if he was the most popular boy in his school, and all. Which of course he said he was—though I personally don't believe being the most popular boy at Versailles (which in Indiana-speak is pronounced Ver-Sales, by the way) High School is such a big accomplishment.

Then she was all, "Do you have a girlfriend?"

Hank got bashful and said that he used to, only "Amber" had ditched him a couple weeks ago for a guy whose father owns the local Outback Steakhouse. Lilly acted all shocked, and said Amber must be suffering from a borderline personality disorder if she couldn't see what a fully self-actualized individual Hank was.

I was so revolted by this display, I could hardly keep my veggie burger down.

Then Lilly started talking about all the fabulous things there are to do in the city, and how Hank really ought to take advantage of them, rather than hanging around here at school with me. She said, "For instance, there's the Transit Museum, which is fascinating."

Seriously. She actually said the *Transit Museum* was fascinating. *Lilly Moscovitz.*

I swear, hormones are way dangerous.

Then she went, "And on Halloween, there's a parade in the Village, and then we are all going to *The Rocky Horror Picture Show.* Have you ever been to that before?"

Hank said that no, he hadn't.

I should have known right then that something was up, but I didn't. The bell rang, and Lilly said she wanted to take Hank to the auditorium to show him the part of the *My Fair Lady* set that she had painted herself (a street lamp). Feeling that even a momentary alleviation from Hank's constant stream of reminders of our last visit together—"Remember that time we left our bikes in the front yard and you were all worried somebody might come in the night and steal them?"—would be a relief, I said, "Okay."

And that was the last any of us saw of them.

I blame myself. Hank is apparently simply too attractive to be released amongst the general population. I ought to have recognized that. I ought to have recognized that the pull of an uneducated but completely gorgeous farm boy from Indiana would be stronger than the pull of a not-so-attractive musical genius from Russia.

Now I have turned my best friend into a two-timer AND a class ditcher. Lilly has never skipped a class in her life. If she gets caught, she will get detention. I wonder if she'll think sitting in the cafeteria for an hour after school with the other juvenile delinquents will be worth the fleeting moments of teenage lust she and Hank are sharing.

Michael is no help. He isn't worried about his sister at all. In fact, he seems to find the situation highly amusing. I have pointed out to him that for all we know, Lilly and Hank could have been kidnapped by Libyan terrorists, but he says he finds that unlikely. He thinks it more reasonable to assume that they are enjoying an afternoon showing at the Sony Imax.

As if. Hank is totally prone to motion sickness. He told us all about it when we drove past the cable car to Roosevelt Island this morning on the way to school.

What are Mamaw and Papaw going to say when they find out I lost their grandson?

TOP FIVE PLACES LILLY AND HANK
COULD BE
1. Transit Museum
2. Enjoying some corned beef at 2nd Avenue Deli
3. Looking up Dionysius Thermopolis's name on the wall of immigrants at Ellis Island
4. Getting tattoos on St. Marks' Place
5. Making wild passionate love back in his room at the SoHo Grand

OH, GOD!

Still no sign of them.

Still nothing.

HOMEWORK

Algebra: solve problems #3, 9, 12 on pg. 147
English: Profound Moment!!
World Civ: read Chapter 10
G&T: please
French: 4 sentences: une blague, la montagne, la mer, il y a du soleil
Biology: ask Kenny

I am so sure—who can concentrate on homework when your best friend and cousin are missing in New York City????

Wednesday, October 29, Algebra review

Lars says he thinks it would be precipitous at this point to call the police. Mr. Gianini agrees with him. He says Lilly is ultimately quite sensible, and it is unrealistic to believe that she might let Hank fall into the hands of Libyan terrorists. I was, of course, only using Libyan terrorists as an example of the type of peril that might befall the two of them. There is another scenario which is much more disturbing:

Supposing Lilly is in love with him.

Seriously. Supposing Lilly, against all reason, has fallen madly in love with my cousin Hank, and he has fallen in love with her. Stranger things have happened. I mean, maybe Lilly is starting to realize that, yeah, Boris is a genius, but he still dresses funny and is incapable of breathing through his nose. Maybe she's willing to sacrifice those long intellectual conversations she and Boris used to have for a boy whose only asset is what is commonly referred to as booty.

And Hank, maybe he's been dazzled by Lilly's superior intellect. I mean, her IQ is easily a hundred points higher than his.

But can't they see that in spite of their mutual attraction, this relationship can only lead to ruin? I mean, suppose they DO IT, or something? And suppose that in spite of all those public service announcements on MTV, they neglect to practice safe sex, like my mom and Mr. G? They'll have to get married, and then Lilly will have to go live in Indiana in a trailer park, because that's where all teen mothers live. And she'll be wearing Wal-Mart housedresses and smoking

Kools while Hank goes off to the rubber tire factory and makes five fifty an hour.

Am I the only one who can see where all of this is heading? What is wrong with everyone?

First—grouping (evaluate with grouping symbols beginning with the innermost one)

Second—evaluate all powers

Third—multiply and divide left to right

Fourth—add and subtract in order left to right

It's all right. They're safe.

Apparently, Hank got back to the hotel around five, and Lilly showed up at her apartment, according to Michael, a little before that.

I would seriously like to know where they were, but all either of them will say is, "Just walking around."

Lilly adds, "God, could you be a little more possessive?"

I am so sure.

But I have bigger things to worry about. Right as I was about to step into Grandmère's suite at the Plaza for my princess lesson today, Dad appeared, looking nervous.

Only two things make my dad nervous. One is my mother.

And the other is his mother.

He said in a low voice, "Listen, Mia, about the wedding situation . . ."

I said, "I hope you had a chance to talk to Grandmère."

"Your grandmother has already sent out the invitations. To the wedding, I mean."

"*What?*"

Oh, my God. Oh, my God. This is a disaster. A *disaster*!

My dad must have known what I was thinking from my expression, since he went, "Mia, don't worry. I'll take care of it. Just leave it to me, all right?"

But how can I not worry? My dad is a good guy and all. At least he tries to be, anyway. But we're talking *Grandmère* here. *GRANDMÈRE*. Nobody goes up against Grandmère, not even the prince of Genovia.

And whatever he might have said to her so far, it certainly hasn't worked. She and Vigo are more deeply absorbed than ever in their nuptial planning.

"We have had acceptances already," Vigo informed me proudly when I walked in, "from the mayor, and Mr. Donald Trump, and Miss Diane Von Furstenberg, and the royal family of Sweden, and Mr. Oscar de la Renta, and Mr. David Hasselhoff, and Miss Martha Stewart—"

I didn't say anything. That's because all I could think was what my mother was going to say if she walked down the aisle and there was David Hasselhoff and Martha Stewart. She might actually run screaming from the room.

"Your dress arrived," Vigo informed me, his eyebrows waggling suggestively.

"My what?" I said.

Unfortunately Grandmère overheard me and clapped her hands so loudly she sent Rommel scurrying for cover, apparently thinking a nuclear missile or something had gone off.

"Do not ever let me hear you say *what* again," Grandmère fire-breathed at me. "Say, *I beg your pardon.*"

I looked at Vigo, who was trying not to smile. Really! Vigo actually thinks it's funny when Grandmère gets mad.

If there is a Genovian medal for valor, he should totally get it.

"I beg your pardon, Mr. Vigo," I said, politely.

"Please, please," Vigo said, waving his hand. "Just Vigo, none of this mister business, Your Highness. Now tell me. What do you think of this?"

And suddenly, he pulled this dress from a box.

And the minute I saw it, I was lost.

Because it was the most beautiful dress I have ever seen. It looked just like Glinda the Good Witch's dress from *The Wizard of Oz*—only not as sparkly. Still, it was pink, with this big poofy skirt, and it had little rosettes on the sleeves. I had never wanted a dress as much as I wanted that one the minute I laid eyes on it.

I had to try it on. I just had to.

Grandmère supervised the fitting, while Vigo hovered nearby, offering often to refresh her Sidecar. In addition to enjoying her favorite cocktail, Grandmère was smoking one of her long cigarettes, so she looked more officious than usual. She kept pointing with the cigarette and going, "No, not that way," and "For God's sake, stop slouching, Amelia."

It was determined that the dress was too big in the bust (what else is new?) and would have to be taken in. The alterations would take until Friday, but Vigo assured us he'd see that they were done in time.

And that's when I remembered what this dress was actually for.

God, what kind of daughter am I? I am terrible. I don't want this wedding to happen. My mother doesn't want this wedding to happen. So what am I doing, trying on a dress I'm supposed to be wearing at this event nobody but Grandmère wants to see happen, and which, if my dad succeeds, isn't going to happen anyway?

Still, I thought my heart might break as I took off the dress and put it back on its satin hanger. It was the most beautiful thing I had ever seen, let alone worn. If only, I couldn't help thinking, Michael could see me in this dress.

Or even Jo-C-rox. He might overcome his shyness and be able to tell me to my face what he'd been able to tell me before only in writing . . . and if it turns out he isn't that chili guy, maybe we could actually go out.

But there was only one appropriate place to wear a dress like this, and that was in a wedding. And no matter how much I wanted to wear that dress, I certainly didn't want there to be a wedding. My mother was barely holding on to her sanity as it was. A wedding at which David Hasselhoff was in attendance—and who knows, maybe even singing—might push her over the edge.

Still, I've never in my life felt as much like a princess as I did in that dress.

Too bad I'll never get to wear it.

Okay, so I was just casually flipping through the channels, you know, taking a little study break and all from thinking up a profound moment to write about in my English journal, when all of a sudden I hit Channel 67, one of the public access channels, and there is an episode of Lilly's show, *Lilly Tells It Like It Is*, that I have never seen before. Which was weird, because *Lilly Tells It Like It Is* is usually on Friday nights.

Then I figured since this Friday is Halloween, maybe Lilly's show was being preempted for coverage of the parade in the Village or something.

So I'm sitting there, watching the show, and it turns out to be the slumber party episode. You know, the one we taped on Saturday, with all the other girls confessing their French-kissing exploits, and me dropping the eggplant out the window? Only Lilly had edited out any scene showing my face, so unless you knew Mia Thermopolis was the one in the pajamas with the strawberries all over them, you would never have known it was me.

All in all, pretty tame stuff. Maybe some really puritanical moms would get upset about the French-kissing, but there aren't too many of those in the five boroughs, which is the extent of the broadcast region.

Then the camera did this funny skittering thing, and when the picture got clear again, there was this close-up of my face. That's right. MY FACE. I was lying on the floor with this pillow under my head, talking in this sleepy way.

Then I remembered: At the slumber party, after everyone else had fallen asleep, Lilly and I had stayed awake, chatting.

And it turned out she'd been FILMING ME THE WHOLE TIME!

I was lying there going, "The thing I most want to do is start a place for stray and abandoned animals. Like I went to Rome once, and there were about eighty million cats there, roaming around the monuments. And they totally would have died if these nuns hadn't fed them and stuff. So the first thing I think I'll do is, I'll start a place where all the stray animals in Genovia will be taken care of. You know? And I'd never have any of them put to sleep, unless they were really sick or something. And there'll just be like all these dogs and cats, and maybe some dolphins and ocelots—"

Lilly's voice, disembodied, went, "Are there ocelots in Genovia?"

I went, "I hope so. Maybe not, though. But whatever. Any animals that need a home, they can come live there. And maybe I'll hire some Seeing Eye dog trainers, and they can come and train all the dogs to be Seeing Eye dogs. And then we can give them away free to blind people who need them. And then we can take the cats to hospitals and old people's homes, and let the patients pet them, because that always makes people feel better—except people like my grandmère, who hates cats. We can take dogs for them. Or maybe one of the ocelots."

Lilly's voice: "And that's going to be your first act when you become the ruler of Genovia?"

I said, sleepily, "Yeah, I think so. Maybe we could just

turn the whole castle into an animal shelter, you know? And like all the strays in Europe can come live there. Even those cats in Rome."

"Do you think your grandmère is going to like that? I mean, having all those stray cats around the castle?"

I said, "She'll be dead by then, so who cares?"

Oh, my God! I hope they don't have public access on the TVs up at the Plaza!

Lilly asked me, "What part of it do you hate the most? Being a princess, I mean."

"Oh, that's easy. Not being able to go to the deli to buy milk without having to call ahead and arrange for a bodyguard to escort me. Not being able just to come over and hang out with you without it being this big production. This whole thing with my fingernails. I mean, who cares how my fingernails look, right? Why does it even matter? That kind of stuff."

Lilly went, "Are you nervous? About your formal introduction to the people of Genovia, in December?"

"Well, not really nervous, just . . . I don't know. What if they don't like me? Like the ladies-in-waiting and stuff? I mean, nobody at school likes me. So chances are, nobody in Genovia will like me, either."

"People at school like you," Lilly said.

Then, right in front of the camera, I drifted off to sleep. Good thing I didn't drool, or worse, snore. I wouldn't have been able to show my face at school tomorrow.

Then these words floated up over the screen: *Don't Believe the Hype! This Is the* Real *Interview with the Princess of Genovia!*

As soon as it was over, I called Lilly and asked her exactly what she thought she'd been doing.

She just went, in this infuriatingly superior voice, "I just want people to be able to see the real Mia Thermopolis."

"No, you don't," I said. "You just want one of the networks to pick up on the interview, and pay you lots of money for it."

"Mia," Lilly said, sounding wounded. "How can you even think such a thing?"

She sounded so taken aback that I realized I must have been wrong about that one.

"Well," I said, "you could have told me."

"Would you have agreed to it?" Lilly wanted to know.

"Well," I said. "No . . . probably not."

"There you go," Lilly said.

I guess I don't come off as quite as much of a big-mouthed idiot in Lilly's interview. I just come off as a whacko who has a thing for cats. I really don't know which is worse.

But the truth is, I'm actually starting not to care. I wonder if this is what happens to celebrities. Like maybe at first, you really care what they say about you in the press, but after a while, you're just like, Whatever.

I do wonder if Michael saw this, and if so, what he thought of my pajamas. They are quite nice ones.

Hank didn't come to school with me today. He called first thing this morning and said he wasn't feeling too well. I am not surprised. Last night Mamaw and Papaw called wanting to know where in Manhattan they could go for a New York strip. Since I do not generally frequent restaurants that serve meat, I asked Mr. Gianini for a suggestion, and he made a reservation at this semi-famous steak place.

And then, in spite of my mother's strenuous objections, he insisted on taking Mamaw and Papaw and Hank and me out, so he could get to know his future in-laws better.

This was apparently too much for my mother. She actually got out of bed, put mascara and lipstick and a bra on, and went with us. I think it was mostly to guard against Mamaw driving Mr. G away with her many references to the number of family cars my mother accidentally rolled over in cornfields while she was learning to drive.

At the restaurant, I am horrified to report, in spite of the increased risk of heart disease and some cancers to which saturated fats and cholesterol have scientifically been linked, my future stepfather, my cousin, and my maternal grandparents—not to mention Lars, whom I had no idea was so fond of meat, and my mother, who attacked her steak like Rosemary attacked that raw chunk of ground round in *Rosemary's Baby* (which I've never actually seen, but I heard about it)—ingested what had to have been the equivalent of an entire cow.

This distressed me very much and I wanted to point out to them how unnecessary and unhealthy it is to eat things that were once alive and walking around, but, remembering my princess training, I merely concentrated on my entree of grilled vegetables and said nothing.

Still, I am not at all surprised Hank doesn't feel well. All that red meat is probably sitting, completely undigested, behind those washboard abs even as we speak. (I am only assuming Hank has washboard abs, since, thankfully, I have not actually seen them).

Interestingly, however, that was the one meal my mother has been able to keep down. This baby is no vegetarian, that's for sure.

Anyway, the disappointment Hank's absence has generated here at Albert Einstein is palpable. Miss Molina saw me in the hall and asked, sadly, "You don't need another guest pass for your cousin today?"

Hank's absence also apparently means that my special dispensation from the mean looks the cheerleaders have been giving me is revoked: This morning Lana reached out, snapped the back of my bra, and asked in her snottiest voice, "What are you wearing a bra for? You don't need one."

I long for a place where people treat each other with courtesy and respect. That, unfortunately, is not high school. Maybe in Genovia? Or possibly that space station the Russians built, the one that's falling apart above our heads.

Anyway, the only person who seems happy about Hank's misfortune is Boris Pelkowski. He was waiting for Lilly by the front doors to the school when we arrived this morning, and as soon as he saw us, he asked, "Where is Honk?"

(Because of his thick Russian accent, that's the way he pronounces Hank's name.)

"Honk—I mean, Hank—is sick," I informed him, and it would not be exaggerating to say that the look that spread across Boris's uneven features was beatific. It was actually a little bit touching. Boris's doglike devotion to Lilly can be annoying, but I know that I really only feel that way about it because I am envious. *I* want a boy I can tell all my deepest secrets to. *I* want a boy who will French-kiss me. *I* want a boy who will be jealous if I spend too much time with another guy, even a total bohunk like Hank.

But I guess we don't always get what we want, do we? It looks like all I'm going to get is a baby brother or sister, and a stepfather who knows a lot about the quadratic formula and who is moving in tomorrow with his foozball table.

Oh, and the rule of the throne of a country, someday.

Big deal. I'd rather have a boyfriend.

Thursday, October 30, World Civ

THINGS TO DO BEFORE MR. G MOVES IN

1. Vacuum
2. Clean out cat box
3. Drop off laundry
4. Take out recycling, esp. any of Mom's magazines that refer to orgasms on the cover—very imp.!!!
5. Remove feminine hygiene products from all bathrooms
6. Clear out space in living room for foozball table/pinball machine/large TV
7. Check medicine cabinet: Hide Midol, Nair, Jolene—very imp.!!!
8. Remove *Our Bodies, Ourselves* and *The Joy of Sex* from Mom's bookshelves
9. Call cable company. Get Classic Sports Network added. Remove Romance Channel.
10. Get Mom to stop hanging bras on bedroom doorknob
11. Stop biting off fake fingernails
12. Stop thinking so much about M. M.
13. Fix lock on bathroom door
14. Toilet paper!!!!

I don't believe this.

They've done it again.

Hank and Lilly have disappeared AGAIN!

I didn't even know about the Hank part until Lars got a call on his cell phone from my mother. She was very annoyed, because her mother had called her at the studio, screaming hysterically because Hank was missing from his hotel room. Mom wanted to know if Hank had shown up at school.

Which, to the best of my knowledge, he had not.

Then Lilly didn't show up for lunch.

She wasn't even very subtle about it, either. We were doing the Presidential Fitness exam in PE, and just as it was her turn to climb the rope, Lilly started complaining that she had cramps.

Since Lilly complains that she has cramps every single time the Presidential Fitness exam rolls around, I wasn't suspicious. Mrs. Potts sent Lilly to the nurse's office, and I figured I'd see her at lunch, miraculously recovered.

But then she didn't show up for lunch. A consultation with the nurse revealed that Lilly's cramps had been of such severity, she'd decided to go home for the rest of the day.

Cramps. I am so sure. Lilly doesn't have cramps. What she has is the hots for my cousin!

The real question is, how long can we keep this from Boris? Remembering the Mahler we'd been subjected to yesterday, everyone is being careful not to remark how coincidental it is that Lilly is sick and Hank is missing in action at the same time. Nobody wants to have to resort to the gym mats again. Those things were heavy.

As a precaution, Michael is trying to keep Boris busy with a computer game he invented called Decapitate the Backstreet Boy. In it, you get to hurl knives and axes and stuff at members of the Backstreet Boys. The person who cuts the heads off the most Backstreet Boys moves up to another level, where he gets to cut off the heads of the boys in 98 Degrees, then 'N Sync, etc. The player who cuts off the most heads gets to carve his initials on Ricky Martin's naked chest.

I can't believe Michael only got a B on this game in his computer class. But the teacher took points off because he felt it wasn't violent enough for today's market.

Mrs. Hill is letting us talk today. I know it's because she doesn't want to have to listen to Boris play Mahler, or worse, Wagner. I went up to Mrs. Hill after class yesterday and apologized for what I said on TV about her always being in the teachers' lounge, even though it was the truth. She said not to worry about it. I'm pretty sure this is because my dad sent her a DVD player, along with a big bunch of flowers, the day after the interview was broadcast. She's been a lot nicer to me since then.

You know, I find all of this stuff about Lilly and Hank very difficult to process. I mean, *Lilly*, of all people, turning out to be such a slave to lust. Because she can't genuinely be in love with Hank. He's a nice enough guy and all—and very good-looking—but let's face it, his elevator does *not* go all the way up.

Lilly, on the other hand, belongs to Mensa—or at least

she could if she didn't think it hopelessly bourgeois. Plus Lilly isn't exactly what you'd call a traditional beauty—I mean, *I* think she's pretty, but according to today's admittedly limited ideal of what "attractive" is, Lilly doesn't really pass muster. She's much shorter than me, and kind of chunky, and has that sort of squished-in face. Not really the type you'd expect a guy like Hank to fall for.

So what do a girl like Lilly and a guy like Hank have in common, anyway?

Oh, God, don't answer that.

HOMEWORK

Algebra: pg. 123, problems 1–5, 7

English: in your journal, describe one day in your life; don't forget profound moment

World Civ: answer questions at end of Chapter 10

G&T: bring one dollar on Monday for earplugs

French: une description d'une personne, trente mots minimum

Biology: Kenny says not to worry, he'll do it for me

Another huge shock. If my life continues along this roller-coaster course, I may have to seek professional counseling.

When I walked in for my princess lesson, there was Mamaw—*Mamaw*—sitting on one of Grandmère's tiny pink couches, sipping tea.

"Oh, she was always like that," Mamaw was saying. "Stubborn as a mule."

I was sure they were talking about me. I threw down my bookbag and went, "I am *not!*"

Grandmère was sitting on the couch opposite Mamaw, a teacup and saucer poised in her hands. In the background, Vigo was running around like a little windup toy, answering the phone and saying things like, "No, the orange blossoms are for the wedding party, the roses are for the center-pieces," and "But *of course* the lamb chops were meant to be appetizers."

"What kind of way is that to enter a room?" Grandmère barked at me in French. "A princess never interrupts her elders, and she certainly never throws things. Now come here and greet me properly."

I went over and gave her a kiss on both cheeks, even though I didn't want to. Then I went over to Mamaw and did the same thing. Mamaw giggled and went, "How continental!"

Grandmère said, "Now sit down, and offer your grandmother a madeleine."

I sat down, to show how unstubborn I can be, and offered

Mamaw a madeleine from the plate on the table in front of her, the way Grandmère had shown me to.

Mamaw giggled again and took one of the cookies. She kept her pinky in the air as she did so.

"Why, thanks, hon," she said.

"Now," Grandmère said, in English. "Where were we, Shirley?"

Mamaw said, "Oh, yes. Well, as I was saying, she's always been that way. Just stubborn as the day is long. I'm not surprised she's dug her heels in about this wedding. Not surprised at all."

Hey, it wasn't me they were talking about after all. It was—

"I mean, I can't tell you we were thrilled when this happened the first time. 'Course, Helen never mentioned he was a prince. If we had known, we'd have encouraged her to marry him."

"Understandably," Grandmère murmured.

"But this time," Mamaw said, "well, we just couldn't be more thrilled. Frank is a real doll."

"Then we are agreed," Grandmère said. "This wedding must—and will—take place."

"Oh, definitely," Mamaw said.

I half expected them to spit in their hands and shake on it, an old Hoosier custom I learned from Hank.

But instead they each took a sip of their tea.

I was pretty sure nobody wanted to hear from me, but I cleared my throat anyway.

"Amelia," Grandmère said, in French. "Don't even think about it."

Too late. I said, "Mom doesn't want—"

"Vigo," Grandmère called. "Do you have those shoes? The ones that match the princess's dress?"

Like magic, Vigo appeared, carrying the prettiest pair of pink satin slippers I have ever seen. They had rosettes on the toes that matched the ones on my maid-of-honor dress.

"Aren't they lovely?" Vigo said, as he showed them to me. "Don't you want to try them on?"

It was cruel. It was underhanded.

It was Grandmère, all over.

But what could I do? I couldn't resist. The shoes fit perfectly, and looked, I have to admit, gorgeous on me. They gave my ski-like feet the appearance of being a size smaller—maybe even two sizes! I couldn't wait to wear them, and the dress, too. Maybe if the wedding was called off, I could wear them to the prom. If things worked out with Jo-C-rox, I mean.

"It would be a shame to have to send them back," Grandmère said with a sigh, "because your mother is being so stubborn."

Then again, maybe not.

"Couldn't I keep them for another occasion?" I asked. Hint, hint.

"Oh, no," Grandmère said. "Pink is so inappropriate for anything but a wedding."

Why me?

When my lesson was over—apparently today's consisted of sitting there listening to my two grandmothers complain about how their children (and grandchildren) don't appreciate them—Grandmère stood up and said to Mamaw, "So we understand each other, Shirley?"

And Mamaw said, "Oh, yes, Your Highness."

This sounded very ominous to me. In fact, the more I think about it, the more convinced I am that my dad hasn't done a single solitary thing to bail Mom out of what is clearly going to be a very messy situation. According to Grandmère, a limo is going to swing by our place tomorrow evening to pick up me, Mom, and Mr. Gianini, and whisk us off to the Plaza. It's going to be pretty obvious to everyone when my mom refuses to get into the car that there isn't going to be any wedding.

I think I am going to have to take matters into my own hands. I know Dad assured me that everything is under control, but we're talking Grandmère. GRANDMÈRE!

During the ride downtown I tried pumping Mamaw for information—you know, about what she and Grandmère meant when they said they "understood" one another.

But she wouldn't tell me a thing . . . except that she and Papaw were too tired, what with all the sightseeing they've been doing—not to mention worrying about Hank, whom they still hadn't heard from—to go out for dinner tonight, and were going to stay in and order room service.

Which is just as well, because I'm pretty sure if I have to hear one more person say the words "medium rare," I might hurl.

Well, Mr. Gianini is all moved in. I have already played nine games of foozball. Boy, are my wrists tired.

It's not really weird having him here on a permanent basis, because he was always hanging around before anyway. The only difference really is the big TV, the pinball machine, the foozball table, and the drum set in the corner where we normally keep Mom's life-size metallic gold bust of Elvis.

But the coolest thing is the pinball machine. It's called Motorcycle Gang, and it has all these very realistic drawings of tattooed, leather-wearing Hell's Angels on it. Also, it has pictures of the Hell's Angels' girlfriends—who don't have very much clothing on at all—bending over and sticking out their enormous bosoms. When you sink a ball, the pinball machine makes the noise of a motorcycle engine revving very loudly.

My mother took one look at it and just stood there, shaking her head.

I know it's misogynistic and sexist and all, but it's also really, really neat.

Mr. Gianini told me today that he thought it would be all right for me to call him Frank now, considering the fact that we are practically related. But I just can't bring myself to do it. So I just call him Hey. I go, "Hey, can you pass the parmesan?" and "Hey, have you seen the remote control?"

See? No names needed. Pretty clever, huh?

Of course, it hasn't exactly been smooth sailing. There's the small fact that tomorrow, there's supposedly going to be this huge celebrity wedding that I know has not been canceled, and that I also know my mother still hasn't the slightest intention of attending.

But when I ask her about it, instead of freaking out, my mom just smiles all secretively, and says, "Don't worry about it, Mia."

But how can I help worrying about it? The only thing that is definitely off is my mom and Mr. G's trip to the courthouse. I asked if they still wanted me to come dressed as the Empire State Building, thinking I should probably start working on my costume, and all, and my mom just got this furtive look in her eyes and said why don't we just hold off on that.

I could kind of tell she didn't want to talk about it, so I clammed up and went and called Lilly. I figured it was about time she gave me some explanation as to just what was going on here.

But when I called her, the line was busy. Which meant there was a good chance Lilly or Michael was online. I took a gamble and instant-messaged Lilly. She wrote back right away.

FtLouie: Lilly, just where did you and Hank disappear to today? And don't lie and say you weren't together.
WmnRule: I fail to see what business it is of yours.
FtLouie: Well, let's just say that if you want to hang on to your boyfriend, you better come up with a good explanation.
WmnRule: I have a very good explanation. But I am not likely to share it with you. You'll just blab it to Beverly Bellerieve. Oh, and twenty-two million viewers.

FTLOUIE: That is so totally unfair. Look, Lilly, I'm worried about you. It isn't like you to skip school. What about your book about high school society? You may have missed out on some valuable material for it.
WMNRULE: Oh, really? Did something happen today worth recording?
FTLOUIE: Well, some of the seniors snuck into the teachers' lounge and put a fetal pig in the mini-fridge.
WMNRULE: Gosh, I'm so sorry I missed that. Is there anything else, Mia? Because I am trying to research something on the Web right now.

Yes, there was something else. Didn't she know how wrong it was to be seeing two boys at the same time? Especially when some of us don't even have *one* boy? Couldn't she see how selfish and mean-spirited that was?

But I didn't write that. Instead, I wrote:

FTLOUIE: Well, Boris was pretty upset, Lilly. I mean, he totally suspects something.
WMNRULE: Boris has got to learn that in a loving relationship, it is important to establish bonds of trust. That is something you might keep in mind yourself, Mia.

I realize, of course, that Lilly is talking about *our* relationship—hers and mine. But if you think about it, it applies to more than just Lilly and Boris, and Lilly and me. It applies to me and my dad, too. And me and my mom. And me and . . . well, just about everybody.

Was this, I wondered, a profound moment? Should I get

out my English journal?

It was right after this that it happened: I got instant-messaged by someone else. By Jo-C-rox himself!

JoCrox: So are you going to *Rocky Horror* tomorrow?

Oh, my God. Oh, my GOD. OH, MY GOD!

Jo-C-rox is going to *Rocky Horror* tomorrow.

And so is Michael.

Really, there is only one logical explanation that can be drawn from this: Jo-C-rox is Michael. Michael is Jo-C-rox. He HAS to be. He just HAS to be.

Right?

I didn't know what to do. I wanted to jump up from my computer and run around my room and scream and laugh at the same time.

Instead—and I don't know where I got the presence of mind to do this, I wrote back:

FtLouie: I hope so.

I can't believe it. I really can't believe it. Michael is Jo-C-rox.

Right?

What am I going to do? What am I going to do?

Friday, October 31, Homeroom

I woke with the strangest feeling of foreboding. I couldn't figure out why for a few minutes. I lay there in bed, listening to the rain patter against my window. Fat Louie was at the end of my bed, kneading the comforter and purring very loudly.

Then I remembered: Today, according to my grandmother, is the day my pregnant mother is supposed to marry my Algebra teacher in a huge ceremony at the Plaza Hotel, with musical accompaniment courtesy of David Hasselhoff.

I lay there for a minute, wishing my temperature was one hundred and two again, so I wouldn't have to get out of bed and face what was sure to be a day of drama and hurt feelings.

And then I remembered my e-mail from the night before, and jumped right out of bed.

Michael is my secret admirer! Michael is Jo-C-rox!

And with any luck, by the end of the night, he'll have admitted it to my face!

Mr. Gianini is not here today. Instead, we have a substitute teacher named Mrs. Krakowski.

It is very strange that Mr. G isn't here, because he was certainly in the loft this morning. We played a game of foozball before Lars showed up in the limo. We even offered Mr. G a ride to school, but he said he was coming in later.

Really later, it looks like.

A lot of people aren't here today, actually. Michael, for instance, didn't catch a ride with us this morning. Lilly says that is because he had last-minute problems printing out a paper that is due today.

But I wonder if it is really because he is too scared to face me after admitting that he is Jo-C-rox.

Well, not that he actually admitted it. But he sort of did. Didn't he?

Mr. Howell is three times as old as Gilligan. The difference in their ages is 48. How old are Mr. Howell and Gilligan?

T = Gilligan
$3T$ = Mr. Howell

$3T - T = 48$
$2T = 48$
$T = 24$

Oh, Mr. G, where ARE you?

Okay.

I will never underestimate Lilly Moscovitz again. Nor will I suspect her of having anything but the most altruistic motives. This I hereby solemnly swear in writing.

It was at lunch when it happened:

We were all sitting there—me, my bodyguard, Tina Hakim Baba and her bodyguard, Lilly, Boris, Shameeka, and Ling Su. Michael, of course, sits over with the rest of the Computer Club, so he wasn't there, but everybody else who mattered was.

Shameeka was reading aloud to us from some of the brochures her father had gotten from girls' schools in New Hampshire. Each one filled Shameeka with more terror, and me with more shame for ever having opened my big mouth in the first place.

Suddenly, a shadow fell over our little table.

We looked up.

There stood an apparition of such godlike stature that for a minute, I think even Lilly believed the chosen people's long lost Messiah had finally shown up.

It turned out it was only Hank—but Hank looking as I had certainly never seen him before. He had on a black cashmere sweater beneath a clinging black leather coat, and black jeans that seemed to go on and on over his long, lean legs. His golden hair had been expertly styled and cut, and—I swear—he looked so much like Keanu Reeves in *The Matrix* that I actually might have believed he had wandered in off the set if it hadn't been for the fact that on his feet, he wore cowboy boots. Black, expensive-looking ones, but cowboy boots, just the same.

I don't think it was my imagination that the entire crowd inside the cafeteria seemed to gasp as Hank slid into a chair at our table—the reject table, I have frequently heard it called.

"Hello, Mia," Hank said.

I stared at him. It wasn't just the clothes. There was something . . . different about him. His voice seemed deeper, somehow. And he smelled . . . well, good.

"So," Lilly said to him, as she scooped a glob of creamy filling out of her Ring Ding. "How'd it go?"

"Well," Hank said, in that same deep voice. "You're looking at Calvin Klein's newest underwear model."

Lilly sucked the filling off her finger. "Hmmm," she said, with her mouth full. "Good for you."

"I owe it all to you, Lilly," Hank said. "If it weren't for you, they never would have signed me."

Then it hit me. The reason Hank seemed so different was that his Hoosier drawl was gone!

"Now, Hank," Lilly said. "We discussed this. It's your natural ability that got you where you are. I just gave you a few pointers."

When Hank turned his gaze toward me, I saw that his sky-blue eyes were damp. "Your friend Lilly," he said, "has done something no one's ever done for me in my life."

I threw an accusing gaze at Lilly.

I knew it. I *knew* they'd had sex.

But then Hank said, "She believed in me, Mia. Believed in me enough to help me pursue my dream . . . a dream I've had since I was a very young boy. A lot of people—including my own Mamaw and Pa—I mean, my grandparents—told me it was a pipe dream. They told me to give it up, that it would never happen. But when I told my dream to Lilly, she held out her hand"—Hank held out his hand to illustrate this, and all of us—me, Lars, Tina, Tina's bodyguard Wahim, Shameeka, and Ling Su—looked at that hand, the nails of which had been perfectly manicured—"and said, 'Come with me, Hank. I will help you achieve your dream.'"

Hank put his hand down. "And do you know what?"

All of us—except Lilly, who went right on eating—were so astonished, we could only stare.

Hank did not wait for us to reply. He said, "It happened. Today, it happened. My dream came true. I was signed by Ford. I am their newest male model."

We all blinked at him.

"And I owe it all," Hank said, "to this woman here."

Then something really shocking happened. Hank got up out of his chair, walked over to where Lilly was sitting, innocently finishing her Ring Ding, not suspecting a thing, and pulled her to a standing position.

Then as everyone in the entire cafeteria looked on—including, I noticed, Lana Weinberger and all her cronies over at the cheerleaders' table—my cousin Hank laid such a kiss on Lilly Moscovitz, I thought he just might suck that Ring Ding right back up again.

When he was done kissing her, Hank let go. And Lilly, looking as if someone had just poked her with an electric prod, sank slowly back down to her seat. Hank adjusted the lapels of his leather coat and turned to me.

"Mia," he said. "Tell Mamaw and Papaw they're going to have to find somebody to cover my shift at the hardware store. I ain't—I mean, I'm *not*—going back to Versailles. Ever."

And with that, he strode from our cafeteria like a cowboy walking away from a gunfight he'd just won.

Or I suppose I should say he *started* to stride from the cafeteria. Unfortunately for Hank, he didn't make it out quite fast enough.

Because one of the people who had observed that searing kiss he'd laid on Lilly was none other than Boris Pelkowski.

And it was Boris Pelkowski—Boris Pelkowski, with his retainer and his sweater tucked into his pants—who stood up and said, "Not so fast, hot shot."

I'm not sure if Boris had just seen the movie *Top Gun* or what, but that *hot shot* came out sounding pretty menacing, considering Boris's accent and all.

Hank kept going. I don't know if he hadn't heard Boris, or if he wasn't about to let some little violin-playing genius mess up his great exit.

Then Boris did something completely reckless. He reached out and grabbed Hank by the arm as he went by and said, "That's *my* girl you had your lips all over, pretty boy."

I am not even joking. Those were his exact words. Oh, how my heart thrilled to hear them! If only some guy (okay, Michael) would say something like that about me. Not the Josiest girl he'd ever met, but *his* girl. Boris had actually referred to Lilly as *his* girl! No boy has ever referred to me as *his* girl. Oh, I know all about feminism and how women aren't property and it's sexist to go around claiming them as such. But, oh! If only somebody (okay, Michael) would say I was *his* girl!

Anyway, Hank just went, "Huh?"

And then, from out of nowhere, Boris's fist went sailing into Hank's face. *Pow!*

Only it didn't really sound like pow. It sounded more like a thud. There was a sickening crunch of bones splintering. All of us girls gasped, thinking that Boris had marred Hank's perfect cover-guy face.

But we needn't have worried: It was Boris's hand that made the crunching sound, not Hank's face. Hank escaped completely unscathed. Boris is the one who has to have his knuckles splinted.

And you know what that means:

No more Mahler.

Whoopee!!!

It's unprincess-like of me, however, to gloat over another's misfortune.

Friday, October 31, French

I borrowed Lars's cell phone and called the SoHo Grand between lunch and fifth period. I mean, I figured someone should let Mamaw and Papaw know that Hank was all right. Well, a Ford model, but all right.

Mamaw must have been sitting by the phone, since she picked up on the first ring.

"Clarisse?" she said. "I still haven't heard from them."

Which is weird. Because Clarisse is Grandmère's name.

"Mamaw?" I said. "It's me, Mia."

"Oh, *Mia*." Mamaw laughed a little. "I'm sorry, honey. I thought you were the princess. I mean, the dowager princess. Your other grandma."

I went, "Uh, yeah. Well, it's not. It's me. And I'm just calling to tell you that I heard from Hank."

Mamaw shrieked so loud, I had to hold the cell phone away from my ear.

"WHERE IS HE?" she yelled. "YOU TELL HIM FROM ME THAT WHEN I GET MY HANDS ON HIM, HE'S—"

"Mamaw," I cried. It was kind of embarrassing, because all sorts of people in the hallway heard her yelling and were looking at me. I tried to make myself inconspicuous by hunching behind Lars.

"Mamaw," I said, "he got a contract with Ford Models, Inc. He's the newest Calvin Klein underwear model. He's going to be a big celebrity, like—"

"UNDERWEAR?" Mamaw yelled. "Mia, you tell that boy to call me RIGHT NOW."

188

"Well, I can't really do that, Mamaw," I said. "On account of the fact that—"

"RIGHT NOW," Mamaw repeated, "or he's in BIG TROUBLE."

"Um," I said. The bell was ringing anyway. "Okay, Mamaw. Is, um, the, uh, wedding still on?"

"The WHAT?"

"The wedding," I said, wishing I could, just for once, be a normal girl who did not have to go around asking people if the royal marriage of her pregnant mother and her Algebra teacher was still on.

"Well, of course it's still on," Mamaw said. "What do you think?"

"Oh," I said. "You, um, talked to my mom?"

"Of course I did," Mamaw said. "Everything is all set."

"Really?" I was immensely surprised. I could not picture my mother going along with this thing. Not in a million years. "And she said she'd be there?"

"Well, of course she'll be there," Mamaw said. "It's her wedding, isn't it?"

Well . . . sort of, I guess. I didn't say that to Mamaw, though. I said, "Sure." And then I hung up, feeling crushed.

For entirely selfish reasons, too, I confess. I was a little bit sad for my mom, I guess, since she really had tried to put up a resistance against Grandmère. I mean, she really had tried. It wasn't her fault, of course, that she'd been going up against such a inexorable force.

But mostly I felt sad for myself. I would NEVER escape in time for *Rocky Horror*. Never, never, *never*. I mean, I know the movie doesn't even start until midnight, but wedding receptions last way longer than that.

And who knows if Michael will ever ask me out again? I mean, not once today has he acknowledged that he is, in fact, Jo-C-rox, nor has he mentioned *Rocky Horror*. Not once. Not even so much as a reference to Rachel Leigh Cook.

And we talked at length during G and T. AT LENGTH. That is on account of how some of us who saw last year's groundbreaking episode of *Lilly Tells It Like It Is* were understandably confused by Lilly's helping Hank to realize his dream of supermodel stardom. The segment was titled "Yes, You as an Individual *Can* Bring Down the Sexist, Racist, Ageist, and Sizeist Modeling Industry" (by "criticizing ads that demean women and limit our ideas of beauty" and "finding ways to make your protest known to the companies advertised" and "letting the media know you want to see more varied and realistic images of women." Also, Lilly urged us to "challenge men who judge, choose, and discard women on the basis of appearance").

The following exchange took place during Gifted and Talented (Mrs. Hill has returned to the teachers' lounge—permanently, one can only hope) and included Michael Moscovitz, who, as you will see, did NOT ONCE mention Jo-C-rox or *Rocky Horror*:

Me: Lilly, I thought you found the modeling industry as a whole sexist and racist and belittling to the human race.

Lilly: So? What's your point?

Me: Well, according to Hank, you helped him realize his

dream of becoming a you know what. A model.

Lilly: Mia, when I recognize a human soul crying out for self-actualization, I am powerless to stop myself. I must do what I can to see that that person's dream is realized.

[Gee, I haven't noticed Lilly doing all that much to help me realize *my* dream of French-kissing her brother. But on the other hand, I have not exactly made that dream known to her.]

Me: Um, Lilly, I hadn't noticed that you had a real foothold in the modeling industry.

Lilly: I don't. I merely taught your cousin how to make the most of his God-given talents. Some simple lessons in elocution and fashion, and he was well on his way to landing that contract with Ford.

Me: Well, why did it have to be such a big secret?

Lilly: Do you have any idea how fragile the male ego is?

[Here Michael broke in.]

Michael: Hey!

Lilly: I'm sorry, but it's true. Hank's self-esteem had already been reduced to nothing thanks to Amber, Corn Queen of Versailles County. I couldn't allow any negative comments to ruin what little self-confidence he had left. You know how fatalistic boys can be.

Michael: Hey!

Lilly: It was vital that Hank be allowed to pursue his dream without the slightest fatalistic influence. Otherwise, I knew, he didn't stand a chance. And so I kept our plan a secret even from those I most cared about. Any one of you, without consciously meaning to, might have torpedoed Hank's chances with the most casual of comments.

Me: Come on. We'd have been supportive.

Lilly: Mia, think about it. If Hank had said to you, 'Mia, I want to be a model,' what would you have done? Come on. You would have laughed.

Me: No, I wouldn't have.

Lilly: Yes, you would have. Because to you, Hank is your whiny, allergy-prone cousin from the boondocks who doesn't even know what a bagel is. But I, you see, was able to look beyond that, to the man Hank had the potential to become. . . .

Michael: Yeah, a man who is destined to have his own pin-up calendar.

Lilly: You, Michael, are just jealous.

Michael: Oh, yeah. I've always wanted a big picture of myself in my underwear hanging up in Times Square.

[Actually, I think that is something I would really enjoy seeing, but Michael was, of course, being sarcastic.]

Michael: You know, Lil, I highly doubt Mom and Dad are going to be so impressed by your tremendous act of charity that they're going to overlook the fact that you skipped school to do it. Especially when they find out you've got detention next week because of it.

Lilly: (looking long-suffering) The most eleemosynary are often martyred.

192

And that was it. That's all he said to me, all day. ALL DAY.

Note to self: look up *eleemosynary*

POSSIBLE REASONS MICHAEL WON'T ADMIT HE IS JO-C-ROX

1. He really is too shy to reveal his true feelings for me.
2. He thinks I don't feel the same way about him.
3. He's changed his mind and doesn't like me after all.
4. He doesn't want to have to bear the social stigma of dating a freshman and he is just waiting until I am a sophomore before asking me out. (Except that by then he'll be a freshman in college and won't want to bear the social stigma of dating a high school girl.)
5. He isn't Jo-C-rox at all and it turns out I am obsessing about something written by that guy from the cafeteria who has the thing about corn.

HOMEWORK

Algebra: none (no Mr. G!)
English: finish Day in a Life! Plus Profound Moment!
World Civ: read and analyze one current event from Sunday Times (200 wd minimum)
G&T: don't forget the dollar!
French: pg. 120, huit phrases (ex. A)
Biology: questions at end of Chapter 12—get answers from Kenny!

ENGLISH JOURNAL

A Day In My Life by Mia Thermopolis
(I chose to write about a night instead.
Is that okay, Mrs. Spears?)

FRIDAY, OCTOBER 31

3:16 p.m.—Arrive home at SoHo loft with bodyguard (Lars). Find it ostensibly empty. Decide mother probably napping (something she does a lot these days).

3:18 p.m.—3:45 p.m.—Play foozball with bodyguard. Win three out of twelve games. Decide must practice foozball in spare time.

3:50 p.m.—Curious as to why riotous game of foozball—not to mention incredibly loud pinball machine—have not awakened mother from nap. Knock gently on bedroom door. Stand there hoping door does not open and reveal view of mother actually sharing bed with Algebra teacher.

3:51 p.m.—Knock louder. Decide perhaps cannot be heard due to intense lovemaking session. Sincerely hope I will not be inadvertent witness to any nakedness.

3:52 p.m.—After receiving no response to my knock, I go into mother's bedroom. No one is there! Check of mother's bathroom reveals crucial items such as mascara, lipstick, and bottle of folic acid tablets missing from medicine cabinet. Begin to suspect something is afoot.

3:55 p.m.—Phone rings. I answer it. It is my father.

Following conversation ensues:

Me: Dad? Mom's missing. And so is Mr. Gianini. He didn't even come to school today.

Father: You still call him Mr. Gianini even though he lives with you?

Me: Dad. Where are they?

Father: Don't worry about it.

Me: That woman is carrying my last chance at having a sibling. How can I help but worry about her?

Father: Everything is under control.

Me: How am I supposed to believe that?

Father: Because I said so.

Me: Dad, I think you should know, I have some very serious trust issues concerning you.

Father: How come?

Me: Well, part of it might be the fact that up until about a month ago, you had lied to me for my entire life about who you are and what you do for a living.

Father: Oh.

Me: So just tell me. WHERE IS MY MOTHER?

Father: She left you a letter. You can have it at eight o'clock.

Me: Dad, eight o'clock is when the wedding is supposed to start.

Father: I am aware of that.

Me: Dad, you can't do this to me. What am I supposed to tell—

Voice: Phillipe, is everything all right?

Me: Who is that? Who *is* that, Dad? Is that Beverly Bellerieve?

Father: I have to go now, Mia.
Me: No, Dad, wait—
CLICK

4:00 p.m.–4:15 p.m.–Tear apartment apart, looking for clues as to where mother might have disappeared to. Find none.

4:20 p.m.–Phone rings. Paternal grandmother on line. Requests to know if mother and I are ready for trip to salon for beauty makeover. Inform her that mother has left already (well, it's the truth, isn't it?). Grandmother suspicious. Inform her that if she has any questions to consult with her son, my father. Grandmother says she fully intends to do so. Also says limo will be by at five o'clock to pick me up.

5:00 p.m.–Limo pulls up. Bodyguard and I get into it. Inside is paternal grandmother (hereafter known as Grandmère) and maternal grandmother (hereafter known as Mamaw). Mamaw is very excited about upcoming nuptials–though excitement is somewhat dampened by cousin's desertion to become male supermodel. Grandmère, on other hand, is mysteriously calm. Says son (my father) has informed her that bride has decided to make own hair and make-up plans. Remembering missing folic acid tablets, I say nothing.

5:20 p.m.–Enter Chez Paolo.

6:45 p.m.–Emerge from Chez Paolo. Amazed at difference Paolo has made with Mamaw's hair. She no longer resembles mom in John Hughes film, but member of upscale country club.

7:00 p.m.—Arrive at Plaza. Father attributes bride's absence to her desire to nap before ceremony. When I surreptitiously force Lars to call home on his cell phone, however, no one answers.

7:15 p.m.—Begins to rain again. Mamaw observes that rain on a wedding day is bad luck. Grandmère says, No, that's pearls. Mamaw says, No, rain. First sign of division within formerly united ranks of grandmas.

7:30 p.m.—I am ushered into little chamber just off the White and Gold Room, where I sit with the other brides-maids (supermodels Gisele, Karmen Kass, and Amber Valletta, whom Grandmère has hired due to fact that my mother refused to supply her with list of her own brides-maids). I have changed into my beautiful pink dress and matching shoes.

7:40 p.m.—None of the other bridesmaids will talk to me, except to comment about how I look so "sweet." All they can talk about is a party they went to last night where someone threw up on Claudia Schiffer's shoes.

7:45 p.m.—Guests begin to arrive. I fail to recognize my maternal grandfather without his baseball cap. He looks quite spry in his tux. A little like an elderly Matt Damon.

7:47 p.m.—Two people arrive who claim to be parents of the groom. Mr. Gianini's parents from Long Island! Mr. Gianini Sr. calls Vigo "Bucko." Vigo looks delighted.

7:48 p.m.—Martha Stewart stands near door, chatting with Donald Trump about Manhattan real estate. She can't find a building with a co-op board that will let her keep her pet chinchillas.

7:50 p.m.—David Hasselhoff has cut his hair. Almost

don't recognize him. Looks faintly babe-like. Queen of Sweden asks him if he is friend of bride or groom. Says groom, for some inexplicable reason, though I happen to know from having looked through Mr. Gianini's CDs that he owns nothing but the Rolling Stones and a little Who.

7:55 p.m.—Everyone goes quiet as David Hasselhoff sits down at baby grand. Pray that my mother is in different hemisphere and cannot see or hear this.

8:00 p.m.—Everyone waits expectantly. I demand that my father, who has joined me and the supermodels, give me letter from my mother. Dad surrenders letter.

8:01 p.m.—I read letter.

8:02 p.m.—I have to sit down.

8:05 p.m.—Grandmère and Vigo in deep consultation. They seem to have realized that neither the bride nor the groom have shown up.

8:07 p.m.—Amber Valletta whispers that if we don't get a move on, she's going to be late for a dinner engagement with Hugh Grant.

8:10 p.m.—A hush falls over the guests as my father, looking excessively princely in his tux (in spite of his bald head) strides to the front of the White and Gold Room. David Hasselhoff stops playing.

8:11 p.m.—My father makes the following announcement:

Father: I want to thank all of you for taking the time out of your busy schedules to come here tonight. Unfortunately, the wedding between Helen Thermopolis and Frank Gianini will not take place . . . at least, not this evening. The happy couple have given us the slip, and this morning they flew to Cancun, where I understand they plan to be married by a justice of the peace.

[A shriek is heard from the far side of the baby grand. It does not appear to have come from David Hasselhoff, but rather, Grandmère.]

Father: You are of course urged to join us in the Grand Ballroom for dinner. And thank you again for coming.

[Father strides off. Bewildered guests gather their belongings and go in search of cocktails. No sound whatsoever is heard from behind baby grand.]

Me: (to no one in particular) Mexico! They must be crazy. If my mother drinks the water, my future brother or sister will be born with flippers for feet!
Amber: Don't worry, my friend Heather got pregnant in Mexico, and she drank the water, and she just gave birth to twins.
Me: And they had dorsal fins coming out of their backs, didn't they?

8:20 p.m.—David Hasselhoff begins to play. At least until Grandmère barks, "Oh, shut up!"

199

What the letter from my mother said:

Dear Mia,
By the time you read this, Frank and I will be married. I am sorry I couldn't tell you sooner, but when your grandmother asks you if you knew (and she will ask you), I wanted to be sure you could say truthfully that you didn't, so there won't be any ill feeling between the two of you.

[Ill feeling between Grandmère and me? Who does she think she's kidding? There's nothing but ill feeling between us!
Well, as far I'm concerned, anyway.]

More than anything, Frank and I wanted you to be there for our wedding. So we have decided that when we get back, we're going to have another ceremony: This one will be kept strictly secret and very private, with just our little family and our friends!

[Well, that certainly should be interesting. Most of my mom's friends are militant feminists or performance artists. One of them likes to stand up on a stage and pour chocolate syrup all over her naked body while reciting poetry.
I wonder how they are going to get along with Mr. G's friends, who I understand like to watch a lot of sports.]

You have been a tower of strength during this crazy time, Mia, and I want you to know how much I—as well as your father, and stepfather—appreciate it. You are the best daughter a mother could have, and this new little guy (or girl) is the luckiest baby in the world to have you as a big sister.

Missing you already—
Mom

I am in shock. I really am.

Not because my mom and my Algebra teacher eloped. That's kind of romantic, if you ask me.

No, it's the fact that my dad—*my dad*—helped them to do it. He actually defied his mother. In a BIG way.

In fact, because of all this, I'm starting to think my dad isn't scared of Grandmère at all! I think he just doesn't want to be bothered. I think he just feels it's easier to go along with her than to fight her, because fighting her is so messy and exhausting.

But not this time. This time, he put his foot down.

And you can bet he's going to pay for it, too.

I may never get over this. I am going to have to readjust everything I ever thought about him. Kind of like when Luke Skywalker finds out his dad is really Darth Vader. Only the opposite.

Anyway, while Grandmère was plotzing behind the baby grand, I went up to Dad and threw my arms around him and was like, "You did it!"

He looked at me curiously. "Why do you sound surprised?"

Oops. I said, totally embarrassed, "Oh, well, because, you know."

"No, I don't know."

"Well," I said. (WHY? WHY do I have such a big mouth?)

I thought about lying. But I think my dad must have realized what I was thinking, since he said, in this warning voice, "*Mia . . .*"

"Oh, okay," I said, grudgingly, letting him go. "It's just that sometimes you give the appearance—just the appearance, mind you—of being a little bit scared of Grandmère."

My dad reached out and wrapped an arm around my neck. He did this right in front of Liz Smith, who was getting up to follow everyone into the Grand Ballroom. She smiled at us as if she thought it was sweet, though.

"Mia," my dad said. "I am not scared of my mother. She really isn't as bad as you think. She just needs proper handling."

This was news to me.

"Besides," my dad said, "do you really think I would ever let you down? Or your mother? I will always be there for you two."

This was so nice, I actually got tears in my eyes for a minute. But it might have been the smoke from all the cigarettes. There were a lot of French people at this party.

"Mia, I haven't done so badly by you, have I?" my dad asked, all of a sudden.

I was surprised by the question. "No, Dad, of course not. You guys have always been okay parents."

My dad nodded. "I see."

I could see I hadn't been complimentary enough, so I added, "No, I mean it. I really couldn't ask for better . . ." I couldn't help adding, "I could probably live without the princess thing, though."

He looked as if he probably would have reached out and

203

ruffled my hair if it hadn't been so full of mousse his hand would have stuck to it.

"Sorry about that," he said. "But do you really think you'd be happy, Mia, being Nancy Normal Teenager?"

Um. Yes.

Except I wouldn't want my name to be Nancy.

We might have gone on to have a really profound moment I could have written about in my English journal if Vigo hadn't come hurrying up just then. He looked frazzled. And why not? His wedding was turning out to be a disaster! First the bride and groom had neglected to show up, and now the hostess, the dowager princess, had locked herself into her hotel suite and would not come out.

"What do you mean, she won't come out?" my father demanded.

"Just what I said, Your Highness." Vigo looked like he was about to start crying. "I have never seen her so angry! She says she has been betrayed by her own family, and she will never be able to show her face in public again, the shame is so great."

My dad looked heavenward. "Let's go," he said.

When we got to the door to the penthouse suite, my dad signaled for Vigo and me to be quiet. Then he knocked on the door.

"Mother," he called. "Mother, it's Phillipe. May I come in?"

No response. But I could tell she was in there. I could hear Rommel moaning softly.

"Mother," my dad said. He tried turning the door

handle, and found it locked. This caused him to sigh very deeply.

Well, you could see why. He had already spent the better part of the day thwarting all of her well-laid plans. That had to have been exhausting. And now *this*?

"Mother," he said. "I want you to open this door."

Still no response.

"Mother," my father said. "You are being ridiculous. I want you to open this door this instant. If you don't do it, I shall fetch the housekeeper, and have her open it for me. Are you trying to force me to resort to this? Is that it?"

I knew Grandmère would sooner let us see her without her makeup than ever allow a member of the hotel staff to be privy to one of our family squabbles, so I laid a hand on my dad's arm and whispered, "Dad, let me try."

My father shrugged, and, with a sort of if-you-want-to look, stepped aside.

I called through the door, "Grandmère? Grandmère, it's me, Mia."

I don't know what I'd expected. Certainly not for her to open the door. I mean, if she wouldn't do it for Vigo, whom she seemed to adore, or for her own son, who, if she didn't adore, was at least her only child, why would she do it for me?

But I was greeted with only silence from behind that door. Well, except for Rommel's whining.

I refused to be daunted, however. I raised my voice and called, "I'm really sorry about my mom and Mr. Gianini, Grandmère. But you have to admit it, I warned you that she didn't want this wedding. Remember? I told you she wanted something small. You might have realized that by the fact that there isn't a single person here who was actually invited by my mother. These are all *your* friends. Well, except for Mamaw and Papaw. And Mr. G's parents. But I mean, come on. My mom does not know Imelda Marcos, okay? And Barbara Bush? I'm sure she's a very nice lady, but not one of my mom's closest buddies."

Still no response.

"Grandmère," I called through the door. "Look, I am really surprised at you. I thought you were always teaching me that a princess has to be strong. I thought you said that a princess, no matter what kind of adversity she is facing, has to put on a brave face and not hide behind her wealth and privilege. Well, isn't that exactly what you're doing right now? Shouldn't you be down there right now, pretending this was exactly the way you planned things to go, and raising a glass to the happy couple in absentia?"

I jumped back as the doorknob to my grandmother's suite slowly turned. A second later, Grandmère came out, a vision in purple velvet and a diamond tiara.

She said, with a great deal of dignity, "I had every intention of returning to the party. I merely came up here to freshen my lipstick."

My dad and I exchanged glances.

"Sure, Grandmère," I said. "Whatever you say."

"A princess," Grandmère said, closing the door to her suite behind her, "never leaves her guests unattended."

"Okay," I said.

"So what are you two doing here?" Grandmère glared at my dad and me.

"We were, um, just checking on you," I explained.

"I see." Then Grandmère did a surprising thing. She slipped her hand through the crook of my elbow. Then, without looking at my dad, she said, "Come along."

I saw my dad roll his eyes at this blatant dis.

But he didn't look scared, the way I would have been.

"Hold on, Grandmère," I said.

Then I slipped my hand through the crook of my dad's elbow, so the three of us were standing in the hallway, linked by . . . well, by me.

Grandmère just sniffed and didn't say anything. But my dad smiled.

And you know what? I'm not sure, but I think it might have been a profound moment for all of us.

Well, all right. At least for *me*, anyway.

The evening wasn't a total bust.

Quite a few people seemed to have a very good time. Hank, for one. He actually showed up just in time for dinner—he'd always been good at that—looking totally gorgeous in an Armani tux.

Mamaw and Papaw were delighted to see him. Mrs. Gianini, Mr. Gianini's mom, took quite a shine to him, too. It must have been his clean-cut good manners. He hadn't forgotten any of Lilly's elocution lessons, and only mentioned his affection for 'muddin' on the weekends once. And later, when the dancing started, he asked Grandmère for the second waltz—Dad got the first—forever cementing him in her mind as the ideal royal consort for me.

Thank God first-cousin marriages were made illegal in Genovia in 1907.

But the happiest people I talked to all evening weren't actually at the party. No, at around ten o'clock, Lars handed me his cell phone, and when I said, "Hello?" wondering who it could be, my mom's voice, sounding very far away and crackly, went, "Mia?"

I didn't want to say the word 'Mom' too loudly, since I knew Grandmère was hovering nearby. And I don't think it likely that Grandmère is going to forgive my parents anytime soon for the fast one they pulled. I ducked behind a pillar and whispered, "Hey, Mom! Mr. Gianini make an honest woman out of you yet?"

Well, he had. The deed was done (a little late, if you ask me, but hey, at least the kid won't be born harboring the stigma of illegitimacy like I've had to all my life). It was only like six o'clock where they were, and they were on a beach somewhere sipping (virgin) piña coladas. I made my mom promise not to have any more, because you can't trust the ice at those places.

"Parasites can exist in ice, Mom," I informed her. "There are these worms that live in the glaciers in Antarctica, you know. We studied them in Bio. They've been around for thousands of years. So even if the water's frozen, you can still get sick from it. You definitely only want to get ice made from bottled water. Here, why don't you put Mr. Gianini on the phone, and I'll tell him exactly what he has to do—"

My mom interrupted me.

"Mia," she said. "How are—" She cleared her throat. "How's my mother taking it?"

"Mamaw?" I looked in Mamaw's direction. The truth was, Mamaw was having the time of her life. She was thoroughly enjoying her gig as mother of the bride. So far, she'd gotten to dance with Prince Albert, who was there representing the royal family of Monaco, and Prince Andrew, who didn't seem to be missing Fergie one bit, if you asked me.

"Um," I said. "Mamaw's . . . really mad at you."

It was a lie, of course, but it was a lie I knew would make my mother happy. One of her favorite things to do is make her parents mad.

"Really, Mia?" she asked, breathlessly.

"Uh-huh," I said, watching as Papaw twirled Mamaw around practically into the champagne fountain. "They'll probably never speak to you again."

"Oh," Mom said happily. "Isn't that too bad?"

Sometimes my natural ability to lie actually comes in handy.

But unfortunately, right then our connection broke up. Well, at least Mom had heard my warning about the ice worms before we lost contact.

As for me, well, I can't say I had the time of my life—I mean, the only person even close to my age was Hank, and he was way too busy dancing with Gisele to talk to me.

Thankfully, around eleven, my dad was like, "Uh, Mia, isn't it Halloween?"

I said, "Yeah, Dad."

"Don't you have someplace you'd rather be?"

You know, I hadn't forgotten the whole *Rocky Horror* thing, but I figured Grandmère needed me. Sometimes family things are more important than friend things—even romance things.

But as soon as I heard that, I was like, "Um, yes."

The movie started at midnight down at the Village Cinema—about fifty blocks away. If I hurried, I could make it. Well, Lars and I could make it.

There was only one problem. We had no costumes: On Halloween, they don't let you into the theater if you come in street clothes.

"What do you mean, you don't have a costume?" Martha Stewart had overheard our conversation.

I held out the skirt of my dress. "Well," I said, dubiously. "I guess I could pass for Glinda the Good Witch. Only I don't have a wand. No crown, either."

I don't know if Martha had too many champagne cocktails, or if she's just like this, but next thing I knew, she was whipping me up a wand from a bunch of crystal drink stir-rers that she tied together with some ivy from the center-piece. Then she fashioned this big crown for me out of some menus and a glue gun she had in her purse.

And you know what? It looked good, just like the one in *The Wizard of Oz*! (She turned the writing so it was on the inside of the crown.)

"There," Martha said, when she was through. "Glinda the Good Witch." She looked at Lars. "And you're easy. You're James Bond."

Lars seemed pleased. You could tell he'd always fanta-sized about being a secret agent.

No one was more pleased than me, however. My fantasy of Michael seeing me in this gorgeous dress was about to be realized. What's more, the outfit was going to give me the confidence I needed to confront him about Jo-C-rox.

So, with my father's blessings—I would have stopped to say good-bye to Grandmère, only she and Gerald Ford were doing the tango out on the dance floor (no, I am not kid-ding)—I was out of there like a shot—

And stumbled right into a thorny patch of reporters.

"Princess Mia!" they yelled. "Princess Mia, what are your feelings about your mother's elopement?"

I was about to let Lars hustle me into the limo without saying anything to the reporters. But then I had an idea. I grabbed the nearest microphone and said, "I just want to say to anyone who is watching that Albert Einstein High School is the best school in Manhattan, maybe even North America, and that we have the most excellent faculty and the best student population in the world, and anyone who doesn't recognize that is just kidding himself, Mr. Taylor."

(Mr. Taylor is Shameeka's dad.)

Then I shoved the microphone back at its owner, and hopped into the limo.

We almost didn't make it. First of all, because of the parade, the traffic downtown was criminal. Secondly, there was a line to get into the Village Cinema that wound all the way around the block! I had the limo driver cruise the length of it, while Lars and I scanned the assorted hordes. It was pretty hard to recognize my friends, because everyone was in costume.

But then I saw this group of really weird-looking people dressed in WWII Army fatigues. They were all covered in fake blood, and some of them had phony stumps in place of limbs. They were holding a big sign that said *Looking for Private Ryan*. Standing next to them was a girl wearing a black lacy slip and a fake beard. And standing next to her was a boy dressed as a Mafioso type, holding a violin case.

The violin case was what did it.

"Stop the car!" I shrieked.

The limo pulled over, and Lars and I got out. The girl in the nightie went, "Oh, my God! You came! You came!"

It was Lilly. And standing next to her, a big pile of bloody intestines coming out of his Army jacket, was her brother, Michael.

"Quick," he said, to Lars and me. "Get in line. I got two extra tickets just in case you ended up making it after all."

There was some grumbling from the people behind us as Lars and I cut in, but all he had to do was turn so that his shoulder holster showed, and they got quiet pretty quick.

Lars's Glock, being real and all, was pretty scary-looking.

"Where's Hank?" Lilly wanted to know.

"He couldn't make it," I said. I didn't want to tell her why. You know, that last time I'd seen him, he'd been dancing with Gisele. I didn't want Lilly to think Hank preferred supermodels to, you know, us.

"He cannot come. Good," Boris said, firmly.

Lilly shot him a warning look, then, pointing at me, demanded, "What are you supposed to be?"

"Duh," I said. "I'm Glinda the Good Witch."

"I knew that," Michael said. "You look really . . .You look really . . ."

He seemed unable to go on. I must, I realized, with a sinking heart, look really stupid.

"You are way too glam for Halloween," Lilly declared.

Glam? Well, glam was better than stupid, I guess. But why couldn't Michael have said so?

I eyed her. "Um," I said. "What, exactly, are you?"

She fingered the straps to her slip, then fluffed out her fake beard.

"Hello," she said, in a very sarcastic voice. "I'm a Freudian slip."

Boris indicated his violin case. "And I am Al Capone," he said. "Chicago gangster."

"Good for you, Boris," I said, noticing he was wearing a sweater, and yes, it was tucked into his pants. He can't help being totally foreign, I guess.

Someone tugged on my skirt. I looked around, and there was Kenny, my Bio partner. He was in Army fatigues, too, and missing an arm.

"You made it!" he cried.

"I did," I said. The excitement in the air was contagious.

Then the line started moving. Michael and Kenny's friends from the Computer Club, who made up the rest of the bloody platoon, started marching and going, "Hut, two, three, four. Hut, two, three, four."

Well, they can't help it. They're in the computer club, after all.

It wasn't until the movie started that I began to realize something weird was going on. I very cleverly maneuvered myself in the aisle so that I would end up sitting next to Michael. Lars was supposed to be on my other side.

But somehow Lars got pushed out, and Kenny ended up on my other side.

Not that it mattered . . . then. Lars just sat behind me. I hardly noticed Kenny, even though he kept trying to talk to me, mostly about Bio. I answered him, but all I could think about was Michael. Did he really think I looked stupid? When should I mention that I happen to know that he is Jo-C-rox? I had this little speech all rehearsed. I was going to be like, Hey, seen any good cartoons lately?

Lame, I know, but how else was I supposed to bring it up?

I could hardly wait for the movie to be over so I could spring my offensive.

Rocky Horror, even if you can't wait for it to end, is pretty fun. Everybody just acts like a lunatic. People were throwing bread at the screen, and putting up umbrellas when it rained in the movie, and dancing the Pelvic Thrust. It really is one of the best movies of all time. It almost beats out

Dirty Dancing as my favorite, except, of course, there's no Patrick Swayze.

Except I forgot there aren't really any scary parts. So I didn't actually get a chance to pretend to be scared so Michael could put his arm around me, or anything.

Which kind of sucks, if you think about it.

But hey, I got to sit by him, didn't I? For like two hours. In the dark. That's something, isn't it? And he kept laughing and looking at me to see whether or not I was laughing, too. That counts, right? I mean, when someone keeps checking to see whether you think the same things are funny that he does? That totally counts for something.

The only problem was, I couldn't help noticing that Kenny was doing the same thing. You know, laughing and then looking at me to see if I was laughing, too.

That should have been my next clue.

After the movie, we all went out to breakfast at Round the Clock. And this is where things got even more weird.

I had been to Round the Clock before, of course—where else in Manhattan can you get pancakes for two dollars?— but never quite this late, and never with a bodyguard. Poor Lars was looking a little worse for wear by that time. He kept ordering cup after cup of coffee. I was jammed in at this table between Michael and Kenny—funny how that kept happening—with Lilly and Boris and the entire Computer Club all around us. Everyone was talking really loud and at the same time, and I was having a really hard time figuring out how I was ever going to bring up the cartoon thing, when all of a sudden, Kenny said, right in my ear, "Had any interesting mail lately?"

215

I am sorry to say that it was only then that the truth dawned.

I should have known, of course.

It hadn't been Michael. *Michael wasn't Jo-C-rox.*

I think a part of me must have known that all along. I mean, it really isn't like Michael to do anything anonymously. He just isn't the type not to sign his name. I guess I'd been suffering from a bad case of wishful thinking, or something.

A REALLY bad case of wishful thinking.

Because of course Jo-C-rox was Kenny.

Not that there's anything wrong with Kenny. There totally isn't. He is a really, really nice guy. I mean, I really like Kenny Showalter. Really, I do.

But he's not Michael Moscovitz.

I looked up at Kenny after he'd made that comment about having any interesting mail lately, and I tried to smile. I really did.

I said, "Oh, Kenny. Are you Jo-C-rox?"

Kenny grinned.

"Yes," Kenny said. "Didn't you figure it out?"

No. Because I am a complete idiot.

"Uh-huh," I said, forcing another smile. "Finally."

"Good." Kenny looked pleased. "Because you really do remind me of Josie, you know. Of *Josie and the Pussycats*, I mean. See, she's lead singer in a rock group, and she solves mysteries on the side. She's cool. Like you."

Oh, my God. *Kenny.* My Bio partner, *Kenny.* Six-foot-tall, totally gawky Kenny, who always gives me the answers in Bio. I'd forgotten he's like this huge Japanese anime fan.

Of course he watches the Cartoon Network. He's practically addicted to it. *Batman* is like his favorite thing of all time.

Oh, someone shoot me. Someone please shoot me.

I smiled. I'm afraid my smile was very weak.

But Kenny didn't care.

"And you know, in later episodes," Kenny said, encouraged by my smile, "Josie and the Pussycats go up into space. So she's also a pioneer into space exploration."

Oh, God, make this be a bad dream. Please make this be a bad dream, and let me wake up and have it not be true!

All I could do was thank my lucky stars that I hadn't said anything to Michael. Could you imagine if I'd gone up to him and said what I'd planned to? He'd have thought I'd forgotten to take my medication, or something.

"Anyway," Kenny said. "You want to go out sometime, Mia? With me, I mean?"

Oh, God. I hate that. I really hate that. You know, when people go "Do you want to go out with me sometime?" instead of "Do you want to go out with me next Tuesday?" Because that way you can make up an excuse. Because then you can always go, "Oh, no, on Tuesday I have this thing."

But you can't go, "No, I don't want to go out with you EVER."

Because that would be too mean.

And I can't be mean to Kenny. I like Kenny. I really do. He's very funny and sweet and everything.

But do I want his tongue in my mouth?

Not so much.

What could I say? "No, Kenny? No, Kenny, I don't want

to go out with you ever, because I happen to be in love with my best friend's brother?"

You can't say that.

Well, maybe some girls can.

But not me.

"Sure, Kenny," I said.

After all, how bad could a date with Kenny be? What doesn't kill us makes us stronger. That's what Grandmère says, anyway.

After that, I had no choice but to let Kenny put his arm around me—the only one he had, the other being tightly secured beneath his costume to give him the appearance of having been severely injured in a land mine explosion.

But we were all jammed in so closely at that table that Kenny's arm, as it went around my shoulders, jostled Michael, and he looked over at us. . . .

And then he looked over at Lars, really fast. Almost like he—I don't know . . .

Saw what was going on, and wanted Lars to put a stop to it?

No. No, of course not. It couldn't be that.

But it is true that when Lars, who was busy pouring sugar into like his fifth cup of coffee that night, didn't look up, Michael stood and said, "Well, I'm beat. What do you say we call it a night?"

Everyone looked at him like he was crazy. I mean, some people were still finishing their food and all. Lilly even went, "What's with you, Michael? Gotta catch up on your beauty sleep?"

But Michael totally took out his wallet and started counting out how much he owed.

So then I stood up really fast and said, "I'm tired, too. Lars, could you call the car?"

Lars, delighted finally to be leaving, whipped out his cell phone and started dialing. Kenny, beside me, started saying stuff like, "It's a shame you have to go so early," and "So, Mia, can I call you?"

This last question caused Lilly to look from me to Kenny and then back again. Then she looked at Michael. Then she stood up, too.

"Come on, Al," she said, giving Boris a tap on the head. "Let's blow this juke joint."

Only of course Boris didn't understand. "What is a juke joint?" he asked. "And why are we blowing it?"

Everyone started digging around for money to pay the bill . . . which was when I remembered that I didn't have any. Money, I mean. I didn't even have a purse to put money in. That was the one part of my wedding ensemble Grandmère had forgotten.

I elbowed Lars and whispered, "Have you got any cash? I'm a little low at the moment."

Lars nodded and reached for his wallet. That's when Kenny, who noticed this, went, "Oh, no, Mia. Your pancakes are on me."

This, of course, completely freaked me out. I didn't want Kenny to pay for my pancakes. Or Lars's five cups of coffee, either.

"Oh, no," I said. "That isn't necessary."

Which didn't have at all the desired effect, since Kenny said, all stiffly, "I insist," and started throwing dollar bills

219

down on the table.

Remembering I'm supposed to be gracious, being a princess and all, I said, "Well, thank you very much, Kenny."

Which was when Lars handed Michael a twenty and said, "For the movie tickets."

Only then Michael wouldn't take my money—okay, it was Lars's money, but my dad totally would have paid him back—either. He looked totally embarrassed, and went, "Oh, no. My treat," even after I strenuously insisted.

So then I had to say, "Well, thank you very much, Michael," when all I really wanted to say was, "Get me out of here!"

Because with two different guys paying for me, it was like I'd been out on a date with both of them at once!

Which, I guess, in a way, I had.

You would think I would be very excited about this. I mean, considering I'd never really been out even with *one* guy before, let alone *two* at the same time.

Except that it was totally and completely *not* fun. Because, for one thing, I didn't actually want to be going out with one of them at all.

And for another, he was the one who'd actually confessed to liking me . . . even if it had been anonymous.

The whole thing was excruciating, and all I wanted to do was go home and get in bed and pull the covers up over my head and pretend it hadn't happened.

Only I couldn't even do that because, what with my mom and Mr. G being in Cancun, I had to stay up at the Plaza with Grandmère and my dad until they got back.

But just when I thought things had sunk to an all-time low, as everyone was piling into the limo (well, a few people asked for rides home, and how could I say no? It wasn't like we didn't have the room) Michael, who ended up standing beside me, waiting for his turn to get into the car, said, "What I meant to say before, Mia, was that you look . . . you look really . . ."

I blinked up at him in the pink-and-blue light from the neon Round the Clock sign in the window behind us. It's amazing, but even bathed in pink-and-blue neon, with fake intestines hanging out of his shirt, Michael still looked totally—

"You look really nice in that dress," he said, all in a rush.

I smiled up at him, feeling just like Cinderella all of a sudden. . . . You know, at the end of the Disney movie, when Prince Charming finally finds her and puts the slipper on her foot and her rags change back into the ball gown and all the mice come out and start singing?

That's how I felt, just for a second.

Then this voice right beside us said, "Are you guys coming, or what?" and we looked over and there was Kenny sticking his head and his one unsevered arm out of the sun roof of the limo.

"Um," I said, feeling totally and utterly embarrassed. "Yes."

And I got into the limo like nothing had happened.

And actually, if you think about it, nothing really had.

Except that the whole way back to the Plaza, this little voice inside my brain was going, "Michael said I looked nice. Michael said *I* looked nice. *Michael* said I looked nice."

221

And you know what? Maybe Michael didn't write those notes. And maybe he doesn't think I'm the Josiest girl in school.

But he thought I looked nice in my pink dress. And that's all that matters to me.

And now I am sitting in Grandmère's suite at the hotel, surrounded by piles of wedding and baby presents, with Rommel trembling down at the other end of the couch in a pink cashmere sweater. I am supposed to be writing thank-you notes, but of course I am writing in my journal instead.

No one seems to have noticed, though, I guess because Mamaw and Papaw are here. They stopped by to say good-bye on their way to the airport before they fly back to Indiana. Right now, my two grandmothers are making lists of baby names and talking about who to invite to the christening (oh, no. Not again.) while my dad and Papaw are talking about crop rotation, as this is an important topic to both Indiana farmers and Genovian olive growers. Even though, of course, Papaw owns a hardware store and Dad is a prince. But whatever. At least they're *talking*.

Hank is here, too, to say good-bye and to try to convince his grandparents they are not doing the wrong thing, leaving him here in New York—though to tell the truth, he isn't doing such a good job of it, since he hasn't once gotten off his cell phone since he arrived. Most of these calls seem to be from last night's bridesmaids.

And I'm thinking that, all in all, things aren't so bad. I mean, I am getting a baby brother or sister and have also acquired not just a stepfather who is exceptionally good at

Algebra, but a foozball table as well.

And my dad proved that there is at least one person on this planet who is not afraid of Grandmère . . . and even Grandmère seems a bit more mellow than usual, in spite of never having made it to Baden-Baden.

Though she still isn't talking to my dad, except when she absolutely has to.

And yes, it is true that later today I have to meet Kenny back at the Village Cinema for a Japanese anime marathon, since I said I would, and all.

But after that I am going down to Lilly's, and we are going to work on next week's show, which is about repressed memories. We are going to try to hypnotize each other and see if we can remember any of our past lives. Lilly is convinced, for instance, that in one of her past lives she was Elizabeth I.

You know what? I, for one, believe her.

Anyway, after that, I am spending the night at Lilly's, and we are going to rent *Dirty Dancing* and *Rocky Horror*-ize it. We plan to yell things in response to the actors' lines and throw things at the screen.

And there is a very good chance that tomorrow morning, Michael will come to the Moscovitzes' breakfast table wearing pajama bottoms and a robe, and forget to tie the robe like he did once before.

Which would actually make for a very profound moment, if you ask me.

A *very* profound moment.

MEG CABOT

Princess *in love*

HARPER TEEN
AN IMPRINT OF HARPERCOLLINS PUBLISHERS

ACKNOWLEDGMENTS

Many thanks to Beth Ader, Jennifer Brown, Barbara Cabot, Sarah Davies, Laura Langlie, Abby McAden, and David Walton.

For Benjamin, with love

"One of Sara's 'pretends' is that she is a princess," said Jessie. "She plays it all the time—even in school. She wants Ermengarde to be one, too, but Ermengarde says she is too fat."

"She is too fat," said Lavinia. "And Sara is too thin."

"Sara says it has nothing to do with what you look like, or what you have. It has only to do with what you think of, and what you do," Jessie explained.

A LITTLE PRINCESS
Frances Hodgson Burnett

Assignment (Due December 8): Here at Albert Einstein High School, we have a very diverse student population. Over one hundred and seventy different nations, religions, and ethnic groups are represented by our student body. In the space below, describe the manner in which your family celebrates the uniquely American holiday, Thanksgiving. Please utilize appropriate margins.

MY THANKSGIVING
by Mia Thermopolis

6:45 a.m.–Roused by the sound of my mother vomiting. She is well into her third month of pregnancy now. According to her obstetrician, all the throwing up should stop in the next trimester. I can't wait. I have been marking the days off on my 'N Sync calendar. (I don't really like 'N Sync. At least, not that much. My best friend, Lilly, bought me the calendar as a joke. Except that one guy really is pretty cute.)

7:45 a.m.– Mr. Gianini, my new stepfather, knocks on my door. Only now I am supposed to call him Frank. This is very difficult to remember due to the fact that at school, where he is my first-period Algebra teacher, I am supposed to call him Mr. Gianini. So I just don't call him anything (to his face).

It's time to get up, Mr. Gianini says. We are having Thanksgiving at his parents' house on Long Island. We have to leave now if we are going to beat the traffic.

8:45 a.m.—There is no traffic this early on Thanksgiving Day. We arrive at Mr. G's parents' house in Sagaponic three hours early.

Mrs. Gianini (Mr. Gianini's mother, not my mother. My mother is still Helen Thermopolis because she is a fairly well known modern painter under that name, and also because she does not believe in the cult of the patriarchy) is still in curlers. She looks very surprised. This might not only be because we arrived so early, but also because no sooner had my mother entered the house than she was forced to run for the bathroom with her hand pressed over her mouth, on account of the smell of the roasting turkey. I am hoping this means that my future half-brother or -sister is a vegetarian, since the smell of meat cooking used to make my mother hungry, not nauseated.

My mother had already informed me in the car on the way over from Manhattan that Mr. Gianini's parents are very old-fashioned and are used to enjoying a conventional Thanksgiving meal. She does not think they will appreciate hearing my traditional Thanksgiving speech about how the Pilgrims are guilty of committing mass genocide by giving their new Native American friends blankets filled with the smallpox virus, and that it is reprehensible that we as a country annually celebrate this rape and destruction of an entire culture.

Instead, my mother said, I should discuss more neutral topics, such as the weather.

I asked if it was all right if I discussed the astonishingly

2

high rate of attendance at the Reykjavik opera house in Iceland (over 98 percent of the country's population has seen *Tosca* at least once).

My mother sighed and said, "If you must," which I take to be a sign that she is beginning to tire of hearing about Iceland.

Well, I am sorry, but I find Iceland extremely fascinating, and I will not rest until I have visited the ice hotel.

9:45 a.m.–11:45 a.m.–I watch the Macy's Thanksgiving Day parade with Mr. Gianini Senior in what he calls the rec room.

They don't have rec rooms in Manhattan.

Just lobbies.

Remembering my mother's warning, I refrain from repeating another one of my traditional holiday rants, that the Macy's Thanksgiving Day parade is a gross example of American capitalism run amok.

At one point during the broadcast, I catch sight of Lilly standing in the crowd outside of Office Max on Broadway and Thirty-Seventh, her videocamera clutched to her slightly squished-in face (so much like a pug) as a float carrying Miss America and William Shatner of *Star Trek* fame passes by. So I know Lilly is going to take care of denouncing Macy's on the next episode of her public access television show, *Lilly Tells It Like It Is* (every Friday night at nine, Manhattan cable channel 67).

12:00 p.m.–Mr. Gianini Junior's sister arrives with her husband, their two kids, and the pumpkin pies. The kids, who are my age, are twins, a boy, Nathan, and a girl,

Claire. I know right away Claire and I are not going to get along, because when we are introduced she looks me up and down the way the cheerleaders do in the hallway at school and goes, in a very snotty voice, "*You're* the one who's supposed to be a princess?"

And while I am perfectly aware that at five foot nine inches tall, with no visible breasts, feet the size of snow-shoes, and hair that sits in a tuft on my head like the cotton on the end of a Q-tip, I am the biggest freak in the freshman class of Albert Einstein High School for Boys (made coeducational circa 1975), I do not appreciate being reminded of it by girls who do not even bother finding out that beneath this mutant facade beats the heart of a person who is only striving, just like everybody else in this world, to find self-actualization.

Not that I even care what Mr. Gianini's niece Claire thinks of me. I mean, she is wearing a pony-skin miniskirt. And it is not even imitation pony skin. She must know that a horse had to die just so she could have that skirt, but she obviously doesn't care.

Now Claire has pulled out her cell phone and gone out onto the deck, where the reception is best (even though it is thirty degrees outside, she apparently doesn't mind. She has that pony skin to keep her warm, after all). She keeps looking in at me through the sliding glass doors and laughing as she talks on her phone.

Nathan—who is dressed in baggy jeans and has a pager, in addition to a lot of gold jewelry—asks his grandfather if he can change the channel. So instead of traditional Thanksgiving viewing options, such as football or the Lifetime Channel's made-for-TV movie marathon, we are now forced to watch MTV2. Nathan knows all the songs and sings along with them. Most of them have dirty words that have been bleeped out, but Nathan sings them anyway.

1:00 p.m. – The food is served. We begin eating.

1:15 p.m. – We finish eating.

1:20 p.m. – I help Mrs. Gianini clean up. She says not to be ridiculous, and that I should go "have a nice gossip" with Claire.

It is frightening, if you think about it, how clueless old people can be sometimes.

Instead of going to have a nice gossip with Claire, I stay where I am and tell Mrs. Gianini how much I am enjoying having her son live with us. Mr. G is very good about helping around the house, and has even taken over my old job of cleaning the toilets. Not to mention the thirty-six-inch TV, pinball machine, and foozball table he brought with him when he moved in.

Mrs. Gianini is immensely gratified to hear this, you can just tell. Old people like to hear nice stuff about their kids, even if their kid, like Mr. Gianini, is thirty-nine and a half years old.

3:00 p.m. – We have to leave if we are going to beat the traffic home. I say good-bye. Claire does not say good-bye back to me, but Nathan does. He advises me to keep it real. Mrs. Gianini gives us a lot of leftover turkey. I thank her, even though I don't eat turkey, being a vegetarian.

6:30 p.m. – We finally make it back into the city, after

spending three and a half hours in bumper-to-bumper traffic along the Long Island Expressway. Though there is nothing very express about it, if you ask me.

I barely have time to change into my baby-blue floor-length Armani sheath dress and matching ballet flats before the limo honks downstairs, and Lars, my bodyguard, arrives to escort me to my second Thanksgiving dinner.

7:30 p.m.—Arrive at the Plaza Hotel. I am greeted by the concierge, who announces me to the masses assembled in the Palm Court:

"Presenting Her Royal Highness Princess Amelia Mignonette Grimaldi Thermopolis Renaldo."

God forbid he should just say Mia.

My father, the prince of Genovia, and his mother, the dowager princess, have rented the Palm Court for the evening in order to throw a Thanksgiving banquet for all of their friends. Despite my strenuous objections, Dad and Grandmère refuse to leave New York City until I have learned everything there is to know about being a princess . . . or until my formal introduction to the Genovian people the day before Christmas, whichever comes first. I have assured them that it isn't as if I am going to show up at the castle and start hurling olives at the ladies-in-waiting and scratching myself under the arms. I mean, I am fourteen years old: I do have some idea how to act, for crying out loud.

But Grandmère, at least, does not seem to believe this, and so she is still subjecting me to daily princess lessons. Lilly recently contacted the United Nations to see whether these lessons constitute a human rights violation. She believes it is unlawful to force a minor to sit for hours practicing tipping her soup bowl away from her—"Always, always, *away* from you, Amelia!"—in order to scrape up a few drops of lobster bisque. The UN has so far been unsympathetic to my plight.

It was Grandmère's idea to have what she calls an "old-fashioned" Thanksgiving dinner, featuring mussels in a white wine sauce, squab stuffed with foie gras, lobster tails, and Iranian caviar, which you could never get before because of the embargo. She has invited two hundred of her closest friends, plus the emperor of Japan and his wife, since they were in town anyway for a world trade summit.

That's why I have to wear ballet flats. Grandmère says it's rude to be taller than an emperor.

8:00 p.m.–11:00 p.m.—I make polite conversation with the empress while we eat. Like me, she was just a normal person until one day she married the emperor and became royal. I, of course, was born royal. I just didn't know it until September, when my dad found out he couldn't have any more kids, due to his chemotherapy for testicular cancer having rendered him sterile. Then he had to admit he was actually a prince and all, and that though I am "illegitimate," since my dad and my mom were never married, I am still the sole heir to the Genovian throne.

And even though Genovia is a very small country (population 50,000) crammed into a hillside along the Mediterranean Sea between Italy and France, it is still this very big deal to be princess of it.

Not a big enough deal for anyone to raise my allowance higher than ten dollars a week, apparently. But a big enough deal that I have to have a bodyguard follow me around everywhere I go, just in case some Euro-trash terrorist in a ponytail and black leather pants takes it into his head to kidnap me.

The empress knows all about this—what a bummer it is, I mean, being just a normal person one day, and then having your face on the cover of *People* magazine the next. She even gave me some advice: She told me I should always make sure my kimono is securely fastened before I raise my arm to wave to the populace.

I thanked her, even though I don't actually own a kimono.

11:30 p.m.—I am so tired on account of having gotten up so early to go to Long Island, I have yawned in the empress's face twice. I have tried to hide these yawns the way Grandmère taught me to, by clenching my jaw and refusing to open my mouth. But this only makes my eyes water, and the rest of my face stretch out like I am hurtling through a black hole. Grandmère gives me the evil eye over her salad with pears and walnuts, but it is no use. Even her malevolent stare cannot shake me from my state of extreme drowsiness.

Finally, my father notices, and grants me a royal reprieve from dessert. Lars drives me back to the apartment. Grandmère is clearly upset because I am leaving before the cheese course. But it is either that, or pass out in the *fromage bleu*. I know that in the end,

Grandmère will have retribution, undoubtedly in the form of forcing me to learn the names of every member of the Swedish royal family, or something equally as heinous.

Grandmère always gets her way.

12:00 a.m.–After a long and exhausting day of giving thanks to the founders of our nation–those genocidal hypocrites known as the Pilgrims–I finally go to bed.

And that concludes Mia Thermopolis's Thanksgiving.

Over.

That is what my life is. O-V-E-R.

I know I have said that before, but this time I really mean it.

And why? Why THIS TIME? Surprisingly, it's not because:

Three months ago, I found out that I'm the heir to the throne of a small European nation, and that at the end of this month, I am going to have to go to said small European nation and be formally introduced for the first time to the people over whom I will one day reign, and who will undoubtedly hate me, because given that my favorite shoes are my combat boots and my favorite TV show is *Baywatch*, I am so not the royal-princess type.

Or because:

My mother, who is expecting to give birth to my Algebra teacher's child in approximately seven months, recently eloped with said Algebra teacher.

Or even because:

At school they've been loading us down with so much homework—and after school, Grandmère's been torturing me so endlessly with all the princess stuff I've got to learn by Christmas—that I haven't even been able to keep up with this journal, let alone anything else.

Oh, no. It's not because of any of that. Why is my life over?

Because I have a boyfriend.

At fourteen years of age, I suppose it's about time.

I mean, all my friends have boyfriends. All of them, even Lilly, who blames the male gender for most, if not all, of society's ills.

And okay, Lilly's boyfriend is Boris Pelkowski, who may, at the age of fifteen, be one of the nation's leading violin virtuosos, but that doesn't mean he doesn't tuck his sweater into his pants, or that he doesn't have food in his braces more often than not. Not what I would call ideal boyfriend material, but Lilly seems to like him, which is all that matters.

I guess.

I have to admit, when Lilly—possibly the pickiest person on this planet (and I should know, having been best friends with her since kindergarten)—got a boyfriend, and I still didn't have one, I pretty much started to think there was something wrong with me. Besides my gigantism and what Lilly's parents, the Drs. Moscovitz, who are psychiatrists, call my inability to verbalize my inner rage.

And then, one day, out of the blue, I got one. A boyfriend, I mean.

Well, okay, not out of the blue. Kenny started sending me all these anonymous love letters. I didn't know it was him. I kind of thought (okay, hoped) someone else was sending them. But in the end, it turned out to be Kenny. And by then I was in too deep, really, to get out. So *voilà*! I had a boyfriend.

Problem solved, right?

Not. So not.

And it isn't that I don't like Kenny. I do. I really do. We have a lot in common. For instance, we both appreciate the preciousness of not just human, but *all* life forms, and refuse to dissect fetal pigs and frogs in Bio. Instead, we are writing term papers on the life cycles of various grubs and mealworms.

And we both like science fiction. Kenny knows a lot more about it than I do, but he has been very impressed so far by the extent of my familiarity with the works of Robert A. Heinlein and Isaac Asimov, both of whom we were forced to read in school (though he doesn't seem to remember this).

I haven't told Kenny that I actually find most science fiction boring, since there seem to be very few girls in it.

There are a lot of girl characters in Japanese anime, which Kenny also really likes, and which he has decided to devote his life to promoting (when he is not busy finding a cure for cancer). I have noticed that most of the girls in Japanese anime seem to have misplaced their bras.

Plus I really think it might be detrimental to a fighter pilot to have a lot of long hair floating around in the cockpit while she is gunning down the forces of evil.

But like I said, I haven't mentioned any of this to Kenny. And mostly, we get along great. We have a fun time together. And in some ways, it's very nice to have a boyfriend. Like, I don't have to worry now about not being asked to the Albert Einstein High School Nondenominational Winter Dance (so called because its former title, the Albert Einstein High School Christmas Dance, offended many of our non–Christmas-celebrating students).

And why is it that I do not have to worry about not being asked to the biggest dance of the school year, with the exception of the prom?

Because I'm going with Kenny.

Well, okay, he hasn't exactly asked me yet, but he will. Because he is my boyfriend.

Isn't that great? Sometimes I think I must be the luckiest girl in the whole world. I mean, really. Think about it: I may not be pretty, but I am not grossly disfigured; I live in New York City, the coolest place on the planet; I'm a princess; I have a boyfriend. What more could a girl ask for?

Oh, God.

WHO AM I KIDDING?????

This boyfriend of mine? Here's the scoop:

I DON'T EVEN LIKE HIM.

Well, okay, it's not that I don't like him. But this boyfriend thing, I just don't know. Kenny's a nice enough guy and all—don't get me wrong. I mean, he is funny and not boring to be with, certainly. And he's pretty cute, you know, in a tall, skinny sort of way.

It's just that when I see Kenny walking down the hall, my heart so totally doesn't start beating faster, the way girls' hearts start beating faster in those teen romances my friend Tina Hakim Baba is always reading.

And when Kenny takes my hand, at the movies or whatever, it's not like my hand gets all tingly in his, the way girls' hands do in those books.

And when he kisses me? Those fireworks people always talk about? Forget about it. No fireworks. Nil. Nada.

It's funny, because before I got a boyfriend, I used to spend a lot of time trying to figure out how to get one, and once I got him, how I'd get him to kiss me.

But now that I actually have a boyfriend, mostly all I do

13

is try to figure out how to get out of kissing him.

One way that I have found that works quite effectively is the head turn. If I notice his lips coming toward me, I just turn my head at the last minute, so all he gets is my cheek, and maybe some hair.

I guess the worst thing is, when Kenny gazes deeply into my eyes—which he does a lot—and asks me what I am thinking about, I am usually thinking about this one certain person.

And that person isn't Kenny. It isn't Kenny at all. It is Lilly's older brother, Michael Moscovitz, whom I have loved for, oh, I don't know, MY ENTIRE LIFE.

Wait, though. It gets worse.

Because now it's like everybody considers me and Kenny this big Item. You know? Now we're Kenny-and-Mia. Now, instead of Lilly and me hanging out together Saturday nights, it's Lilly-and-Boris and Kenny-and-Mia. Sometimes my friend Tina Hakim Baba and her boyfriend, Dave Farouq El-Abar, and my other friend Shameeka Taylor and her boyfriend, Daryl Gardner, join us, making it Lilly-and-Boris and Kenny-and-Mia and Tina-and-Dave and Shameeka-and-Daryl.

So if Kenny and I break up, who am I going to hang around with on Saturday nights? I mean, seriously. Lilly-and-Boris and Tina-and-Dave and Shameeka-and-Daryl won't want just plain Mia along. I'll be just like this seventh wheel.

Not to mention, if Kenny and I break up, who will I go to the Nondenominational Winter Dance with? I mean, if he ever gets around to asking me.

Oh, God, I have to go now. Lilly-and-Boris and Tina-and-Dave and Kenny-and-Mia are supposed to go ice-skating at Rockefeller Center.

All I can say is, be careful what you wish for. It just might come true.

I thought my life was over because I have a boyfriend now and I don't really like him in that way, and I have to break up with him without hurting his feelings, which is, I guess, probably impossible.

Yeah, well, I didn't know *how* over my life could actually be.

Not until tonight, anyway.

Tonight, Lilly-and-Boris and Tina-and-Dave and Mia-and-Kenny were joined by a new couple, Michael-and-Judith.

That's right: Lilly's brother Michael showed up at the ice-skating rink, and he brought with him the president of the Computer Club—of which he is treasurer—Judith Gershner.

Judith Gershner, like Lilly's brother Michael, is a senior at Albert Einstein High School.

Judith Gershner, like Michael, is on the honor roll.

Judith Gershner, like Michael, will probably get into every college she applies to, because Judith Gershner, like Michael, is brilliant.

In fact, Judith Gershner, like Michael, won a prize last year at the Albert Einstein High School Annual Biomedical Technology Fair for her science project, in which she actually cloned a fruit fly.

She cloned a fruit fly. At home. In her *bedroom.*

Judith Gershner knows how to clone fruit flies in her bedroom. And me? I can't even multiply fractions.

Hmmm. Gee, I don't know. If you were Michael

Moscovitz—you know, a straight-A student who got into Columbia, early decision—who would you rather go out with? A girl who can clone fruit flies in her bedroom, or a girl who is getting a D in Freshman Algebra, in spite of the fact that *her mother is married to her Algebra teacher?*

Not that there's even a chance of Michael ever asking me out. I mean, I have to admit, there were a couple of times when I thought he might. But that was clearly just wishful thinking on my part. I mean, why would a guy like Michael, who does really well in school and will probably excel at whatever career he ultimately chooses, ever ask out a girl like me, who would have flunked out of the ninth grade by now if it hadn't been for all those extra tutoring sessions with Mr. Gianini, and, ironically, Michael himself?

But Michael and Judith Gershner, on the other hand, are perfect for each other. Judith even looks like him, a little. I mean, they both have the same curly black hair and pale skin from being inside all the time, looking up stuff about genomes on the Internet.

But if Michael and Judith Gershner are so suited for each other, how come when I first saw them walking toward us while we were lacing up our rental skates, I got this very bad feeling inside?

I mean, I have absolutely no right to be jealous of the fact that Michael Moscovitz asked Judith Gershner to go skating with him. Absolutely no right at all.

Except that when I first saw them together, I was shocked. I mean, Michael hardly ever leaves his room, on account of always being at his computer, maintaining his webzine, *Crackhead.* The last place I'd ever expected to see him is the ice-skating rink at Rockefeller Center during the height of the Christmas-tree–lighting hysteria. Michael generally avoids places he considers tourist traps, like pretty much everywhere north of Bleecker Street.

But there he was, and there was Judith Gershner, in her overalls and Rockports and ski parka, chatting away with him about something—probably something really smart, like DNA.

I nudged Lilly in the side—she was lacing up her skates—and said, in this voice that I hoped didn't show what I was feeling inside, "Look, there's your brother."

And Lilly wasn't even surprised to see him! She looked over and saw him and went, "Oh, yeah. He said he might show up."

Show up with a *date*? Did he mention *that*? And would it have been too much for you, Lilly, to have mentioned this to me beforehand, so I could have had time for a little mental preparation?

Only Lilly doesn't know how I feel about her brother, so I guess it never occurred to her to break it to me gently.

Here's the subtle way in which I handled the situation. It was really smooth (NOT).

As Michael and Judith were looking around for a place to put on their skates:

Me: (Casually, to Lilly) I didn't know your brother
        and Judith Gershner were going out.
Lilly: (Disgusted for some reason) Please. They're
        not. She was just over at our place, working
        with Michael on some project for the stupid

	Computer Club. They heard we were all going skating, and Judith said she wanted to come, too.
Me:	Well, that sounds like they're going out to me.
Lilly:	Whatever. Boris, must you constantly *breathe* on me?
Me:	(To Michael and Judith as they walk up to us) Oh, hi, you guys. Michael, I didn't know you knew how to ice-skate.
Michael:	(shrugging) I used to be on a hockey team.
Lilly:	(snorting) Yeah, Pee Wee Hockey. That was before he decided that team sports were a waste of time because the success of the team was dictated by the performance of all the players as a whole, as opposed to sports determined by individual performance such as tennis and golf.
Michael:	Lilly, don't you ever shut up?
Judith:	I love ice-skating! Although I'm not very good at it.

And she certainly isn't. Judith is such a bad skater, she had to hold on to both of Michael's hands while he skated backwards in front of her, just to keep from falling flat on her face. I don't know which astonished me more: that Michael can skate backwards, or that he didn't seem to mind having to tow Judith all around the rink. I mean, I may not be able to clone a fruit fly, but at least I can remain upright unaided in a pair of ice skates.

Kenny, however, seemed to really think Michael and

Judith's method of skating was way preferable to skating the old-fashioned way—you know, solo—so he kept coming up and trying to get me to let him tow me around the way Michael was towing Judith.

And even though I was all, "Duh, Kenny, I know how to skate," he said that that wasn't the point. Finally, after he'd bugged me for like half an hour, I gave in, and let him hold both my hands as he skated in front of me, backwards.

Only the thing is, Kenny isn't very good at skating backwards. I can skate forward, but I'm not good enough at it that if someone is wobbling around in front of me, I can keep from crashing into him if he falls down.

Which was exactly what happened. Kenny fell down, and I couldn't stop, so I crashed into him, and my chin hit his knee and I bit my tongue and all this blood filled up my mouth, and I didn't want to swallow it so I spat it out. Only unfortunately it went all over Kenny's jeans and onto the ice, which clearly impressed all of the tourists standing along the railings around the rink, taking pictures of their loved ones in front of the enormous Rockefeller Center Christmas tree, since they all turned around and started taking pictures of the girl spitting up blood on the ice below, a truly New York moment.

And then Lars came *shoosh*ing over—he is a champion ice-skater, thanks to his Nordic upbringing; quite a contrast to his bodyguard training in the heart of the Gobi desert—picked me up, looked at my tongue, gave me his handkerchief and told me to keep pressure on the wound, and then said, "That's enough skating for one night."

And that was it. Now I've got this bloody gouge in the

tip of my tongue, and it hurts to talk, and I was totally humiliated in front of millions of tourists who'd come to look at the stupid tree at stupid Rockefeller Center, not to mention in front of my friends and, worst of all, Judith Gershner, who it turns out also got accepted early decision at Columbia (great, the same school Michael's going to in the fall), where she will be pre-med, and who advised me that I should go to the hospital, as it seemed likely to her that I might need stitches. In my *tongue*. I'm lucky, she said, I didn't bite the tip of it off.

Lucky!

Oh, yeah, I'll tell you how lucky I am: I'm so lucky that while I lie here in bed writing this, with no one but my twenty-five-pound cat, Fat Louie, to keep me company (and Fat Louie only likes me because I feed him), the boy I've been in love with since like forever is up at midtown right now with a girl who knows how to clone fruit flies and can tell if wounds need stitches or not.

One good thing about this tongue, though: if Kenny was thinking about moving on to Frenching, we totally can't until I heal. And that could, according to Dr. Fung—whom my mom called as soon as Lars brought me home—take anywhere from three to ten days.

Yes!

TEN THINGS I HATE ABOUT THE HOLIDAY SEASON IN NEW YORK CITY

1. Tourists who come in from out of town in their giant sports utility vehicles and try to run you over at the crosswalks, thinking they are driving like aggressive New Yorkers. Actually, they are driving like morons. Plus there is enough pollution in this city. Why can't they just take public transit, like normal people?
2. Stupid Rockefeller Center tree. They asked me to be the person who throws the switch to light it this year, as I am considered "New York's own Royal" in the press, but when I told them how cutting down trees contributes to the destruction of the ozone layer, they rescinded their invitation and had the mayor do it instead.
3. Stupid Christmas carols blaring from outside all the stores.
4. Stupid ice-skating with stupid boys who think they can skate backwards when they can't.
5. Pressure to buy stupid "meaningful" gifts for everyone you know.
6. Final exams.
7. Stupid lousy New York weather. No snow, just cold, wet rain, every single day. Whatever happened to a white Christmas? I'll tell you: Global warming. You know why? Because everybody keeps driving SUVs and cutting down trees!
8. Stupid manipulative Christmas specials on TV.

9. Stupid manipulative Christmas commercials on TV.
10. Mistletoe. This stuff should be banned. In the hands of adolescent boys, it becomes a societally approved excuse to demand kisses. This is sexual harassment, if you ask me.

Plus all the wrong boys have it.

Sunday, December 7

Just got back from dinner at Grandmère's. All of my efforts to get out of having to go—even my pointing out that I am currently suffering from a perforated tongue—were in vain.

And this one was even worse than usual. That's because Grandmère wanted to go over my itinerary for my trip to Genovia, which, by the way, looks like this:

Sunday, December 21
3 p.m.
Arrive in Genovia

3:30 p.m.–5 p.m.
Meet and greet palace staff

5 p.m.–7 p.m.
Tour of palace

7 p.m.–8 p.m.
Change for dinner

8 p.m.–11 p.m.
Dinner with Genovian dignitaries

Monday, December 22
8 a.m.–9:30 a.m.
Breakfast with Genovian public officials

10 a.m.–11:30 a.m.
Tour of Genovian public schools

12 p.m.–1 p.m.
Meet with Genovian schoolchildren

1:30 p.m.–3 p.m.
Lunch with members of Genovian Teachers Association

3:30 p.m.–4:30 p.m.
Tour of Port of Genovia and Genovian naval cruiser
(the *Prince Phillipe*)

5 p.m.–6 p.m.
Tour of Genovian General Hospital

6 p.m.–7 p.m.
Visit with hospital patients

7 p.m.–8 p.m.
Change for dinner

8 p.m.–11 p.m.
Dinner with the dowager princess, prince, and
Genovian military advisors

Tuesday, December 23
8 a.m.–9 a.m.
Breakfast with members of Genovian Olive Growers
Association

10 a.m.–11 a.m.
Christmas Tree Lighting ceremony, Genovia Palace
Courtyard

11:30 a.m.–1 p.m.
Meet with Genovian Historical Society

1 p.m.–3 p.m.
Lunch with Genovian Board of Tourism

3:30 p.m.–5:30 p.m.
Tour of Genovian National Art Museum

6 p.m.–7 p.m.
Visit Genovian War Veterans Memorial,
place flowers on grave of Unknown Soldier

7:30 p.m.–8:30 p.m.
Change for dinner

8:30 p.m.–11:30 p.m.
Dinner with Royal Family of Monaco

And so on.

It all culminates in my appearance on my dad's annual
nationally televised Christmas Eve address to the people of
Genovia, during which he will introduce me to the populace.
I am then supposed to make a speech about how thrilled I am
to be Dad's heir, and how I promise to try to do as good a
job as he has at leading Genovia into the twenty-first century.

Nervous? Me? About going on TV and promising fifty thousand people that I won't let their country down?

Nah. Not me.

I just want to throw up every time I think about it, that's all.

Whatever. Not that I thought my trip to Genovia was going to be like going to Disneyland, but still. You'd think they'd have scheduled in *some* fun time. I'm not even asking for Mr. Toad's Wild Ride. Just, like, some swimming or horseback riding.

But apparently, there is no time for fun in Genovia.

As if going over my itinerary wasn't bad enough, I also had to meet my cousin Sebastiano. Sebastiano Grimaldi is my dead grandfather's sister's daughter's kid. Which I guess actually makes him my cousin a couple times removed. But not removed enough that, if it weren't for me, he wouldn't be inheriting the throne to Genovia.

Seriously. If my dad had died without ever having had a kid, Sebastiano would be the next prince of Genovia.

Maybe that's why my dad, every time he looks at Sebastiano, heaves this big shudder.

Or maybe it's just because my dad feels about Sebastiano the way I feel about my cousin Hank: I like him in theory, but in actual practice, he kind of bugs me.

Sebastiano doesn't bug Grandmère, though. You can tell that Grandmère just loves him. Which is really weird, because I always supposed Grandmère was incapable of loving anyone. Well, with the exception of Rommel, her miniature poodle.

But you can tell she totally adores Sebastiano. When she

introduced him to me, and he bowed with this big flourish and kissed the air above my hand, Grandmère was practically beaming beneath her pink silk turban. Really.

I have never seen Grandmère beam before. Glare, plenty of times. But never beam.

Which might be why my dad started chewing the ice in his whiskey and soda in a very irritated manner. Grandmère's smile disappeared right away when she heard all that crunching.

"If you want to chew ice, Phillipe," Grandmère said, coldly, "you can go and have your dinner at McDonald's with the rest of the proletariat."

My dad stopped chewing his ice.

It turns out Grandmère brought Sebastiano over from Genovia so that he could design my dress for my nationally televised introduction to my countrymen. Sebastiano is a very up-and-coming fashion designer—at least according to Grandmère. She says it is important that Genovia supports its artists and craftspeople, or they will all flee to New York, or even worse, Los Angeles.

Which is too bad for Sebastiano, since he looks like the type who might really enjoy living in LA. He is thirtyish, with long, dark hair tied back in a ponytail, and is all tall and flamboyant-looking. Like for instance, tonight, instead of a tie, Sebastiano was wearing a white silk ascot. And he had on a blue velvet jacket with leather pants.

I am fully prepared to forgive Sebastiano for the leather pants if he designs me a dress that is nice enough. A dress that, should he happen to see me in it, will make Michael Moscovitz forget all about Judith Gershner and her fruit flies, and fill his head with nothing but thoughts of me, Mia Thermopolis.

Only of course the chances of Michael ever actually seeing me in this dress are very slim, as my introduction to the Genovian people is only going to be on Genovian television, not CNN or anything.

Still, Sebastiano seemed ready to rise to the challenge. After dinner, he even took out a pen and began sketching—right on the white tablecloth!—a design he thought might accentuate what he called my narrow waist and long legs.

Only, unlike my dad, who was born and raised in Genovia but speaks fluent English, Sebastiano doesn't have a real keen grasp of the language. He kept forgetting the second syllables of words. So *narrow* became "nar." Just like *coffee* became "coff," and when he described something as magical, it came out as "madge." Even the butter wasn't safe. When Sebastiano asked me to please pass him the "butt," I had to practically stuff my napkin in my mouth to keep from laughing out loud.

All my efforts to stifle myself didn't do any good, though, since Grandmère caught me and, raising one of her drawn-on eyebrows, went, "Amelia, kindly do not make light of other people's speech habits. Your own are not even remotely perfect."

Which is certainly true, considering the fact that, with my swollen tongue, I can't really say any word that starts with *s*.

Not only did Grandmère not mind Sebastiano saying the word *butt* at the dinner table, she didn't mind his drawing on the tablecloth, either. She looked down at his sketch and said, "Brilliant. Simply brilliant. As usual."

Sebastiano looked very pleased. "Do you real think so?" he asked.

Only I didn't think his sketch was so brilliant. It just looked like an ordinary dress to me. Certainly nothing to make anyone forget the fact that I'm about as likely to clone a fruit fly as I am to use animal-tested hair products.

"Um," I said. "Can't you make it a little more . . . I don't know . . . sexy?"

Grandmère and Sebastiano exchanged looks. "Sexy?" Grandmère echoed, with an evil laugh. "How? By making it lower cut? But you haven't got anything there to show!"

Now, seriously. I would expect to hear this kind of thing from the cheerleaders at school, who have made demeaning other people—especially me—a sort of new Olympic sport. But what kind of person says things like this to her only grandchild? I had meant, of course, a side slit, or maybe some fringe. I wasn't asking for anything Jennifer Lopez-ish.

But trust Grandmère to turn it into something like that. Why do I have to be cursed with a grandmother who shaves off her eyebrows and seems to enjoy making light of my inadequacies? Why can't I have a normal grandmother, who bakes me cookies and can't stop bragging to her friends in her bridge club about how wonderful I am?

It was while Grandmère and Sebastiano were cackling to themselves over this great witticism at my expense that my dad abruptly got up and left the table, saying he had to make a call. I suppose it's every man for himself where Grandmère is concerned, but you would think my own father would stick up for me once in a while.

I don't know, maybe I was feeling odd about the giant hole in my tongue (which doesn't even have a nice hypoallergenic stud in it so I can pretend to have done it on purpose to be controversial). I sat there listening to Grandmère and Sebastiano chatter away about how pathetic it was that I would never be able to wear anything strapless, unless some miracle of nature occurred one night that inflated me from a 32A to a 34C, and I couldn't help thinking that probably, given my luck, it will turn out that Sebastiano isn't in town just to design me a dress for my royal introduction, but to kill me so that he can assume the throne of Genovia himself.

Or, as Sebastiano would say, "ass" the throne.

Seriously. That kind of stuff happens on *Baywatch* all the time. You wouldn't believe the number of royal family members Mitch has had to save from assassination.

Like supposing I put on the dress that Sebastiano has designed for me to wear when I'm introduced to the people of Genovia, and it ends up squeezing me to death, just like that corset Snow White puts on in the original version of the story by the Brothers Grimm. You know, the part they left out of the Disney movie because it was too gruesome.

Anyway, what if the dress squeezes me to death, and then I'm lying in my coffin, looking all pale and queenly, and Michael comes to my funeral and ends up gazing down at me and doesn't realize until right then that he has always loved me?

Then he'll *have* to break up with Judith Gershner.

Hey. It could happen.

Okay, well, probably not, but thinking about that was better than listening to Grandmère and Sebastiano talk about me as if I weren't even there. Seriously. I was roused from my pleasant little fantasy about Michael pining for me for the rest of his life by Sebastiano saying suddenly, "She has bute bone struck," which, when I realized I was the *she* he was referring to, I took to be a compliment about my bone structure.

Only a second later it wasn't such a compliment when he went, "I put makeup on her that make her look like a mod."

Implying I don't look like a model without makeup (although of course I don't).

Grandmère certainly wasn't about to come to my defense, however. She was feeding bits of her leftover veal marsala to Rommel, who was sitting on her lap, shivering as usual, since all of his fur has fallen out due to canine allergies.

"I wouldn't count on her father letting you," she said to Sebastiano. "Phillipe is hopelessly old-fashioned."

Which is so the pot calling the kettle black! I mean, Grandmère still thinks that cats go around trying to suck the breath out of their owners while they are sleeping. Seriously. She is always trying to convince me to give Fat Louie away.

So while Grandmère was going on about how old-fashioned her son is, I got up and joined him on the balcony.

He was checking his messages on his cell phone. He's supposed to play racquetball tomorrow with the prime minister of France, who is in town for the same summit as the emperor of Japan.

"Mia," he said, when he saw me. "What are you doing out here? It's freezing. Go back inside."

"I will, in a minute," I said. I stood there next to him and looked out over the city. It really is kind of awe-inspiring, the view of Manhattan from the penthouse of the Plaza Hotel. I mean, you look at all those lights in all those windows, and you think, for each light there's probably at least one person, but maybe even more, maybe even like ten people, and that's, well, pretty mind-boggling.

I've lived in Manhattan my whole life. But it still impresses me.

Anyway, while I was standing there looking at all the lights, I suddenly realized that one of them probably belonged to Judith Gershner. Judith was probably sitting in her room right this moment cloning something new. A pigeon, or whatever. I got yet another flashback of her and Michael looking down at me after I'd split open my tongue. Hmmm, let me see: girl who can clone things, or girl who bit her own tongue? I don't know, who would *you* choose?

My dad must have noticed something was wrong, since he went, "Look, I know Sebastiano is a bit much, but just put up with him for the next couple of weeks. For my sake."

"I wasn't thinking about Sebastiano," I said sadly.

My dad made this grunting noise, but he made no move to go back inside, even though it was about forty degrees out there, and my dad, well, he's completely bald. I could see that the tips of his ears were getting red with cold, but still he didn't budge. He didn't even have a coat on, just another one of his charcoal-gray Armani suits.

I figured this was invitation enough to go on. You see, ordinarily my dad is not who I would go to first if I had a problem. Not that we're not close. It's just that, you know, he's a guy.

On the other hand, he's had a lot of experience in the romance department, so I figured he might just be able to offer some insight into this particular dilemma.

"Dad," I said. "What do you do if you like someone, but they don't, you know, know it?"

My dad went, "If Kenny doesn't know you like him by now, then I'm afraid he's never going to get the message. Haven't you been out with him every weekend since Halloween?"

This is the problem with having a bodyguard who is on your father's payroll: All of your personal business totally gets discussed behind your back.

"I'm not talking about Kenny, Dad," I said. "It's someone else. Only like I said, he doesn't know I like him."

"What's wrong with Kenny?" my dad wanted to know. "I like Kenny."

Of course my dad likes Kenny. Because the chances of me and Kenny ever getting past first base are like, nil. What father doesn't want his teenage daughter to date a guy like that?

But if my dad has any serious hope of keeping the Genovian throne in the hands of the Renaldos, and not allowing it to slip into Sebastiano's control, he had better get over the whole Kenny thing, because I'm pretty sure that Kenny and I will not be doing any procreating. In this lifetime, anyway.

"Dad," I said. "Forget Kenny, okay? Kenny and I are just friends. I'm talking about someone else."

My dad was looking over the side of the balcony railing like he wanted to spit. Not that he ever would. I don't think. "Do I know him? This someone else, I mean?"

I hesitated. I've never really admitted to anyone out loud that I have a crush on Michael. Really. Not to anybody. I mean, who could I tell? Lilly would just make fun of me, or worse, tell Michael. And Mom, well, she's got her own problems.

"It's Lilly's brother," I said in a rush, to get it over with.

My dad looked alarmed. "Isn't he in college?"

"Not yet," I said. "He's going in the fall." When he still looked alarmed, I said, "Don't worry, Dad. I don't stand a chance. Michael is very smart. He'd never like someone like me."

Then my dad got all offended. It was like he couldn't figure out which to be, worried about my liking a senior, or angry that that senior didn't like me back.

"What do you mean, he'd never like someone like you?" my father demanded. "What's wrong with you?"

"Duh, Dad," I said. "I practically flunked Algebra, remember? Michael is going to an Ivy League school in the fall, for crying out loud. What would he want with a girl like me?"

Now my dad was *really* annoyed: "You may take after your mother as far as your aptitude with numbers is concerned, but you take after me in every other respect."

This was surprising to hear. I stuck out my chin and tried to believe it. "Yeah," I said.

"And you and I, Mia, are not unintelligent," my dad went on. "If you want this Michael fellow, you must let him know it."

"You think I should just go up to him and be like, 'Hey, I like you'?"

My dad shook his head in disgust. "No, no, no," he said. "Of course you must be more subtle than that. Tell him by *showing* how you feel."

"Oh," I said. I may take after my father in every respect except my math aptitude, but I had no idea what he was talking about.

"We'd better get back in," my father said. "Or your grandmother will suspect us of plotting against her."

So what else is new? Grandmère is always suspecting somebody of plotting something against her. She thinks the launderers at the Plaza are plotting against her. She blames the soap they use on their linens for making all of Rommel's fur fall out.

Reminded of plots, I asked my dad, "Do you think Sebastiano's plotting to kill me so he can ascend the throne himself?"

My dad made a strangled noise, but he managed not to burst out laughing. I guess that wouldn't have seemed very princely.

"No, Mia," he said. "I do not."

But my dad, he really doesn't have much of an imagination. I have decided to stay on alert about Sebastiano, just in case.

My mom just poked her head into my room to say that Kenny is on the phone for me.

I suppose he wants to ask me to the Nondenominational Winter Dance. Really, it is about time.

Sunday, December 7, 11 p.m.

Okay. I am in shock. Kenny so did NOT ask me to the Nondenominational Winter Dance. Instead, this is how our conversation went:

Me: Hello?
Kenny: Hi, Mia. It's Kenny.
Me: Oh, hi, Kenny. What's the matter?

Kenny sounded funny, which is why I asked.

Kenny: Well, I just wanted to see if you were okay. I mean, if your tongue was okay.
Me: It's a little better, I guess.
Kenny: Because I was really worried. You know. I really, really didn't mean to—
Me: Kenny, I know. It was just an accident.

This is when I started realizing I'd asked my dad the wrong question. I should have asked him what's the best way to break up with somebody, not what's the best way to let someone know you like them.

Anyway, to get back to what Kenny said:

Kenny: Well, I just wanted to call and wish you a good night. And say that I hope you feel better. And also to let you know . . . well, Mia, that I love you.
Me: . . . .

I didn't say anything right away, because I was completely FREAKED OUT!!!! It wasn't exactly as if it happened out of the blue, because we are sort of going out, after all.

But still, what kind of guy calls a girl on the phone and says I love you??? Except for weird psycho stalkers? And Kenny's not a weird psycho stalker. He's just Kenny. So what's he doing calling me on the phone and telling me he loves me????

And then, brilliant me, here's what I do. Because he was still on the phone, waiting for an answer, and all. So I go:

Me: Um, okay.

Um, okay.
A boy says he loves me, and this is how I respond: "Um, okay." Oh, yeah, good thing my future career lies in the diplomatic corps.

So then, poor Kenny, he's like waiting for some response other than "Um, okay," as anybody would.

But I am perfectly incapable of giving him one. Instead, I just go:

Me: Well, see you tomorrow.

AND I HUNG UP!!!!!
Oh, my God, I am the meanest, most ungrateful girl in the world. After Sebastiano kills me, I am going to burn in hell. Seriously.

TO DO BEFORE LEAVING FOR GENOVIA

1. Detailed list for Mom and Mr. G: How to care for Fat Louie while I am away
2. Stock up on cat food, litter
3. Christmas/Hannukah presents! For:
   Mom—electric breast pump? Check on this.
   Mr. G—new drumsticks
   Dad—book on vegetarianism. He should eat better if he wants to keep his cancer in remission.
   Lilly—what she always wants, blank videotapes for her show
   Lars–See if Prada makes a shoulder holster that would fit his Glock
   Kenny—gloves? Something NON-romantic
   Fat Louie—catnip ball
   Grandmère–What do you get for the woman who has everything, including an eighty-nine-carat sapphire pendant given to her by the Sultan of Brunei? Soap on a rope?
4. Break up with Kenny. . . . Only how can I? He LOVES me.

But not enough to ask me to the Nondenominational Winter Dance, I've noticed.

Lilly doesn't believe me about Kenny calling and saying he loves me. I told her in the car on the way to school this morning (thank God Michael had a dentist appointment and wasn't there. I would sooner die than discuss my love life in front of him. It's bad enough having to discuss it in front of my bodyguard. If I had to discuss it in front of this person I've been worshiping for half my life, I think I'd probably go completely borderline personality disorder).

Anyway, so Lilly went, "I categorically refuse to believe Kenny would do something like that."

"Lilly," I said. I had to keep my voice down so the driver wouldn't hear. "I am dead serious. He told me he loves me. *I love you.* That is what he said. It was completely random and weird."

"He probably didn't say that. He probably said something else, and you misunderstood him."

"Oh, what? I *glove* you?"

"Well, of course not," Lilly said. "That doesn't even make any sense."

"Well, then what? What could Kenny have said that sounded like *I love you*, but wasn't *I love you*?"

Lilly got mad then. She went, "You know, you have been acting weird about Kenny for the past month. Since the two of you started going out, practically. I don't know what's wrong with you. All I ever heard before was 'Why don't I have a boyfriend? How come everybody I know has a boyfriend but me? When am I going to get a boyfriend?' And now you've got one and you aren't the least bit appreciative of him."

Even though what she was saying was true, I acted offended, because I have been trying really hard not to let the fact that I am not in love with Kenny show.

"That is so false," I said. "I completely appreciate Kenny."

"Oh, yeah? I think the truth of the matter is, you, Mia, simply aren't ready to have a boyfriend."

Boy did I see red after *that* remark.

"*Me*? Not ready to have a boyfriend? Are you kidding? I've been waiting my whole life to have a boyfriend!"

"Well, if that's true"—Lilly was looking very superior—"why won't you let him kiss you on the lips?"

"Where did you hear *that*?" I demanded.

"Kenny told Boris, of course, who told me."

"Oh, great," I said, trying to remain calm. "So now our boyfriends are talking about us behind our backs. And you're condoning this?"

"Of course not," Lilly said. "But I do find it intriguing, from a psychological point of view."

This is the problem with being best friends with someone whose parents are psychiatrists. Everything you do is interesting to them from a psychological point of view.

"Where I let anybody kiss me," I exploded, "is *my* business! Not yours, and not Boris's, either."

"Well," Lilly said. "I'm just saying, if Kenny did say what you say he said—you know, the L word—then maybe he said it because he can't express the depth of his feelings any other way. You know. Other than *verbally*. Since you won't *let* him, physically."

So I suppose that technically I should be thankful that

Kenny chose merely to *say* the words I love you, rather than enacting them physically, which, God knows, might have actually involved his tongue.

Oh, God, I don't even want to think about it anymore.

They just passed out the final exam schedules. Here is mine:

FINAL EXAM SCHEDULE

December 15
Reading Day

December 16
Periods One and Two

For me, that means the Algebra and English finals will be on the same day. But that's okay. I'm doing pretty good in English. Well, except for that sentence diagramming thing. As if I'll ever need to do *that* in my future role as princess of the smallest nation in Europe.

Unfortunately, Algebra, I am told, I will probably need to know. DAMN!

December 17
Periods Three and Four

World Civ: Easy. I mean, Grandmère has told me enough stories about post–World War II Europe for me to pass any test. I probably know more about it than the teacher. And PE? How can you give a final in PE? We already had the Presidential Fitness Test (I did okay on everything but the V-sit reach).

43

December 18
Periods Five, Six, and Seven

Gifted and Talented? No exam there. They don't give finals in classes that are basically study hall. That will be a snap. I have French sixth period. I do okay in oral, not so great in written. Fortunately Tina's in the same class. Maybe we can study together.

But I have Bio seventh period. That won't be so easy. The only reason I'm not flunking Bio is because of Kenny. He slips me most of the answers.

And if I break up with him, that will be the end of that.

December 19
Nondenominational Winter Carnival and Dance

The Winter Carnival should be fun. All the different school clubs and groups are going to have booths, with traditional winter fare, like hot cider. This will be followed in the evening by the dance I am supposed to go to with Kenny. If he ever asks me to it, I mean.

Unless, of course, I do the right thing and break up with him.

In which case, I won't be able to go at all, because you can't go without a date.

I wish Sebastiano would just hurry up and off me already.

Monday, December 8, Algebra

WHY???? WHY can't I ever remember my Algebra notebook?????

FIRST—Evaluate exponents
SECOND—Multiply and divide in order, left to right
THIRD—Perform addition and subtraction in order, left to right
EXAMPLE: $2 \times 3 - 15 \div 5 = 6 - 3 = 3$

Oh, God. Lana Weinberger just tossed me a note.

What now? This can't be good. Lana's had it out for me forever. Don't ask me why. I mean, I could kind of understand her resenting me for when Josh Richter asked me to the Cultural Diversity Dance instead of her. But he only asked me because of the princess thing—and they got back together right after. Besides, Lana hated me long before that.

So I open the note. Here's what it says:

I heard what happened to you at the skating rink this weekend. Guess the BF is going to have to wait a little longer if he wants to see any tongue action, huh?

Oh, my God. Does *everyone* in the entire school know that Kenny and I have not yet French kissed?

It is all Kenny's fault, of course.

What next? The cover of the *Post*?

I'm telling you, if our parents knew what actually goes on every day in the typical American high school, they would totally opt for homeschooling.

It's clear what I have to do.

I've always known it, of course, and if it hadn't been for, you know, the dance, I would have done it long before now.

But it is clear now that I cannot afford to wait until after the dance. I should have done it last night when he called, but you can't really do something like that over the phone. Well, I mean, a girl like Lana Weinberger probably could, but not me.

No, I don't think I can put it off another day: I have got to break up with Kenny. I simply cannot continue living this lie.

Fortunately, I do have the support of at least one person in this plan: Tina Hakim Baba.

I didn't want to tell her. I didn't plan on telling anybody. But it all sort of slipped out today in the girls' room between second and third periods while Tina was putting on her eye makeup. Her dad won't let her wear makeup, you see, so Tina has to wait until she gets to school to put it on. She has a deal with her bodyguard, Wahim. Tina won't tell her parents how much Wahim flirts with Mademoiselle Klein, our French teacher, if Wahim doesn't tell Mr. and Mrs. Hakim Baba about Tina's Maybelline addiction.

Anyway, all of a sudden I just couldn't take it anymore, and I ended up telling Tina what Kenny said last night on the phone—

And a lot more than that actually.

But first the part about Kenny's phone call:

Unlike Lilly, *Tina* believed me.

But Tina also had the totally wrong reaction. She thought it was great.

"Oh, my God, Mia, you are so lucky," she kept saying. "I wish Dave would tell me he loves me! I mean, I know he is fully committed to our relationship, but his idea of romance is paying to have my fries super-sized at Mickey D's."

This was so not the kind of support I was looking for.

"But, Tina," I said. I felt Tina, with her extensive reading of romances, would understand. "The thing is, I don't love him."

Tina widened her mascaraed eyes at me. "You don't?"

"No," I said, miserably. "I mean, I really like him, as a friend. But I'm not in love, or anything. Not with him."

"Oh, God," Tina said, reaching out and grabbing my wrist. "There's someone else, isn't there?"

We only had a few minutes before the bell rang. We both had to get to class.

And yet, for some reason, I chose this moment to make my big confession. I don't know why. Maybe since I'd already spilled it to my dad, it didn't seem too hard to tell someone else, especially Tina. Also, I can't stop thinking about what my dad said. You know, about showing the guy I like how I feel. Tina, I felt, was the only person I knew who would know how to help me do that.

So I went, "Yes."

Tina nearly spilled her cosmetics bag, she was so excited.

"I knew it!" she yelled. "I knew there was a reason you wouldn't let him kiss you!"

My jaw dropped. "*You* know about that, too?"

"Well." Tina shrugged. "Kenny told Dave, who told me."

Jeez! What's that Oprah always complaining about, about how men aren't in touch with their emotions, and don't share enough? It sounds to me like Kenny's been doing enough sharing recently to make up for several centuries' worth of masculine reticence.

"So who is he?" Tina asked, all eager as she packed up her eyelash curler and lipliner. "The guy you like?"

I went, "It doesn't matter. Besides, the whole thing is completely futile. He sort of has a girlfriend. I think."

Tina whipped her head around to look at me, making her thick, black braid smack her in her own face, which is chubby, but in a good way.

"It's Michael, isn't it?" she demanded, grabbing my arm again. She was holding on so tight it hurt.

My instinct, of course, was to deny it. In fact, I even opened my mouth, all set to have the word *No* come out of it.

But then I was like, Why? Why should I deny it to Tina? Tina wouldn't tell anyone. And Tina might be able to help me.

So instead of saying No, I took a deep breath, and said, "If you tell anyone, I'll kill you, understand? KILL YOU."

Tina did a strange thing then. She let go of my arm and started jumping up and down in a circle.

"I knew it, I knew it, I knew it," she said, as she jumped. Then she stopped jumping and grabbed my arm again. "Oh, Mia, I always thought you two would make the cutest couple. I mean, I like Kenny and all, but he's, you know." She wrinkled up her nose. "Not Michael."

If I had thought it felt strange last night telling my dad the truth about my feelings for Michael, that was nothing—

NOTHING—compared to how it felt to be telling someone my own age. The fact that Tina hadn't burst out laughing or gone, "Yeah, right," in a sarcastic way meant more to me than I ever would have expected.

And the fact that she seemed to understand—even applaud—my feelings for Michael made me want to fling my arms around her and give her a great big hug.

Only there was no time for that, since the bell was about to ring.

Instead, I gushed, "Really? You really don't think it's stupid?"

"Duh," Tina said. "Michael is *hot. And* he's a senior." Then she looked troubled. "But what about Kenny? And Judith?"

"I know," I said, my shoulders slumping in a manner that would have caused Grandmère to rap me on the back of the head, if she'd seen them. "Tina, I don't know what to do."

Tina's dark eyebrows furrowed with concentration.

"I think I read a book where this happened once," she said. "*Listen to My Heart,* it was called, I think. If I could just remember how they resolved everything—"

But before she could remember, the bell rang. We were both totally late to class.

But if you ask me, it was worth it. Because now, at least, I don't have to worry alone. I have somebody else worrying with me.

Lunch was a disaster.

Considering that everybody in the entire school seems to know, in the minutest detail, exactly what I've been doing—or not doing—with my tongue lately, I guess I shouldn't have been surprised. But it was even worse than I could have imagined.

That's because I ran into Michael at the salad bar. I was creating my usual chickpea-and-pinto-bean pyramid when I saw him headed for the burger grill (despite my best efforts, both Moscovitzes remain stubbornly carnivorous).

Seriously, all I did was say "Fine" when he asked how I was doing. You know, on account of how last time he saw me, I was bleeding out of the mouth (what a nice picture that must have been. I am so glad that I have been able to maintain an appearance of dignity and beauty at all times in front of the man I love).

Anyway, then I asked him, just to be polite, you know, how his dentist appointment went. What happened next was not my fault.

Which was that Michael started telling me about how he'd had to have this cavity filled, and that his lips were still numb from the novocaine. Seeing as how I have experienced a certain amount of sensation-deadening, what with my gouged tongue, I could relate to this, so I just sort of, you know, *looked* at Michael's lips while he was talking, which I have never really done before. I mean, I have looked at other parts of Michael's body (particularly when he comes into the kitchen in the morning with no shirt on, like he does every time I have a sleepover at Lilly's). But I've never really looked at his lips. You know. Up close.

Michael actually has very nice lips. Not thin lips, like mine. I don't know if you should say this about a boy's lips, but Michael's lips look like if you kissed them, they'd be very soft.

It was while I was noticing this about Michael's lips that the very bad thing happened: I was looking at them, you know, and wondering if they'd be soft to kiss, and as I looked, I sort of actually pictured us kissing, you know, in my head. And right then I got this very warm feeling—the one they talk about in all of Tina's romance novels—and RIGHT THEN was when Kenny went by on his way to get his usual lunch: Coke and an ice-cream sandwich.

I know Kenny can't read my mind—if he could, he totally would have broken up with me by now—but maybe he caught some hint as to what I was thinking, and that's why he didn't say *Hi* back, when Michael and I said "Hi" to him.

Well, that and the whole part where I said, "Um, okay," after he said he loved me.

Kenny must have known something was up, if my face was anywhere near as red-hot as it felt. Maybe *that*'s why he didn't say *Hi* back. Because I was looking so guilty. I'd certainly *felt* guilty. I mean, there I was, looking at another guy's lips and wondering what it would be like to kiss them, and my boyfriend goes walking by.

I am so going to bad-girl hell when I die.

You know what I wish? I wish everyone *could* read my mind. Because then Kenny would never have asked me out. He'd have known I don't think of him that way. And Lilly wouldn't make fun of me for not letting Kenny kiss me. She would know the reason I don't is that I'm in love with someone else.

The bad part is, she'd know who that someone else is.

And that someone probably won't even speak to me again, because it's totally uncool for a senior to go out with a freshman. Especially one who can't go anywhere without a bodyguard.

Besides, I'm almost positive he's going out with Judith Gershner, because after he came back from the grill, he went and sat down next to her.

So that settles that.

I wish I were leaving for Genovia tomorrow instead of in two weeks.

In spite of that disastrous incident at lunch, I had a pretty good time in Gifted and Talented. In fact, it was almost like old times again. I mean, before we all started going out with each other and everyone became so obsessed with the inner workings of my mouth, and all that.

Mrs. Hill spent the whole class period in the teachers' lounge across the hall, yelling at American Express on the phone, leaving us free to do what we usually do during her class . . . whatever we wanted. For instance, those of us who, like Lilly's boyfriend Boris, wanted to work on our individual projects (Boris's is learning to play some new sonata on his violin), which is what Gifted and Talented class is supposedly for, did so.

Those of us, however, like Lilly and me, who did not want to work on our individual projects (mine is studying for Algebra; Lilly's is working on her cable access TV show) did not.

This was especially satisfying, because Lilly had completely forgotten about the whole kissing thing between Kenny and me. The reason for this is that now she's mad at Mrs. Spears, her honors English teacher, who shot down her term paper proposal.

It really was unfair of Mrs. Spears to turn it down, because it was actually very well thought out, and quite creative. I made a copy of it:

How to Survive High School

by Lilly Moscovitz

Having spent the past two months locked in that institution of secondary education commonly referred to as high school, I feel that I am a qualified authority on the subject. From pep rallies to morning announcements, I have observed high-school life and all of its complexities. Sometime in the next four years, I will be granted my freedom from this festering hell-hole, and then I will publish my carefully compiled *High School Survival Guide.*

Little did my peers and teachers know that as they went about their daily routines, I was recording their activities for study by future generations. With my handy guide, every ninth grader's sojourn in high school can be a little more fruitful. Students of the future will learn that the way to settle their differences with their peers is not through violence, but through the sale of a really scathing screenplay—featuring characters based on those very individuals who tormented them all those years—to a major Hollywood movie studio. That, not a Molotov cocktail, is the path to true glory.

Here, for your reading pleasure, are a few examples of the topics I will explore in *How to Survive High School*, by Lilly Moscovitz:

1. High-School Romance, or How I Cannot Open My Locker Because Two Oversexed Adolescents are Leaning Up Against It, Making Out

2. Cafeteria Food: Can Corndogs Legally Be Listed as a Meat Product?
3. How to Communicate with the Subhumans Who Populate the Hallways
4. Guidance Counselors: Who Do They Think They're Kidding?
5. Get Ahead by Forging: The Art of the Hall Pass

Does that sound good, or what? Now look what Mrs. Spears had to say about it:

Lilly—Sorry as I am to hear that your experience thus far at AEHS has not been a positive one, I am afraid I am going to have to make it worse by asking you to find another topic for your term paper. A for creativity, as usual, however.

—Mrs. Spears

Can you believe that? Talk about unfair! Lilly's been censored! By rights, her proposal ought to have brought the school's administration to its knees. Lilly says she is appalled by the fact that, considering how much our tuition costs, this is the kind of support we can expect from our teachers. Then I reminded her that that isn't true of Mr. Gianini, who really goes beyond the call of duty by staying after school every day to conduct help sessions for people like me, who aren't doing so well in Algebra.

Lilly says Mr. Gianini probably only started pulling that staying-after-school thing so that he could ingratiate himself to my mother, and now he can't stop, because then she'll realize it was all just a setup and divorce him.

I don't believe that, however. I think Mr. G would have stayed after school to help me whether he was dating my mom or not. He's that kind of guy.

Anyway, the upshot of it all is that now Lilly has launched another one of her famous campaigns. This is actually a good thing, as it will keep her mind off me and where I am putting (or not putting) my lips. Here's how it started:

Lilly:	The real problem with this school isn't the teachers. It's the apathy of the student body. For instance, let's say we wanted to stage a walkout.
Me:	A walkout?
Lilly:	You know. We all get up and walk out of the school at the same time.
Me:	Just because Mrs. Spears turned down your term paper proposal?
Lilly:	No, Mia. Because she's trying to usurp our individuality by forcing us to bend to corporate feudalism. Again.
Me:	Oh. And how is she doing that?
Lilly:	By censoring us when we are at our most fertile, creatively speaking.
Boris:	(leaning out of the supply closet, where Lilly made him go when he started practicing his latest sonata) Fertile? Did someone say *fertile*?
Lilly:	Get back in the closet, Boris. Michael, can you send a mass e-mail tonight to the entire student

	body, declaring a walkout tomorrow at eleven?
Michael:	(working on the booth he and Judith Gershner and the rest of the Computer Club are going to have up at the Winter Carnival) I can, but I won't.
Lilly:	WHY NOT?
Michael:	Because it was your turn to empty the dishwasher last night, but you weren't home, so I had to do it.
Lilly:	But I TOLD Mom I had to go down to the studio to edit the last few finishing touches on this week's show!

Lilly's TV program, *Lilly Tells It Like It Is*, is now one of the highest-ranked shows on Manhattan cable. Of course, it's public access, so it's not like she's making any money off it, but a bunch of the major networks picked up this interview she did of me one night when I was half asleep and played it. I thought it was stupid, but I guess a lot of other people thought it was good, because now Lilly gets tons of viewer mail, whereas before the only mail she got was from her stalker, Norman.

Michael:	Look, if you're having time-management issues, don't take it out on me. Just don't expect me to meekly do your bidding, especially when you already owe me one.
Me:	Lilly, no offense, but I don't think this week's a good time for a walkout, anyway. I mean, after all, it's almost finals.

Lilly:	SO???
Me:	So some of us really need to stay in class. I can't afford to miss any review sessions. My grades are bad enough as it is.
Michael:	Really? I thought you were doing better in Algebra.
Me:	If you call a D plus better.
Michael:	Aw, come on. You have to be making better than a D plus. Your mom is married to your Algebra teacher!
Me:	So? That doesn't mean anything. You know Mr. G doesn't play favorites.
Michael:	I would think he'd cut his own stepdaughter a little slack, is all.
Lilly:	WOULD YOU TWO PLEASE PAY ATTENTION TO THE SITUATION AT HAND, WHICH IS THE FACT THAT THIS SCHOOL IS IN VITAL NEED OF SERIOUS REFORM?

Fortunately at that moment the bell rang, so no walkout tomorrow as far as I know. Which is a good thing, because I really need the extra study time.

You know, it's funny about Mrs. Spears not liking Lilly's term paper proposal, because she was very enthusiastic about my proposal, *A Case Against Christmas Trees: Why We Must Curtail the Pagan Ritual of Chopping Down Pine Trees Every December if We Are Going to Repair the Ozone Layer.*

And my IQ isn't anywhere near as high as Lilly's.

Kenny just passed me the following note:

> *Mia–I hope what I said to you last night didn't*
> *make you feel uncomfortable. I just wanted you to know*
> *how I feel.*
> *Sincerely,*
> *Kenny*

Oh, God. *Now* what am I supposed to do? He's sitting here next to me, waiting for an answer. In fact, that's what he thinks I'm writing right now. An answer.

What do I say?

Maybe this is my perfect opportunity to break up with him. *I'm sorry, Kenny, but I don't feel the same way—let's just be friends.* Is that what I should say?

It's just that I don't want to hurt his feelings, you know? And he is my Bio partner. I mean, whatever happens, I am going to have to sit next to him for the next two weeks. And I would much rather have a Bio partner who likes me than one who hates me.

And what about the dance? I mean, if I break up with him, who am I going to go to the Nondenominational Winter Dance with? I know it is horrible to think things like this, but this is the first dance in the history of my life to which I already have a date.

Well, I mean, if he'd ever get around to asking me.

And how about that final, huh? Our Bio final, I mean.

No way am I going to be able to pass without Kenny's notes. NO WAY.

But what else can I do? I mean, considering what happened today at the salad bar.

This is it. Good-bye, date for the Nondenominational Winter Dance. Hello, Friday-night television.

Dear Kenny,
It isn't that I don't think of you as a very dear friend.
It's just that—

Okay, so the bell rang before I had time to finish my note.

That doesn't mean I'm not going to tell Kenny exactly how I feel. I totally am. Tonight, as a matter of fact. I don't care if it's cruel to do something like that over the phone. I just can't take it anymore.

HOMEWORK

Algebra: review questions at the end of Chapters 1–3
English: term paper
World Civ: review questions at the end of Chapters 1–4
G & T: none
French: review questions at the end of Chapters 1–3
Biology: review questions at the end of Chapters 1–5

All right. So I didn't break up with him.

I totally meant to.

And it wasn't even because I didn't have the heart to do it over the phone, either.

It was something *Grandmère*, of all people, said.

Not that I feel right about it. Not breaking up with him, I mean. It's just that after Algebra review, I had to go to the showroom where Sebastiano is flogging his latest creations, so that he could have his flunkies take my measurements for my dress. Grandmère was going on about how from now on, I should really only wear clothes by Genovian designers, to show my patriotism, or whatever. Which is going to be hard, because, uh, there's only one Genovian clothing designer that I know of, and that's Sebastiano. And let's just say he doesn't make very much out of denim.

But whatever. I so had more important things to worry about than my spring wardrobe.

Which I guess Grandmère must have caught on to, because midway through Sebastiano's description of the beading he was going to have sewn onto my gown's bodice, Grandmère shouted, "Amelia, what is the matter with you?"

I must have jumped about a foot in the air. "What?"

"Sebastiano asked if you prefer a sweetheart or square-cut neckline."

I stared at her blankly. "Neckline for what?"

Grandmère gave me the evil eye. She does this quite frequently. That's why my father, even though he has the neighboring hotel suite, never stops by during my princess lessons.

"Sebastiano," my grandmother said. "You will please leave the princess and me for a moment."

And Sebastiano—who was wearing a new pair of leather pants, these in a tangerine color (the new gray, he told me; and white, you might be surprised to know, is the new black)—bowed and left the room, followed by the slinky ladies who'd been taking my measurements.

"Now," Grandmère said imperiously. "Something is clearly troubling you, Amelia. What is it?"

"It's nothing," I said, turning all red. I knew I was turning all red because: a) I could feel it, and b) I could see my reflection in the three full-length mirrors in front of me.

"It is not nothing." Grandmère took in a healthy drag from her Gitanes, even though I have asked her repeatedly not to smoke in my presence, as breathing secondhand smoke can cause just as much lung damage as actually smoking. "What is it? Trouble at home? Your mother and the math teacher fighting already, I suppose. Well, I never expected *that* marriage to last. Your mother is much too flighty."

I have to admit, I kind of snapped when she said that. Grandmère is always putting my mother down, even though Mom has raised me pretty much single-handedly and I certainly haven't gotten pregnant or shot anyone yet.

"For your information," I said, "my mom and Mr. Gianini are blissfully happy together. I wasn't thinking about them at all."

"What is it, then?" Grandmère asked in a bored voice.

"Nothing," I practically yelled. "I just—well, I was thinking about the fact that I have to break up with my boyfriend tonight, that's all. Not that it's any of your business."

Instead of taking offense at my tone, which any self-respecting grandparent would have found insolent, Grandmère only took a sip of her drink and suddenly looked way interested.

"Oh?" she said, in a totally different tone of voice—the same tone of voice she uses when someone mentions a stock tip she thinks might be useful for her portfolio. "What boyfriend is this?"

God, what did I ever do to be cursed with such a grandmother? Seriously. Lilly and Michael's grandma remembers the names of all their friends, makes them rugelach all the time, and always worries that they're not getting enough to eat, even though their parents, the Drs. Moscovitz, are wholly reliable at bringing home groceries, or at least ordering out.

Me? I get the grandma with the hairless poodle and the nine-carat diamond rings whose greatest joy in life is to torture me.

And why is that, anyway? I mean, why does Grandmère love to torture me so much? I've never done anything to her. Nothing except be her only grandchild, anyway. And it isn't exactly like I go around advertising how I feel about her. You know, I've never actually *told* her I think she's a mean old lady who contributes to the destruction of the environment by wearing fur coats and smoking filterless French cigarettes.

"Grandmère," I said, trying to remain calm. "I have only one boyfriend. His name is Kenny." I've only told you about fifty thousand times, I added, in my head.

"I thought this Kenny person was your Biology partner," Grandmère said, after taking a sip of her sidecar, her favorite drink.

"He is," I said, a little surprised that she'd managed to remember something like that. "He's also my boyfriend. Only last night he went completely schizo on me, and told me he loves me."

Grandmère patted Rommel, who was sitting in her lap looking miserable (his habitual expression), on the head.

"And what is so wrong," Grandmère wanted to know, "about a boy who says he loves you?"

"Nothing," I said. "Only I'm not in love with him, see? So it wouldn't be fair of me to, you know, lead him on."

Grandmère raised her painted-on eyebrows. "I don't see why not."

How had I ever gotten into this conversation? "Because, Grandmère. People just don't go around *doing* things like that. Not nowadays."

"Is that so? Well, my observations of people are to the contrary. Except, of course, if one happens to be in love with someone else. Then shedding an unwanted suitor might be considered wise, so that one can make oneself available to the man one truly desires." She eyed me. "Is there someone like that in your life, Amelia? Someone—ahem—special?"

"No." I lied, automatically.

Grandmère snorted. "You're lying."

"No, I'm not." I lied again.

"Indeed you are. I oughtn't tell you this, but I suppose as it is a bad habit for a future monarch, you ought to be made aware of it, so that in the future, you can try to prevent it: When you lie, Amelia, your nostrils flare."

I threw my hands up to my nose. "They do not!"

"Indeed," Grandmère said, clearly enjoying herself immensely. "If you do not believe me, look in the mirror."

I turned around to face the nearby full-length mirrors. Taking my hands from my face, I examined my nose. My nostrils weren't flaring. She was crazy.

"I'll ask you again, Amelia," Grandmère said, in a lazy voice, from her chair. "Are you in love with anyone right now?"

"No." I lied, automatically. . . .

And my nostrils flared right out!

Oh, my God! All these years I've been lying, and it turns out whenever I do, my nostrils totally give me away! All anyone has to do is look at my nose when I talk, and they'll know for sure whether or not I'm telling the truth.

How could no one have pointed this out to me before? And Grandmère—Grandmère, of all people—was the one who figured it out! Not my mother, with whom I've lived for fourteen years. Not my best friend, whose IQ is higher than Einstein's.

No. Grandmère.

If this got out, my life was over.

"Fine," I cried dramatically, spinning away from the mirror to face her. "All right, yes. Yes, I am in love with somebody else. Are you happy now?"

Grandmère raised her painted-on eyebrows.

"No need to shout, Amelia," she said, with what I might have taken for amusement in anyone other than her. "Who might this special someone be?"

"Oh, no," I said, holding out both my hands. If it wouldn't have been totally rude, I'd have made a little cross out of my index fingers and held it up toward her—that's how much she scares me. And if you think about it, with her tattooed eyeliner, she does look a little like Nosferatu. "You are not getting that information out of me."

Grandmère stamped out her cigarette in the crystal ashtray Sebastiano had provided, and went, "Very well. I take it, then, that the gentleman in question does not return your ardor?"

There was no point in lying to her. Not now. Not with my nostrils.

My shoulders sagged. "No. He likes this other girl. This really smart girl who knows how to clone fruit flies."

Grandmère snorted. "A useful talent. Well, never mind that now. I don't suppose, Amelia, that you are acquainted with the expression dirty dishwater is better than none?"

I guess she must have been able to tell from my perplexed expression that this was one I hadn't heard before, since she went on, "Do not throw away this Kenny until you have managed to secure someone better."

I stared at her, horrified. Really, my grandmother has said—and done—some pretty cold things in her time, but this one took the cake.

"Secure someone better?" I couldn't believe she actually meant what I thought she meant. "You mean I shouldn't break up with Kenny until I've got someone else?"

Grandmère lit another cigarette. "But of course."

"But Grandmère." I swear to God, sometimes I can't figure out if she's human or some kind of alien life force sent down from some other planet to spy on us. "You can't do that. You can't just string a guy along like that, knowing that you don't feel the same way about him that he feels about you."

Grandmère exhaled a long plume of blue smoke. "Why not?"

"Because it's completely unethical!" I shook my head. "No. I'm breaking up with Kenny. Right away. Tonight, as a matter of fact."

Grandmère stroked Rommel under the chin. He looked more miserable than ever, as if instead of stroking him, she was peeling the skin away from his body. He really is the most heinous excuse for a dog I have ever seen.

"That," Grandmère said, "is your prerogative, of course. But allow me to point out to you that if you break off your relationship with this young man, your Biology grade will suffer."

I was shocked. But mostly because this was something I had already thought of myself. I was amazed Grandmère and I had actually shared something.

Which was really the only reason I exclaimed, "Grandmère!"

"Well," Grandmère said, flicking ash from her cigarette into the ashtray. "Isn't it true? You are only making what, a C, in this class? And that is only because that young man allows you to copy his answers to the homework."

"Grandmère!" I squealed again. Because, of course, she was right.

She looked at the ceiling. "Let me see," she said. "With your D in Algebra, if you get anything less than a C in Biology, your grade-point average will take quite a little dip this semester."

"Grandmère." I couldn't believe this. She knew all about my grades! And she was right. She was so right. But still. "I am not going to postpone breaking up with Kenny until after the final. That would be just plain wrong."

"Suit yourself," Grandmère said with a sigh. "But it certainly will be awkward having to sit beside him for the next—how long is it until the end of the semester?—Oh, yes, two weeks. Especially considering the fact that after you break things off with him, he probably won't even speak to you anymore."

God, so true. And not something I hadn't thought of myself. If Kenny got mad enough over me breaking up with him to not want to speak to me anymore, seventh period was going to be plenty unpleasant.

"And what about this dance?" Grandmère rattled the ice in her sidecar. "This Christmas dance?"

"It's not a Christmas dance," I said. "It's a nondenominational—"

Grandmère waved a hand. This spiky charm bracelet she was wearing tinkled.

"Whatever," she said. "If you stop seeing this young man, who will you go to the dance with?"

"I won't go with anybody," I said, firmly, even though, of course, my heart was breaking at the thought. "I'll just stay home."

"While everyone else has a good time? Really, Amelia, you aren't being at all sensible. What about this other young man?"

"What other young man?"

"The one you claim to be so in love with. Won't he be at this dance with the housefly girl?"

"Fruit fly," I corrected her. "And I don't know. Maybe."

The thought that Michael might ask Judith Gershner to the Nondenominational Winter Dance had never occurred to me. But as soon as Grandmère mentioned it, I felt that same sickening sensation I'd felt at the ice-skating rink when I'd first seen them together: kind of like the time when Lilly and I were crossing Bleecker Street and this Chinese food delivery man crashed into us on his bicycle, and I had the wind completely knocked out of me.

Only this time, it wasn't just my chest that hurt, but my tongue. It had been feeling a lot better, but now it started to throb again.

"It seems to me," Grandmère said, "that one way to get this young man's attention might be to show up at this dance on the arm of this other young man, looking perfectly divine in an original creation by Genovian fashion designer Sebastiano Grimaldi."

I just stared at her. Because she was right. She was so right. Except . . .

"Grandmère," I said. "The guy I like? Yeah, he likes girls who can clone *insects*. Okay? I highly doubt he is going to be impressed by a *dress*."

I didn't mention that I had, of course, just the night before, been hoping that very thing. But almost as if she could read my mind, Grandmère just went, "Hmmm," in this knowing way.

"Suit yourself," she continued. "Still, it seems a bit cruel to me, your breaking things off with this young man at this time of year."

"Why?" I asked, confused. Had Grandmère inadvertently stumbled across some TV channel playing *It's a Wonderful Life*, or something? She had never shown one speck of holiday spirit before now. "Because it's *Christmas*?"

"No," Grandmère said, looking very disgusted with me, I guess over the suggestion that she might ever be moved by the anniversary of the birth of anyone's savior. "Because of your exams. If you truly wish to be kind, I think you might at least wait until after the final exams are over before breaking the poor little fellow's heart."

I had been all ready to argue with whatever excuse for me not breaking up with Kenny Grandmère came up with next— but this one, I had not expected. I stood there with my mouth hanging open. I know it was hanging open, because I could see it reflected in the three full-length mirrors.

"I cannot imagine," Grandmère went on, "why you do not simply allow him to believe that you return his ardor until your exams are over. Why compound the poor boy's stress? But you must, of course, do what you think is best. I suppose this—er—Kenny is the sort of boy who bounces back easily from rejection. He'll probably do quite well on his exams, in spite of his broken heart."

Oh, God! If she had stabbed a fork in my stomach and twisted my intestines around the tines like spaghetti, she couldn't have made me feel worse. . . .

And, I have to admit, a little relieved. Because of course I can't break up with Kenny now. Never mind my Bio grade and the dance: You can't break up with someone right before finals. It's, like, the meanest thing you can do.

Well, aside from the kind of stuff Lana and her friends pull. You know, girls' locker-room stuff, like going up to someone who is changing and asking her why she wears a bra when she obviously doesn't need one, or making fun of her just because she doesn't happen to like being kissed by her boyfriend. That kind of thing.

So here I am. I *want* to break up with Kenny, but I can't.

I *want* to tell Michael how I feel about him, but I can't do that either.

I can't even quit biting my fingernails. I am going to gross out an entire European nation with my bloody cuticles.

I am a pathetic mess. No wonder in the car this morning—after I accidentally closed the door on Lars's foot—Lilly said that I should really look into getting some therapy, because if there's anybody who needs to find inner harmony between her conscious and her subconscious, it's me.

TO DO BEFORE LEAVING FOR GENOVIA

1. Get cat food, litter for Fat Louie
2. Stop biting fingernails
3. Achieve self-actualization
4. Find inner harmony between conscious and subconscious
5. Break up with Kenny—but not until after finals/Nondenominational Winter Dance

Tuesday, December 9, English

What was THAT just now in the hallway? Did Kenny Showalter just say what I think he said to you?

Yes. Oh, my God, Shameeka, what am I going to do? I'm shaking so hard I can barely write.

What do you mean, what are you going to do? The boy is warm for your form, Mia. Go for it.

People can't just be allowed to go around saying things like that. Especially so loud. Everyone must have heard him. Do you think everyone heard him?

Everybody heard him, all right. You should have seen Lilly's face. I thought she was going to suffer one of those synaptic breakdowns she's always talking about.

You think EVERYBODY heard him? I mean, like the people coming out of the Chemistry lab? Do you think they heard?

How could they not? He yelled it pretty loud.

Were they laughing? The people coming out of Chemistry? They weren't laughing, were they?

Most of them were laughing.

Oh, God! Why was I ever born????

Except Michael. He wasn't laughing.

He WASN'T? REALLY? Are you pulling my leg?

No. Why would I do that? And what do you care what Michael Moscovitz thinks, anyway?

I don't. I don't care. What makes you think I care?

Um, for one thing because you won't shut up about it.

People shouldn't go around laughing at other people's misfortunes. That's all.

I don't see what the big misfortune is. So the guy loves you?
A lot of girls would really like it if their boyfriend yelled that at
them between first and second period.
    Yeah, well, NOT ME!!!!

Use <u>transitive verbs</u> to create brief, vigorous sentences.

<u>Transitive</u>: He soon regretted his words.
<u>Intransitive</u>: It was not long before he was very
sorry that he had said what he said.

Gifted and Talented was so not fun today. Not that Bio is any better, on account of the fact that I am stuck here next to Kenny, who seems to have calmed down a little since this morning.

Still, I really think that people who are not actually enrolled in certain classes have no business showing up in them.

For instance, just because Judith Gershner has study hall for fifth period is no reason that she should be allowed to hang around the Gifted and Talented classroom for fifty minutes during that period. She should never have been let out of study hall in the first place. I don't think she even had a pass.

Not that I would turn her in, or anything. But this kind of flagrant rule-breaking really shouldn't be encouraged. If Lilly is going to go through with this walkout thing, which she is still trying to garner support for, she should really add to her list of complaints the fact that the teachers in this school play favorites. I mean, just because a girl knows how to clone things doesn't mean she should be allowed to roam the school freely any time she wants.

But there she was when I walked in, and there's no doubt about it: Judith Gershner has a total crush on Michael. I don't really know how he feels about her, but she was wearing tan-colored panty hose instead of the black cotton tights she normally wears, so you *know* something is up. No girl wears tan panty hose without a good reason.

And okay, so maybe they are working on their booth for

the Winter Carnival, but that is no reason for Judith to drape her arm across the back of Michael's chair like that. Plus he used to help me with my Algebra homework during G and T, but now he can't, because Judith is monopolizing all his time. I would think he might resent the intrusion.

Plus Judith really has no business butting into my private conversations. She hardly even knows me.

But did that stop her from letting me know, when she overheard Lilly's formal apology for not having believed me about Kenny's weird phone call—any doubts about the veracity of which he managed to scatter today with his display of unbridled passion in the third floor hallway—that she feels sorry for him? Oh, no.

"Poor kid," Judith said. "I heard what he said to you in the hallway. I was in the chem lab. What was it again? 'I don't care if you don't feel the same way, Mia, I will always love you,' or something like that?"

I didn't say anything. That's because I was busy picturing how Judith would look with a pencil sticking out of the middle of her forehead.

"It's really sweet," Judith said. "If you think about it. I mean, the guy's clearly got it bad for you."

This is the problem, see. Everyone thinks what Kenny did was so cute and everything. Nobody seems to understand that it wasn't cute. It wasn't cute at all. It was completely humiliating. I don't think I've ever been so embarrassed in my whole life.

And believe me, I've lived through more than my fair share of embarrassing incidents, especially since this whole princess thing started.

But I'm apparently the only person in this entire school who thinks what Kenny did was the least bit wrong.

"He's obviously very in touch with his emotions." Even Lilly was taking Kenny's side in the whole thing. "Unlike *some* people."

I have to say, this makes me so mad when I think about it, because the truth is, ever since I started writing things down in journals, I have gotten very in touch with my emotions. I usually know almost exactly how I feel.

The problem is, I just can't tell anyone.

I don't know who was the most surprised when Michael suddenly came to my defense against his sister—Lilly, Judith Gershner, or me.

"Just because Mia doesn't go around shouting about how she feels in the third floor hallway," Michael said, "doesn't mean she isn't in touch with her emotions."

How does he do that? How is it that he is able to magically put into words exactly what I feel, but seem to have so much trouble saying? This, you see, is why I love him. I mean, how could I not?

"Yeah," I said triumphantly.

"Well, you could have said something back to him." Lilly always gets disgruntled when Michael comes to my rescue—especially when he does it while she is attacking me about the lack of honesty in my emotional life. "Instead of just leaving him hanging there."

"And what," I demanded—injudiciously, I now realize—"should I have said to him?"

"How about," Lilly said, "that you love him back?"

WHY? That's all I want to know. WHY was I cursed

with a best friend who doesn't understand that there are some things you just don't say in front of EVERYONE IN THE ENTIRE GIFTED AND TALENTED CLASSROOM, INCLUDING HER BROTHER????

The problem is, Lilly has never been embarrassed about anything in her life. She simply does not know the meaning of the word *embarrassment*.

"Look," I said, feeling my cheeks begin to burn. I couldn't lie, of course. How could I lie, considering what I now knew about my nostrils? And okay, Lilly hadn't figured it out yet, but it was only a matter of time. I mean, if *Grandmère* knew . . . "I really and truly value Kenny's companionship," I said, carefully. "But love. I mean, *love*. That is a very big thing. I'm not, I mean, I don't . . ."

I dribbled off pathetically, acutely aware that everyone in the room, most especially Michael, was listening.

"I see," Lilly said, narrowing her eyes. "Fear of commitment."

"I do not fear commitment," I insisted. "I just—"

But Lilly's dark eyes were already shining in eager anticipation. She was getting ready to psychoanalyze me, one of her favorite hobbies, unfortunately.

"Let's examine the situation, shall we?" she said. "I mean, here you've got this guy going around the hallways, screaming about how much he loves you, and you just stare at him like a rat caught in the path of the D train. What do you suppose that means?"

"Have you ever considered," I demanded, "that maybe

the reason I didn't tell him I love him back is because I—"

I almost said it. Really. I did. I almost said that I don't love Kenny.

But I couldn't. Because if I'd said that, somehow it would have gotten back to Kenny, and that would be even worse than my breaking up with him. I couldn't do it.

So all I said instead was, "Lilly, you know perfectly well I do not fear commitment. I mean, there are lots of boys I—"

"Oh, yeah?" Lilly seemed to be enjoying herself way more than usual. It was almost as if she was playing to an audience. Which, of course, she was. The audience of her brother and his girlfriend. "Name one."

"One what?"

"Name a boy that you could see yourself committing to for all eternity."

"What do you want, a list?" I asked her.

"A list would be nice," Lilly said.

So I drew up the following list:

GUYS MIA THERMOPOLIS COULD
SEE HERSELF COMMITTING TO FOR
ALL ETERNITY

1. Wolverine of the *X-Men*
2. Orlando Bloom as Legolas
3. James Franco as Tristan in *Tristan and Isolde*
4. Tarzan from the Disney cartoon
5. The Beast from *Beauty and the Beast*

6. That hot soldier guy from *Mulan*
7. The guy Brendan Fraser played in *The Mummy*
8. Christian Bale as Batman
9. Jake Gyllenhaal in *Donnie Darko*
10. Justin Baxendale

But this list turned out to be no good, because Lilly totally took it and analyzed it, and it works out that almost half the guys on it are actually cartoon characters; one is an elf; and one is a mutant who can make spikes shoot out of his knuckles.

In fact, except for Justin Baxendale—the good-looking senior who just transferred from Trinity and who a lot of girls at Albert Einstein High School are already in love with—all the guys I listed are fictional creations. Apparently, the fact that I could list no guy I had a hope of actually getting together with—or who even lives in the third dimension—is indicative of something.

Not, of course, indicative of the fact that the guy I like was actually in the room at the time, sitting next to his new girlfriend, and so I couldn't list him.

Oh, no. Nobody thought of *that*.

No, the lack of actual attainable men on my list was apparently indicative of my unrealistic expectations where men are concerned, and further proof of my inability to commit.

Lilly says if I don't lower my expectations somewhat, I am destined for an unsatisfactory love life.

As if the way things have been going, I've ever expected anything else.

Kenny just tossed me this note:

Mia—I'm sorry about what happened today in the hallway. I understand now that I embarrassed you. Sometimes I forget that even though you are a princess, you are still quite introverted. I promise never to do anything like that again. Can I make it up to you by taking you to lunch at Big Wong on Thursday? —Kenny

I said yes, of course. Not just because I really like Big Wong's steamed vegetable dumplings, or even because I don't want people thinking I fear commitment. I didn't even say yes because I suspect that, over dumplings and hot tea, Kenny is finally going to ask me to the Nondenominational Winter Dance.

I said yes because in spite of it all, I really do like Kenny, and I don't want to hurt his feelings.

And I'd feel the same way even if I weren't a princess, and always had to do the right thing.

HOMEWORK

Algebra: review questions at the end of Chapters 4–7
English: term paper
World Civ: review questions at the end of Chapters 5–9
G & T: none
French: review questions at the end of Chapters 4–6
Biology: review questions at the end of Chapters 6–8

Tuesday, December 9, 4 p.m., in the limo on the way to the Plaza

The following conversation took place between Mr. Gianini and me today after Algebra review:

Mr. G: Mia, is everything all right?

Me: (Surprised) Yes. Why wouldn't it be?

Mr. G: Well, it's just that I thought you'd pretty much grasped the FOIL method, but on today's pop quiz, you got all five problems wrong.

Me: I guess I've sort of had a lot on my mind.

Mr. G: Your trip to Genovia?

Me: Yeah, that, and . . . other things.

Mr. G: Well, if you want to talk about the, um, other things, you know I'm always here for you. And your mother. I know we might seem preoccupied with the baby coming and everything, but you're always number one on our list of priorities. You know that, don't you?

Me: (Mortified) Yes. But there's nothing wrong. Really.

Thank God he doesn't know about my nostrils.

And really, what else *could* I have said? "Mr. G, my boyfriend is a nut case but I can't break up with him on account of finals, and I'm in love with my best friend's brother?"

I highly doubt he'd be able to offer any meaningful advice on any of the above.

Tuesday, December 9, 7 p.m.

I don't believe this. I'm home before *Baywatch Hawaii* starts for the first time in, like, months. Something must be wrong with Grandmère. Although she seemed pretty normal at our lesson today. I mean, for her. Except that she stopped me in the middle of my reciting the Genovian pledge of allegiance (which I have to memorize, of course, for when I am visiting schools in Genovia. I don't want to look like an idiot in front of a bunch of five-year-olds for not knowing it) to ask me what I'd decided to do about Kenny.

It's kind of funny about her taking an interest in my personal life, since she certainly never has before. Well, not very much, anyway.

And she kept on saying stuff about how ingenious it had been of Kenny, sending me those anonymous love letters last October, the ones I thought (well, okay, *hoped*, not really thought) Michael was writing.

I was all, "What was so ingenious about *that?*" to which Grandmère just replied, "Well, you're his girlfriend now, aren't you?"

Which I never really thought about, but I guess she's right.

Anyway, my mom was so surprised to see me home so early, she actually let me be in charge of choosing the take-out (pizza margherita for me. I let her get rigatoni bolognese, even though the sausage in the sauce is probably steeped in nitrates that could harm a developing fetus. Still, it was sort of a special occasion, what with me actually being home for dinner for a change. Even Mr. Gianini got a little wild and had something with porcini mushrooms in it).

I am psyched to be home early, because you wouldn't believe all the studying I have to do, plus I should probably start my term paper, then there's figuring out what I'm going to get people for Christmas and Hannukah, not to mention going over the thank-you speech I have to make to the people of Genovia in my nationally televised (in Genovia, anyway) introduction to the people I will one day rule.

I had really better buckle down and get to work!

Tuesday, December 9, 7:30 p.m.

Okay, so I was taking a study break, and I just realized something. You can learn *a lot* from watching *Baywatch*. Seriously.

I have compiled this list:

THINGS I HAVE LEARNED FROM WATCHING BAYWATCH

1. If you are paralyzed from the waist down, you just need to see a kid being attacked by a murderer, and you will be able to get up and save him.
2. If you have bulimia, it is probably because two men love you at the same time. Just tell the two of them you only want to be friends, and your bulimia will go away.
3. It is always easy to get a parking place near the beach.
4. Male lifeguards always put a shirt on when they leave the beach. Female lifeguards don't need to bother.
5. If you meet a beautiful but troubled girl, she is probably either a diamond smuggler or suffering from split personality disorder: Do not accept her invitation to dinner.
6. Dick van Patten, though a senior citizen, can be surprisingly hard to quell in a fistfight.
7. If people are mysteriously dying in the water, it is probably because a giant electric eel has escaped from a nearby aquarium.

8. A girl who is thinking about abandoning her baby should just leave it on the beach. Chances are, a nice lifeguard will take it home, adopt it, and raise it as his own.
9. It is very easy to outswim a shark.
10. Wild seals make adorable and easily trained pets.

I just got an e-mail from Lilly. I'm not the only one who got it, either. Somehow she figured out how to do a mass e-mail to every kid in school.

Well, I shouldn't be surprised, I guess. She *is* a genius. Still, she has clearly developed atrophy of the brain from too much studying, because look what she wrote:

ATTENTION ALL STUDENTS AT
ALBERT EINSTEIN HIGH SCHOOL

Stressed from too many exams, term papers, and final projects? Don't just passively accept the oppressive workload handed down to us by the tyrannical administration! A silent walkout has been scheduled for tomorrow. At 10 A.M. exactly, join your fellow students in showing our teachers how we feel about inflexible exam schedules, repressive censorship, and having only one reading day on which to prepare for our finals. Leave your pencils, leave your books, and gather on East 75th Street between Madison and Park (use doors by main administration offices, if possible) for a rally against Principal Gupta and the trustees. Let your voice be heard!

I am so sure. I can't walk out tomorrow at 10 A.M. That's right in the middle of Algebra. Mr. Gianini's feelings will be so hurt if we all just get up and leave.

But if I say I'm not going to take part in it, Lilly will be furious.

But if I do take part in it, my dad will kill me. Not to mention my mom. I mean, we could all get suspended, or something. Or hit by a delivery truck. There are a lot of them on 75th at that time of day.

Why? Why must I be saddled with a best friend who is so clearly a sociopath?

I just got the following Instant Message from Michael:

CracKing: Did you just get that whacked-out mass e-mail from my sister?

I replied at once.

FtLouie: Yes.
CracKing: You're not going along with her stupid walkout, are you?
FtLouie: Oh, right. She won't be too mad if I don't, or anything.
CracKing: You don't have to do everything she says, you know, Mia. I mean, you've stood up to her before. Why not now?

Um, because I have enough to worry about right now—for instance, finals; my impending trip to Genovia; and, oh, yeah, the fact that I love you—without adding a fight with my best friend to the list.

But I didn't say that, of course.

FtLouie: I find that the path of least resistance is often the safest one when dealing with your sister.
CracKing: Well, I'm not doing it. Walking out, I mean.
FtLouie: It's different for you. You're her brother. She has to remain on speaking terms with you. You live together.
CracKing: Not for much longer. Thank God.

Oh, right. He's going away to college soon.

Well, not too far away. But about a hundred blocks or so.

FtLouie: That's right. You got accepted to Columbia. Early decision, too. I never did congratulate you. So congratulations.

CracKing: Thanks.

FtLouie: You must be happy that you'll know at least one other person there. Judith Gershner, I mean.

CracKing: Yeah, I guess so. Listen, you're still going to be in town for the Winter Carnival, right? I mean, you're not leaving for Genovia before the 19th are you?

All I could think was, *Why is he asking me this? I mean, he can't be going to ask me to the dance. He must know I'm going with Kenny. I mean, if Kenny ever gets around to asking me, that is. Besides, it isn't as if Michael is available. Isn't he going with Judith? Well? ISN'T HE?*

FtLouie: I'm leaving for Genovia on the 20th.

CracKing: Oh, good. Because you should really stop by the Computer Club's booth at the Carnival, and check out this program I've been working on. I think you'll like it.

I should have known. Michael isn't going to ask me to any dance. Not in this lifetime, anyway. I should have known it was just his stupid computer program he wanted me to see. Who even cares? I suppose dumb army guys will pop out at me, and I'll have to shoot them, or whatever. Judith's idea, I'm sure.

I wanted to write to him, *Don't you have the slightest idea what I'm going through? That the only person with whom I can see myself committing to for all eternity is YOU? Don't you KNOW that by now????*

But instead I wrote:

FTLOUIE: Can't wait. Well, I have to go. Bye.

Sometimes I completely hate myself.

Wednesday, December 10, 3 a.m.

You're never going to believe this. Something *Grandmère* said is keeping me awake.

Seriously. I was dead asleep—well, as asleep as you can be with a twenty-five pound cat purring on your abdomen—when all of a sudden, I woke up with this totally random phrase going around in my head:

"Well, you're his girlfriend now, aren't you?"

That's what Grandmère said when I asked her what was so ingenious about Kenny's having sent me those anonymous love letters.

And do you know what?

SHE'S RIGHT.

It seems totally bizarre to admit that Grandmère might be right about something, but I think it's true. Kenny's anonymous love letters *did* work. I mean, I *am* his girlfriend now.

So what's to keep me from writing some anonymous love letters to the boy *I* like? I mean, really? Besides the fact that I already have a boyfriend, and the guy I like already has a girlfriend?

I think this is a plan that might have some merit. It needs more work, of course, but hey, desperate measures call for desperate times. Or something like that. Too sleepy to figure it out.

Okay, I was up all night thinking about it, and I'm pretty sure I've got it figured out. Even as I sit here, my plan is being put into action, thanks to Tina Hakim Baba and a stop at Ho's Deli before school started.

Actually, Ho's didn't really have what I wanted. I wanted a card that was blank inside, with a picture on the front that was sophisticated but not too sexy. But the only blank cards they had at Ho's (that weren't plastered with pictures of kittens) were ones with photos of fruit being dipped into chocolate sauce.

I tried to choose a non-phallic fruit, but even the strawberry I got is kind of sexier than I would have liked. I don't know what's sexy about fruit with chocolate sauce dripping off it, but Tina was like, "Whoa," when she saw it.

Still, she gamely agreed to print my poem on the inside of the card, so Michael won't recognize my handwriting. She even liked my poem, which I came up with at five this morning:

> *Roses are Red*
> *Violets are Blue*
> *You may not know it*
> *But someone loves you.*

Not my best work, I will admit, but it was really hard to come up with something better after only three hours of sleep.

I hesitated somewhat over the use of the L word. I thought

maybe I should substitute *like* for *love*. I don't want him to think there's a creepy stalker after him, and all.

But Tina said *love* was absolutely right. Because, as she put it, "It's the truth, isn't it?"

And since it's anonymous, I guess it doesn't matter that I am laying open my soul.

Anyway, Tina goes by Michael's locker right before we have PE, so she's going to slip it to him then.

I can't believe that this is the low I have stooped to. But like Dad once told me, Faint heart never won fair lady.

Lars just pointed out that I'm not exactly risking anything, seeing as how I didn't sign the card and even went to the extreme of having someone else write out the poem for me (Lars knows all about this, on account of I had to explain to him why we had to go into Ho's at eight fifteen in the morning). He helped pick the card, but I would be happy if that was the extent of his contribution to this particular project. Because he's a man, I cannot imagine his input is at all valuable.

Besides, he's been married like four times, so I highly doubt he knows anything about romance.

Also, he should know by now we're not allowed to talk during Homeroom.

Wednesday, December 10, Algebra, 9:30 a.m.

I just saw Lilly in the hallway. She whispered, "Don't forget! Ten o'clock! Don't let me down!"

Well, the truth is, I did forget. The walkout! The stupid walkout!

And poor Mr. Gianini, standing up there going over Chapter Five, not suspecting a thing. It's not his fault Mrs. Spears didn't like Lilly's term paper topic. Lilly can't just arbitrarily punish all the teachers in school for something one teacher did.

It's already nine thirty-five. What am I going to do?

Lana just leaned back and hissed, "You gonna walk out with your fat friend?"

I take real objection to this. Only in a culture as screwed up as ours, where girls like Christina Aguilera are held up as models of beauty when clearly they are in fact suffering from some sort of malnutrition (scurvy?), would Lilly ever be considered fat. Because Lilly isn't fat. She is just round, like a puppy.

I hate it here.

Wednesday, December 10, Algebra, 9:50 a.m.

Ten minutes until the walkout. I can't take this. I'm getting out.

Okay. I'm standing in the hallway next to the fire alarm by the second-floor drinking fountain. I got a hall pass from Mr. G. I told him I had to go to the bathroom.

Lars is with me, of course. I wish he'd stop laughing. He does not seem to realize the seriousness of the situation. Plus Justin Baxendale just walked by with a hall pass of his own, and he gave us this really weird look.

And yeah, I probably do look a little strange, hanging out in the hallway with my bodyguard, who is currently experiencing a fit of the giggles, but still—I do not need to be looked at weirdly by Justin Baxendale.

His eyelashes are really long and dark and they make his eyes look sort of smoky. . . .

OH, MY GOD! I CAN'T BELIEVE I AM WRIT-ING ABOUT JUSTIN BAXENDALE'S EYELASHES AT A TIME LIKE THIS!

I mean, I am in a real bind here:

If I do not walk out with Lilly, I'll lose my best friend.

But if I do walk out with everyone, I will be totally diss-ing my stepfather.

So I really only have one choice.

Lars just offered to do it for me. But I can't let him. I can't let him take the fall for me if we get caught. I am the princess. I have to do it myself.

I just told him to get ready to run. This is one time being so tall comes in handy. I have a pretty long stride.

Well, here goes.

I don't get why she's so mad. I mean, yeah, if everyone evacuates the building due to a fire alarm going off, it's not the same thing as everyone leaving in protest against the repressive teaching techniques of some of the teachers.

But we're still all standing in the middle of the street in the rain, and nobody has coats on because they wouldn't let us stop at our lockers for fear we'd all be consumed in a fiery conflagration, so we're probably going to get hypothermia from the cold and die.

That's what she wanted, right?

But no. She can't even be happy about that.

"Somebody ratted us out!" she keeps yelling. "Somebody told! Why else would they schedule a fire drill for exactly the same time as my walkout? I'm telling you, these bureaucrats will stop at nothing to keep us from speaking out against them. Nothing! They'll even make us stand out in freezing drizzle, hoping to weaken our immune systems so we'll no longer have the strength to fight them. Well, I for one refuse to catch cold! I refuse to succumb to their petty abuses!"

I suggested to Lilly that she write her term paper on the suffragettes, because they, like us, had to put up with numerous indignities in their battle for equal rights.

Lilly, however, told me not to be facile.

God, being best friends with a genius is hard.

Wednesday, December 10, G & T

I can't tell if Michael got the note or not!!!!

Worse, stupid Judith Gershner is here AGAIN. Why can't she stay in her own class? Why is she always hanging around ours? We were all getting along perfectly well until *she* came along.

My life is pathetic.

I thought about going across the hall to the teachers' lounge and asking Mrs. Hill a question about something—like why she had the custodians remove the door to the supply closet so we can't lock Boris in there anymore—so she'd maybe look over and NOTICE that there's a girl in our classroom who is *not* supposed to be there.

But I couldn't bring myself to do it, because of Michael. I mean, Michael obviously *wants* Judith here, or else he'd tell her to go away.

RIGHT?????

Anyway, with Michael so busy and all with Miss Gershner, I guess I am on my own with the whole Algebra review thing.

That's all right. I'm completely fine with that. I can study on my own just fine. Watch:

A, B, C = disjoint partition of universal set
Collection of non-empty subsets of U that are pairwise disjoint and whose union is equal to the set of U

I get that. I totally get what that means. Who needs

Michael's help? Not me. I am totally cool with the collection of non-empty subsets.
TOTALLY COOL WITH IT.

*Oh, Michael
You have made my heart
a disjoint partition.*

*Why can't you see
that we were meant to be
a universal set?*

*Instead, you have turned my soul
into a collection
of non-empty subsets.*

*I cannot believe
that our love was meant to be
pairwise disjoint.*

*But rather
a union—
equal to the set of
U and me.*

You know what else I just realized? That if this thing works—you know, if I do manage to get Michael away from Judith Gershner, and I break up with Kenny, and I end up, you know, in a potentially romantic situation with Lilly's brother—I will not know what to do.

Seriously.

Take kissing, for instance. I have only ever kissed one person before, and that's Kenny. I cannot believe that what Kenny and I did really encompassed the whole of the kissing experience, because it certainly wasn't as fun as people always make it look on TV.

This is a very disturbing thought, and has led me to an equally disturbing conclusion: I know very little about kissing.

In fact, it seems to me that if I am going to be doing any kissing with anybody, I should get some advice beforehand. From a kissing expert, I mean.

Which is why I am consulting Tina Hakim Baba. She may not be allowed to wear makeup to school, but she has been kissing Dave Farouq El-Abar—who goes to Trinity— for close to three months now, *and* liking it, so I consider her an expert on the subject.

I am enclosing the results of this highly scientific document for future reference.

Tina—
I need to know about kissing. Can you please answer
each of the following questions IN DETAIL????
And DO NOT show this to anyone!!!! DO NOT lose
this paper!!!! —Mia

1. Can a boy tell if the person he is with is inexperienced?
How does an inexperienced kisser kiss (so I can avoid
that)?

> The guy may sense a feeling of nervousness coming from
> you, or that you are uneasy, but everyone is nervous when
> they are kissing someone new. It's natural! But kissing is
> easy to catch on to—believe me! An inexperienced kisser
> might break away too soon because he or she is scared or
> whatever. But that is normal. It's SUPPOSED to be
> weird. That's what makes it fun.

2. Is there such a thing as a great kisser? If so, what are
the qualifications? (So I know what to practice.)

> Yes, there is such a thing as a great kisser. A great kisser
> is always affectionate and gentle and patient and not
> demanding.

3. How much pressure do you exert on his lips? I mean,
do you push, or like in a handshake, are you just supposed
to be firm? Or are you just supposed to stand there and
let him do all the work?

If you want a gentle kiss (a caring one) don't apply too much pressure (this is also true if he is wearing braces—you don't want to cause any lacerations). If you give a guy a "harsh" kiss (too much pressure), he might think you are desperate or that you want to go further than you probably do.

Of course you aren't supposed to just stand there and let him do all the work: kiss him back! But always kiss him the way YOU want to be kissed. That is how guys learn. If we didn't show them how to do everything, we'd never get anywhere!

4. How do you know when it's time to stop?

Stop when he stops, or when you feel like you've had enough, or don't want to go any further. Just gently (so you don't freak him out) move your head back, or if the moment is right, you can change the kiss into a hug, then step back.

5. If you are in love with him, is it still gross?

Of course not! Kissing is never gross!

Well, okay, I guess I could see that maybe with Kenny, it might be. It is always better with someone you actually like.

Of course, even with someone you really like, sometimes kissing can be gross. Once Dave licked me on the chin, and I was all, Get away. But I think that was by accident (the licking).

6. If he is in love with you, does he even care if you are bad? (Define bad kisser. See above.)

If the guy likes/loves you, he won't care if you are a good kisser or not. In fact, even if you are a bad kisser, he will probably think you are a good one. And vice versa. He should like you for what you are—not how you kiss.

DEFINITION OF BAD KISSER: A bad kisser is someone who gets your face all wet, slobbers on you, sticks his tongue in when you're not ready, has bad breath, OR sometimes there can be kissers whose tongues are all dry and prickly like a cactus but I have never experienced one of those, just heard about them.

7. When do you know if it's time to open your mouth (thus turning it into a French)?

You will probably feel his tongue touch your lips. If you want to pursue the idea, open your lips a little. If not, keep them closed.

Coming au demain–Chapter II: How to French!!!!

HOMEWORK

Algebra: review questions at the end of Chapters 8–10
English: English Journal: Books I Have Read
World Civ: review questions at the end of Chapters 10–12
G & T: none
French: review questions at the end of Chapters 7–9
Biology: review questions at the end of Chapters 9–12

I am so tired I can hardly write. Grandmère made me try on every single dress in Sebastiano's showroom. You wouldn't believe the number of dresses I've had on today. Short ones, long ones, straight-skirted ones, poufy-skirted ones, white ones, pink ones, blue ones, and even a lime-green one (which Sebastiano declared brought out the 'col' in my cheeks).

The purpose of all this dress-trying-on business was to choose one to wear on Christmas Eve, during my first official televised speech to the Genovian people. I have to look regal, but not too regal. Beautiful, but not too beautiful. Sophisticated, but not too sophisticated.

I tell you, it was a nightmare of hollow-cheeked women in white (the new black) buttoning and zipping and snapping me in and out of dresses. Now I know how all those supermodels must feel. No wonder they do so many drugs.

Actually, it *was* kind of hard to choose my dress for my first big televised event, because surprisingly, Sebastiano turned out to be a pretty good designer. There were several dresses I actually wouldn't be embarrassed to be caught dead in.

Oops. Slip of the tongue. I wonder, though, if Sebastiano really does want to kill me. He seems to like being a fashion designer, which he couldn't do if he were prince of Genovia: He'd be too busy turning bills into law and stuff like that.

Still, you can tell he'd totally enjoy wearing a crown. Not

that, as ruler of Genovia, he'd ever get to do this. I've never seen my dad in a crown. Just suits. And shorts when he plays racquetball with other world leaders.

Ew, I wonder if I will have to learn to play racquetball.

But if Sebastiano became prince of Genovia, he would totally wear a crown all the time. He told me nothing brings out the sparkles in someone's eyes like pear-shaped diamonds. He prefers Tiffany's. Or as he calls it, Tiff's.

Since we were getting so chummy and all, I told Sebastiano about the Nondenominational Winter Dance, and how I have nothing to wear to it. Sebastiano seemed disappointed when he learned I would not be wearing a tiara to my school dance, but he got over it and started asking me all these questions about the event. Like "Who do you go with?" and "What he look like?" and stuff like that.

I don't know what it was, but I found myself actually telling Sebastiano all about my love life. It was so weird. I totally didn't want to, but it all just started spilling out. Thank God Grandmère wasn't there. . . . he'd gone off in search of more cigarettes, and to have her sidecar refreshed.

I told Sebastiano all about Kenny and how he loves me but I don't love him, and how I actually like someone else, but he doesn't know I'm alive.

Sebastiano is actually quite a good listener. I don't know how much, if anything, he understood of what I said, but he didn't take his eyes off my reflection as I talked, and when I was done, he looked me up and down in the mirror, and just said one thing: "This boy you like. How you know he no like you back?"

"Because," I said. "He likes this other girl."

Sebastiano made an impatient motion with this hands. The gesture was made more dramatic by the fact that he was wearing sleeves with these big frilly lace cuffs.

"No, no, no, no, no," he said. "He help you with your Al home. He like you, or he no do that. Why he do that, if he no like you?"

I took "He help you with your Al home" to mean "He helps you with your Algebra homework." I thought for a minute about why Michael had always been so willing to do that. Help me with my Algebra, I mean. I guess just because I am his sister's best friend, and he isn't the type of person who can sit around and watch his sister's best friend flunk out of high school without, you know, at least trying to do something about it.

While I was thinking about that, I couldn't help remembering how Michael's knees, beneath our desks, sometimes brush against mine as he's telling me about integers. Or how sometimes he leans so close to correct something I've written wrong that I can smell the nice, clean scent of his soap. Or how sometimes, like when I do my Lana Weinberger imitation or whatever, he throws back his head and laughs.

Michael's lips look extra nice when he is smiling.

"Tell Sebastiano," Sebastiano urged me. "Tell Sebastiano why this boy help you, if he no like you."

I sighed. "Because I'm his little sister's best friend," I said sadly. Really, could there *be* anything more humiliating? I mean, clearly Michael has never been impressed with my keen intellect or ravishing good looks, given my low grade-point average and of course my gigantism.

Sebastiano tugged on my sleeve and went, "You no worry. I make dress for dance, this boy, he no think of you as little sister's best friend."

Yeah. Sure. Whatever. Why must all my relatives be so weird?

Anyway, we picked out what I'm going to wear on Genovian national TV during my introduction. It's this white taffeta job with a huge poufy skirt and this light blue sash (the royal colors are blue and white). But Sebastiano had one of his assistants take photos of me in all the dresses, so I can see how I looked in them and then decide. I thought this was fairly professional for a guy who calls breakfast "breck."

But all that isn't what I want to write about. I'm so tired, I hardly know what I'm doing. What I want to write about is what happened today after Algebra review.

Which was that Mr. Gianini, after everyone but me had left, went, "Mia, I heard a rumor that there was supposed to have been some kind of student walkout today. Had you heard that?"

Me:	(freezing in my seat) Um, no.
Mr. Gianini:	Oh. So you wouldn't know then if somebody—maybe in protest of the protest—threw the second-floor fire alarm? The one by the drinking fountain?
Me:	(wishing Lars would stop coughing suggestively) Um, no.
Mr. Gianini:	That's what I thought. Because you know

	the penalty for pulling one of the fire alarms—when there is, in fact, no sign of a fire—is expulsion.
Me:	Oh, yes. I know that.
Mr. Gianini:	I thought you might have seen who did it, since I believe I gave you a hall pass shortly before the alarm went off.
Me:	Oh, no. I didn't see anybody.

Except Justin Baxendale, and his smoky eyelashes. But I didn't say that.

Mr. Gianini:	I didn't think so. Oh, well. If you ever hear who did it, maybe you could tell her from me never to do it again.
Me:	Um. Okay.
Mr. Gianini:	And tell her thanks from me, too. The last thing we need right now, with tensions running so high over finals, is a student walkout. (Mr. Gianini picked up his briefcase and jacket.) See you at home.

Then he winked at me. WINKED at me, like he knew I was the one who'd done it. But he couldn't know. I mean, he doesn't know about my nostrils (which were fully flaring the whole time; I could *feel* them!) Right? RIGHT????

Lilly is going to drive me crazy.

Seriously. Like it's not enough I have finals and my introduction to Genovia and my love life and everything to worry about. I have to listen to Lilly complain about how the administration of Albert Einstein High is out to get her. The whole way to school this morning she just droned on and on about how it's all a plot to silence her because she once complained about the Coke machine outside the gym. Apparently the Coke machine is indicative of the administration's efforts to turn us all into mindless soda-drinking, Gap-wearing clones, in Lilly's opinion.

If you ask me, this isn't really about Coke, or the attempts by the school's administration to turn us into mindless pod-people. It's really just because Lilly's still mad she can't use a chapter of the book she's writing on the high-school experience as her term paper.

I reminded Lilly if she doesn't submit a new topic, she's going to get an F as her nine-week grade. Factored in with her A for the last nine weeks, that's only like a C, which will significantly lower her grade-point average, and put her chances of getting into Berkeley, which is her first-choice school, at risk. She may be forced to fall back on her safety school, Brown, which I know would be quite a blow.

She didn't even listen to me. She says she's having an organizational meeting of this new group (of which she is president) Students Against the Corporatization of Albert Einstein High School (SACAEHS) on Saturday, and I have to come, because I am the group's secretary. Don't ask me how *that* happened. Lilly says I write everything down anyway, so it shouldn't be any trouble for me.

I wish Michael had been there to protect me from his sister, but like he has every day this week, he took the subway to school early so he could work on his project for the Winter Carnival.

I wouldn't doubt Judith Gershner has been showing up to school on the early side, too, this week.

Speaking of whom, I picked up another greeting card, this one from the Plaza gift shop on the way to Sebastiano's showroom last night. It's a lot better than that stupid one with the strawberry. This one has a picture of a lady holding a finger to her lips. Inside, it says, *Shhhh . . .*

Under that, I am having Tina write:

> *Roses are red*
> *But cherries are redder*
> *Maybe she can clone fruit flies*
> *But I like you better.*

What I meant was that I like him more than Judith Gershner does, but I'm not really sure that comes through in the poem. Tina says it does, but Tina thinks I should have used love instead of like, so who knows if her opinion is of any value? This is a poem clearly calling for a like and not a love.

I should know. I write enough of them.

Poems, I mean.

This semester, we have read several novels, including *To Kill a Mockingbird*, *Huckleberry Finn*, and *The Scarlet Letter*. In your English journal, please record your feelings about the books we have read, and books in general. What have been your most meaningful experiences as a reader? Your favorite books? Your least favorite?

Please utilize <u>transitive</u> verbs.

Books I Have Read, and What They Meant to Me
by Mia Thermopolis

Books that were good:

1. *Jaws*—I bet you didn't know that in the book version of this, Richard Dreyfuss and Roy Scheider's wife have sex. But they do.
2. *The Catcher in the Rye*—This is totally good. It has lots of bad words.
3. *To Kill a Mockingbird*—This is an excellent book. They should do a movie version of this with Mel Gibson as Atticus, and he should blow Mr. Ewell away with a flame thrower at the end.
4. *A Wrinkle in Time*—Only we never find out the most important thing: whether or not Meg has breasts. I'm thinking she probably did, considering the fact that she already had the glasses and braces. I mean, all of that, and flat-chested, too? God wouldn't be so cruel.
5. *Emanuelle*—In the eighth grade, my best friend and I

found this book on top of a trash can on East Third
Street. We took turns reading it out loud. It was very,
very good. At least the parts I remember. My mom
caught us reading it and took it away before we'd
gotten a chance to finish it.

Books that sucked*
1. *The Scarlet Letter*—You know what would have been
cool? If there had been a rift in the space-time
continuum, and one of those Euro-trash terrorists Bruce
Willis is always chasing in the *Die Hard* movies
dropped a nuclear bomb on the town where Arthur
Dimmesdale and all those losers lived, and blew it sky
high. That's about the only thing I can think of that
would have made this book even remotely interesting.
2. *Our Town*—Okay, this is a play and not a book, but they
still made us read it, and all I have to say about it is that
basically, you find out when you die that nobody cared
about you and we're all alone forever, the end. Okay!
Thanks for that! I feel much better now!
3. *The Mill on the Floss*—I don't want to give anything
away here, but midway through the book, just when
things were going good and there were all these hot
romances (not as hot as in *Emanuelle*, though, so don't
get your hopes up) someone very crucial to the plot
DIES, which if you ask me is just a cop-out so the
author could make her deadline on time.
4. *Anne of Green Gables*—All that blah-blah-blah about
imagination. I tried to imagine some car chases or
explosions that would actually make this book good, but

115

I must be like all of Anne's drippy unimaginative friends, because I couldn't.

5. *Little House on the Prairie*—Little yawn on the big snore. I have all ninety-seven thousand of these books, because people kept on giving them to me when I was little, and all I have to say is if Half Pint had lived in Manhattan, she'd have gotten her you-know-what-kicked from here to Avenue D.

---

* Mrs. Spears, I believe the word *sucked* is transitive in this instance.

No PE today!

Instead there is an assembly.

And it's not because there's a sporting event they want us all to show our support for. No! This was no pep rally. There wasn't a cheerleader in sight. Well, okay, there were cheerleaders in sight, but they weren't in uniform or anything. They were sitting in the bleachers with the rest of us. Well, not really with the rest of us, since they were in the best seats, the ones in the middle, all jostling to see who could sit next to Justin Baxendale, who has apparently ousted Josh Richter as hottest guy in school, but whatever.

No. Instead, it appears that there has been a major disciplinary infraction at Albert Einstein High School. An act of random vandalism that has shaken the administration's faith in us. Which was why they called an assembly, so that they could better convey their feelings of—as Lilly just whispered in my ear—disillusionment and betrayal.

And what was this act that has Principal Gupta and the trustees so up in arms?

Why, someone pulled a fire alarm yesterday, that's what.

Oops.

I have to say, I have never done anything really bad before—well, I dropped an eggplant out a sixteenth floor window a couple of months ago, but no one got hurt or anything—but there really is something sort of thrilling about it. I mean, I would never want to do anything *too* bad, like anything where someone might get hurt.

But I have to say, it is immensely gratifying to have all

these people coming up to the microphone and decrying my behavior.

I probably wouldn't feel so good about it if I'd gotten caught, though.

I am being urged to come forward and turn myself in even as I write this. Apparently, the guilt for my action is going to hound me well past my teen years, possibly even into my twenties and beyond.

Okay, can I just tell you how much I'm NOT going to think about high school when I am in my twenties? I am going to be way too busy working with Greenpeace to save the whales to worry about some stupid fire alarm I pulled in the ninth grade.

The administration is offering a reward for information leading to the identity of the perpetrator of this heinous crime. A reward! You know what the reward is? A free movie pass to the Sony Imax theater. That's all I'm worth! A movie pass!

The only person who could possibly turn me in isn't even paying attention to the assembly. I can see Justin Baxendale has got a Gameboy out, and is playing it with the sound off, while Lana and her fellow cheer cronies look over his broad shoulders, probably panting so hard they're fogging up the screen.

I guess Justin hasn't put two and two together yet. You know, about seeing me in the hallway just before that fire alarm went off. With any luck, he never will.

Mr. Gianini, though. That's another story. I see him over there, talking to Mrs. Hill. He has obviously not told anyone that he suspects me.

Maybe he doesn't suspect me. Maybe he thinks Lilly did it, and I know about it. That could be. I can tell Lilly really wishes she'd done it, because she keeps on muttering under her breath about how, when she finds out who did it, she's going to kill that person, etc.

She's just jealous, of course. That's because now it seems like some kind of political statement, instead of what it actually was: a way to prevent a political statement.

Principal Gupta is looking at us very sternly. She says that it is always natural to want to burn off a little steam right before finals, but that she hopes we will choose positive channels for this, such as the penny drive the Community Outreach Club is holding in order to benefit the victims of Tropical Storm Fred, which flooded several suburban New Jersey neighborhoods last November.

Ha! As if contributing to a stupid penny drive can ever give anybody the same kind of thrill as committing a completely random act of civil disobedience.

LILLY MOSCOVITZ'S LIST OF THE
TOP TEN BEST MOVIES OF ALL TIME
(with commentary by Mia Thermopolis)

Say Anything: Kick-boxing iconoclast Lloyd Dobler, as played by John When-is-He-Going-to-Run-for-President-So-We-Can-Have-Someone-Cute-in-the-Oval-Office Cusack, goes after the class brain (Ione Skye), who soon learns what we all know: Lloyd is every girl's dream date. He understands us. He longs to protect us from broken glass in the parking lot of the local Seven Eleven. Need we say more? (*This movie also contains classic song,* Joe Lies.)

Reckless: Rebel from wrong side of tracks (Aidan Quinn) goes after straight-arrow cheerleader (Daryl Hannah). A classic example of teens struggling to break the yoke of parental expectation. (*Plus you get to see Aidan Quinn's you-know-what!*)

Desperately Seeking Susan: Bored suburban housewife finds man of her dreams in East Village. An Eighties manifesto about female empowerment. Also starring Madonna and that lady who played Roseanne's sister Jackie. (*Also starring Aidan Quinn as the East Village hottie, only you don't really get to see his you-know-what in this one. But you do get to see his butt!*)

Ladyhawke: Star-crossed lovers are caught in an evil spell that only Matthew Broderick can help them break.

Rutger Hauer makes a powerful Navarre, a knight who lives only to exact vengeance upon the man who wronged his fair Isabeau, played by Michelle Pfeiffer. An elegant and moving love story. (*But what is with Matthew Broderick's hair?*)

Dirty Dancing: Spoiled teenage Baby learns a lot more than the cha-cha from long-haired summer resort dance instructor Johnny. A classic tale of coming-of-age in the Catskills, with important messages about the class system in America. (*Only you don't get to see anyone's butt.*)

Flashdance: A welder by day and an exotic dancer by night, Jennifer Beals's Alex is a feminist in a thong, the Elizabeth Cady Stanton of the lap dance, who longs to audition for the Pittsburgh ballet. (*But first she sleeps with her totally hot boss Michael Nouri and throws a big rock through his window!*)

The Cutting Edge: Former hockey stud D.B. Sweeney is paired with figure skater and prissy rich girl Moira Kelly in an unlikely quest for Olympic gold. Interesting for its strategic build-up of sexual tension through ice dancing. (*Toe-pick. Toooooooe-pick.*)

Some Kind of Wonderful: Victory of tomboy Mary Stuart Masterson over prissy Lea Thompson for the heart of Eric Stolz. As usual, keen insight by John Hughes into the teen psyche/social structure. (*Last movie in which Eric Stolz was actually cute.*)

Reality Bites: Who will indie filmmaker Winona Ryder choose, smart aleck slacker Ethan Hawke, or clean-cut go-getter Ben Stiller? (*Isn't it obvious?*)

Footloose: Out-of-towner flaunts small town's anti-dancing laws. Starring Kevin Bacon, who saves Lori Singer from her abusive hick boyfriend. Most notable for scene at the PTA meeting in which Kevin Bacon's character reveals he has actually done homework, as illustrated by his quoting from several Biblical passages which support dancing. (*In the movies* Wild Thing *and* Hollow Man *you get to see Kevin Bacon's you-know-what.*)

Today was my lunch with Kenny at Big Wong.

I really don't have anything to say about it, except that he didn't ask me to the Nondenominational Winter Dance. Not only that, but it appears that Kenny's passion for me has ebbed significantly since it hit its zenith on Tuesday.

I of course was beginning to suspect this, since he's stopped calling me after school, and I haven't had one Instant Message from him since before the great Ice-Skating Debacle. He says it's because he's so busy studying for finals and all, but I suspect something else:

He knows. He knows about Michael.

I mean, come on. How can he not?

Well, okay, maybe he doesn't know about Michael *specifically,* but Kenny must know *generally* that he is not the one who lights my fire.

If I had a fire, that is.

No, Kenny is just being nice.

Which I appreciate, and all, but I just wish he'd come out and say it. All of this kindness, this solicitousness, it's just making me feel worse. I mean, how could I? Really? How could I have ever agreed to be Kenny's girlfriend, knowing full well I liked someone else? By rights, Kenny should go to *Majesty* magazine and spill all. "Royal Betrayal," they could call it. I totally would understand it, if he did.

But he won't. Because he's too nice.

Instead, he ordered steamed vegetable dumplings for me, and pork buns for him (one encouraging sign that

Kenny might not love me as much as he used to insist: he's eating meat again) and talked about Bio and what had happened at assembly (I didn't tell him it was me who pulled the alarm, and he didn't ask me, so there was no need to shield my nostrils). He mentioned again how sorry he was about my tongue, and asked how I was doing in Algebra, and offered to come over and tutor me if I wanted (Kenny tested out of freshman Algebra), even though of course I live with an Algebra teacher. Still, you could tell he meant to be nice.

Which just makes me feel worse. Because of what I'm going to have to do after finals and all.

But he didn't ask me to the dance.

I don't know if this means we aren't going, or if it means he considers the fact we are going a given.

I swear, I do not understand boys at all.

As if lunch wasn't bad enough, G and T isn't too great, either. No, Judith Gershner isn't here . . . but neither is Michael. The guy is AWOL. Nobody knows where he is. Lilly had to tell Mrs. Hill, when she took attendance, that her brother was in the bathroom.

I wonder where he really is. Lilly says that since he started writing this new program that the Computer Club will be unveiling at the Winter Carnival, she's hardly seen him.

Which is no real change, since Michael hardly comes out of his room anyway, but still. You'd think he'd come home once in a while to study.

But I guess, seeing as how he already got into his first-choice college, his grades don't really matter anymore.

Besides, like Lilly, Michael is a genius. What does he need to study for?

Unlike the rest of us.

I wish they'd put the door back on the supply closet. It is extremely hard to concentrate with Boris scraping away on his violin in there. Lilly says this is just another tactic by the trustees to weaken our resistance, so we will remain the mindless drones they are trying to make us, but I think it's just on account of that time we all forgot to let him out, and he was stuck in there until the night custodian heard his anguished pleas to be released.

Which is Lilly's fault, if you think about it. I mean, she's his girlfriend. She should really take better care of him.

HOMEWORK

Algebra: practice test
English: term paper
World Civ: practice test
G & T: none
French: l'examen pratique
Biology: practice test

Thursday, December 11, 9 p.m.

Grandmère is seriously out of control. Tonight she started quizzing me on the names and responsibilities of all of my dad's cabinet ministers. Not only do I have to know exactly what they do, but also their marital status and the names and ages of their kids, if any. These are the kids I am supposedly going to have to hang out with while celebrating Christmas at the palace. I am figuring they will probably hate me as much, if not more, than Mr. Gianini's niece and nephew hated me at Thanksgiving.

All of my holidays from now on are apparently going to be spent in the company of kids who hate me.

You know, I would just like to say that it is totally not my fault I am a princess. They have no right to hate me so much. I have done everything I could to maintain a normal life in spite of my royal status. I have totally turned down opportunities to be on the covers of *CosmoGirl*, *Teen Vogue*, *Seventeen*, *Twist*, and *Girl's Life*. I have refused invitations to go on *TRL* and introduce the number-one video in the country, and when the mayor asked if I wanted to be the one to press the button that drops the ball in Times Square on New Year's Eve, I said no (aside from the fact I am going to be in Genovia for New Year's, I oppose the mayor's mosquito spraying campaign, as runoff from the pesticides used to kill the mosquitos that may be carrying the West Nile virus has infected the local horseshoe crab population. A compound in the blood of horseshoe crabs, which nest all along the eastern seaboard, is used to test the purity of every drug and vaccine administered in the U.S. The crabs are routinely gathered, drained of a third of their blood, then re-released into the sea . . . a sea which is now killing them as well as many other arthropods, such as lobsters, thanks to the amount of pesticide in it).

Anyway, I am just saying, all the kids who hate me should just chill, because I have never once sought the spotlight I have been thrust into. I've never even called my own press conference.

But I digress.

So Sebastiano was there, drinking aperitifs and listening as I rattled off name after name (Grandmère has made flashcards out of the pictures of the cabinet ministers—kind of like those bubble gum cards you can get of the boy-band members, only the cabinet ministers don't wear as much leather). I was kind of thinking maybe I was wrong about Sebastiano's commitment to fashion, and that maybe Sebastiano was there to try and pick up some pointers for after he's thrust me into the path of an oncoming limo or whatever.

But when Grandmère paused to take a phone call from her old friend Imelda Marcos, Sebastiano started asking me all these questions about clothes, in particular what clothes my friends and I like to wear. What were my feelings, he wanted to know, on velvet stretch pants? Spandex tube tops? Sequins?

I told him all of that sounded, you know, okay for Halloween or Jersey City, but that generally in my day-to-day life I prefer cotton. He looked saddened by this, so I told him that I really felt orange was going to be the next pink, and that perked him right up, and he wrote a bunch of stuff down in this notebook he carries around. Kind of like I do, now that I think about it.

When Grandmère got off the phone, I informed her— quite diplomatically, I might add—that, considering how much progress we'd made in the past three months, I felt more than prepared for my impending introduction to the people of Genovia, and that I did not feel it would be necessary to have lessons next week, as I have FIVE finals to prepare for.

But Grandmère got totally huffy about it! She was all, "Where did you get the idea that your academic education is more important than your royal training? Your father, I suppose. With him, it's always education, education, education. He doesn't realize that education is nowhere near as important as deportment."

"Grandmère," I said. "I need an education if I'm going to run Genovia properly." Especially if I'm going to convert the palace into a giant animal shelter—something I'm not going to be able to do until Grandmère is dead, so I see no point in mentioning it to her now . . . or ever, for that matter.

Grandmère said some swear words in French, which wasn't very dowager-princessy of her, if you ask me. Thankfully right then my dad walked in, looking for his Genovian Air Force medal, since he had a state dinner to go to over at the embassy. I told him about my finals and how I really needed time off from princess stuff to study, and he was all, "Yes, of course."

When Grandmère protested, he just went, "For God's sake, if she hasn't got it by now, she never will."

Grandmère pressed her lips together and didn't say anything more after that. Sebastiano used the opportunity to ask me about my feelings on rayon. I told him I didn't have any. For once, I was telling the truth.

Friday, December 12, Homeroom

HERE'S WHAT I HAVE TO DO:

1. Stop thinking about Michael, especially when I should be studying.
2. Stop telling Grandmère anything about my personal life.
3. Start acting more:
   A. Mature
   B. Responsible
   C. Regal
4. Stop biting my fingernails.
5. Write down everything Mom and Mr. G need to know about how to take care of Fat Louie while I'm gone.
6. CHRISTMAS/HANNUKAH PRESENTS!
7. Stop watching *Baywatch* when I should be studying.
8. Stop playing Pod-Racer when I should be studying.
9. Stop listening to music when I should be studying.
10. Break up with Kenny.

Well, I guess it's official now:

I, Mia Thermopolis, am a juvenile delinquent.

Seriously. That fire alarm I pulled was only the beginning, it appears.

I really don't know what's come over me lately. It's like the closer I get to actually going to Genovia and performing my first official duties as its princess, the less like a princess I act.

I wonder if I'll be expelled.

If I am, it is totally unfair. Lana started it. I was sitting there in Algebra, listening to Mr. G go on about the Cartesian plane, when suddenly Lana turns around in her seat and slaps a copy of *USA Today* down in front of me. There is a headline screaming:

TODAY'S POLL
Most Popular Young Royal

Fifty-seven percent of readers say that **Prince William of England** is their favorite young royal, with Will's little brother **Harry** coming in at 28 percent. America's own royal, **Princess Mia Renaldo of Genovia**, comes in third, with 13 percent of the votes, and Prince Andrew and Sarah Ferguson's daughters, **Beatrice** and **Eugenie**, round out the votes with 1 percent each.

The reasons given for Princess Mia's third-place finish? "Not outgoing" is the most common answer. Ironically, Princess Mia is perceived as being as shy as Princess Diana—the mother of William and Harry—when she first stepped into the harsh glare of the media spotlight.

Princess Mia, who only recently learned she was heir to the throne of Genovia, a small principality located on the Cote d'Azur, is expected to make her first official trip to that country next week. A representative for the princess describes her as looking forward to her visit with "eager anticipation." The princess will continue her education in America, and will reside in Genovia only during the summer months.

I read the stupid article and then passed the paper back to Lana.

"So?" I whispered to her.

"So," Lana whispered. "I wonder how popular you'd be—especially with the people of Genovia—if they found out their future ruler goes around pulling fire alarms when there isn't any fire."

She was only guessing, of course. She couldn't have seen me. Unless . . .

Unless maybe Justin Baxendale did figure it out! You know, seeing me in the hallway like that, just before the alarm went off—and he mentioned it to Lana. . . .

No. Not possible. I am so far out of the sphere of Justin Baxendale's consciousness as to be nonexistent to him. He didn't tell Lana anything. Lana, like Mr. G, obviously thinks it's a little coincidental that on that fateful Wednesday, the fire alarm went off about two minutes after I'd disappeared from class with the pass to the bathroom.

But even so. Even though she could only have been guessing, it seemed to me like she knew, like she was going to make sure I never heard the end of it.

I really don't know what came over me. I don't know if it was

A. The stress of finals
B. My impending trip to Genovia
C. This thing with Kenny
D. The fact that I'm in love with this guy who is going out with a human fruit fly
E. The fact that my mother is going to give birth to my Algebra teacher's baby
F. The fact that Lana has been persecuting me practically my whole life and pretty much getting away with it, or
G. All of the above.

Whatever the reason, I snapped. Just snapped. Suddenly, I found myself reaching for Lana's cell phone, which was lying on her desktop beside her calculator.

And then the next thing I knew, I had put the tiny little pink thing on the floor, and crushed it into a lot of pieces beneath the heel of my size-ten combat boot.

I guess I can't really blame Mr. G for sending me to the principal's office.

Still, you would expect a little sympathy from your own stepfather.

Uh-oh. Here comes Principal Gupta.

Well, that's it then. I'm suspended.

Suspended. I can't believe it. ME! Mia Thermopolis! What is happening to me? I used to be such a good kid!

And okay, it's just for one day, but still. It's going on my permanent record! What are the Genovian cabinet ministers going to say?

I am turning into Lindsay Lohan.

And yeah, it's not like I'm not going to get into college because I was suspended for one day in the first semester of my freshman year, but how totally embarrassing! Principal Gupta treated me like I was some kind of *criminal* or something.

And you know what they say: Treat a person like a criminal, and pretty soon, she'll end up like one. At least I think that's what they say. The way things are going, I wouldn't be surprised if pretty soon I start wearing ripped-up fishnet stockings and dying my hair black. Maybe I'll even start smoking and get my ears double pierced or something. And then they'll make a TV movie about me, and call it *Royal Scandal*. It will show me going up to Prince William and saying, "Who's the most popular young royal now, huh, punk?" and then headbutting him or something.

Except I practically fainted the first time I got my ears pierced, and smoking is really bad for you, and I always thought it must hurt to headbutt someone.

I guess I don't have the makings of a juvenile delinquent after all.

My dad doesn't think so, either. He's all ready to set the

royal Genovian lawyers on Principal Gupta. The only problem, of course, is that I won't tell him—or anybody else, for that matter—what Lana said to make me assault her cell phone. It's kind of hard to prove the attack was provoked if the attacker won't say what the provocation was. My dad pleaded with me for a while when he came to pick me up from school, after having received The Call from Principal Gupta. But when I wouldn't tell him what he wanted, and Lars just looked carefully blank, my dad just went, "Fine," and his mouth got all scrunchy like it does when Grandmère has one too many sidecars and starts calling him Papa Cueball.

But how can I tell him what Lana said? If I do that, then everyone will know I'm guilty of not just one crime, but two!

Anyway, now I'm home, watching the Lifetime channel with my mother. She hasn't been doing much painting at her studio since she got pregnant. This is on account of her being exhausted. It's quite hard to paint lying down, she's discovered. So instead she has been doing a lot of sketching from bed, mostly line drawings of Fat Louie, who seems to enjoy having someone home all day with him. He sits for hours on her bed, watching the pigeons on the fire escape outside her window.

But since I'm home today, Mom did some drawings of me. I think she is making my mouth too big, but I'm not saying anything, as Mr. Gianini and I have discovered it's better not to upset my mother in her current hormonal state. Even the slightest criticism—like asking her why she left the phone bill in the vegetable crisper—can lead to an hour-long crying jag.

While she sketched me, I watched a very excellent movie called *Mother, May I Sleep With Danger?* starring Tori Spelling, of *Beverly Hills 90210* fame, as a girl who has an abusive boyfriend. I really don't get why any girl would stay with a guy who hits her, but my mom says it's all about self-esteem and your relationship with your father. Except that my mom doesn't have that great a relationship with Papaw, and if any guy ever tried to slug her, you can bet she'd put him in the hospital, so go figure.

As my mom drew, she tried to get me to spill my guts to her, you know, about what Lana said that made me go on a cell-phone-stomping rampage. You could tell she was trying really hard to be all TV mom about it.

I guess it must have worked, because all of a sudden I found myself telling her all of it, every last thing: the stuff about Kenny and about my not liking to kiss him and about him telling everybody, and about how I plan to break up with him as soon as finals are over.

And along the way, I mentioned Michael and Judith Gershner and Tina and the greeting cards and the Winter Carnival and Lilly and her protest group and how I'm secretary of it, and just about everything else, except the part about pulling the fire alarm.

After a while my mom stopped drawing and just looked at me.

Finally, when I was done, she said, "You know what I think you need?"

And I said, "What?"

And she said, "A vacation."

So then we had a sort of vacation, right there on her bed.

I mean, she wouldn't let me go study. Instead, she made me order a pizza, and together we watched the satisfying but completely unbelievable end of *Mother, May I Sleep with Danger?*, which was followed, much to our joy, by the dishiest made-for-TV movie ever, *Midwest Obsession*, in which Courtney Thorne-Smith plays the local Dairy Princess, who goes around in a pink Cadillac wearing cow earrings and kills people like Tracey Gold (deep in the throes of her post–*Growing Pains* anorexia) for messing with her boyfriend. And the best part was, it was all *based on a true story*.

For a while, there on my mom's bed, it was almost like old times. You know, before my mom met Mr. Gianini and I found out I was a princess.

Except, of course, not really, because she's pregnant, and I'm suspended.

But why quibble?

Friday, December 12, 8 p.m., the loft

Oh, my God, I just checked my e-mail. I am being inundated with supportive messages from my friends!

They all want to congratulate me on my decisive handling of Lana Weinberger. They sympathize with my suspension and encourage me to stay firm in my refusal to back down from my stand against the administration (what stand against the administration? All I did was destroy a cell phone. It has nothing to do with the administration). Lilly went so far as to compare me with Mary, Queen of Scots, who was imprisoned and then beheaded by Elizabeth I.

I wonder if Lilly would still think that if she knew that the reason I smashed Lana's cell phone was because she was threatening to spill the beans about my having pulled the fire alarm that ruined Lilly's walkout.

Lilly says it's all a matter of principle, that I was banished from the school for refusing to back down from my beliefs. But actually, I was banished from school for destroying someone else's private property—and I only did it to cover up for another crime that I committed.

No one knows that but me, though. Well, me and Lana. And even she doesn't know for sure why I did it. I mean, it could have been just one of those random acts of violence that are going around.

Everyone else, however, is seeing it as this great political act. Tomorrow, at the first meeting of the Students Against the Corporatization of Albert Einstein High School, my case is going to be held up as an example of one of the many unjust decisions of the Gupta Administration.

I think tomorrow I might develop a case of weekend strep throat.

Anyway, I wrote back to everyone, telling them how much I appreciate their support, and not to make a bigger deal out of this than it actually is. I mean, I'm not proud of what I did. I would much rather have NOT done it, and stayed in school.

One bright note: Michael is definitely getting the cards I've been sending him. Tina walked by his locker today after PE and saw him take the latest one out and put it in his backpack! Unfortunately, according to Tina, he did not wear an expression of dazed passion as he slipped the card into his bag, nor did he gaze at it tenderly. He did not even put it away very carefully: Tina regretted to inform me that he slipped his iMac laptop into his backpack next, undoubtedly squashing the card.

But he wouldn't, Tina hastened to assure me, have done that if he'd known it was from you, Mia! Maybe if you'd signed it . . .

But if I signed it, he'd know I like him! More than that, he'd know I love him, since I do believe the L word was mentioned in at least one card. And what if he doesn't feel the same way about me? How embarrassing! Way worse than being suspended.

Oh, no! As I was writing this, I got Instant Messaged by, of all people, Michael himself! I freaked out so bad, I shrieked and scared Fat Louie, who was sleeping on my lap as I wrote. He sank all of his claws into me, and now I have little puncture marks all over my thighs.

Michael wrote:

CRACKING: Hey, Thermopolis, what's this I hear about you getting suspended?

I wrote back:

FTLOUIE: Just for one day.
CRACKING: What'd you do?
FTLOUIE: Crushed a cheerleader's cellular phone.
CRACKING: Your parents must be so proud.
FTLOUIE: If so, they've done a pretty good job of disguising it so far.
CRACKING: So are you grounded?
FTLOUIE: Surprisingly, no. The attack on the cell phone was provoked.
CRACKING: So you'll still be going to the Carnival next week?
FTLOUIE: As secretary to the Students Against the Corporatization of Albert Einstein High School, I believe my attendance is required. Your sister is planning for us to have a booth.
CRACKING: That Lilly. She's always looking out for the good of mankind.
FTLOUIE: That's one way of putting it.

We probably would have talked longer, but right then my mom yelled at me to get off line, since she's waiting to hear from Mr. Gianini, who, surprisingly, still wasn't home from school, even though it was past dinnertime. So I logged off.

This is the second time Michael's asked if I'm going to the Winter Carnival. What's up with that?

Friday, December 12, 9 p.m., the loft

Now we know why Mr. G was so late getting home:
He stopped along the way to buy a Christmas tree.

Not just any Christmas tree, either, but a twelve-footer
that must be at least six feet wide at the base.

I didn't say anything negative, of course, because my
mom was so happy and excited about it, and immediately
lugged out all of her Dead Celebrity Christmas ornaments
(my mom doesn't use pretty glass balls or tinsel on her
Christmas tree, like normal people. Instead, she paints
pieces of tin with the likenesses of celebrities who have died
that year, and hangs those on the tree. Which is why we
probably have the only tree in North America with ornaments commemorating Richard and Pat Nixon, Elvis,
Audrey Hepburn, Kurt Cobain, Jim Henson, John Belushi,
Rock Hudson, Alec Guiness, Divine, John Lennon, and
many, many more).

And Mr. Gianini kept looking over at me, to see if I was
happy, too. He got the tree, he said, because he knew what
a bad day I'd had, and he didn't want it to be a total loss.

Mr. G, of course, has no idea what my English term
paper topic is.

What was I supposed to say? I mean, he'd already gone
out and bought it, and you know a tree that size had to have
cost a lot of money. And he'd meant to do a nice thing. He
really had.

Still, I wish the people around here would consult me
about things before just going out and doing them. Like the
whole pregnancy thing, and now this tree. If Mr. G had

asked me, I would have been like, Let's go to the Big Kmart on Astor Place and get a nice fake tree so we don't contribute to the destruction of the polar bear's natural habitat, okay?

Only he didn't ask me.

And the truth is, even if he had, my mom would never have gone for it. Her favorite part of Christmas is lying on the floor with her head under the tree, gazing up through the branches and inhaling the sweet tangy smell of pine sap. She says it's the only memory of her Indiana childhood she actually likes.

It's hard to think about the polar bears when your mom says something like that.

Saturday, December 13, 2 p.m., Lilly's apartment

Well, the first meeting of the Students Against the Corporatization of Albert Einstein High School is a complete bust.

That's because nobody showed up but me and Boris Pelkowski. I am a little miffed that Kenny didn't come. You would think that if he really loves me as much as he says he does, he would take any opportunity whatsoever to be near me, even a boring meeting of the Students Against the Corporatization of Albert Einstein High School.

But I guess even Kenny's love is not that great. As should be obvious to me by now, considering the fact that there are exactly six days until the Nondenominational Winter Dance, and Kenny STILL HASN'T ASKED ME IF I WANT TO GO WITH HIM.

Not that I'm worried, or anything. I mean, a girl who set off a fire alarm AND smashed Lana Weinberger's cell phone, worried about not having a date to a stupid dance?

All right. I'm worried.

But not worried enough to pull a Sadie Hawkins and ask *him* to the dance.

Lilly is pretty much inconsolable over the fact that no one but Boris and me showed up for her meeting. I tried to tell her that everybody is too busy studying for finals to worry about privatization at the moment, but she doesn't seem to care. Right now she is sitting on the couch, with Boris speaking to her in a soothing voice. Boris is pretty gross and all—with his sweaters that he always tucks into his pants, and that weird retainer his orthodontist makes him wear—

but you can tell he genuinely loves Lilly. I mean, look at the tender way he is gazing at her as she sobs about how she is going to call her congressmember.

It makes my heart hurt, looking at Boris looking at Lilly. I guess I must be jealous. I want a boy to look at *me* like that. And I don't mean Kenny, either. I mean a boy who I actually like back, as more than just a friend.

I can't take it anymore. I am going into the kitchen to see what Maya, the Moscovitzes' housekeeper, is doing. Even helping to wash things has to be better than this.

Maya wasn't in the kitchen. She was here, in Michael's room, putting away his school uniform, which she just finished ironing. Maya is going around picking up Michael's things and telling me about her son Manuel. Thanks to the help of the Drs. Moscovitz, Manuel was recently released from the prison in the Dominican Republic where he'd been wrongfully held for suspicion of having committed crimes against the state. Now Manuel is starting his own political party, and Maya is just as proud as can be, except she is worried he might end up back in prison if he doesn't tone down the anti-government stuff a little.

Manuel and Lilly have a lot in common, I guess.

Maya's stories about Manuel are always interesting, but it is much more interesting to be in Michael's room. I have been in it before, of course, but never while he was gone (he is at school, even though it is Saturday, working in the computer lab on his project for the Carnival; apparently the school's modem is faster than his. Also, I suppose, though I hate to admit it, he and Judith Gershner can freely practice their downloading there, without fear of parental interruption).

So I am lying on Michael's bed while Maya putters around, folding shirts and muttering about sugar, one of her native land's main exports and apparently a source of some consternation to her son's political platform, while Michael's dog, Pavlov, sits next to me, panting on my face. I can't help thinking, *This is what it's like to be Michael: This is what*

Michael sees when he looks up at his ceiling at night (he has put glow-in-the-dark stars up there, in the form of the spiral galaxy Andromeda) and *This is how Michael's sheets smell* (springtime fresh, thanks to the detergent Maya uses) and *This is what the view of Michael's desk looks like from his bed.*

Except that looking over at his desk, I just noticed something. It's one of my cards! The one with the strawberry on it!

It isn't exactly on display, or anything. It's just sitting on his desk. But hey, that's a far cry from being crumpled at the bottom of his backpack. It shows that the cards mean something to him, that he hasn't buried them under all the other junk on his desk—the DOS manuals and anti-Microsoft literature—or worse, thrown them away.

This is somewhat heartening.

Uh-oh. I just heard the front door open. Michael??? Or the Drs. Moscovitz???? I better get out of here. Michael doesn't have all those Enter At Your Own Risk signs on the door for nothing.

Saturday, December 13, 3 p.m., Grandmère's

How, you might ask, did I go from the Moscovitzes' apartment to my grandmother's suite at the Plaza in the space of a mere half hour?

Well, I'll tell you.

Disaster has struck, in the form of Sebastiano.

I always suspected, of course, that Sebastiano was not the sweet-tempered innocent he pretended to be. But now it looks like the only murder Sebastiano needs to worry about is his own. Because if my dad ever gets his hands on him, Sebastiano is one dead fashion designer.

Looking at it objectively, I think I can safely say I'd prefer to have been murdered. I mean, I'd be dead and all, which would be sad—especially since I still haven't written down those instructions for caring for Fat Louie while I'm gone—but at least I wouldn't have to show up for school on Monday.

But now, not only do I have to show up for school on Monday, but I have to show up for school on Monday knowing that every single one of my fellow classmates is going to have seen the supplement that arrived in the *Sunday Times*: the supplement featuring about twenty photos of ME standing in front of a triple mirror in dresses by Sebastiano, with the words "Fashion Fit for a Princess" emblazoned all over the place.

Oh, yes. I'm not kidding. Fashion Fit for a Princess.

I can't really blame him, I guess. Sebastiano, I mean. I suppose the opportunity was too much for him to resist. He is, after all, a businessman, and having a princess model your clothes . . . well, you can't buy exposure like that.

Because you know all the other papers are going to pick up on the story. You know, Princess of Genovia Makes Modeling Debut. That kind of thing.

So with just one little photo spread, Sebastiano is going to get virtual worldwide coverage of his new clothing line.

A clothing line that it looks like I have endorsed.

Grandmère doesn't understand why my dad and I are so upset. Well, I think she gets why my dad is upset. You know the whole "My daughter is being used" thing. She just doesn't get why *I'm* so unhappy. "You look perfectly beautiful," she keeps saying.

Yeah. Like that helps.

Grandmère thinks I am overreacting. But hello, have I ever aspired to tread in Gisele's footsteps? I don't think so. Fashion is so not what I'm about. What about the environment? What about the rights of animals? What about the HORSESHOE CRABS??????

People are not going to believe I didn't pose for those photos. People are going to think I am a sellout. People are going to think I am a stuck-up model snob.

I would so rather that they think I am a juvenile delinquent, I can't tell you.

Little did I know when I heard the front door to the Moscovitzes' apartment opening, and I hustled out of Michael's room, that I was about to be greeted by the disastrous news. It was only Lilly's parents, after all, coming home from the gym, where they'd met with their personal trainers. Afterward, they'd stopped to have a latte and read the *Sunday Times*, large sections of which arrive, for reasons no one understands, on Saturday, if you have a subscription.

What a surprise they had had, when they'd opened up the paper and saw the Princess of Genovia hawking this hot new fashion designer's spring collection.

What a surprise I had, when the Drs. Moscovitz congratulated me on my new modeling career, and I was all, "What are you talking about?"

So, while Lilly and Boris looked on with curiosity, Dr. Moscovitz opened her paper and showed me:

And there it was, in all of its four-color-layout glory.

I'm not going to lie and say I looked bad. I looked okay. What they had done was, they had taken all the photos Sebastiano's assistant had snapped of me trying to decide which dress to wear to my introduction to the people of Genovia and laid them all out on this purple background. I'm not smiling in the pictures, or anything. I'm just looking at myself in the mirror, clearly going, in my head, *Ew, could I look more like a walking toothpick?*

But of course, if you didn't know me, and didn't know WHY I was trying on all these dresses, I'd seem like some freak who cares WAY too much about how she looks in a party dress.

Which is exactly the kind of person I've always wanted to be portrayed as.

NOT!!!!!!!

I have to admit, I am a little hurt. I'd thought, when he'd asked me all those questions about Michael, Sebastiano and I had kind of made a connection. But I guess not. Not if he could do something like this.

My dad has already called the *Times* and demanded that

they remove the supplement from all the papers that haven't been delivered yet. He has called the concierge of the Plaza and insisted on Sebastiano being listed as persona non grata, which means the cousin to the prince of Genovia won't be allowed to set foot on hotel property.

I thought this was a little harsh, but not as harsh as what my dad *wanted* to do, which was call the NYPD and press charges against Sebastiano for using the likeness of a minor without the consent of her parents. Thank God Grandmère talked him out of that. She said there'd be enough publicity about this without the added humiliation of a royal arrest.

My dad is still so mad he can't sit still. He is pacing back and forth across the suite. Rommel is watching him very nervously from Grandmère's lap, his head moving back and forth, back and forth, his eyes following my dad as if he were watching the US Open or something.

I bet if Sebastiano *were* here, my dad would smash up a lot more than just his cell phone.

Well.

All I can say is, Grandmère's really done it this time.

I'm serious. I don't think my dad is ever going to speak to her again.

And I know *I* never will.

And okay, she's an old lady and she didn't know that what she was doing was wrong, and I should really be more understanding.

But for her to do *this*—for her not to even take into consideration my feelings—I frankly don't think I will ever be able to forgive her.

What happened was, Sebastiano called right before I was getting ready to leave the hotel. He was completely perplexed about why my dad is so mad at him. He tried to come upstairs to see us, he said, but Plaza security stopped him.

When my dad, who'd answered the phone, told Sebastiano that the reason Plaza security stopped him was because he'd been PNG'd, and then explained why, Sebastiano was even more upset. He kept going, "But I had your permish! I had your permish, Phillipe!"

"My permission to use my daughter's image to promote your tawdry rags?" My father was disgusted. "You most certainly did not!"

But Sebastiano kept insisting he had.

And little by little, it came out that he *had* had permission, in a way. Only not from me. And not my dad, either. Guess who, it appears, gave it to him?

Grandmère went, all indignantly, "I only did it, Phillipe,

because Amelia, as you know, suffers from a terrible self-image, and needed a boost."

But my dad was so enraged, he wouldn't even listen to her. He just thundered, "And so to repair her self-image, you went behind her back and gave permission for her photo to be used in an advertisement for *women's clothing?*"

Grandmère didn't have much to say after that. She just stood there, going "Uhn . . . uhn . . . uhn . . . " like someone in a horror movie who'd been pinned to a wall with a machete but wasn't quite dead yet (I always close my eyes during parts like this, so I know exactly what it sounds like).

It became clear that even if Grandmère had had a reasonable excuse for her behavior, my father wasn't going to listen to it—or let me listen to it, either. He stalked over to me, grabbed my arm, and marched me right out of the suite.

I thought we were going to have a bonding moment, like fathers and daughters always do on TV, where he'd tell me that Grandmère was a very sick woman and that he was going to send her somewhere where she could take a nice, long rest, but instead all he said was, "Go home."

Then he handed me over to Lars—after slamming the door to Grandmère's suite VERY loudly behind him, before storming off in the direction of his own suite.

Jeez.

It just goes to show, even a royal family can be dysfunctional.

Couldn't you just see us on *The Tyra Banks Show?*

Tyra:	Clarisse, tell us: Why did you allow Sebastiano to put your granddaughter's photos in that *Times* advertising supplement?
Grandmère:	That's Your Royal Highness to you, Ms. Banks. I did it to boost her self-esteem.

I just know that when I get to school on Monday, everybody is going to be all, "Oh, look, here comes Mia, that big FAKE, with her vegetarianism and her animal-rights activism and her looks-aren't-important-it's-what's-on-the-inside-that-matters-ism. But I guess it's all right to pose for *fashion photo shoots*, isn't it, Mia?"

As if it wasn't enough to be suspended. Now I am going to be sneered at by my peers, too.

I'm home now, trying to pretend none of it ever happened. This is difficult, of course, because when I walked back into the loft, I saw that my mom had already pulled the supplement out of our paper and drawn little devil horns coming out of my head in every picture, then stuck the whole thing onto the refrigerator.

While I appreciate this bit of whimsy, it does not make the fact that I will have to show my face—now plastered all over advertising supplements throughout the tristate area—in school on Monday any easier.

Surprisingly, there is one good thing that's come out of all of this: I know for sure I look best in the white taffeta number with the blue sash. My dad says over his dead body am I going to wear it, or any other Sebastiano creation, again. But there isn't another designer in Genovia who could do as good a job, let alone finish the dress in time. So it looks like the dress by Sebastiano, which got delivered to the loft this morning, is it.

Which is one thing off my mind, anyway.

I guess.

I've already gotten seventeen e-mails, six phone calls, and one visitor (Lilly) about the fashion thing. Lilly says it's not as bad as I think, and that most people throw the supplements away without even looking at them.

If that's true, I said, why are all these people calling and e-mailing me?

She tried to make out like it was all members of the Students Against the Corporatization of Albert Einstein High School, calling to show their solidarity with my suspension, but I think we both know better:

It's all people who want to know what I was thinking, selling out like that.

How am I ever going to explain that I had nothing to do with it, that I didn't even *know* about it? Nobody is going to believe that. I mean, the proof is right there: I'm *wearing* the proof. There's photographic evidence of it.

My reputation is going down the drain, even as I sit here. Tomorrow morning, millions of subscribers to *The New York Times* are going to open their papers and be like, "Oh, look, Princess Mia. Sold out already. Wonder how much she got paid? You wouldn't think she'd need the money, what with being royal, and all."

Finally I had to ask Lilly to please go home, because I'd developed a bad headache. She tried to cure it with some shiatsu, which her parents frequently employ on their patients, but it didn't work. All that ended up happening was that I think she burst a blood vessel or something between my thumb and index finger, since it really hurts.

Now I am determined to start studying, even though it's Saturday night, and everyone else my age is out having fun. But haven't you heard? Princesses never get to have any fun.

HERE IS WHAT I HAVE TO DO

Algebra: review Chapters 1–10
English: term paper, 10 pages, double spaced; utilize appropriate margins; also, review Chapters 1–7
World Civ: review Chapters 1–12
G & T: none
French: revue Chapitres Un–Neuf
Biology: review Chapters 1–12
Write out instructions on how to care for Fat Louie
Christmas/Hannukah shopping:
    Mom—Bon Jovi maternity T
    Dad—Book on anger management
    Mr. G—Swiss Army knife
    Lilly—blank videotapes
    Tina Hakim Baba—copy of *Emanuelle*
    Kenny—combination TV/VCR (I don't think this is too extravagant. And no, it's not guilt, either. He really wants one.)
    Grandmère—NOTHING!!!!!!
Paint fingernails (maybe presence of foul-tasting polish will prevent biting them off)
Break up with Kenny
Organize sock drawer

I am going to start with the sock drawer, because that is clearly the most important. You can't really concentrate on anything if your socks aren't right.

Then I will move on to Algebra because that is my worst subject, and also my first test. I am going to pass it if it's the last thing I do. NOTHING is going to distract me. Not this thing with Grandmère, not the fact that four of those seventeen e-mails are from Michael, not the fact that two are from Kenny, not the fact that I am leaving for Europe at the end of next week, not the fact that my mother and Mr. Gianini are in the next room watching *Die Hard*, my favorite Christmas movie, NOTHING.

I WILL PASS ALGEBRA THIS SEMESTER, and NOTHING IS GOING TO DISTRACT ME FROM STUDYING FOR THE FINAL!!!!!!!!!!!!

Saturday, December 13, 9 p.m., the loft

I just had to go out and see the part where Bruce Willis throws the explosives down the elevator shaft, but now I am back at work.

Saturday, December 13, 9:30 p.m., the loft

I was really curious about what Michael could possibly want, so I read his e-mails—just his. One was about the supplement (Lilly had told him, and he wanted to know if I was thinking of abdicating, ha ha) and the other three were jokes that I guess were supposed to make me feel better. They weren't very funny, but I laughed anyway.

I bet Judith Gershner doesn't laugh at Michael's jokes. She's too busy cloning things.

HOW TO CARE FOR FAT LOUIE
WHILE I AM AWAY

A.M.:

In the morning, please fill Fat Louie's bowl with DRY FOOD. Even if there is already food in the bowl, he likes to have some fresh served on top so he can feel like he is having breakfast like the rest of us.

In my bathroom is a BLUE PLASTIC CUP sitting by the bathtub. Please fill that every morning with water from the bathroom sink. You must use water from the bathroom sink, because water from the kitchen sink isn't cold enough. And you have to put it in the BLUE CUP because that is the cup Fat Louie is used to drinking out of while I am brushing my teeth.

He has a bowl in the hallway outside my room. Rinse that out and fill it with water from the WATER FILTER PITCHER in the refrigerator. It must be water from the WATER FILTER PITCHER because even though New York tap is said to be contaminant-free, it is good for Louie to get at least some water that is definitely pure. Cats need to drink a lot of water to flush out their systems and prevent kidney and urinary tract infections, so always leave lots of water out, and not just by his food bowls, but other places as well.

161

Do not confuse the bowl in the hall with the BOWL BY THE CHRISTMAS TREE. That bowl is there to discourage Louie from drinking out of the tree holder. Too much tree resin could make him constipated.

In the morning, Fat Louie likes to sit on the windowsill in my room and look at the pigeons on the fire escape. NEVER OPEN THIS WINDOW, but be sure the curtains are open so he can see out.

Also, sometimes he likes to look out the windows by the TV. If he cries while he is doing this, it means you should pet him.

P.M.:

At dinnertime, give Fat Louie CANNED FOOD. Fat Louie only likes three flavors: CHICKEN AND TUNA FEAST (FLAKED), SHRIMP AND FISH FEAST (FLAKED), and OCEAN FISH FEAST (FLAKED). He won't eat anything with BEEF or PORK. He must have the contents of the can on a new, CLEAN saucer, or he won't eat. Also, he won't eat if the contents don't retain their CANLIKE SHAPE on the plate, so don't chop up his food.

After eating his canned food, Fat Louie likes to stretch out on the carpet in front of the front door. This is a good time to give him his exercise. When he stretches out, just put your hand under his front legs and straighten them (he likes this) until he bends like a comma. Then dig your thumbs between his shoulder blades and give him a kitty massage. He will purr if you do it right. If you do it wrong you will know, because he will bite you.

Fat Louie gets bored very easily, and when he gets bored, he walks around crying, so here are some games he likes to play:

Take some pieces of CAT TREAT and line them up on top of the stereo for Fat Louie to knock off and chase.

Put Fat Louie in my COMPUTER CHAIR and then hide behind the bookshelf and throw one end of a shoelace over the back of the chair so he can't see where it is coming from.

Make a FORT out of pillows on my bed and put Fat Louie inside of it and then stick your hand into any openings between the pillows (I recommend wearing an oven mitt during this game).

Put some catnip in an OLD SOCK and throw it to Fat Louie. Then leave him alone for four to five hours, because catnip makes him a little free with his claws.

THE LITTER BOX

Mr. Gianini, this one is for you. Mom must not clean out the litter box or touch anything that may have come in contact with it, or she might develop toxoplasmosis, and the baby might get sick. Always wash' your hands in warm, soapy water after changing Fat Louie's litter box, even if you don't think you got anything on your hands.

Fat Louie's box needs to be scooped out EVERY DAY. Always use clumping litter, and then just scoop out the clumps into a Grand Union bag and dispose. Nothing could be simpler. He tends to do number 2 about two hours after his evening meal. You will be able to tell from the odor wafting from his box in my bathroom.

MOST IMPORTANT OF ALL

Remember not to disturb Fat Louie's SPECIAL AREA BEHIND THE TOILET in my bathroom. That is where he keeps his collection of shiny objects. If he takes something of yours and you find it there, be sure not to take it out while he is looking, or for weeks he will try to bite you every time he sees you. I talked to the vet about it, but she said short of hiring an animal behaviorist at $70/hr there is nothing that can be done. We just have to put up with it.

ABOVE ALL, BE SURE TO PICK FAT LOUIE UP SEVERAL TIMES A DAY AND HUG AND SQUEEZE HIM!!!!! (HE LIKES THIS.)

Saturday, December 13, Midnight, the loft

I can't believe it's midnight already, and I am still only on Chapter One of *An Introduction to Algebra*!

This book is incomprehensible. I sincerely hope whoever wrote it did not make very much money off of it.

I should just go and ask Mr. G what's going to be on the final.

No, that would be cheating.

Wouldn't it?

Sunday, December 14, 10 a.m., the loft

Only forty-eight hours until the Algebra final, and I am still on Chapter One.

Lilly just came over again. She wants to study for World Civ together. I told her I can't worry about World Civ when I am only on Chapter One in my Algebra review, but she said we could alternate: She would quiz me on Algebra for an hour, then I could quiz her on World Civ for an hour. I said okay, even though it really isn't fair: She is getting an A in Algebra, so her quizzing me isn't really helping her any, while my quizzing her in World Civ helps me study for it, too.

But that's what friends are for, I guess.

Tina just called. Her little brother and sisters are driving her crazy. She wanted to know if she could come down and study here. I said sure.

What else could I say? Besides, she promised to stop at H and H for bagels and vegetable cream cheese. And she said she thought the photos of me in the supplement were beautiful and that I shouldn't care if people call me a sellout, because I look so hot.

Sunday, December 14, Noon, the loft

Michael told Boris where Lilly is, so now Boris is here, too. Lilly's right. Boris really does breathe too loudly. It's very distracting.

And I wish he wouldn't put his feet on my bed. The least he could do is take his shoes off first. But when I suggested it, Lilly said that would be a bad idea.

Ew. I don't know why Lilly puts up with a boyfriend who is not only a mouth breather but also has stinky feet.

Boris may be a musical genius, but he has a lot to learn about hygiene, if you ask me.

Sunday, December 14, 12:30 p.m., the loft

Now Kenny's here. I don't know how I am supposed to get any studying done with all of these people around. Plus, Mr. Gianini has decided that now would be a good time to practice his drums.

I told Lilly, and she agreed, that once Boris and Kenny showed up, the whole studying thing kind of went down the drain. Plus, Mr. G's drumming didn't help. So we decided it would be best to take a study break and go to Chinatown for dim sum.

We had a good time at Great Shanghai eating vegetable dumplings and dried sauteed string beans with garlic sauce. I ended up sitting by Boris, and he really made me laugh, engineering it so that whenever the waiters brought something new, the only empty spot on the table was in front of him, so they had to put it there, and then Boris and I got first dibs on it.

Which made me realize that in spite of the sweaters and the mouth-breathing, Boris really is a funny and nice person. Lilly is so lucky. I mean, that the boy she loves actually loves her back. If only I could love Kenny the way Lilly loves Boris!

But I don't seem to have any control over who I fall in love with. Believe me, if I did, I would NOT love Michael. I mean, for one thing, he is my best friend's older brother, and if Lilly ever found out I liked him, she would NOT understand. Also, of course, he is a senior and is graduating soon.

And oh, yeah, he already has a girlfriend.

But what am I supposed to do? I can't *make* myself fall in love with Kenny any more than I can *make* him stop liking me, you know, in that special way.

Although he still hasn't asked me to the dance. Or mentioned it, anyway. Lilly says I should just call him and be like,

"So are we going, or not?" After all, she keeps pointing out, I had the guts to smash up Lana's cell phone. Why don't I have the guts to call my own boyfriend and ask him whether or not he is taking me to the school dance?

But I smashed up Lana's cell phone in the heat of passion. I cannot summon up anything like passion where Kenny is concerned. There is a part of me that doesn't want to go to the dance with him at all, and that part of me is relieved that he hasn't mentioned anything about it.

Okay, it is a very small part of me, but it's still *there*.

So actually, even though I was having fun sitting by Boris at the restaurant and all, it was also a little depressing, on account of the whole Kenny thing.

And then things got even more depressing. That's because some little Chinese-American girls came up to me as I was opening my fortune cookie and wanted to know if they could have my autograph. Then they handed me pens and the advertising supplement that had appeared in that day's *Times* for me to sign.

I seriously thought about killing myself, only I couldn't think how I'd do it, except for maybe stabbing myself through the heart with a chopstick.

Instead I just signed the stupid thing for them and tried to smile. But inside, of course, I was FREAKING OUT, especially when I saw how happy the little girls were to have met me. And why? No, not because of my tireless work on behalf of the polar bears or the whales or starving kids. Which I haven't actually done yet, but I fully intend to do.

No, because I'd been in a magazine in a bunch of pretty

dresses, and I'm tall and skinny like a model.

Which is no accomplishment at all!

After that, my headache came back, and I said I had to go home.

Nobody protested very much, I think because everybody realized all of a sudden how much time we'd wasted, and how much studying we all had left to do. So we left, and now I am home again, and my mom says that while I was gone, Sebastiano called four times, AND he had another dress delivered.

Not just any dress, either. It is a dress Sebastiano designed just for me, to wear to the Nondenominational Winter Dance. It's not sexy. It isn't sexy at all. It's dark green velvet with long sleeves and a wide, square neckline.

But when I put it on and looked at my reflection in the mirror in my room, something funny happened:

I looked good. *Really* good.

There was a note attached to the dress that said,

Please forgive me.
I promise this dress will not make him think of you
as his little sister's best friend.
S.

Which is very sweet. Sad, but sweet. Sebastiano can't know, of course, that the Michael situation is completely hopeless, and that no *dress* is going to make any difference, no matter how nice I look in it.

But hey, at least Sebastiano *apologized*. That's a lot more,

I've noticed, than Grandmère has done.

Of course I forgive Sebastiano. I mean, none of it is his fault, really.

And I guess someday I'll probably forgive Grandmère, since she's too old to know any better.

But the person I will never, ever forgive is myself, for getting into this situation in the first place. I totally should have known better. I should have told Sebastiano, No photos, please. Only I was so carried away, looking at myself in all those beautiful dresses, that I forgot that being a princess is more than just wearing pretty dresses: It's being an example to a lot of people . . . people you don't even know and may not ever even meet.

Which is why if I don't pass this Algebra test, I am dead.

Here are the number of students at Albert Einstein High School who (so far) have felt compelled to make comments to me about my smashing Lana Weinberger's cell phone last Friday: 37

Here are the number of students at Albert Einstein High School who (so far) have felt compelled to mention my suspension last Friday: 59

Here are the number of students at Albert Einstein High School who (so far) have felt compelled to make comments to me about my appearance in an advertising supplement to *The New York Times* over the weekend: 74

Total number of comments made to me so far today by students at Albert Einstein High School: 170

Oddly, after wading through all of this, when I got to my locker, I found something that seemed extremely out of place: a single yellow rose, sticking out of the door.

What can this mean? Can there be someone in this school who does not despise me?

Apparently so. But when I looked around, wondering who my one supporter could be, I saw only Justin Baxendale, being stalked (as usual) by a horde of worshipful girls.

I suppose my anonymous rose-leaver must be Kenny, trying to cheer me up. He will not admit it, but who else could it be?

It is Reading Day today, which means we are supposed to spend the whole day—except for lunch—sitting in Homeroom, studying for our finals, which begin tomorrow.

This is fine by me, since at least this way, there's no chance I'll run into Lana. Her homeroom is on a whole other floor.

The only problem is that Kenny's in this class. We have to sit alphabetically, so he's way up at the front of this row, but he keeps passing notes back to me. Notes that say things like, *Keep on smilin'!* and *Hang in there, Sunshine!*

He won't fess up to the rose thing, though.

By the way, want to know the total number of comments made to me so far today by Michael Moscovitz? 1

And it wasn't even really a comment. He told me in the hallway that my combat boot had come untied.

And it had.

My life is so over.

Four days until the Nondenominational Winter Dance, and still no date.

Distance formula: $d - 10xrt$

$r = 10$

$t = 2$

$d = 10 + (10)(2)$

$\quad = 10 + 20 = 30$

Variables are placeholders for numbers (letters)

Distributive law

$5x + 5y - 5$

$5 (x + y - 1)$

$2a - 2b + 2c$

$2 (-1) - 2(-2) + 2 (5)$

$-2 + 4 + 10 = 12$

Four times a number is added to three. The result is five times the number.

Find the number.

$x =$ *the number*

$4x + 3 = 5x$

$\underline{-4x \qquad\quad -4x}$

$\qquad 3 = x$

Regardes les oiseaux stupides.

Cartesian coordinate system divides the plane into four parts called quadrants

Quadrant 1 (positive, positive)

Quadrant 2 (negative, positive)

Quadrant 3 (negative, negative)
Quadrant 4 (positive, negative)

Slope: slope of a line is line denoted m

Find slope
negative slopes
positive slopes
zero slope
Vertical line has no slope
Horizontal line has 0 slope
Collinear—points that lie on the same line
Parallel lines have the same slope

$$4x + 2y = 6$$
$$2y = -4x + 6$$
$$y = -2x + 3$$

Active voice indicates that the subject of the verb is acting

Passive voice indicates that the subject of the verb is being acted upon

Tuesday, December 16

Algebra and English finals completed.
Only three more, plus term paper, to go.

76 comments today, 53 of them negative:
"Sellout" = 29 times
I-Must-Think-I'm-All-That = 14 times
Here Comes Miss Thang = 6 times

Lilly says, "Who cares what people are saying? You know the truth, right? And that's all that matters."
That's easy for Lilly to say. Lilly's not the one who people are saying all those mean things about. *I* am.

Somebody left another yellow rose in my locker. What is up with that? I asked Kenny again if it was him, but he denied it. Strangely, he seemed to get very red in the face about it. But this might have been because Justin Baxendale, who was walking by at the time, stepped on Kenny's foot. Kenny has very large feet, larger even than mine.

Three more days until the Nondenominational Winter Dance, and nada on the date front.

Wednesday, December 17

World Civ exam *finis*.
Two more, plus term paper, to go.

62 comments, 34 negative:
Don't give up your day job = 12 times
Sellout = 5 times
"If I was flat-chested like you, Mia, I could be a model, too" = 6 times

One rose, yellow, still no indication who left it. Perhaps someone is mistaking my locker for Lana's. She is, after all, always hanging out in that area, waiting for Josh Richter, whose locker is next door to mine, so that the two of them can suck face. It's possible that someone thinks he is leaving roses for her.

God knows no one at Albert Einstein High School would want to leave flowers for me. Unless I were dead, maybe, and they could fling them onto my grave and say, "Good riddance, Miss Thang."

Two more days until the dance. Still nothing.

Thursday, December 18, 1 a.m.

It just occurred to me:

Maybe Kenny is lying about the roses. Maybe they really *are* from him. Maybe he's leaving them as kind of teasers, leading up to asking me to the dance tomorrow night.

Which is kind of insulting, really. I mean, him waiting this long to finally ask. For all he knows, I could have said yes to somebody else by now.

As if somebody else might have asked.

HA!

THAT'S IT!!!!!
I'M DONE!!!!!!
DONE WITH FINALS!!!!!!!!!!!!!
And guess what?

I'm pretty sure I passed all of them. Even Algebra. The grades aren't posted until tomorrow, during the Winter Carnival, but I bugged Mr. G so much he finally said, "Mia, you did fine. Now leave me alone, all right?"

Got that????? He said I did FINE!!!!!!!!!! You know what *fine* means, don't you?

IT MEANS I PASSED!!!!!!!!!!!!!!!!

Thank God all of that's over. Now I can concentrate on what's important:

My social life.

I am serious. It is in a state of total disrepair. Everyone at school—with the exception of my friends—thinks I am this total sellout. They're like, "You talk the talk, Mia, but you don't walk the walk."

Well, I'm going to show them. Right after the World Civ exam yesterday, it hit me like a ton of bricks. I knew *exactly* what to do. It's what Grandmère would do.

Well, okay, maybe not *quite* what Grandmère would do, but it will solve the whole problem. Granted, Sebastiano isn't going to like it very much. But then, he should have asked ME, not Grandmère, if it was all right to run those photos in an ad for his clothes. Right?

I have to say, this is the most princessy thing I've done so far. I am very, very nervous. Seriously. You wouldn't believe how much my palms are sweating.

But I cannot continue to lie back and meekly take this abuse. Something must be done about it, and I think I know what.

The best part is, I am doing it all by myself, with no help from anyone.

Well, all right, the concierge at the Plaza helped by getting me a room, and Lars helped by making all the calls on his cell phone.

And Lilly helped me write down what I was going to say, and Tina did my makeup and hair just now.

But other than that, it was all me.

Okay, we're here.

Here goes nothing.

Thursday, December 18, 7 p.m.

I have now watched myself on all four major networks, plus New York 1, CNN, Headline News, MSNBC, and Fox News Channel. Apparently, they are also going to show it on *Entertainment Tonight*, *Access Hollywood*, and *E! Entertainment News*.

And I have to say, for a girl who supposedly has issues with her self-image, I think I did a fine job. I didn't mess up, not even once. If I maybe spoke a little too fast, well, you could still *understand* me. Unless, you know, you're a non–English-speaker or something.

I looked good, too. I probably should have worn something other than my school uniform, but you know, royal blue comes off pretty good on TV.

The phone has been ringing off the hook ever since the press conference was first aired. The first time it rang, my mom picked it up, and it was Sebastiano, screaming incomprehensibly about how I've ruined him.

Only he can't say ruined. It just came out "rued."

I felt really bad. I mean, I didn't mean to ruin him. Especially after he was so nice about designing me that dress for the dance.

But what was I supposed to do? I tried to make him look on the bright side:

"Sebastiano," I said, when I got on the phone, "I haven't ruined you. Really. It's just the proceeds from the sales of the dresses I'm wearing in the ad that will go to Greenpeace."

But Sebastiano completely failed to look at the big

picture. He kept screaming, "Rued! I'm rued!"

I pointed out that, far from ruining him, his donating all the proceeds from sales of the dresses I modeled to Greenpeace was going to be perceived in the industry as a brilliant stroke of marketing genius, and that I wouldn't be surprised if those dresses flew off the racks, since girls like me, who are really the people his fashions are geared for, care a great deal about the environment.

I must have picked up a thing or two during my princess lessons with Grandmère, since in the end, I totally won him over. By the time I hung up, I think Sebastiano almost believed the whole thing had been his idea in the first place.

The next time the phone rang, it was my dad. I may have to scratch the plan to get him a book on anger management, because he was laughing his head off. He wanted to know if it had been my mom's idea, and when I said, "No, it was all me," he went, "You really *have* got the princess thing down, you know."

So, in a weird way, I feel like I passed that final, too.

Except of course that I'm still not speaking to Grandmère. Not a single one of the calls I've gotten tonight—from Lilly and Tina and Mamaw and Papaw back in Indiana, who saw the broadcast on a local affiliate—have been from her.

Really, I think she should be the one to apologize, because what she did was totally underhanded.

Almost as underhanded, my mom pointed out to me over dinner from Number One Noodle Son, as what *I* did.

Which is sort of shocking. I mean, I never thought about it before, but it's true: What I did tonight—it was as sneaky as anything Grandmère's ever done.

But I guess that shouldn't be very surprising. We *are* related, after all.

Then again, so were Luke Skywalker and Darth Vader.

Must go. *Baywatch* is on. This is the first time in a while I've been home to watch it.

Tina just called. She didn't want to talk about the press conference. She wanted to know what I got from my Secret Snowflake. I was all, "Secret Snowflake? What are you talking about?"

"You know," Tina said. "Your Secret Snowflake. You remember, Mia. We signed up for it like a month ago. You put your name in the jar, and then someone draws it, and they have to be your Secret Snowflake for the last week of school before Winter Break. They're supposed to surprise you with little gifts and stuff. You know, as a stress breaker. Since it's finals week, and all."

I dimly remembered, one day before Thanksgiving Break, Tina dragging me over to a folding table where some nerdy-looking kids from the student government were sitting on one side of the cafeteria with a big jar filled with little pieces of paper. Tina had made me write my name on a slip of paper, then pick someone else's name out of the jar.

"Oh, my God!" I cried. With all the stress of finals and everything, I had forgotten all about it!

Worse, I had forgotten that I had drawn Tina's name. No real coincidence, since she'd stuffed her slip of paper into the jar right before I picked. Still, what kind of heinous friend am I, that I would forget something like this?

Then I realized something else. The yellow roses. They hadn't been put in my locker by mistake! And they really weren't from Kenny, either! They had to be from my Secret Snowflake.

Which was kind of upsetting in a way. I mean, it's really starting to look as if Kenny has no intention whatsoever of asking me to tomorrow night's dance.

"I can't believe you forgot about it," Tina said, sounding amused. "You *have* been getting stuff for your Secret Snowflake, haven't you, Mia?"

I felt a rush of guilt. I had totally blown it. Poor Tina!

"Uh, sure," I said, wondering where I was going to find a present for her by tomorrow morning, the last day of the Secret Snowflake thing. "Sure, I have."

Tina sighed. "I guess nobody picked me," she said. "Because I haven't gotten anything."

"Oh, don't worry," I said, hoping the guilt washing over me wasn't noticeable in my voice. "You will. Your Secret Snowflake is probably waiting, you know, until the last day because she's—or he's—gotten you something really good."

"Do you think so?" Tina asked, wistfully.

"Oh, yes," I gushed.

Reassured, Tina got businesslike.

"Now," she said, "that finals are over . . ."

"Um, yes?"

". . . when are you going to tell Michael that you're the one who sent him those cards?"

Shocked, I went, "How about never?"

To which Tina replied, tartly, "Mia, if you don't tell him, then what was the point of sending those cards?"

"To let him know that there are other girls out there who might like him, besides Judith Gershner."

Tina said, severely, "Mia, that's not enough. You've got to tell him it was you. How are you ever going to get him if he doesn't know how you feel?" Tina Hakim Baba, surprisingly, has a lot in common with my dad. "Remember Kenny? That's how Kenny got you. He sent the anonymous notes, but then he finally fessed up."

"Yeah," I said, sarcastically. "And look how great *that* turned out."

"It'll be different with you and Michael," Tina insisted. "Because you two are destined for each other. I can just *feel* it. You've got to tell him, and it's got to be tomorrow, because the next day, you are leaving for Genovia."

Oh, God. In my self-congratulations over having successfully maneuvered my first press conference, I'd forgotten about that, too. I am leaving for Genovia the day after tomorrow! With Grandmère! To whom I am not even speaking anymore!

I told Tina that I'd confess to Michael tomorrow. She hung up all happy.

But it was a good thing she hadn't been able to see my nostrils, because they were flaring like crazy, on account of the fact that I was totally lying to her.

Because there is no way I am ever telling Michael Moscovitz how I feel about him. No matter what my dad says. I *can't*.

Not to his face.

Not ever.

They are holding us hostage here in Homeroom until they've passed out our final semester grades. Then we are free to spend the rest of the day at the Winter Carnival in the gym, and then, later this evening, the dance.

Really. We don't have any more classes after this. We are just supposed to have fun.

As if. I am so never having fun again.

That is because—you know, aside from my many other problems, including the fact that I don't love my boyfriend, who also apparently does not love me anymore, at least not enough to ask me to the school dance, but I do love my best friend's brother, who is not even remotely aware of my feelings—that I think I know who my Secret Snowflake is.

Really, there is no other explanation. Why else would Justin Baxendale—who, even though he's so new, is still totally popular, not to mention way good-looking—be hanging around my locker so much? I mean, seriously. This is the third time I've spotted him lurking around there this week. Why else would he be hanging around there, except to leave those roses?

Unless he's planning on blackmailing me about the whole fire-alarm thing.

But Justin Baxendale doesn't exactly strike me as the blackmailer type. I mean, he looks to me like somebody who'd have something better to do than blackmail a princess.

Which leaves only one other explanation for why he could possibly be spending so much time around my locker:

He is my Secret Snowflake.

And how totally embarrassing is it going to be when I go out there when the bell rings, and Justin comes up to me to confess—because that's the rule, it turns out: You have to reveal your identity to your Secret Snowflake today—and I have to look up into his smoky eyes with those long lashes and give a big fake smile and go, "Oh, gee, thanks, Justin. I had no idea it was you!"

Whatever. This is actually the least of my problems, right? I mean, considering that I am the only girl in this entire school who does not have a date to the dance tonight. And that tomorrow I have to leave for a country I am princess of, with my lunatic grandmother who isn't speaking to my father, and who, I know from past experience, is not above smoking in the airplane lavatory if the urge strikes her.

Really. Grandmère is a flight attendant's worst nightmare.

But that's not even half of it. I mean, what about my mom and Mr. Gianini? Sure, they're acting like they don't mind my spending the holidays in another country, and yes, we're going to have our own private little Christmas among ourselves before I leave, but really, I bet they mind. I bet they mind a lot.

And what about my grade in Algebra? Oh, Mr. Gianini says it's fine, but what is fine, exactly? A D? A D is not fine. Not considering the number of hours I've put into raising my grade from an F, it isn't. A D is *not* acceptable.

And what—oh God, *what*—am I going to do about Kenny?

At least I got Tina's present out of the way. I went on line last night and signed her up for a teen romance book-of-the-month club. I printed out the certificate, saying she is an official member, and will give it to her when the bell rings.

When the bell rings, which is also when I have to go out there and face Justin Baxendale.

It wouldn't be so bad if it weren't for those eyes of his. Why does he have to be so good-looking? And why did a good-looking person have to pick me as his Secret Snowflake? Beautiful people, like Lana and Justin, can't help but be repulsed by ordinary-looking people, like me.

He probably didn't even pull my name from that jar at all. Probably, he picked Lana's name and has been putting those roses in my locker, thinking it's Lana's, seeing as how God knows she never hangs out in front of her own locker.

What's even worse is, Tina told me yellow roses mean love *everlasting*.

Which of course was why I figured maybe it was Kenny after all.

Oh, great. They are passing around the printouts with our grades on them. I am not looking. I don't even care. I DO NOT CARE ABOUT MY GRADES.

Thank God for the bell. I'm just going to slip out of here—not looking at my grades, totally not looking at my grades—and go about my business like nothing out of the ordinary is going on.

Except of course when I get to my locker, Justin is there, looking for someone. Lana is there, too, waiting for Josh.

You know, I really don't need this. Justin revealing that

he is my Secret Snowflake right in front of Lana, I mean. God only knows what she's going to say, the girl who has been suggesting I wear Band-Aids instead of a bra every day since the two of us hit puberty. Plus, it isn't like she's been super happy with me since the whole cell-phone thing. I'll bet she'll have something extra mean all prepared for the occasion. . . .

"Dude," Justin says.

Dude? I'm not a dude. Who is Justin talking to?

I turn around. Josh is standing there, behind Lana.

"Dude, I've been looking for you all week," Justin says, to Josh. "Do you have those Trig notes for me, or not? I've got to make up the final in one hour."

Josh says something, but I don't hear him. I don't hear him because there's a roaring sound in my ears. There's a roaring sound in my ears because standing behind Justin is Michael. *Michael Moscovitz.*

And in his hand is *a yellow rose.*

Oh, God.

I am in so much trouble.

Again.

And it isn't even my fault this time. I mean, I couldn't help myself. It just *happened*, you know? And it doesn't mean anything. It was just, you know, one of those things.

And besides, it's not what Kenny thinks. Not even. I mean, if you think about it, it is a complete and total letdown. For me, anyway.

Because of course the first thing Michael says, when he sees me standing there gaping at him while he is holding that flower, is, "Here. This just fell out of your locker."

I took it from him in a complete daze. I swear to God my heart was beating so hard, I thought I was going to pass out.

Because I thought they'd been from him. The roses, I mean. For a minute there, I really did think Michael Moscovitz had been leaving me roses.

But of course this time, there's a note attached to the rose. It says:

Good luck on your trip to Genovia! See you when you get back!
Your Secret Snowflake,
Boris Pelkowski

Boris Pelkowski. Boris Pelkowski is the one who's been leaving those roses. Boris Pelkowski is my Secret Snowflake.

Of course Boris wouldn't know that a yellow rose represents love everlasting. Boris doesn't even know not to tuck his sweater into his pants. How would he know the secret language of flowers?

I don't know which was actually stronger, my feeling of relief that it wasn't Justin Baxendale leaving those roses after all . . .

. . . or my feeling of disappointment that it wasn't Michael.

Then Michael went, "Well? What's the verdict?"

To which I responded by staring at him blankly. I still hadn't quite gotten over it. You know, those brief few seconds when I'd thought—I'd actually thought, fool that I am—that he loved me.

"What did you get in Algebra?" he asked, slowly, as if I were dense.

Which, of course, I am. So dense that I never realized how much in love with Michael Moscovitz I was until Judith Gershner came along and swept him right out from under my nose.

Anyway, so I opened the computer printout containing my grades, and would you believe that I had raised my F in Algebra all the way up to a B minus?

Which just goes to show that if you spend nearly every waking moment in your life studying something, the likelihood is that you are going to retain at least a little of it.

Enough to get a B minus on the final, anyway.

I'm trying really hard not to gloat, but it's difficult. I mean, I'm so happy.

Well, except for the whole not-having-a-date-to-the-dance thing.

Still, it's hard to be unhappy. There is absolutely no way

I got this grade because the teacher happens to be my step-father. In Algebra, either you get the right answer, or you don't. There's nothing subjective about it, like in English. There's no interpretation of the facts. Either you're right, or you're not.

And I was right. Eighty percent of the time.

Of course it helped that I knew the answer to the final's extra-credit question: What instrument did Ringo, in the Beatles, play?

But that was only worth two points.

Anyway, here's the part where I got into trouble. Even though, of course, it isn't my fault.

I was so happy about my B minus, I completely forgot for a minute how much I am in love with Michael. I even forgot, for a change, to be shy around him. Instead, I did something really unlike me.

I threw my arms around him.

Seriously. Threw my arms right around his neck and went, "Wheeeeeee!!!!!"

I couldn't help it. I was so happy. Okay, the whole rose thing had been a little bit of a bummer, but the B minus made up for it. Well, almost.

It was just an innocent hug. That's *all* it was. Michael had, after all, tutored me almost the whole semester. He had some stake in that B minus, too.

But I guess Kenny, who Tina now tells me came around the corner right as I was doing it—hugging Michael, I mean—doesn't see it that way. According to Tina, Kenny thinks there's something going on between Michael and me.

To which, of course, I can only say, I WISH!

But I can't say that. I have to go find Kenny now, and let him know, you know, it was just a friendly hug.

Tina's all, "Why? Why don't you tell him the truth—that you don't feel the same way about him that he feels about you? This is your big chance!"

But you can't break up with someone during the Winter Carnival. I mean, really. How mean.

Why must my life be so fraught with trauma?

Well, I still haven't found Kenny, but I really have to hand it to the administrators: Grasping they might be, but they sure do know how to throw a party. Even Lilly is impressed.

Of course, signs of corporatization are everywhere: There are McDonald's orange drink dispensers on every floor, and it looks as if there was a run on Entenmann's, there are so many cake-and-cookie-laden tables scattered around.

Still, you can tell they are really trying to show us a good time. All of the clubs are offering activities and booths. There's ballroom dancing in the gym, courtesy of the Dance Club; fencing lessons in the auditorium, thanks to the Drama club; even cheerleading lessons in the first-floor hallway, brought to us by—you guessed it—the junior varsity cheerleaders.

I couldn't find Kenny anywhere, but I ran into Lilly at the Students for Amnesty International booth (Students Against the Corporatization of Albert Einstein High School did not submit their application for a booth in time to get one, so Lilly is stuck running the Amnesty International booth instead). And guess what? Guess who got an F in something?

That's right.

Lilly. I couldn't believe it.

"Mrs. Spears gave you an F in English? *YOU* got an F?"

She didn't seem too bothered by it, though.

"I had to take a stand, Mia," she said. "And sometimes, when you believe in something, you have to make sacrifices."

"Sure," I said. "But an *F*? Your parents are going to kill you."

"No, they won't," Lilly said. "They'll just try to psychoanalyze me."

Which is true.

Oh, God. Here comes Tina.

I hope she doesn't remember—

She does.

We're going over to the Computer Club's booth right now.

I don't want to go to the Computer Club's booth. I already looked over there, and I know what's going on. Michael and Judith and the rest of the computer nerds are sitting there behind all these color monitors. When somebody comes up, they get to sit down in front of one of the monitors, and play a computer game the club designed where you walk through the school and all of the teachers are in funny costumes. Like Principal Gupta is wearing a leather dominatrix's outfit, and holding a whip, and Mr. Gianini is in footie pajamas with a teddy bear that looks exactly like him.

They used a different program when the club applied to be part of the Carnival, of course, so none of the teachers or administrators know what everyone is sitting there looking at. You would think they'd wonder why all of the kids are laughing so hard.

Whatever. I don't want to do it. I don't want to go anywhere near it.

But Tina says I have to.

"Now's the perfect time to tell him," she says. "I mean, Kenny's nowhere to be seen."

Oh, God. This is what comes from telling your friends anything.

Well, I'm in the girls' room again. And I think I can state with certainty that this time, I'm never coming out.

No, I think I'll just stay in here until everyone has gone home. Only then will it be safe. Thank God I am leaving the country tomorrow. Maybe by the time I get back, everyone involved in this little incident will have forgotten about it.

But I doubt it. Not with my luck, anyway.

Why do these kinds of things always happen to me? I mean, seriously? What did I ever do to turn the gods against me? Why don't these kinds of things ever happen to Lana Weinberger? Why me? Why always *me*?

All right, so here's what happened.

I had no intention whatsoever of actually telling Michael anything. I mean, let me get that out right away. I was only going along with Tina because, well, it would have looked weird if I had completely avoided the Computer Club's booth. Plus Michael had asked me so many times to make sure I stopped by. So there was no way I could avoid it.

But I never intended to say a word about You-Know-What. I mean, Tina was just going to have to learn to live with the disappointment. You don't love somebody for, like, as long as I have loved Michael and then just go up to him at a school fair and be like, "Oh, by the way, yeah, I love you."

Okay? You don't *do* that.

But whatever. So I went up to the stupid booth with Tina. Everyone was all giggly and excited, because their program was so popular that there was this really long line to see it. But Michael saw us, and went, "Come on up!"

Like we were supposed to cut in front of all these other people. I mean, we did it, of course, but everyone behind us grumbled, and who can blame them? They'd been waiting a long time.

But I guess because of the thing the night before—you know, when I explained on national television that the only reason I'd done that clothing ad was because the designer was donating all the proceeds to Greenpeace—I have been noticeably more popular (positive comments so far: 243. Negative: 1. From Lana, of course). So the grumbling wasn't as bad as it could have been.

Anyway, Michael was all, "Here, Mia, sit at this one." And he pulled out a chair in front of this one computer monitor.

So I sat down and waited for the stupid thing to come on, and all around me other kids were laughing at what they were seeing on their screens. I just sat there thinking, for some reason, *Faint heart never won fair lady.*

Which was stupid, because, number one, I was NOT going to tell him I like him and number two, Michael is dark-haired, *not* fair. And he isn't a lady either, obviously.

Then I heard Judith go, "Wait, what are you doing?"

And then I heard Michael say, "No, that's okay. I have a special one for her."

Then the screen in front of my eyes flickered. I sighed. *Okay*, I thought. *Here goes the stupid teacher thing. Be sure to laugh so they think you like it.*

So I was sitting there, and I was actually kind of depressed, because I really didn't have anything to look forward to, if you think about it. I mean, everybody else was all excited, because later on they were going to the dance, but no one had asked me to the dance—not even my supposed boyfriend—so I didn't even have that to look forward to. And everyone else I knew was going skiing or to the Bahamas or wherever for Winter Break, but what did I get to do? Oh, hang out with a bunch of members of the Genovian Olive Growers Society. I'm sure they are all really nice people, but come on.

And before I even leave for my boring trip to Genovia, I have to break up with Kenny, something I totally don't want to do, because I really do like him, and I don't want to hurt his feelings, but I guess I sort of have to.

Although I have to say, the fact that he still hasn't so much as mentioned the dance is making the idea of breaking up with him seem a lot less heinous.

Then tomorrow, I thought, *I'll leave for Europe on a plane with Dad and Grandmère, who still aren't speaking to each other* (and since I'm not speaking to Grandmère either, it should be a really fun flight), *and when I come back, knowing my luck, Michael and Judith will be engaged.*

That's what I was sitting there thinking in the split second the screen in front of me flickered. That, and, *You know, I'm not really in the mood to see any of my teachers in funny outfits.*

Only when the flickering stopped, that's not what I saw. What I saw instead was this castle.

Seriously. It was a castle, like out of the Knights of the Round Table, or *Beauty and the Beast*, or whatever. The picture zoomed in until we were over the castle walls and inside this courtyard, where there was a garden. And in the garden, all these big, fat, red roses were blooming. Some of the roses had lost their petals, and you could see them lying on the courtyard floor. It was really, really pretty, and I was like, *Hey, this is cooler than I thought it would be.*

And I sort of forgot I was sitting there in front of a computer monitor at the Winter Carnival, with like two dozen people all around me. I began to feel like I was actually *in* that garden.

Then this banner waved across the screen, in front of the roses, like it was blowing in the wind. The banner had some words written on it in gold leaf. When it stopped flapping, I could read what the words said:

Roses are red
Violets are blue
You may not know it
But I love you, too

I screamed and jumped up out of my chair, tipping it over behind me.

Everyone started laughing. I guess they thought I'd seen Principal Gupta in her leather catsuit.

Only Michael knew I hadn't.

And Michael wasn't laughing.

Only I couldn't look at Michael. I couldn't look anywhere, really, except at my own feet. Because I couldn't believe what had just happened. I mean, I couldn't process it. What did it *mean*? Did it mean Michael knew I was the one who'd been sending him those notes, and that he felt the same way?

Or did it mean he knew I was the one who'd been sending him those notes, and he was trying to get back at me, as a kind of joke?

I didn't know. All I knew was that if I didn't get out of there, I was going to start crying . . .

. . . and in front of everyone in the entire school.

I grabbed Tina by the arm and yanked her, *hard*, after me. I guess I was figuring I could tell her what I'd seen, and maybe *she'd* be able to figure out what it meant, since I sure couldn't.

Tina shrieked—I must have grabbed her harder than I thought—and I heard Michael call, "Mia!"

But I just kept going, lugging Tina behind me, and pushing through the crowd for the door, thinking only one thing:

Must get to the girls' room. Must get to the girls' room before I start bawling my head off.

Somebody, with about as much force as I'd grabbed Tina, grabbed me. I thought it was Michael. I knew if I so much as looked at him, I'd burst into big baby sobs. I said, "Get *off*," and jerked my arm away.

It was Kenny's voice that said, "But Mia, I *have* to talk to you!"

"Not *now*, Kenny," Tina said.

But Kenny was totally inflexible. He went, "Yes, *now*," and you could tell from his face he meant it.

Tina rolled her eyes and backed off. I stood there, my back to the Computer Club's booth, and prayed, *Please, please don't come over here, Michael. Please stay where you are.*

205

Please, please, please *don't come over here.*

"Mia," Kenny said. He looked more uncomfortable than I'd ever seen him, and I've seen Kenny look plenty uncomfortable. He's an awkward kind of guy. "I just want to . . . I mean, I just want you to know. Well. That I know."

I stared at him. I had no idea what he was talking about. Seriously. I'd forgotten all about that hug he'd seen in the hallway. The one I'd given Michael. All I could think was, *Please don't come over here, Michael. Please don't come over here, Michael. . . .*

"Look, Kenny," I said. I don't even know how I got my tongue to work, I swear. I felt like a robot somebody had switched into the Off position. "This really isn't a good time. Maybe we could talk later—"

"Mia," Kenny said. He had a funny look on his face. "I *know.* I saw him."

I blinked.

And then I remembered. Michael, and the B-minus hug.

"Oh, Kenny," I said. "Really. That was just . . . I mean, there's nothing—"

"You don't have to worry," Kenny said. And then I realized why his face looked so funny. It was because he was wearing an expression on it that I had never seen before. At least, not on Kenny. The expression was resignation. "I won't tell Lilly."

Lilly! Oh, God! The last person in the world I wanted to know how I felt about Michael!

Maybe it wasn't too late. Maybe there was still a chance I could . . .

But no. No, I couldn't lie to him. For once in my life,

I could not summon up a lie.

"Kenny," I said. "I am so, so sorry."

I didn't realize until I said it that it was too late to run for the girls' room: I had already started crying. My voice broke, and when I put my hands to my face, they came away wet. Great. I was crying, and in front of the entire student body of Albert Einstein High School.

"Kenny," I said, sniffling. "I honestly meant to tell you. And I really do like you. I just don't . . . love you."

Kenny's face was very white, but he didn't start crying—not like me. Thank God. In fact, he even managed to smile a little in that weird, resigned way as he said, shaking his head, "Wow. I can't believe it. I mean, when it first hit me, I was like *no way*. Not Mia. No way would she do that to her best friend. But . . . well, I guess it explains a lot. About, um, us."

I couldn't look him in the face any longer. I felt like a worm. Worse than a worm, because worms are very environmentally helpful. I felt like . . . like . . .

Like a fruit fly.

"I guess I've suspected for a long time that there was someone else," Kenny went on. "You never . . . well, you never exactly seemed to return my ardor when we . . . you know."

I knew. Kissed. Nice of him to bring it up though, here in the gym, in front of everyone.

"I knew you just weren't saying anything because you didn't want to hurt my feelings," Kenny said. "That's the kind of girl you are. And that's why I put off asking you to the dance," Kenny admitted. "Because I figured you'd just say no. On account of you, you know, liking someone else.

I mean, I know you'd never lie to me, Mia. You're the most honest person I've ever met."

HA! Was he joking? *Me?* Honest? Obviously, he did not have the slightest clue about my nostrils.

"That's how I know how much this must be tearing you up inside. I just think you'd better tell Lilly soon," Kenny said somberly. "I started to suspect, you know, at the restaurant. And if I figured it out, other people will, too. And you wouldn't want her to hear it from somebody else."

I had reached up to try to wipe some of my tears away with my sleeve, but paused with my hand only halfway there, and stared at him. "Restaurant? What restaurant?"

"You know," Kenny said, looking uncomfortable. "That day we all went to Chinatown. You and he sat next to each other. You kept laughing. . . . You looked pretty chummy."

Chinatown? But Michael hadn't gone with us that day to Chinatown. . . .

"And you know," Kenny said, "I'm not the only one who's noticed him leaving you those roses all week, either."

I blinked. I could barely see him through my tears. "W–what?"

"You know." He looked around, then dropped his voice to a whisper. "Boris. Leaving you all those roses. I mean, come on, Mia. If you two want to carry on behind Lilly's back, that's one thing, but—"

The roaring in my ears that had been there just after I'd read Michael's poem came back. BORIS. BORIS PELKOWSKI. My boyfriend just broke up with me because he thinks I am having an affair with BORIS PELKOWSKI.

208

BORIS PELKOWSKI, who always has food in his braces.

BORIS PELKOWSKI, who wears his sweaters tucked inside his pants.

BORIS PELKOWSKI, my best friend's boyfriend.

Oh, God. My life is so over.

I tried to tell him. You know, the truth. That Boris isn't my secret love, but my Secret Snowflake.

But Tina darted forward, grabbed me by the arm, and went, "Sorry, Kenny, Mia has to go now." Then she dragged me into the girls' room.

"I have to tell him," I kept saying, over and over, like a crazy person, as I tried to break free of her grip. "I have to tell him. I have to tell him the truth."

"No, you do not," Tina said, pushing me past the toilet stalls. "You two are broken up. Who cares why? You're through, and that's all that matters."

I blinked at my tear-stained reflection in the mirror above the sinks. I looked awful. Never in your life have you seen anyone who looked less like a princess than I did just then. Just looking at myself made me break out into a fresh new wave of tears.

Of course Tina says she's sure Michael wasn't trying to make fun of me. Of course she says that he must have figured out that I was the one who was sending him those cards and was trying to let me know that he felt the same way about me.

Only of course I can't believe that. Because if that were true—*if that were true*—why did he let me go? Why didn't he try to stop me?

Tina has pointed out that he did try. But my shrieking when I read his poem, and then running in tears from the room, might not have seemed to him like a very encouraging sign. In fact, it might have actually looked to him like I was displeased by what I'd seen. Furthermore, Tina pointed out, even if Michael had tried to go after me, there'd been Kenny cornering me on my way out. It had certainly looked as if the two of us were Having A Moment—which we most certainly were—and didn't wish to be disturbed.

All of which could be true.

But it could also be true that Michael had just been joking. It was a very mean joke, under the circumstances, but Michael doesn't know that I adore him with every fiber of my being. Michael doesn't know that I've been in love with him all my life. Michael doesn't know that without him, I will never, ever achieve self-actualization. I mean, to Michael, I'm just his kid sister's best friend. He probably didn't mean to be cruel. He probably thought he was being funny.

It isn't his fault that my life is over, and that I am never, ever leaving this bathroom.

I'll just wait until everybody is gone, and then I'll sneak out, and no one will see me again until next semester starts, by which time, hopefully, all of this will have blown over.

Or, better yet, maybe I'll just stay in Genovia. . . .

Hey, yeah. Why not?

Friday, December 19, 5 p.m., the loft

I don't know why people can't just leave me alone.

Seriously. I may be done with finals, but I still have a lot
to do. I mean, I have to pack, don't I? Don't people know
that when you are leaving for your royal introduction to the
people over whom you will one day reign, you have to do a
lot of packing?

But no. No, people keep on calling, and e-mailing, and
coming over.

Well, I'm not talking to anybody. I think I have made
that perfectly clear. I am not speaking to Lilly or Tina or
my dad or Mr. Gianini or my mother and ESPECIALLY
not Michael, even though at last count, he'd called four
times.

I am *way* too busy to talk to anybody.

And with my headphones on, I can't even hear them
pounding on the door. It's kind of nice, I have to say.

Friday, December 19, 5:30 p.m., the fire escape

People have a right to their privacy. If I want to go into my room and lock the door and not come out or have to deal with anyone, I should have a right to. People should *not* be allowed to take the hinges off of my door and *remove* it. That is completely unfair.

But I have found a way to foil them. I am out on the fire escape. It's about thirty degrees out here, and snowing, by the way, but guess what? So far no one has followed me.

Fortunately I bought one of those pens that's also a flashlight, so I can see to write. The sun went down a while ago, and I have to admit, my butt is freezing. But it's actually sort of nice out here. All you can hear is the hiss of the snow as it lands on the metal of the fire escape, and the occasional siren or car alarm. It is restful, in a way.

And you know what I'm finding out? I need a rest. Big time.

Really. I need to like, go and lie on a beach somewhere, or something.

There's a nice beach in Genovia. Really. With white sand, palm trees, the whole bit.

Too bad while I'm there, I'm never going to have time to visit it, since I'm going to be too busy christening battleships, or whatever.

But if I *lived* in Genovia . . . you know, moved there, and lived there full time . . .

Oh, I'll miss my mom, of course. I've already considered that. She's leaned out the window about twenty times already, begging me to come inside or at least put on a coat.

My mom's a nice lady. I'll really miss her.

But she can come visit me in Genovia. At least up until her eighth month. Then air travel might be a little risky. But she can come after my baby brother or sister is born. That would be nice.

And Mr. G, he's okay, too. He just leaned out and asked if I wanted any of the four-alarm chili he just made. He left out the meat, he says, just for me.

That was nice of him. He can come visit me in Genovia, too.

It will be nice to live there. I can hang out with my dad all the time. He's not such a bad guy, either, once you get to know him. He wants me to come in off the fire escape, too. I guess my mom must have called him. He says he's really proud of me, on account of the press conference and my B minus in Algebra and all. He wants to take me out to dinner to celebrate. We can go to the Zen Palate, he says. A totally vegetarian restaurant. Isn't that nice of him?

Too bad he let Lars take my door down, or I might have gone with him.

Ronnie, our next door neighbor, just looked out her window and saw me. Now she wants to know what I'm doing, sitting out on the fire escape in December.

I told her I needed some privacy, and that this appears to be the only way I can get it.

Ronnie went, "Honey, don't I know how that is."

She said I was going to freeze without a coat though, and offered me her mink. I politely declined, as I cannot wear the skins of dead animals.

So she loaned me her electric blanket, which she has

plugged into the outlet beneath her air conditioner. I must say, this is an improvement.

Ronnie's getting ready to go out. It's nice to watch her put on her makeup. As she does it, she keeps up a running conversation with me through her open window. She asked me if I was having trouble at school, and if that was why I'm on the fire escape, and I said I was. She asked what kind, and I told her. I told her I am being persecuted: that I am in love with my best friend's brother, but that to him it is apparently all this really big joke. Oh, and also that everyone apparently thinks I am having an affair with a mouth-breathing violinist who happens to be my best friend's boyfriend.

Ronnie shook her head and said it was good to know things haven't changed since she was in high school. She says she knows what it is like to be persecuted, because Ronnie used to be a man.

I told Ronnie that it really doesn't matter, because I'm moving to Genovia. Ronnie said she was sorry to hear that. She'll miss me, as I have really improved conditions in the apartment building's incinerator room since I insisted on installing separate recycling bins for newspapers and cans and bottles.

Then Ronnie said she has to go because she's meeting her boyfriend for cocktails at the Carlyle. She said I could keep using the electric blanket, though, so long as I remember to return it when I'm done.

God. Even my next door neighbor, who used to be a man, has a boyfriend. WHAT IS WRONG WITH ME????

Uh-oh. I hear footsteps in my room. Who's coming now?

Well. You could knock me over with a feather.

Guess who just came out onto the fire escape and sat with me for half an hour?

Grandmère.

I'm not even kidding.

I was sitting here, feeling all depressed, when all of a sudden this big furry sleeve appeared out my window, and then a foot in a high-heeled shoe, and then a big blonde head, and next thing I knew, Grandmère was sitting there, blinking at me from the depths of her full-length chinchilla.

"Amelia," she said, in her most no-nonsense tone. "What are you doing out here? It's snowing. Come back inside."

I was shocked. Shocked that Grandmère would even consider coming out onto the fire escape (it's an indelicate thing for a princess to mention, but there is actually a lot of bird poop out here), but also that she would dare to speak to me, after what she did.

But she addressed that issue right away.

"I understand that you are upset with me," she said. "And you have a right to be. But I want you to know that what I did, I did for you."

"Oh, right!" Even though I swore I was never going to speak to her again, I couldn't help myself. "Grandmère, how can you possibly say that? You completely humiliated me!"

"I didn't mean to," Grandmère said. "I meant to show you that you are just as pretty as those girls in the magazines you are always wishing you look like. It's important that you know that you are not this hideous creature that you apparently think you are."

"Grandmère," I said. "That's nice of you and all—I guess—but you shouldn't have done it that way."

"What other way could I do it?" Grandmère demanded. "You will not pose for any of the magazines that have offered to send photographers. Not for *Vogue*, or *Harper's Bazaar*. Don't you understand that what Sebastiano said about your bone structure is really true? You really are quite beautiful, Amelia. If only you'd just have a little more confidence in yourself, show off once in a while. Think how quickly that boy you like would leave the housefly girl for you!"

"Fruit fly," I said. "And Grandmère, I told you, Michael likes her because she's really smart. They have a lot of stuff in common, like computers. It has nothing to do with how she looks."

"Oh, Mia," Grandmère said. "Don't be naive."

Poor Grandmère. It really wasn't fair to blame her, because she comes from such a different world. In Grandmère's world, women are valued for being great beauties—or, if they aren't great beauties, they are revered for dressing impeccably. What they do, like for a living, isn't important, because most of them don't do anything. Oh, maybe they do some charity work, or whatever, but that's it.

Grandmère doesn't understand, of course, that today being a great beauty doesn't count for much. Oh, it matters in Hollywood, of course, and on the runways in Milan. But nowadays, people understand that perfect looks are the result of DNA, something the person has nothing to do with. It's not like it's any great accomplishment, being beautiful. That's just genetics.

No, what matters today is what you do with the brain *behind* those perfect blue eyes, or brown eyes, or green, or whatever. In Grandmère's day, a girl like Judith, who could clone fruit flies, would be viewed as a piteous freak, unless she managed to clone fruit flies *and* look stunning in Dior.

And even in this remarkably enlightened age, girls like Judith still don't get as much attention as girls like Lana—which isn't fair, since cloning fruit flies is probably way more important than having totally perfect hair.

The really pathetic people are the ones like me: I can't clone fruit flies, *and* I've got bad hair.

But that's okay. I'm used to it by now.

Grandmère's the one who still needs convincing that I am an absolutely hopeless case.

"Look," I said to Grandmère. "I told you. Michael is not the type of guy who is going to be impressed because I'm in a *Sunday Times* supplement in a strapless ballgown. *That's why I like him.* If he were the kind of guy who was impressed by stuff like that, I wouldn't want anything to do with him."

Grandmère didn't look very convinced.

"Well," she said. "Perhaps you and I must agree to disagree. In any case, Amelia, I came over to apologize. I never meant to distress you. I meant only to show you what you can do, if you'd only try." She spread her gloved hands apart. "And look how well I succeeded. Why, you planned and executed an entire press conference, all on your own!"

I couldn't help smiling a little at that one. "Yes," I said. "I did."

"And," Grandmère said, "I understand that you passed Algebra."

I grinned wider. "Yes. I did."

"Now," Grandmère said, "there is only one thing left for you to do."

I nodded. "I know. I've been thinking a lot about it, and I think it might be best if I extended my stay in Genovia. Like maybe I could just live there from now on. What do you think about that?"

Grandmère's expression, I could see in the light coming from my room, was one of disbelief.

"Live in . . . live in Genovia?" For once, I'd caught her off guard. "What are you talking about?"

"You know," I said. "They have schools there. I could just finish ninth grade there. And then maybe I could go to one of those Swiss boarding schools you're always going on about."

Grandmère just stared at me. "You'd hate it."

"No," I said. "It might be fun. No boys, right? That would be great. I mean, I'm kind of sick of boys right now."

Grandmère shook her head. "But your friends . . . your mother . . ."

"Well," I said, reasonably. "They could come visit."

Then Grandmère's face hardened. She peered at me from between the heavily mascaraed slits her eyes had become.

"Amelia Mignonette Grimaldi Renaldo," she said. "You are running away from something, aren't you?"

I shook my head innocently. "Oh, no, Grandmère," I said. "Really. I'd like to live in Genovia. It'd be neat."

"NEAT?" Grandmère stood up. Her high heels went through the slots between the metal bars of the fire escape, but she didn't notice. She pointed imperiously at my window.

"You get inside right now," she ordered, in a voice I had never heard her use before.

I have to admit, I was so startled, I did exactly what she said. I unplugged Ronnie's electric blanket and crawled right back into my room. Then I stood there while Grandmère crawled back in, too.

"You," she said, when she'd straightened out her skirt, "are a princess of the royal house of Renaldo. A princess," she said, going to my closet, and rifling through it, "does not shirk her responsibilities. Nor does she run at the first sign of adversity."

"Um, Grandmère," I said. "What happened today was hardly the first sign of adversity, okay? What happened today was the last straw. I can't take it anymore, Grandmère. I'm getting out."

Grandmère pulled from my closet the dress Sebastiano had designed for me to wear to the dance. You know, the one that was supposed to make Michael forget that I am his little sister's best friend.

"Nonsense," Grandmère said.

That was all.

Just nonsense. Then she stood there, tapping her toes, staring at me.

"Grandmère," I said. Maybe it was all that time I'd spent

outside. Or maybe it was that I was pretty sure my mom and Mr. G and my dad were all in the next room, listening. How could they not be? There was no *door*, or anything, to separate my room from the living room.

"You don't understand," I said. "I can't go back there."

"All the more reason," Grandmère said, "for you to go."

"No," I said. "First of all, I don't even have a date for the dance, okay? And P.S., only losers go to dances without dates."

"You are not a loser, Amelia," Grandmère said. "You are a princess. And princesses do not run away when things become difficult. They throw their shoulders back, and they face what disaster awaits them head on. Bravely, and without complaint."

I said, "Hello, we are not talking about marauding visigoths, okay, Grandmère? We are talking about an entire high school that seems to think that I am in love with Boris Pelkowski."

"Which is precisely," Grandmère said, "why you must show them that it doesn't matter to you what they think."

"Why can't I show them that it doesn't matter by not going?"

"Because that," Grandmère said, "is the cowardly way. And you, Mia, as you have shown amply this past week, are not a coward. Now get dressed."

I don't know why I did what she said. Maybe it was because somewhere deep inside, I knew that for once, Grandmère was right.

Or maybe it was because secretly, I guess I was a little curious to see what would happen.

But I think the real reason was because, for the first time in my entire life, Grandmère didn't call me Amelia.

No. She called me Mia.

And because of my stupid sentimentalism, I am in a car right now, going back to stupid, crappy Albert Einstein High School, the dust from which I thought I'd managed to shake permanently from my feet not four hours ago.

But no. Oh, no. I'm going back, in the stupid velvet party dress Sebastiano designed for me. I'm going back, with no date. I'm going back, and I will probably be ridiculed for being the dateless biological freak that I am.

I am, however, a princess, and apparently that means I am expected to take whatever is dished out at me, no matter how cruel, unfair, or undeserved it might be.

And regardless of what happens, I can always comfort myself with the knowledge of one thing:

Tomorrow, I will be thousands of miles away from all of this.

Oh, God. We're here.

I think I'm going to be sick.

When I was about to turn six years old, all I wanted for my birthday was a cat.

I didn't care what kind of cat. I just wanted one. I wanted a cat of my very own. We had been to visit my mom's parents at their farm in Indiana, and they had a lot of cats. One of them had had kittens, little fluffy orange and white ones, which purred loudly when I held them under my chin, and liked to curl up inside the bib of my overalls and take naps. More than anything in the world, I wanted to keep one of those kittens.

I should mention that at the time, I had a thumb-sucking problem. My mother had tried everything to get me to stop sucking my thumb, including buying me a Barbie, in spite of her fundamental stand against Barbie and all that she stands for, as a sort of bribe. Nothing worked.

So when I started whining to her about wanting a kitten, my mom came up with a plan. She told me she would get me a kitten for my birthday if I quit sucking my thumb.

Which I did, immediately. I wanted a cat of my own *that badly.*

Yet, as my birthday rolled around, I had my doubts my mother would live up to her end of the bargain. For one thing, even at the age of six, I knew my mom wasn't the most responsible person. Why else was our electricity always being turned off? And about half the time I would show up at school wearing a skirt AND pants, because my mother let *me* decide what to wear. So I wasn't sure she'd remember about the kitten—or that, if she did remember, she'd know where to get one.

So as you can imagine, when the morning of my sixth birthday rolled around, I wasn't holding out much hope.

But when my mother came into my bedroom holding this tiny ball of yellow and white fur, and plopped it into my chest, and I looked into Louie's (he didn't become Fat Louie until about twenty-something pounds later) great big blue eyes (this was before they turned green), I knew a joy such as I had never known before in my life, and never expected to feel again.

That is, until last night.

I am totally serious.

Last night was the best night of my ENTIRE life. After that whole fiasco with Sebastiano and the photos, I thought I would never ever feel anything like gratitude to Grandmère EVER again.

But she was SO RIGHT to make me go to that dance. I am SO GLAD I went back to Albert Einstein, the best, the loveliest school in the whole country, if not the whole world!!!!!!!

Okay, here's what happened:

Lars and I pulled up in front of the school. There were twinkly white lights in all the windows, that I guess were supposed to represent icicles, or whatever.

I was sure I was going to throw up and I mentioned this to Lars. He said I couldn't possibly throw up because to his certain knowledge I hadn't eaten anything since the Entenmann's cake way before lunch, and that was probably all digested by now. With that piece of encouraging information, he escorted me up the steps and into the school.

There were masses of people teeming around the coat check in the front entrance. Lars checked our coats while I stood there waiting for someone to come up and ask me what I was doing there without a date. All that happened, however, was that Lilly-and-Boris and Tina-and-Dave descended upon me and started acting all nice and said how happy they were that I'd come (Tina told me later that she'd already explained to everyone that Kenny and I had broken up, although she hadn't told them why, THANK GOD).

So, fortified, by my friends, I went into the gym, which was decorated all wintry, with cut-out paper snowflakes, one of those disco balls, and fake snow everywhere, which I must say looked a lot whiter and cleaner than the snow that was starting to pile up on the ground outside.

There were tons of people there. I saw Lana and Josh (ugh), Justin Baxendale with his usual flock of adoring fans, and Shameeka and Ling Su and a bunch of other people. Even Kenny was there, though when he saw me, he turned bright red and turned around and started talking to this girl from our Bio class. Oh well.

Everyone was there, except the one person I'd been most dreading. Or hoping to see. I didn't know which.

Then I saw Judith Gershner. She had changed out of her overalls and looked quite pretty in this red Laura Ashley-ish dress.

But she wasn't dancing with Michael. She was dancing with some boy I'd never seen before.

So I looked around for Lilly, and finally spotted her using one of the pay phones. I went up to her and was like,

"Where's your brother?"

Lilly hung up the phone. "How should I know?" she demanded. "It's not my turn to baby-sit him."

Oddly comforted by her demeanor—which simply proved that no matter how much other things change, Lilly always stayed the same—I went, "Well, Judith Gershner is here, so I just figured—"

"For God's sake," Lilly said. "How many times do I have to tell you? *Michael and Judith are not going out.*"

I went, "Oh, right. Then why have they spent every waking moment together for the past two weeks?"

"Because they were working on that stupid computer program for the Carnival," she said. "Besides, Judith Gershner already has a boyfriend." Lilly grabbed me by the shoulders and turned me around so I could see Judith on the dance floor. "He goes to Trinity."

I looked at Judith Gershner as she slow-danced with a boy who looked a lot like Kenny, only older and not as uncoordinated.

"Oh," I said.

"*Oh* is right," Lilly said. "I don't know what is wrong with you today, but I can't deal with you when you're acting like such a freak. Sit down right here—" She pulled out a chair. "And don't you dare get up. I want to know where to find you when I need to."

I didn't even ask Lilly why she might need to find me. I just sat down. I felt like I couldn't stand up anymore. I was *that* tired.

It wasn't that I was disappointed. I mean, I didn't want to see Michael. At least, part of me didn't.

Another part of me *really* wanted to see him and ask him just what he'd meant by that poem.

But I was sort of afraid of the answer.

Because it might not be the one I was hoping it would be.

After a while, Lars and Wahim came and sat down next to me. I felt like a complete tool. I mean, there I was, sitting at a dance with two bodyguards, who were deep in a discussion about the advantages versus the disadvantages of rubber bullets. Nobody was asking me to dance. Nobody would, either. I mean, I'm a huge, colossal loser. A huge, colossal loser without a date.

Who, by the way, is supposedly in love with Boris Pelkowski.

Why was I even staying? I had done what Grandmère said. I had shown up. I had proved to everyone that I wasn't a coward. Why couldn't I leave? I mean, if I wanted to?

I stood up. I said to Lars, "Come on. We've been here long enough. I still have a lot of packing to do. Let's go."

Lars said okay, and started to get up. Then he stopped. I saw that he was looking at something behind me. I turned around.

And there was Michael.

He had obviously just gotten there. He was out of breath. His bow tie wasn't tied. And there was still snow in his hair.

"I didn't think you were coming," he said.

I knew my face had gone as red as Judith Gershner's dress. But there wasn't anything I could do about that. I said, "Well, I almost didn't."

He said, "I called you a bunch of times. Only you wouldn't come to the phone."

I said, "I know." I was wishing the floor of the gym would open up, like in *It's a Wonderful Life*, and that I'd fall into the pool underneath it and drown and not have to have this conversation.

"Mia," he said. "With that thing today. I didn't mean to make you cry."

Or the floor would open and I could just fall, and keep falling, forever and ever and ever. That would be okay, too. I stared at the floor, willing it to crack apart and swallow me up.

"It didn't." I lied. "I mean, it wasn't that. It was something Kenny said."

"Yeah," Michael said. "Well, I heard you two broke up."

Yeah. Probably by now the whole school had. Now, I knew, my face was even redder than Judith's dress.

"The thing is," Michael went on, "I knew it was you. Who was leaving those cards."

If he had reached inside my chest, pulled out my heart, flung it to the floor, and kicked it across the room, it could not possibly have hurt as much as hearing that. I could feel my eyes filling up with tears all over again.

"You did?" You know, it's one thing to have your heart broken. But to have it happen at a school dance, in front of everyone . . . well, that's harsh.

"Of course I did," he said. He sounded impatient. "Lilly told me."

For the first time, I looked up into his face.

"*Lilly* told you?" I cried. "How did *she* know?"

He waved his hand. "I don't know. Your friend Tina told her, I guess. But that's not important."

I looked around the gym and saw Lilly and Tina on the far

side of it, both staring in my direction. When they saw me looking at them, they turned around really fast and pretended to be deeply absorbed in conversation with their dates.

"I'm going to kill them," I murmured.

Michael reached out and grabbed both my shoulders. "Mia," he said, giving me a little shake. "It doesn't *matter*. What matters is that I meant what I wrote. And I thought you did, too."

I didn't think I could have heard him right. I went, "Of course I meant it."

He shook his head. "Then why did you freak out like that today at the Carnival?"

I stammered, "Well, because . . . because . . . I thought . . . I thought you were making fun of me."

"Never," he said.

And that's when he did it.

No fuss. No asking my permission. No hesitation whatsoever. He just leaned down and kissed me, right on the lips.

And I found out, right then, that Tina was right:

It *isn't* gross if you're in love with the guy.

In fact, it's the nicest thing in the whole world.

And do you know what the best part is?

I mean, aside from Michael being in love with me, and having kept it a secret almost as long as I have, if not longer?

And Lilly knowing all along but not saying anything up until a few days ago because she found it an interesting social experiment to see how long it would take us to figure it out on our own (a long time, it turned out)?

And the fact that Michael's going to Columbia next year, which is only a few subway stops away, so I'll still be able to see him as much as I want?

Oh, and Lana walking by while we were kissing, and going, in this disgusted voice, "Oh, God, get a room, would you please?"

And slow dancing with him all night long, until Lilly finally came up and said, "Come on you guys, it's snowing so hard, if we don't leave now, we'll never get home"?

And kissing good night outside the stoop to my loft, with the snow falling all around us (and grumpy Lars complaining he was getting cold)?

No, the best part is that we moved right into Frenching without any trouble at all. Tina was right—it just seemed perfectly natural.

And now the royal Genovian flight attendant says we have to put away our tray tables for takeoff, so I'll have to quit writing in a minute.

Dad says if I don't stop talking about Michael, he's going to go sit up front with the pilot for the flight.

Grandmère says she can't get over the change in me. She says I seem taller. And you know, maybe I am. She thinks it's because I'm wearing another one of Sebastiano's original creations, designed just for me, just like the dress that was supposed to make Michael see me as more than just his little sister's best friend . . . except that it turned out he did anyway. But I know that's not it.

And it isn't love, either. Well, not entirely.

I'll tell you what it is: self-actualization.

Well, that and the fact that it turns out I'm really a princess, after all. I must be, because guess what?

I'm living happily ever after.

Ali Smith

MEG CABOT

is the author of the bestselling, critically acclaimed Princess Diaries books, which were made into the wildly popular Disney movies of the same name. Her other books for teens include PANTS ON FIRE, JINX, and the manga series Avalon High: Coronation. She also writes books for adults, including BIG BONED and QUEEN OF BABBLE IN THE BIG CITY. She is still waiting for her real parents, the king and queen, to restore her to her rightful throne. Meg lives in Key West with her husband and a one-eyed cat named Henrietta as well as various backup cats.

To read Meg's blog and catch up on all the latest news about her books, visit her online at **www.megcabot.com**.

For exclusive information on your favorite authors and artists, visit www.authortracker.com.